DUNGEONS

OF THE

CROOKED MOUNTAINS

a novel

by Alexey Osadchuk

To my Dear Reader, with gratitude,
Alexey Osadchuk.

UNDERDOG

BOOK ONE

Magic Dome Books

Dungeons of the Crooked Mountains
Underdog, Book #1
Published by Magic Dome Books, 2019
Copyright © A. Osadchuk 2019
Cover Art © Valeria Osadchuk 2019
Designer Vladimir Manyukhin
English Translation Copyright © Andrew Schmitt 2019
All Rights Reserved
ISBN: 978-80-7619-072-6

ALSO BY ALEXEY OSADCHUK:

Mirror World LitRPG series:

Project Daily Grind

The Citadel

The Way of the Outcast

The Twilight Obelisk

TABLE OF CONTENTS:

Chapter One.. 1

Chapter Two.. 20

Chapter Three... 35

Chapter Four.. 45

Chapter Five... 67

Chapter Six.. 81

Chapter Seven.. 94

Chapter Eight.. 118

Chapter Nine... 133

Chapter Ten.. 148

Chapter Eleven.. 164

Chapter Twelve.. 175

Chapter Thirteen.. 197

Chapter Fourteen... 214

Chapter Fifteen.. 235

Chapter Sixteen... 255

Chapter Seventeen....................................... 273

Chapter Eighteen... 293

Chapter Nineteen... 312

Chapter Twenty... 331

Chapter Twenty-One..................................... 351

Chapter Twenty-Two..................................... 371

Chapter Twenty-Three................................... 390

Chapter Twenty-Four.................................... 409

Chapter Twenty-Five.................................... 430

CHAPTER 1

"**F**OREMAN AREN, it's a boy..."

The head of one of the most prosperous mining crews in Orchus, Foreman Aren looked deeply into the gloomy gaze of the woman who delivered his wife's baby and was sincerely perplexed. What possible reason could there be for someone to tell him such joyous news with a sour face? But a few moments later, it began to reach him. The child was born, but he can't hear crying...

"Is he dead?"

Aren was a man who had seen all manner of things in this life, but still the words didn't come easily to him.

"He is alive," the healer woman answered darkly and quickly added softly, nearly in a whisper:

"But he'd be better off not..."

Aren squinted his eyes predatorily and took

a step forward. If his gaze could burn, even the ash pile he'd have quickly reduced her to would have been incinerated by this point. Dalia calmly bore the miner's hateful stare and said:

"But there is also good news. Your wife took the birth marvelously."

That extinguished the newly-lit fire of rage in the soul of the new father. With a bit of effort, he composed himself and continued the questioning. This woman is the only healer of her level in the whole region. What's more, it's remarkable luck that she's still even in Orchus. She was supposed to leave for the capital ages ago. It's all down to the rainy season, which came a week ahead of schedule. Now, Sleepy Pass would be closed for two months. Only a crazy person would even think of traveling through the mountains at a time like this. And fortunately for Aren and his wife, Dalia was sound of mind.

"Speak," the foreman grunted shortly.

No matter how he wanted to be at Liana and his son's side, business came first.

"He's nulled," the healer squeezed out drily.

Aren's face went completely blank. His immovability could inspire envy even in Black Crag, the great stone where northerly storms of the Dead Ocean first broke. But inside, he felt a cold grip clenching around his heart. The poor boy! How could this be?!

Meanwhile, the healer continued:

"First I thought he was born dead. But then

I looked at his life and energy supplies. Just ten points each... And the lower limit usually is twenty."

"But how is that possible?!"

"I don't know," Dalia shrugged, perplexed. "I have never encountered anything like it before. But Never even heard about it. One of Bug's tricks, no two ways about it."

"Do you blaspheme, crone?" Aren's calm again showed a crack. "What does the malevolent spirit have to do with this? Or do you not believe that everything in this world happens by the will of the Great System?"

Hearing that, the healer's face twisted up like she just ate a lemon.

"As a matter of fact, I do believe that..."

"Then where does the evil spirit come into it?"

"Alright," relenting to the foreman's pressure, the healer began speaking wearily:

"But first swear that you will not drag me off to the nearest temple of the Great System to be slain as a heretic."

"You have my word," the foreman promised gloomily.

The healer, receiving a system message that the oath had been accepted, shifted to a hushed tone and began:

"As you know, when we are born, the Great System grants us our first level, fills our supplies and awards us our first characteristic tablets. And their number is defined by the god Random. Most get ten or twelve. The most tablets I've ever heard of is fifteen."

Aren nodded in silence. Ivar, his firstborn had received fourteen when he was born. A shadow slowly crawled across the foreman's face. It had been just two years since he and Liana received the news that Ivar died in battle in the Wastes. He was hoping the birth of a second son would drive off the gloom that had taken root in their home after Ivar's death. But apparently it was not to be...

"But some have also received less than ten tablets. They all had rough childhoods. They were weaker than their peers... But with time, many of them worked their way up to a respectable life."

"Yes," Aren agreed. "Some of the men in my crew were born that way."

His face lit up a bit. How could he forget! Does that mean his son can live a normal life in the future? Right then and there, he made a promise to himself. Of course he can! Aren will see to it!

Seeing the foreman's mood, the healer hurried to bring him back down to earth:

"I know what you're thinking, Aren. You're under the impression that your son is like them. But you are mistaken. Your baby is nulled. He did not receive level one or the tablets due to him. And his supplies are pitifully low. I don't believe Random had any hand in this. It was all Bug..."

It hurt to even look at Aren. Hope just gave

him a little wink but now the very concept of hope was being dragged through the mud.

Meanwhile, Dalia continued:

"As you know, Bug is known by many names. Glitch, Failure, Virus, but there is one more. My teacher read it in a manuscript of the Ancients. The Departed called him System Error. Do you understand? Error! That means the Great System is not perfect and can make mistakes! There were many other things written in that book, but I do not wish to speak of them. And they aren't for your ears..."

Aren collapsed wearily on a bench.

"Level zero," he whispered. "But that's..."

"Yes," the healer nodded sadly. "He will not progress. He cannot use tablets. Even if you gave him your experience essences, nothing would come of it. Almost everything created by the Great System has a limitation: minimum level one."

"But then what can we do?" Aren asked fatedly.

Dalia sat down on the bench next to the foreman. Her face, lined with deep wrinkles, was frozen in deep thought.

"How old is she?" he suddenly thought. Everyone knows healers have long lives. They also say they have discovered the secret of eternal youth. The man chuckled to himself... Nonsense of course... But Bug works in mysterious ways... And if Dalia looked seventy, that number could safely be doubled, maybe even tripled...

"Ha!" the woman exclaimed at a surprising volume. Her dark blue eyes glimmered with joy. "I've got it!"

Rubbing her bone-dry palms together, Dalia turned to the workman:

"Strange that it took me so long to think of this. I'm getting old... You aren't doing much better..."

Aren stared at the woman in confusion.

"Okay," she waved a hand. "Let me explain. I can see you're not much for thinking... For now, the only solution is artifacts of the Ancients."

"You mean to say..."

"Precisely... They are the only items without restrictions. In fact, they have no requirements at all. But you have to understand... They are a rarity and cost dearly. But your son will only need two or three items with plusses to main characteristics..."

The old woman said a bit more, but Aren was only half listening. He was already imagining where and how he would buy artifacts of the Departed. And he wasn't thinking of money... His son's life — that was his main concern...

14 years later

"YOU'RE A HEAVY sumabitch!" flatulating and cursing through his teeth, a fat mover was dragging a heavy armchair over to the front door.

My great grandfather's "throne." Father loved to sit in it after dinner, warming his feet by the fire and smoking a pipe. That always put him in a very tender mood and he told me many stories, tales and legends while sitting in it...

"Yeah all their furniture weighs a ton!" a peevish voice from the dining room echoed.

"Old oaken armchair — one," the bank clerk stated in a calm voice, ignoring the mover's cursing and farting. His long desiccated fingers fluttered a white goose-feather quill, carefully taking down every object removed from the home. Three sheets were already fully covered in his small calligraphic handwriting.

A wiry bearded man emerged from the kitchen. A cracked tureen in his quavering hands. The cloudy gaze of his reddish eyes paused on the gaunt figure of the clerk.

"This thing looks like trash. We gonna take it?"

My mother's favorite tureen. Every time she placed it on the table, we heard the same old adage. "Who cares if it's got a crack! It keeps soup warm a long time!" Then she would scurry back to the kitchen for another dish, and father would whisper that all women have a hard time parting with material things. Meanwhile, with a smile, he would pat his old vest, which mom was constantly threatening to throw out.

The clerk tore his gaze from his notes and looked at the bearded man. His small narrow-set eyes were full of obvious scorn.

"Tox," he rasped. "You were given a simple

instruction: 'remove everything from the home and load it onto the carts.' Exactly what part of that did you not understand?"

"Well it's just so..." Tox tried to object but another man, a giant, came into the house and interrupted him rudely:

"Shut your fat mouth and do as you're told! And move your butt!"

The bearded Tox, his head slumped between his shoulders, tried to slip away out the front door.

"Where do you think you're going?" the giant barked.

Tox gave a blank stare to the immense man, his boss, who was standing in the doorway, arms crossed over his chest and a big gut sticking out in front.

"Did you think I was gonna let you just bring out one tureen at a time? Come on, step to. Back to the kitchen and do your job!"

Tox blew away like the wind.

"Mr. Dreher, you could stand to be a bit more selective with your choice of staff," the clerk noted acridly.

"I don't remember asking you, filing weasel," the big-bellied Dreher waved it off and headed for my parents' bedroom, batting the thin clerk's notes carelessly.

The white sheets of paper flew out of his hands like a flock of startled pigeons and slid around the floor. The "filing weasel" then gave a loud feminine gasp and fell to his knees to recover his treasure. His body was shaking in indignation, a line of green snot drooping down from his long birdlike nose.

Fitfully crawling around the floor, the clerk grunted a curse at the idiot movers and their boorish leader. Mocking the pencil pusher's humiliating position, a rude whinnying came from a few tinny throats in the dining room. The clerk's face instantly turned crimson and tears of anger welled up in the corners of his little eyes.

Finally, his dry old fingers carefully put all the papers back in order. The clerk, clutching an inkwell hanging from a cord around his neck, got up from his knees. Patting the dust from his pants with his right hand and giving a few slaps to his very worn but neat frock, he settled down.

At that very moment, our gazes met...

I was sitting on a kitchen stool in the corner of the entryway and awaiting my fate. Only yesterday had I learned that the bank would be taking our house to pay back my parents' debts. In fact, just one day before that was when I learned my parents lost their lives in a nearby mine.

"What are you staring at, half-baked whelp?" the clerk hissed.

He really is a weasel, I chuckled to myself.

"You think this is funny?" in the weasel's eyes, a mixture of sincere puzzlement and acrimony. "After all, everything happening now is your doing!"

I don't get it... What is he talking about?

"Haha! I can see you aren't getting it."

Dreher appeared in the doorway of my parents' bedroom, his arms loaded with mom's ceramics. He looked gloomily first at me, then at the clerk.

"Shut it, office rat!" he barked. "If you don't leave the kid alone, you'll be going home without teeth!"

Giving me an encouraging wink, the big bellied guy left the house.

Based on his angrily gnarled lips, the weasel wanted to say something, but a shout from above broke off his tirade before it could begin.

"Don't do it, Sakis. Better hold your tongue."

We raised our heads simultaneously. There was a man standing on the stairs leading to the second floor. His head, bald as an egg, was looking down at some notes, his full lips moving in time with the letters being written. His inkwell wasn't so much hanging from the chain around his neck as perched on his gut.

"But Velen! You must see! This whelp isn't showing me the respect I deserve as a bank employee!" Sakis howled.

"Just don't," the fat clerk repeated and continued down the stairs, continuing to take notes all the while. And then, tearing himself from the papers, he added:

"And really, leave the boy alone. He is none of our concern."

"What do you mean?" Sakis asked,

surprised. "I thought the bank..."

"No," Velen interrupted. "The remaining debt was purchased by Bardan."

The weasel's narrow face stretched out so much his face looked flat.

"That Bardan?!"

"Uh huh," Velen answered casually, again sinking into his notes.

Sakis slowly turned his head in my direction. A moment of pity flickered in his eyes.

"Ahem-m-m..." he drew out. "I do not envy you, half-baked whelp."

Enjoying the confusion and disquiet on my face, he gradually made his way to the exit, his head raised proudly.

I couldn't help but overhear a muffled conversation from the two movers in the dining room.

"Listen, Tox, why does that bank rat keep calling the kid half-baked?" I couldn't see who was talking, but I recognized the voice. It was Roy, a big dumpy guy with blond hair and a body like a beer keg.

"Well, that's what he is. He's been like crippled ever since he was born," Tox answered carelessly.

"Hmm," Roy answered in surprise. "You'd never know it to look at him. I guess he is a bit scrawny, and has bags under his eyes. So, you reckon he fell ill recently? Well, he did lose his mom and dad a couple days ago. That must be why he's pale as death."

"Naaah," Tox objected. "He was born that way. Hmm... I guess old Aren, Random rest his soul, had bad luck with sons..."

For some time, the conversation in the dining room ceased. They were both contemplating.

Roy was first to break the silence:

"Say... We've still got half a day's work here, and the time passes quicker when we talk..."

"Yeah there's not really much to tell," Tox answered in strain, clearly moving something heavy. "As you can see, the family had means. A two story house. The farm is doing pretty well. Horses, cows, pigs."

"That's for sure," notes of envy slipped through in Roy's voice.

"The Bergmans are a family of miners," Tox continued. "His father had the strongest crew. And that whole crew just died in a cave-in."

"Yi-iikes..."

"Bergman's wife and another couple ladies were bringing their husbands lunch in the mine, too... And basically they all passed on as well...."

Based on Tox's vocal timbre, he was truly bothered by the death of my parents and their friends.

"And what about the sons?" Roy asked.

"He had bad luck with sons. Well, it all started well. Really well, actually! When his first was born, he got a good set of characteristics. He was the strongest of his age group. By age fourteen, he was working in the mine with his father. And in the winter of that same year, he also won the tournament. And that was when the Baron hired him to serve in his retinue as a novice."

"Woah! What's so unlucky about that?!" Roy exclaimed, baffled.

"Well, one month later, the Bergmans received news that their son died..."

"Ah, there it is..."

"Yep, so..."

The movers fell silent again, digesting the information. But not for long. This time Tox was first to speak up:

"The years of grief passed and Aren's wife got pregnant again. And you'd think that might be cause for joy, but here's the thing... The baby was born with a slight flaw. Actually, a bit worse... At first they thought he was just dead. No crying, no movement, eyes closed. But they hired a very capable medicine woman as midwife and she noticed he was breathing. Barely, but breathing."

"Yi-iikes..." Roy drew out.

"Ha!" Tox exclaimed. "You haven't even heard the most important part yet. Aren paid out the butt for a healer from the capital."

"I bet!"

"Anyway, she saw that the kid was born nulled, level zero!" Tox said triumphantly.

It sounded like Roy's jaw fell down to the floor with a thundering crash. But then I realized the movers had just gotten to father's tools.

"Well, you don't see that every day!" I heard Roy say, amazed.

To be frank, I was surprised. He got my story almost exactly right... A few of the details were off, but the gist was overall accurate... My father had told me the story of my birth many times.

"Hey, you two chumps!" the sudden roar from Dreher made me shudder. "Move your butts! I'm not paying you idiots to talk!"

The giant lead mover suddenly appeared in the front doorway and shot a glare at the workmen as they scurried over to the door.

"Lazy bastards," he growled under his breath. "Don't you worry, we'll have plenty of time to talk when you come around asking for your money..."

He spent a bit longer watching the yard then turned toward me. His gaze had warmed slightly.

"Get ready, kid," he said sadly, nodding at the exit. "Your ride is here."

Weirdly, I catch myself on the thought that I've been impatiently waiting for this since morning. If anyone could know what I'm thinking right now, they'd say I lost my mind.

Ugh... At a certain level, they'd be close to the truth.

Two days ago my world, never the most wonderful to begin with, approximately what a cripple like me could expect, just ceased to exist.

Watching distantly as our home was plundered, I suddenly realized that I was all alone. Just me and the world, one on one. My big strong father would not be coming to help me again. My talkative and tender mom would never again be drying my tears of despair and anger.

I felt a lump coming up my throat. My eyes started stinging, betraying my feelings. No! I will not burst into tears. At least not here, not now — that would just amuse the marauders looting my family home. After this is all over, I can find some hole to cower in. There I'll let my feelings run wild. But not here and not now. Otherwise I'll betray my father's memory. He taught me to be strong.

I watched them moving out my parents' favorite things. Demolishing the history of our family. And I understood that this place ceased to be my home the moment they died... I didn't realize it at the time, but I had penetrated one of life's greatest truths — home is where the people who love you live.

I slowly crawled off the stool. That was all the speed I was capable of with my two points of agility. But I was happy to have even that.

I was two years old when I took my first step. That was also when I said my first word. Luck finally shined on father that year, and he was able to buy me my first artifact of the Ancients on the black market in the capital of our Barony.

Out of old habit, my arm reached for my chest.

- Rock Monitor Bone Button.
- Category: Simple.
- Agility +2.
- Strength +1.
- Mind +3.
- Restrictions — None.
- Durability — 25/25.

Some probably think it funny how happy those pitiful six characteristic points made me... But for me, after two long years confined to a bed like a plank of wood, unfeeling and unable to speak, my father's gift was and still is the best thing that ever happened...

I was holding a small knapsack in my hands. In it, I had a small portrait of my parents, two boiled eggs and a crust of bread. Madam Horst, a neighbor, brought me some food for the road. I always used to think she was evil and quarrelsome, but in the end she managed to surprise me. She was the only one who came around to ask what would become of me.

My normal belt, level zero like all my clothing, had a small compartment where I kept a small pocketknife.

- Dragonfly Pocketknife.
- Category: Simple.
- Damage +2.
- Restrictions — None.
- Durability — 55/55.

It was the last artifact father obtained. My parents gave it to me as a birthday present. Just a few hours before they died...

Somehow, my pitiful three strength points were able to handle both my own body and the little knapsack. And that was all thanks to a meagre little ring.

- Steel Ring.
- Category: Simple.
- Strength +2.
- Restrictions — None.
- Durability — 30/30.

I once asked father why these simple items were so valuable. As it turned out, the reasons were fairly significant.

First of all, artifacts of the Ancients have no restrictions. That means anyone can wear them regardless of level or characteristics.

Second, despite the low bonuses, I could improve them in the future. For now, I just don't know how.

Third, though this is just rumored, improving them would not only raise my already existing characteristics but add new ones.

And the last reason is that these objects, these sca...scalaaa... scal-ab-les... They mean my level will be added to all the item's characteristics. If I were level one now, all the characteristics of my artifacts would be improved by one. Ah... dreams...

dreams...

Also... Dalia told me this. Handiwork of the Ancients can only be recognized by those with high Mind. For normal folks, they look like normal items, totally unremarkable.

And as for their appearance... Well, expensive jewelry like a gold ring is sure to attract the wrong kind of attention on the finger of a miner's son. So it's perfect that they appear plain and inconspicuous. After all, all things crafted by the Departed are one of a kind, expensive. There's no reason to draw unneeded attention. That's one of the first rules father taught me.

That was exactly why every time a new artifact came to our house, Dalia the healer, first just my mother's midwife, came as well. And she soon became a friend of the family. Thanks to that little trick, no one ever asked questions. Like for example, when I started to walk after spending more than two years motionless on my back.

It also created a logical explanation for why the foreman of a miner crew was always going to the bank for more loans. Healers are expensive. Especially healers like Dalia. By the way, mom once spilled that it was none other than the old healer woman who tracked down the handicrafts of the Ancients for me. Father paid her a small finder's fee for the trouble.

I'd always suspected my parents were spending lots of money so their son could live like a normal child. But when I actually saw how much debt they'd accrued with all the runaway interest, it made an impression. Enough that the bank took our house, land and whole farm. And I was still in debt to the bank for almost a hundred gold. But the bank sold that debt... So now I'd have to pay back some guy named Bardan...

Walking out the door of my parents' house for the very last time, I turned to the lead mover:

"Mr. Dreher, would you mind telling me who this Bardan is?"

The giant took a heavy sigh and, hiding a gloomy look, answered:

"Bardan is a lanista. He owns gladiator pits."

CHAPTER 2

Two years prior

"SO THEN, listen up!"
Came trainer Droom, his voice booming through the cave. The tough red-head was from a mining crew that competed with my father's, and was teaching us the basics of the art of mining.

"Today you will all learn to handle a pickaxe!" he barked, staring gloomily into our young faces.

After that, the barbed gaze of his black eyes paused on me.

"Except for Eric Bergman, obviously." His wide toad-like mouth spread into an acrid smile, revealing a row of crooked yellow teeth.

My former classmates all looked at me right on cue and started laughing with glee. A blonde named Mia, the prettiest girl in class, laughed especially hard. Surrounded by a crowd of friends, also cute but not quite as pretty, she looked like a queen.

Mia's father Hrut, one of the twelve elders of Orchus, was at daggers with my father. Once, he just about broke old Hrut's face, and it was topic of discussion in the city for quite some time after. It all started when the stuffy elder started raising a stink about a Bugged cripple studying alongside his daughter.

Honestly, the matter even ended up going to trial. Hrut had the support of the other elders, and my classmates' parents were unanimously behind them. In their words, my deficiency was slowing down the rest of the class. When hunting for example, my mere presence weakens the whole group. I don't do damage, but still I supposedly lay claim to the spoils. Plus, they said, I am no end of trouble for the trainers, who are constantly making sure the "half-baked whelp" doesn't accidentally get struck dead by some mob. After all, my life supply is just ten points... One bite from a large garbage rat.

In theory, that was exactly how it worked but, in practice, no one ever shared anything with me. And the trainers didn't give a damn about my safety. If I survived, good. If I died, it was my own fault.

Gathering resources was also an issue. The tools and resources all had a restriction: minimum level one. And that was the least of my troubles! I couldn't even eat all mother's food. Only the dishes with a little zero. The most basic food like bread, butter and honey. Simple fare like meat or porridge, no accoutrements. Seeing the other kids wolf down sweets was a very particular kind of torture...

In the end, the court decided I should be expelled from school. But I was allowed to sit in and observe. Just be present at lessons. The basic idea was: "look, but don't touch..." And naturally, the trainers would bear no responsibility if I got hurt...

A SMALL PICKAXE appeared in Droom's hands. Father had shown me one like it. Little, for training. Five points of damage.

"I'll only be explaining this one time!" the trainer barked. "You hold it here, by the handle! Wind up, swing! Hit!"

The steel, shooting dozens of tiny sparks, struck ore. Without particular effort, Droom applied pressure to the handle and popped out his first rock.

"Presto! Everyone get it?!"

A dissonant chorus of children's voices answered in the affirmative.

"Okay then, let's see. Who's gonna be first?!"

A tall strong figure quickly broke off from the cluster of students.

Haakon, son of Ulvar the hunter. Hair black

as tar. A supple stature. Soft animalistic movements. The group of girls headed by Mia was watching him, dazed.

They say when he was born, Random granted him a generous fourteen tablets. Exactly the same as my older brother Ivar got once upon a time... And alas I never even met him.

Thanks to the Great System's generous gift, Haakon was progressing much faster than his peers. A week ago, he left with his father and older brother to hunt at level two. He came back five. My former classmates worshipped him for his strength and agility.

"Master Droom, could you maybe give me a better tool?!" Haakon shouted with defiance.

Chest puffed out, hands on hips. Poser...

Droom croaked back happily.

"I don't see why not."

And extended him a more substantial "adult" pickaxe.

"Woah!" marveled Thomas, a bigger kid, also a miner's son like me. "Level five! Like my dad's! That thing must be heavy!"

If Haakon was the least bit worried, no one noticed. His handsome face was just beaming with the same self-satisfied smile as ever.

Walking up almost face to face with the trainer, the hunter's son extended his right hand for the tool. Droom extended the heavy pickaxe with ease, as if it were light as a feather.

"Better use two hands," he said with a smile.

Despite his self-confident appearance, Haakon took the precaution, for which the teacher rewarded him with a nod of approval.

All that time we were standing in silence, holding our breath and watching Haakon. He grasps the handle with both hands. Nods at the trainer. Droom lets go. I see the veins on Haakon's forehead bulge. His hands are quivering in strain, but still he keeps hold of the pick.

A heavy swing and the steel tip cuts into ore. It looks like he's working a little harder than Droom, but it doesn't matter...

Haakon leverages all his bodyweight onto the handle and, with enormous effort, to the admiring gasps of his classmates, pops out quite a large piece of stone.

"Well done!" the master barked and patted the boy on the shoulder.

A satisfied smile froze on Haakon's face. His eyes ran over some system notifications only he could see.

"What did you get?"

"What?"

"What is it?"

Questions leapt in, vying with one another.

Haakon raised a hand demandingly.

"Quiet!" shouted Skeggi, Haakon's best friend. "Read, bro!"

Haakon concentrated on the invisible text and began reading it at his leisure. Was I the only one who noticed how slowly he read? He must have less Mind than even me.

"Attention you have acquired four pounds of ore! Congratulations! You receive..."

Haakon ran a sly meaningful look over all of us and continued:

"Clay tablet of strength!"

Everyone shouted for joy.

"Clay tablet of agility!"

"Yeaaah!" Everyone yelled in concert.

"Clay tablet of endurance! Clay tablet 'Mining!' Clay tablet of carrying capacity! Experience essences — five!"

As Haakon read through his loot, I unwittingly imagined myself in his place. What must it be like to be strong and agile? To achieve everything you desire? To catch the prettiest girls staring at you with stars in their eyes?

It took me a second to realize that Haakon had stopped boasting and everyone was staring at me. I looked around, not understanding.

"Did you see his face?!" shouted Snorri, another of Haakon's flunkies, pointing a grubby finger at me. "That defective is drooling over Haakon's loot!"

A wave of loud whinnying boomed through the cave. They all had their fingers trained on me. They were making faces that must have been imitating how they thought I looked.

Unable to bear it any longer, I turned and ran for the exit. Well, so it seemed to me to me. It would be more accurate to say I crawled slowly like a turtle. I mean, a turtle would have honestly been faster. My "epic" run caused another burst of laughter. Snotty Snorri and fat Thomas even cheered.

I don't remember getting home. I only remember that I wept all night. The anger and humiliation made me want to fall through the earth. But most of all I hated myself for my shameful retreat.

That very day, around morning, before falling into a restless dream, I promised myself that I would never again show my back to an enemy...

Present day

"ERIC BERGMAN?"

Thin as a decaying tree, the old man stared half-blind at a rumpled sheet of paper. A little bald head, narrow bony shoulders, a hunched stature. Just level nine. I wonder what he did all his life. Another failure like me. Actually, no. I'm the only one like me. At the very least that's what Dalia told me.

"Yes, that's me."

The old man finally tore himself from the paper and looked closely at the words over my head.

"What the..." the old man's faded teary eyes went round. He even blinked a few times.

"My old lady told me to stop drinking that moonshine," he rasped out angrily. "Now I'm hallucinating zeroes."

A mover walking past guffawed.

"What, Burdoc? Finally drink yourself silly?"

"What are you laughing about, loafer? Now I'm gonna have to fork over a wad of cash to some healer."

"Oh, you'll learn what it means to force nasty stuff down your throat!" the mover kept laughing.

Burdoc spat in anger and, again frowning, started looking closer at my level.

I decided to take pity on the old man.

"Mr. Burdoc, don't you worry. You're not hallucinating. I really am nulled."

I thought I was reassuring the poor fellow. Little did I know! That only horrified him further.

"How can that be? Oh, Great System!" he lamented, clutching at his head. "What will I ever say to Mr. Bardan?! He'll flay me alive for bringing him a defective!"

"How is that your problem, old fool?" the lead mover jumped in. "Bardan made a deal with the bank. He bought the peonage certificates. If he didn't look at who he was buying, that's his problem. Not yours, old man."

"That's true!" the geezer spread his arms happily. "After all, I'm just a cog in the machine. My job is merely to transport the people on this list!"

"Exactly," Dreher smiled. "And you were about to bury yourself."

"Thank you, sweet man, you've set my soul at ease," Burdoc quickly bowed to the lead mover and turned to me. "And you, kid, climb up on my cart. We have more peons to pick up."

It was around evening when we finally arrived. To my surprise, I took the journey well. My head buried in a pile of sweet-smelling hay, I slept the whole way. I opened my eyes only when Burdoc stopped to pick up more peons. It was hard to sleep with all the heart-rending screaming of women and children. A family sending off one of their own into peonage is not a spectacle for the faint of heart.

I had never seen such a thing before, but Burdoc was eager to explain what all was going on. For an old man, he was actually pretty talkative.

"Let's say a man comes to the bank and takes out a loan," the old man said. "How does the bank stand to benefit from throwing gold around willy-nilly? Exactly, they don't. They need to make a profit, that's why they're a bank. And so they give the man a little cash to grow. Then that racks up interest. If he's got the gold to pay them back on schedule, then good. But if he doesn't, the debt gets bought up by someone like my master. He's always in need of more people... And when that time comes, they have to work for him until they've paid off their whole debt. Ahem, see I still haven't even gotten to the worst part... It's good when a family has strong sons. Usually their fathers give them up to peonage, and themselves try to quickly get the money together to buy their boy back. Well, that's for good fathers... Sometimes, children spend half their lives toiling for their parents' creditors. Sometimes they even die in peonage..."

The last family we went to had no sons. They had children, but only five girls. The very oldest looked to be about my age. And she was who we were taking. Her name was Jay and, surprisingly, her mother was not crying, though her gloomy face was affixed with a mask of pain and despair. The youngest sisters, wiping away tears and snot, were whimpering pitifully like puppies.

I looked at Jay's old house, at her mother embracing her eldest daughter with tense arms. I saw her father, a man who looked like he never crawled out of the bottle. I realized it would be a long time before she'd be able to pay off her debt... If that ever came.

BARDAN'S HOME was impressively large. Three stories. Granite walls. All the windows fitted with massive steel grates. Not a home but a fortress. And his fairly sizable property was entirely surrounded by a tall stone fence. At the gates and front door, there were well-armed guards. By all appearances, this Bardan was made of money.

Our cart of quiet peons rolled over to the barracks, which were a distance from the master's home. There were people waiting for us.

Two men. One subtly reminded me of the bank clerk Sakis. An identical inkwell around his neck, the same mustache, scrutinizing gaze. Gaunt. An unhealthy tinge to his face. A born clerk.

The second was his complete opposite. Tall, broad-shouldered. Hands like excavator shovels. Green eyes burning with energy and power.

Burdoc fitfully lined us up next to the cart and extended a familiar rumpled paper to the "clerk:"

"Here you go, mister steward. Just as the list says, six new peons. Four men, one girl and one boy."

The steward accepted the paper with disgust, using only two fingers and quickly scanned our names. When he reached me, his eyes went wide.

"What have you brought me?!" he shouted. "Doddering old fool, did you not see who the Bergmans were trying to slip you!!! What will I tell my master now?! Valgard, order this idiot flogged!"

The red-bearded giant, previously standing blankly, took a threatening lurch forward. Burdoc lost all his affinity for speech and collapsed to his knees before the raging steward. But he just flew deeper and deeper into a fit of anger. Valgard loomed over the poor man. His wide palms came down on the bony shoulders of the now weeping geezer.

"Mister steward!" I think even I shuddered at the sound of my own voice. "Permission to speak!"

Bug must have pulled that out of my big

stupid mouth! But it was too late to take it back!

An oppressive silence hung over the courtyard. My companions in misfortune stared at me, dumbfounded. Even Burdoc stopped his howling.

The "clerk" squinted predatorily and barked:

"Speak! But keep in mind, if you interrupted me for no reason, you'll be getting a lashing alongside this muttonhead! Got it?"

"Yes, mister steward. I accept the risk." It took effort to keep my voice from quavering.

"Continue!"

"Mr. Burdoc is not at fault. As a matter of fact, he carried out your orders dutifully."

"Then why are you here and not your father, older brother or sister?"

"Well, mister steward, I don't have a sister and never have. My older brother fell in battle in the Wastes fighting for our Baron, and my father and mother died two days ago in a mine collapse... I am all alone... So you see, Mr. Burdoc had no choice."

Out of the corner of my eye, I caught an intrigued glance from Jay. During our trip, I inconspicuously got a good look at her. Much to my surprise, she was level five. Based on her flexible figure and smooth cat-like movements, she had invested heavily in Agility. A lock of fiery red hair stuck out from under her kerchief. Her eyes are like two dark emeralds. The freckles on her slightly upturned little nose and pale cheeks don't diminish her beauty in the slightest. Quite the opposite...

"Is he speaking the truth?" The steward was still angry but, by his tone of voice, I could tell the storm had passed.

"Yes, sir," the old man bleated. "I swear it was so!"

Clearly having received a system message confirming the oath, the steward's rage morphed into sweetness.

"Alright," he crowed at the old man. "Get everyone a place to stay. Tomorrow I'll decide what to do with them..."

Burdoc quickly hopped up and led all the peons to the farthest barrack.

I wanted to also turn and go but suddenly heard:

"But you won't be getting off so easy..."

The barbed gaze of his squinty eyes hooked into me. I forgot how to breathe.

"Master will be outraged. The bank mucked up, and now we're left to pick up the pieces... After all, you're utterly worthless. Just think! Level zero! How are you even still alive...? And where are we going to stick you?"

"Ing," the red-bearded giant unexpectedly spoke up. "Look how dainty he is. Skorx's scout crew has been asking for someone like him a long time."

"Have you lost your mind?" the leader replied, distraught. "Send a null like him out to the mine? For what, so he can keel over before the end of his first hour?"

I think I gulped. My heart was just about to jump out of my chest.

"Well, who cares if he does?" Valgard continued. "Then you can file a grievance against Skorx saying he damaged master's property. You might even come out ahead."

"Are you out of your mind? His debt is almost a hundred gold! Skorx won't accept a risk like that. For that kind of dough, he could hire a few dozen boys like this!"

"Who are you talking about?" the big fellow laughed. "Skorx, who would sell his own mother for ten copper? Haha! You're a funny guy! That miser would never say no to fresh meat if he doesn't have to pay. And who's to say the little guy is gonna kick the bucket on day one. He comes from a family of miners. At the end of the day, he's a Bergman."

After that, Valgard shot me a happy wink. It made a chill run over my skin.

"Yeah but why does he want small kids?" Ing asked, intrigued.

"Well, to scout out long tunnels. Only tiny bodies can fit into the burrows of the stone worms."

"I see," said the steward, stroking his beard in thought.

"Think for yourself," Valgard applied some pressure, seeing that Ing was about to give in. "Did he put out a request for scrawny kids? He did. Did you send him one? You did. And now it's up to Skorx to decide. If he sends him into the tunnels, it's his responsibility. If he sends him back, no big deal. You can set the kid up somewhere in the kitchen before master comes around. They say he's not coming for two weeks."

"Yes," Ing agreed. "He's busy buying up new gladiators. Marshal Vestar's supply train just got to the capital. They have lots of prisoners of war, orcs and goblins."

"All the better. Master will hardly notice some new whelp. And you'll have a great chance to get back at Skorx. After all, didn't he send master a grievance against you last month?"

Based on Ing's angry face, the seeds had hit fertile soil. To my immense pity, Valgard hadn't only invested in strength. He had a way with words as well.

"And Skorx will also never learn the size of the boy's debt. The kid will give us an oath not to tell," said the big fellow, adding his final argument.

After those words, Ing shot a gaze at me. Brr... Cold as ice.

"Well then bigmouth, looks like you'll be following in the footsteps of your dearly departed daddy."

CHAPTER 3

"**H**ERE SWEETHEART, eat. I expect you haven't had anything all day."

A thin little old lady extended me a clay bowl full of vittles that smelled stupendous. I held my breath, swallowed a mouthful of saliva, and looked for the level of the dish. As if reading my thoughts, the old lady said reassuringly:

"Don't you fear, sweetie. It's common vegetable soup. Level zero."

And with a chuckle, as she left the barracks, she added:

"We don't have any other food here."

Despite my savage hunger, I did my best to take the bowl delicately.

"Oh, Great System, what a wonderful smell!" My eyes rolled back.

The traveling food Madam Horst put together for me, Random bless her, ran out this morning.

Thankfully Burdoc was generous and gave me a bit of dried onion and the end piece of some slightly stale bread. I wouldn't say I was accustomed to delicacies in my usual diet, but mom always tried to give me my fill, even if it was just normal food. Father once explained that it was her way of soothing an unfounded feeling of guilt.

Remembering my parents, the tears came right back to my eyes. I still felt like this whole nightmare would be coming to an end any time now. My dad's broad-shouldered figure would be appearing in the doorframe of the dirty barrack where I was temporarily sheltered. Then mom would jump out from behind him, hug me, squeeze me to her chest and we would get in a carriage and ride back home over a raucous retelling of the ludicrous mix-up that landed me here.

I finished the food so quickly it was as if there never was any to begin with. Carefully, as not to damage the valuable pieces of carrot, I sopped up the remaining soup with the end of a piece of bread. I drank down the cool water and sat back satisfied on a dusty hay-filled sack serving as my bed.

"Well, how are you doing? That perk you up a bit?"

A quiet raspy voice to my right tore me from the pleasant embrace of sleep. On the next bag over, half a step from me, someone turned over.

"I guess so," I answered just as quietly. In the dark barrack, there were at least thirty other people. All of them already asleep. The whole day of work obviously had them very tired. I didn't want to wake them.

"I love aunty Agatha's vegetable soup," I heard notes of satisfaction in the unseen man's voice. "It's a world away from when that brainless idiot Hrika makes it. You no doubt got twice as much carrot and cabbage."

"I didn't notice," I answered. "I finished the soup so fast."

"Well you did," the unknown person whispered in a confident tone. Seemingly, I caught a head nod through the darkness.

"But why would she give me more?" I decided to ask.

"What do you mean why?" the voice asked, resentful. "You saved her husband's life today."

"What do you mean? I didn't save anyone."

"What about Burdoc? You think he would have survived today's punishment? Last month when they caned the old bat, it was a miracle he recovered. They say Agatha gave almost all her savings to a medicine man. Just so he'd get better."

My throat ran dry. After all, with my little life supply, just one whip would be more than enough to end my life.

"And by the way, you got fed for free today," the voice shared some more wisdom from the darkness.

"For free?"

"Well sure. What, did you think they were gonna feed us here just because it's the nice thing to do? You gotta pay for grub. Where are you going next?"

"The mine they said, something about Skorx."

"Oh, bucko," I could hear notes of compassion in the voice of the unseen man. "That's bad luck... Skorx is a real animal. And his mine is basically a cesspit."

I felt a nasty chill run down my spine.

"Let me give you some free advice, kid. Try to keep your head down over there. Don't flaunt your valuables. Grow eyes on the back of your head. It isn't only peons down at Skorx's mine. They have lots of convict laborers, too. All kinds of thugs and killers. And the mine tunnels are teeming with subterranean creatures, too. You'd barely make a mouthful to them. But they aren't the ones you need to be afraid of. No, the real monsters in that gods-forsaken place are Skorx and his lowlife helpers. Follow my advice and you might make it out alive... But boy, don't you spend too much time down there..."

He said the last sentence very quietly, but I still heard it. And that made my heart beat all the harder.

"Th-thanks," I whispered back, hiccupping. But no answer followed. Clearly he thought our conversation was over and fell asleep.

I spent a long time lying there and listening

in the darkness. What if the stranger said something else useful all of a sudden? But he was unfortunately already asleep.

Turning over a few times on the bag, smoothing out the especially poky pieces of hay, I finally was able to relax and fall into a restive sleep to the measured snoring of my comrades in misfortune. Unprompted, some events of two days earlier popped into my head...

Two days prior. Several hours before the death of my parents.

I LOVE THIS DAY! Although, what am I talking about? Who doesn't love their own birthday?! At the very least, I've never met someone so foolish.

The excellent mood I woke up with wasn't even spoiled by the rain, which had been pouring since yesterday evening. I was awoken by a muted jingling of dishes from the kitchen. I spent a few minutes lying there and grinning like an idiot. I love these sounds. They can only mean one thing. Mom is cooking something yummy.

Following the sounds, a stupendous smell came into the room which made my stomach groan loudly.

Oh, Great System! Mom is baking my favorite thing - sugar bread! For some, the dish may be too simple, but not for me. There's nothing tastier than a slice of warm fresh-baked sugar bread with a thick layer of fresh fatty cheese on top and doused in amber honey. Every bite is an unforgettable explosion of sweet and sour delight followed by a big swallow of still-warm fresh milk.

On that day, it was as if the housekeepers didn't notice me. But it's all a game! It's always like that. First they put on serious faces as if it were a normal day but then they shower you with birthday wishes and gifts. How I love this day!

A few days ago, mom said something she shouldn't have. Father has a special gift prepared. Unlike anything I got before. Ever since, I'd been burning in impatience. And the closer I got to the long-awaited day, the more bothered I became.

I washed up and brushed my teeth, then went down into the dining room. My parents were already sitting at the table and talking in a low voice.

Trying to look manly, like a grown-up, I wished them good morning as I sat at the table. I might have gotten away with it, but my quivering arms betrayed my excitement.

A few weeks earlier, father went to the market in the capital. He brought back many necessities. Flour, honey, fabric. A few pieces of jewelry for mother. But he also brought a little bundle which he hadn't shown anyone. He placed it in a special hiding place where he kept all our savings and important papers. Even mom wasn't allowed to touch it. Well, at the very least that was what she told me. To be honest, there was such a tricky smile on her face when she said it. Only the biggest sucker in the world would have really believed her.

I asked mom about the bundle almost every day, but she remained firm. Just as expected, that bundle was now sitting on the opposite end of the table! And father and mother, pretending not to notice, just kept up their peaceful conversation. Huh, I'd lose my mind in no time at this rate...

The morning meal finally came to an end. Even the tasty food couldn't distract me from the mysterious object lying just an arm's-length away.

After thanking mom for the food, father finally looked at me. There was a happy and cunning smile dancing on his face.

"Alright mother," he chuckled. "Enough teasing our little silly goose."

Then to me:

"Come over here."

And, with a stupid smile, I walk over to my parents on cottony legs. Father unfolds the bundle. A leather case. A simple bone handle. When I realized what I was seeing, I lost my breath! A knife! A weapon! Damage! If I could do damage, I could earn experience essences and tablets!

"This is Dragonfly!" Smiling happily, father extended me the gift. "It's yours!"

"Happy birthday, son!" mom said, kissing me on the forehead.

Absent-mindedly replying to their congratulations, I took the knife out of the case, my hands shivering.

"Here is the switch," father told me.

I immediately pressed where he showed me. A narrow steel blade the length of my palm abruptly jumped out of the bone handle.

"See," father commented. "A bit curved. Like a dragonfly's wing. It's only sharp on one side. It looks like a simple field knife. But it has a very sharp tip, so it's also good for stabbing."

I turned it over in my hands a few times, taking it in. This was the first tool I could use for work. Perhaps, depending on the situation, it was also my first weapon. Finally! It's silly damage figures didn't even bother me. I was elated!

"Yes the damage is just two, but don't you worry," father justified. "That's temporary. When your level starts going up, the damage will go up too and very quickly. It's a scalable item and those are no laughing matter! Hehe! I spent fourteen years saving up for this thing! Without Dalia, I don't know what we'd have done..."

I stood up and gave father a very big hug. Then mom...

"Thank you... I'm so grateful to have you..."

Mom, smiling, kissed me another few times. After that, wiping a welled up tear with the edge of her apron, she hurried into the kitchen.

"Well, well. You've really touched your mother," father chuckled and immediately asked:

"Will you wait for me? Wanna do an experiment together? As soon as I'm back from the mines, we'll go into the woods and test out your new knife. What do you say?"

"Of course, father! I'll be waiting!"

"Wonderful! Who knows, maybe you'll hit level one by the time we get back? Huh?" Father was enthusiastic.

I don't know who was happier, him or me. I might have asked... But neither he nor mom ever came back...

Present day

"HERE, TAKE THIS. Aunty Agatha put you together some travelling food."

Jay was standing next to the cart with a few other people headed to the Crooked Mountains. That was where Mr. Bardan's old copper mine was located. I didn't want to think bad thoughts, but seemingly that would be my final stop.

"Th-thank you," I said, hiccupping in anxiety and taking the small package.

She's so pretty she could even give Mia a run for her money. But their beauty is different. Mia's beauty is cold like ice. Jay's is like a flame. Her affinity for fire comes from long, thick, red curls. Yesterday, when we were in the cart, she removed her kerchief to fix her hair. It startled me. I lost my breath. What beauty! I could even smell her hair. It smelled of grass and spring.

The gaze of her dark emerald eyes turned me inside out. What's happening to me? That never happened before!

"Take care of yourself out there, boy," she said protectively and walked toward the barrack where the kitchen was.

Boy? She saw me as nothing but a boy? My right arm squeezed the bundle tight. It was not anger. No. it was more like annoyance at myself for my helplessness and weakness.

Suddenly I saw Valgard standing nearby. He was staring at Jay's supple figure, his red-bearded face frozen in a lustful smile.

Was it just me, or did she see him? And it didn't embarrass or frighten her. I didn't totally understand the game they were playing, but I quickly realized that Jay was much older than I first thought.

"Hey, kiddo, climb up on the cart," Burdoc commanded. "If we hurry, we might get there by evening."

CHAPTER 4

"SO THEN, listen son," the cart driver, a bear of a man named Kril said didactically to his seven-year-old boy. "Once upon a time, there were three brothers. A warrior, a hunter and a mage. And they embarked upon a journey to distant lands in search of wealth and glory..."

The fire gave a measured flickering, driving back the darkness. Sparks, like newborn fireflies, flew up into the sky to quickly fade and fall back to earth as tiny little flecks of ash.

In the end, we didn't reach the mine by evening. One of our carts broke a wheel. We had to stop, fix the break and prepare the area for a night's rest. None of us wanted to have a chance encounter out here at this time of night, so we thought it better to stay put.

We had already all eaten, and those who hadn't yet made it to sleep were sitting around a big fire. The conversations fell silent. Everyone was thinking about their tough fate and what awaited them at our destination. The only person in high enough spirits to speak was Kril. He had to bring his son, because the boy's mother died prematurely. He was telling an old folk tale in a hushed tone — the adventures of the three brothers.

My father used to tell me the same one. I didn't know it then, but a trainer named Roglex later told us it was a way parents taught their children the basics of personal development.

The Tales of the Three Brothers are about a warrior, a hunter and a mage who can only achieve their goal by working together. Alone they never get anywhere. Just like in the story Kril is telling now. First, the big strong warrior can't handle a nasty monster without the agile hunter and book-smart mage.

There Kril ends the story and shifts from fable to moral. I gave a furtive smile, wrapped myself tighter in a blanket thoughtfully shared by Burdoc and got ready to hear Kril's lesson just as I'd done many years before from my father.

"So then, son," said the carriage driver, stroking his mop-headed boy's hair. "The Great System gave us three branches of development - Strength, Agility and Mind. And it granted us silver tablets when we were born, each giving one point to any of these characteristics so we can choose our own path. Which of the brothers do you like the best?"

"Warrior, of course!" Tim answered without thinking.

That made me laugh again. It was the exact answer I'd given my own father. Based on the thoughtful smiles on the bearded faces of the men listening to our conversation, all of them must have seen themselves in him.

"Hehe," chuckled Kril and patted his mop-headed boy's hair. "Strength is nice. But without Agility you can't apply it properly. And of course without Mind, you will spend it twice as fast and never get what you're after. Do you understand?"

"Yes," the boy nodded seriously.

"The three main branches are intertwined. If you only work on one of them, the other two will wither. What would have happened to Warrior without his brothers, if he fought the big monster all alone?"

"He would have died," Tim answered softly.

"Exactly!" his father raised his pointer finger in the air instructively. "Never forget that."

In response, Tim nodded slowly, then after a bit of thought asked:

"Hey dad, how do you grow the branches?"

"Good question, son. The Great System gives us tablets for that. There are different kinds. Clay, stone, iron, bronze..."

"And silver like I got?" the kid asked, smiling.

"Exactly right. The same kind you got from

the Great System on the day of your birth. They are very valuable."

"Why?"

"Because they can give a whole point to any characteristic. That's so your mom and I could choose which of your branches to invest in when you were born. All parents do it."

Listening to the placid conversation between father and son, I saw Burdoc making a sad, pensive face. The old man must have been overcome by memories...

"What other kinds of tablets are there?" Tim continued his interrogation.

"Gold, diamond and iridescent."

"Iridescent?" the scamp's eyes lit up.

"Yes," Kril nodded. "But you know son, everyone's heard of them, but no one has seen them. At the very least no one I know. Iridescent tablets are probably more of a legend."

"Woah! Legendary tablets!" Tim admired.

"Exactly, son," his father laughed. "Exactly right. Legendary."

The men all nodded happily.

The look of admiration on Tim's face was suddenly replaced with perplexity.

"But father, where do tablets come from?"

"Good question, son," Kril praised. "You can earn tablets in war, on hunts, and by gathering resources or performing very difficult tasks. And when increasing your level with experience essences. Every time you level-up, the Great

System gives you three silver tablets."

"Ess... Ess-eh-nces?" Tim asked, struggling with the word.

"Correct," his father answered. "They can be earned the same way as tablets. Every essence is one point of experience. Go look how many essences you need to get to level two."

Tim's eyes froze for a moment. His lips moved as he tried to work something out.

"It says zero then a slash, a two and three more zeroes," Tim squeezed out.

Hm, clearly Brother Mage was not favored in Kril's family. They must have put just one or two tablets into Tim's Mind.

"That means," Kril explained patiently. "You need to earn two thousand essences."

"Woah! Are you gonna help me?"

"Of course I will, but you're gonna have to do most of the work on your own. Such is the law of the Great System!"

"And can I fight with a sword or a spear like Brother Warrior?!" Tim's eyes glimmered in anticipation of future adventures.

"You can," Kril answered confidently and then slightly cooled his son's jets:

"But you'll have to earn many tablets by using the corresponding skills. And you'll have to increase your energy supply."

"And how do I do that?"

"Get endurance tablets and practice. Plus carrying capacity. After all, like Brother Warrior, you will be wearing armor and carrying a weapon. Then increase damage. You're at level one right now. That means your natural damage is just one. And don't forget about health and agility, either. Remember? Without Brother Hunter, Brother Warrior never would have gotten anywhere."

Kril doesn't often talk about Brother Mage. But that's basically the same as everyone I know. The Mind branch is the least popular of the three. Although, according to my father's tales, it is the most powerful. But alas, it's also the hardest to use and thus improve.

We only enter this world with two supplies — life and energy. Even someone as Bugged as me got those from the Great System. But the third supply, mana is something you have to earn.

In order to unlock it, you need a tablet of Intellect. Even the most basic kind, clay, will do. But the catch is that the only way to earn one is by gathering a magical resource or killing a creature with magical abilities, which is even harder.

And of course, all secondary characteristics that derive from the Mind branch are activated the same way as Intellect. Oh yeah, I totally forgot! There's one other way of earning tablets of any kind or quality. They can be bought, as can experience essences. Honestly, I'm scared to even imagine how much a Mind-branch tablet must cost.

I considered it and didn't notice that Kril was no longer by the fire. He must have been putting his son to bed in the cart. I looked around wearily. By the looks of things the only ones not asleep were me and two sentries watching the fire. I lay down just a step from them. I close my eyes. Time for me to hit the hay, too. Then through my dream, I hear the squeaky voice of one of the sentries. I don't know his name, but everyone calls him Flea.

"You know what's with old man Burdoc today?"

"What do you mean?" a raspy voice answered his question with a question. That's Hart. Despite his whole head of gray hair, he is not yet an old man. Level fifteen. Many scars on his hands, arms and face. His predatory gaze penetrates into the marrow. One of Skorx's cutthroats. That's what the others say behind his back.

"Yeah, I saw his old face go blank while he was listening to Kril," Flea explained.

"Ah, there you go," Hart answered understandingly. "That old bump on a log must have remembered his childhood when he heard about the tablets."

"Can you tell me?" I could hear impatience and intrigue in Flea's squeaky voice.

"Sure, why not?" Hart rasped. "We've gotta sit around another few hours anyway. And as we know, time passes quicker when we talk."

"Yep, yep..."

"About the old man? Alright, I'll tell you...

Not many know this, but Burdoc was born in the barony of Arundel."

"And where is that? I'm not sure I've ever heard of such a place..."

"That's because you're young. And it hasn't existed for a long time. It's in the east. You probably know it by a different name."

"But the only place east of here is..."

"Exactly. The Wastes."

"Old man Burdoc was born in the Wastes?" Flea asked in surprise.

I also shuddered when I heard the familiar name. It was where my older brother died.

"But steppe orcs control the Wastes!" Clearly learning our coachman's origin did a lot to awaken Flea's imagination. He was really worked up.

"Hey, settle down, blockhead! You're gonna wake everybody up," Hart snapped at his younger comrade. "Yes, he was born in the Wastes! And why are you yelling? It's no shock to me. You know how many of our brothers were born into orcish slavery? No? Well let me tell you, too many to count! Almost every family in the east has someone who spent some time enslaved by the grayskins. Some get captured in battle, others just get snatched up on a raid. Some like Burdoc were just born into it. Our pregnant women are just about the biggest prize for those steppe nomads."

"Why is that?" Flea asked quietly.

By the looks of things, he hadn't been especially focusing on the Mind branch either.

Even I could see why the orcs would want pregnant women.

"Too dim to guess?" Hart asked bitingly. "Don't look at me like that, dolt. It isn't the ladies they want, it's the future people they carry in their womb. And to be even more accurate, it's the silver tablets the Great System awards newborns."

"Bastards!" I could hear hate and indignation in Flea's voice.

And I felt solidarity. My right hand clutched the bone handle of my knife in outrage.

"Bastards is exactly right," Hart agreed in a calm voice. "In a word, inhuman. The shamans give sleeping potions to the mothers so they can't quickly use the tablets on their children and they take everything the Great System grants the child. But that is not all. When the kids grow up, they are given the simplest possible gear for stats and sent out to earn tablets and essences for the tribe. That is why our Burdoc is so weak. He spent half his life working for the orcs."

"Hmm... well cuh-rap..." Flea drew out the word, dazed. "And how did he get here? Did he run?"

"Run from the orcs?" Hart laughed. "From the steppes? No-ope... Not many have the strength for that."

"Then what?"

"Flea, as long as I've known you, it's always surprised me how daft you can be. Don't be so stingy next time and invest a bit in Mind. Hehe...

Haven't you heard the tales of the brothers? Or didn't your mom not tell you fairy tales when she put you to bed?"

"Well, I uhh..." Flea burbled.

"You're a dolt," Hart put it briefly. "Use your brains a little bit. How could he have gotten out here from orcish slavery? I see two options. Either the orcs sold him or the orcs were themselves enslaved. As for Burdoc, it was option two. Our Baron's retinue broke a tribe of steppe warriors. All the slaves of the orcs became peons of the baron. Our master bought many of their debts, including Burdoc's. And that's the whole story."

Could that have been the battle in the Wastes that took my brother? I'd have to find out exactly when that battle took place. If that was so, it meant old man Burdoc was freed partially thanks to my brother. Although it was hard to call peonage freedom. It was basically the same as slavery, just a slightly shifted view. And if anyone came out most ahead it was our Baron Berence without a doubt. That was why my father didn't like nobles. He always called them monsters who grew fat on our blood...

The Crooked Mountains greeted us with a cold rain. Due to the huge torrents of water falling from the sky, the road among the gray cliffs gradually turned into a raging river. A few times, I got the impression the carts were about to careen into the abyss but, thanks to our driver's mastery of his trade, not a single bag or box of provisions was lost.

Burdoc, for the record, caught me by surprise. Despite his frailty, he displayed true marvels of cart-driving. He had probably been investing in that skill all his life. I guess he really was worth his salt.

When we finally reached the miners' village, we were soaked to the bone and no less tired than the horses.

While we strolled the main street, I managed to see the living quarters of the locals. Mostly it was old barracks, but there were also some separate newer little houses. In some of the windows, I saw the faces of women and children.

We stopped for a few minutes outside one of the homes. The doors flew open and a woman hopped out onto the street wrapped in a gray down shawl. To look at her, I would say she was fifty. To my surprise, her face looked familiar. She ran over to Kril's cart, grabbed Tim, who was wrapped in a leather shawl and scurried back into the house. That was when I realized the woman, Kril and his little son all bore a certain resemblance to one another. It instantly dawned on me. She was Tim's grandma!

I distantly remembered stories of my own relatives. The Bergmans hadn't always lived in Orchus. My father and mother were born in the western lands. And that was also where they got married. On their wedding day, two strong clans were bonded. And by the end of the year, mom said she was expecting the heir to both families. But their happiness was darkened by news of a horrible epidemic raging on the western coast. In order to prevent my expectant mother falling ill, my grandparents convinced my parents to move to Orchus for a time. To wait out the disaster. The city had already sent riders to the healers' guild in the capital, but it wouldn't be safe until the sickness cleared.

And hindsight proved they made the right choice. The messengers never even reached the capital. The illness took them on the way. Then over the course of a week, the plague ate through almost the whole city. Not many survived. Among my relatives, none. The local Baron, in order to keep the infection from spreading, ordered the town burned to the ground. Along with the remaining survivors. I think that was the very moment my father began to hate nobles with such a passion...

We rode another few minutes down the main village street and our wagon train turned right down an alley. After that, we turned again, and again... A few more turns and we finally stopped next to a large barn, which was behind a tall stockade fence and guarded by five warriors. Provisions must have been very expensive here, seeing how they were guarded so closely.

Just then, a crowd of beggars appeared at the heavy gates holding clay bowls and mugs. It was mostly old folks, but also there were children.

When they spotted us from afar, they ran out to meet us, badgering and begging us to give them a bit of food or money.

Hart, Flea and the other two warriors who accompanied our caravan, without delay and not being especially careful, drove off the poor folks with lashes.

When he saw me looking dazed, Hart bared his teeth and barked:

"Look, kid. Take this as a warning! If you're lazy, you'll fall to the level of these unfortunate souls!"

When the warrior turned back around, someone shook me by the sleeves. I looked down. It was a kid, eight years old. A mop of black uncombed hair. Colorless simple clothes. A pitiful gaze in hazel eyes. A grubby face.

"Please, some bread?" he squeaked.

I shuddered. It put me beside myself. I understood that my position was not exactly enviable, but I was feeling like a rich man compared to this little kid.

"Sorry, boy," I shrug my shoulders. "No bread, but I do have this here..."

I take a little green apple from my bundle and extend it to the kid. I see his admiring gaze. The fruit disappears almost magically and the boy, without saying a word, starts off for the nearest alley.

"Pointless."

Hart's raspy voice makes me shudder

despite myself.

"You'll come to regret that very soon," he said and walked toward the guardsmen coming our way.

The newcomers, including me, were lined up outside despite the downpour of icy rain. Two steps from the entrance into the warm and dry barracks. On the doorstep, under a wide visor and surrounded by guards, stood Knud. He was second in command after Skorx, who was now away.

A thin and spiteful old man with a ravenous gaze. Thin lips, rotten teeth, a nose sharp as a bird's beak, a greasy clump of gray hair on his chin — an unsavory type. The only feature I liked was the lack of a right ear.

He'd lost it at the hands, or more accurately teeth of one of the peons. Truth be told, it was said that Knud later arranged a "mining accident" for the sap who did it to him. Based on his spiteful rat-like face and harsh gaze — One-ear, as he was called around here, was capable of much worse than that.

"Mark this well, I will say it only once!" Knud began our intake session unhurriedly with a monotone voice. "You are standing here up to your knees in shit because you shit the bed. The bank was so kind and generous as to lend you their hard-earned cash, and you failed to pay them back."

One-ear led a harsh tenacious stare over us and continued.

"Let me warn you assholes right away. If you lose your marbles, and get it in your stupid head to do something we don't like — our conversation will be short and sweet."

The old man nodded toward ten posts at the far wall of a barrack. A few of them had bloodied naked bodies tied to them. Giving us time to take in the ghastly spectacle, Knud continued:

"Now onto the main event. How you will repay your debt to my master. All of you are peons, and that means that, other than the principal, you must pay off three percent interest each month with your labor. Believe you me, Mr. Bardan is merciful and generous. Other masters charge much higher rates."

After making some crude calculations in my head, I fell into a stupor. In my case, that's about three gold per month. That means I need to somehow earn ten silver every day...

"If you haven't paid back your interest by the end of the month, they will add that to the principal and the rate for the next month will be calculated off that," Knud continued beating it into us. "For one daily quota of ore, you will be given three silver coins."

Highway robbery. As son of a miner, I can confidently say that the minimum for one quota is generally around six coins. And if the ore is valuable, it could be even more. Probably Skorx is taking a bit off the top. Honestly, that doesn't affect me either way. I couldn't harvest ore anyhow.

As if hearing my thoughts, the old man continued:

"Other work will be judged in measure with its use. Low-skilled labor is valued at one silver per day maximum."

Only then did it start to reach me what a serious debt hole I'd fallen into.

"For a bed in a barrack and food from the common pot, you'll have to pay. You'll pay for your tools as well. If you don't have the money — we can loan you some for a place to sleep and food to get you started. If it takes too long to pay back... hm... Let me give you some advice. It's in your interest to pay us back as quickly as possible. Remember, you have no rights here, like cattle. And until you can repay my master, you cannot leave this place."

I suspected that Hart's prediction would come true, but I wasn't expecting it to come so fast...

Now I was sitting on the floor of an old barrack. Soaked to the bone. My teeth were chattering so hard I could feel them coming loose. A fierce damp wind howled up through a gap in the rotten boards, chilling me straight to the marrow.

When Knud finished his intake lecture, all of us in turn gave an oath promising we'd repay the debt and the Great System confirmed. Now I have only two ways out. Either on my own two feet after repaying the debt, or feet first into a pauper's grave. Based on the conditions us peons are kept in, the latter is more likely.

Thankfully, Burdoc gave me a thin blanket as a parting gift and now it was sheltering me from the cold, but just barely. Before he left, the old man also advised me to stay away from the northern tunnels. They were said to be the most ancient and dangerous part of the mine. Just a deadly place...

Oooh! I want to eat so bad! My stomach is just in knots. The night before, no one had any plans of feeding us. We all had to get by on our own rations. And I had given my last apple to some street urchin out of the goodness of my heart. I had no money, so I had to get started here on an empty stomach.

My energy supply was already not doing great, but now it had been sitting at a mere two for quite some time. Strangely, I never regretted giving away the apple... well, so far... We'll see how I start to feel when my supply runs dry...

Of course, at a time like this, I couldn't help but think about a backup option. I always had one up my sleeve. Even when I was sitting on the stool in the corner of the entryway of my parents' home and watching my family belongings be plundered, I knew it was there. I just ordered myself no matter what happened to never think about it.

My stomach turned again and, despite myself, my gaze caught on the knife. That was my alternate way out of this shit. The artifact of the Departed. If I sold it, all my problems would be over.

First I considered the ring or button, but I quickly decided against those options. I couldn't get by without characteristics. I could at least live without damage.

As soon as I started thinking about selling the artifacts, I remembered father and mother. Had all their efforts been in vain? Father spent so long hunting for each of these artifacts. He went into debt. He risked being found out or robbed. He paid tons of money for each item and all so his son could just give into weakness and sell them for a pittance? Just to fill his stomach and warm his body? Though honestly, my parents would hardly have wanted me to die here of cold and hunger either.

But no! I won't give in so easy! Tomorrow is another day. I'll think of something!

"Hey kid, you alive over there?!"

The sound of a voice from the darkness made me shudder.

"F-for now, yes," I answered, my teeth chattering. My hand reached for the knife all on its own.

A powerful figure dove out of the darkness and a joyful flaxen-haired head loomed over me. Big blue eyes, a slightly upturned snub nose. An open smile. A boy of twenty years. Level eleven. His dress was simple but sound, and clean. His face beamed kindness and inspired trust but, out of decency I frowned and shrunk.

"Hey, hey, kid! Calm down!" he said, seeing my reaction. "Sorry I scared you. I saw you in this crap heap shivering from cold and decided hey, why not come over? I figured I'd ask if maybe you need some help."

"You help everyone around here?" I ask untrustingly, my voice skeptical.

"No, of course not," he answered seriously and immediately added pointedly:

"Only those who are willing to help others. I saw you share an apple with Crum back there. So then, what are you doing here? It's been a long time since anyone stayed in this barrack..."

"No money."

"How about a loan? Lots of people here started out that way. Me included."

"Knud said I wasn't allowed. He said I'm useless. And to let Skorx decide what to do with me."

"Well the Marked One won't be back for a week."

"Who?"

"The Marked One. That's what everyone calls Skorx around here. You'll see soon. You'll understand."

"Then what should I do?"

"First of all, get a bite to eat, warm up and get some sleep."

He smiled disarmingly and extended a hand:

"By the way, I forgot to introduce myself. The name's Frodi."

"Eric," I responded, also matching his firm handshake.

"Happy to meet you, Eric," Frodi said and nodded at the exit:

"Let's go. There's nothing for you here."

"Uh, wh-where?" I asked, worried. But still I got up from the cold floor.

"Let's go, come on then," my new acquaintance said in a friendly manner and then asked as if in passing:

"You like porridge with mushrooms?"

My stomach groaned treacherously, answering for us both. Frodi laughed loudly at my peculiar response. I looked at him. His kind open face, his tidy appearance. Listening to his endearing vocal timbre, I was sincerely confused — why did I still have doubts? My stomach gave another unintentional burble. As if to say, "what are you waiting for, master? There is warmth and mushroom porridge to be had!" And that was the final argument.

Frodi patted me on the shoulder like an old friend and said:

"Let's go quick! Otherwise they'll eat it all without us!"

My new acquaintance lived in a small but new and warm barrack with fresh floorboards. There were another seven men living there as well. All higher than level ten. They were strong and well equipped. Truthfully, none of their faces were as kind as Frodi's. Everywhere I looked, I saw the faces of cutthroats.

Noticing my perplexity at the entrance to the barrack, Frodi laughed:

"Come in, don't be afraid. Everyone here is a friend. Isn't that right, boys?"

He was answered by a discordant chorus of hoarse and smoky voices. And by the way, none of them paid me any mind.

"Frodi, you little jerk! Close the door!" Someone shouted angrily from a distance. "You'll let all the heat out!"

The boy gave my back a gentle push and quickly slammed the door.

"Let's go," he nodded toward a small stove.

I walked on cottony legs past some pretty beat up plank beds which was what these men used for sleeping, sitting or just lying around. Up close they seemed even stranger and more dangerous.

It was very warm in the barrack, even hot. So they were all stripped to the waist. Based on all the tattoos on the men's bodies, I realized what kind of place Frodi had brought me to. This was a barrack for convict laborers.

"Sit here next to the stove," he said, pointing me to a stool. "I'll get us some food."

I sat timidly on the edge of the stool, ready to run for the exit at any time. For the record, they're all still ignoring me as if I'm not here at all.

A few moments later, Frodi came with two deep bowls in his hands. I could smell the stupendous mushroom aroma from a distance.

"Here," he extended me a bowl of steaming porridge. "Shovel it down while it's still warm."

There was a rye rusk in the bowl along with the porridge, which I used for a spoon.

As expected, I wolfed down the porridge very quickly. The food and warmth quickly made me sleepy. As I put down the last "spoonfuls," I was already dozing off. I only had the strength to slowly crawl off the stool and curl up in a ball on the floor in a corner a step away from the stove.

A few seconds before I passed out, I heard a fragment of a conversation.

"How'd it all go?" one of them asked in a raspy powerful voice.

"Fine," Frodi answered.

"One-ear?"

"He doesn't mind."

"Good," I heard satisfaction in the hoarse voice. "Take him to the mine tomorrow."

CHAPTER 5

THAT NIGHT I had a wonderful dream. Both my mom and dad were there. They were speaking, smiling... I wasn't allowed to finish the dream. Someone was shaking my shoulder demandingly.

"That's enough sleep for you today, kid," Frodi said happily.

Is he ever serious, I wonder?

"Morning already?" I ask, looking around sleepily.

"Sun's coming up soon," the boy nodded. "We've gotta go."

"Are we in a hurry?" I rub my eyes.

All the barrack residents are still snoring peacefully on their plank beds.

"Of course!" Frodi exclaims and, after following my gaze, says:

"Don't you look at them. They have their own tasks. Here you go — to keep your strength up."

He extended me three thick slices of fresh bread, ten or so small prunes and a mug of water.

"Eat up and let's move out."

It never takes long to talk me into eating. Quickly taking down the basic meal, I looked eagerly to my older pal. Truth be told, I stashed one big slice of bread and five prunes for later.

How I would repay all this generosity was something I didn't want to consider. I decided for the time being to stick to the principle: "take what's offered." There's no other way. My life is on the line. If I get hungry, my Energy supply will run out. And as soon as that happens, it will start taking from my Life supply to fill itself... And I have just ten points there...

Despite the early morning hour, everyone in the village was already awake. A few well-armed people were driving a small herd of goats somewhere. And those five there, based on the miner's outfits, must have been on their way to gather ore. Frodi and I, leaving the gates, spent some time walking in their tracks. But then we turned down a very overgrown path that split off from the main road.

"This is an old road to some abandoned tunnels no one mines anymore."

"So, w-why are we g-going there?" I asked, alarmed.

He stopped and, smiling, looked at me.

"Kid what's with you? Scared?"

The same open and ingratiating facial expression.

"N-no," I try put on a brave face. "But still..."

"Come on, don't have a cow," Frodi dismissed it. "As I said, there's something I want to show you. I hope it can help you earn some coin for food and a bed. Up at the level me and the guys are at, everything in this place is worthless. But it could be just the thing for a zero like you."

A bit later, when the sun was really beaming, we reached a fairly wide opening in the cliffside.

"Here!" Frodi said triumphantly. "This is the spot! Let's go..."

"You sure there's nothing nasty in there? I only have ten life points. One bite is enough to kill me."

"No, there's nobody there, nothing," Frodi reassured me. "Don't worry. Just wait a second, I'm gonna light a torch."

He ducked into the darkness of the cave and a bit later a fire shone from its womb.

"Come over here, kid!" he shouted. "It's safe!"

After a bit of hesitation, I decided to follow this to the end. This person wants to help me, and I'm acting like some cowardly stray dog.

In the cave it was damp and gloomy, but Frodi's careless demeanor gave me a certain confidence. Beyond that, my father was a miner and wasn't afraid to go into scarier shafts than this, even as a child. I was constantly pounding that fact into my head like a magic spell. If he could do it, so can I. Bizarrely, that helped push my fears into the background for a bit.

The wide tunnel wound a bit and led us into a wide cave.

"This is a crossing," my guide explained. "A few big sections get their start here."

I glanced at the dark tunnel entrances and shuddered involuntarily. Was it just me or could I hear a muted howling from the farthest one?

"That's just the wind," Frodi explained and nodded at the nearest passage:

"We're headed that way."

The nearly straight tunnel (I counted forty-six steps), led to a cave with an underground lake. Here it was unexpectedly bright due to the many holes in the stone ceiling. The water, glassy calm, reflected the rays of the sun, casting glints of light onto the walls.

I opened my mouth, astounded.

"Pretty, right?!" Frodi commented.

"Very."

"And not that scary."

That's right! Distracted by the gorgeous view, I had totally forgotten about my fears!

"But we aren't here to look at pretty stuff," Frodi brought me down to earth. "Look."

He pointed at a stone wall with a thick coating of gray moss. I walked up closer and stopped one step from where he pointed.

"What do you see?" the boy asked.

"A wall and some moss."

"Can you cut a bit off?"

I looked.

"Yes, I can. It's level zero."

"Alright, give it a try. Let's see what the Great System gives you."

"Hmm, other than the moss itself — nothing," I warned. "I've tried to gather level zero resources many times, but I never got anything."

"Well try again," Frodi winked conspiratorially. "Maybe this time will be different."

"Well okay, but only because you asked," I said with a shrug of my shoulders, taking out the knife.

I really had tried gathering level-zero resources the whole way to the Crooked Mountains. I cut grasses, popped out little rocks, and cut bark off trees, but I never got any tablets or essences for my trouble.

I spotted a small piece of moss and, with a few fairly awkward motions, cut it down off the wall and instantly froze, my mouth open, dumbfounded...

- *You have acquired Gray Moss.*

- *Congratulations! You receive:*
- *Experience essence (5).*
- *Clay tablet "Herbalism."*
- *Clay tablet of Agility.*

- *Clay tablet "Knife Proficiency."*

I looked at the system notification and couldn't believe my eyes. I reread it a few times, then took a glance at my sack. Was that really it?! Did it really work?! I wanted to shout and jump for joy! How long I'd waited for this! Fourteen whole years! And am I gonna get level one now, too?! Can I level like everyone else?! That would make my parents so happy!

My hands shaking, I again open my knapsack and start taking out my riches. The more times I reread the characteristics of my first real loot, the more the stupid happy smile crawled off my face, gradually changing into a grimace of confusion, then anger.

"What's the matter?" Frodi's voice sounded out right over my head.

I was distantly surprised at how quickly and, more importantly, silently he walked up behind me. Though it's easy to understand my mood...

With a loud exhale, I fell down on the stone floor feeling defeated and covered my face with my hands. I wanted to bawl in anger.

"Hey, what's the matter?" My older pal raised his voice again. "Activate the essences and jump up to level one."

Was it just me, or was there a little club in his hand all of a sudden? I looked again... No... It was just me... Just a shadow on his hand...

"I can't," I exhaled in rage.

"Why might that be?"

Why was he so tense? And where'd his careless smile go?

"The essences and tablets have a restriction. Level one," I answer shortly.

"Why would they have that?!" Frodi is surprised. "I don't see the logic. Both you and the resources are zero. That means the loot should all be zero, too."

"A wise medicine woman once said the Malevolent Bug made me as a joke. It looks like she was right and I will always be a freak."

"Cuh-rap," the boy drew out thoughtfully. "Tough luck... and what am I gonna tell him now?"

"Who?" I asked in surprise.

"Ah don't you worry about it, kid," he waved it off. "And chin up. In fact, you can be happy you got some loot."

"Five essences and three tablets. I just don't understand why..."

"Well that's actually quite simple. Read the characteristics of the moss."

I followed his advice, intrigued.

- *Gray Moss.*
- *Weight: 1.75 ounces.*
- *Value: Extremely low.*
- *Quality: Fresh (will change in 12 hours).*

"Okay. And what?"

"You slow or something? You don't see anything?"

I reread it a few times and my gaze stopped on the "value" line.

"Looking at your face, I can see that you figured it out," Frodi smiled.

Seemingly, his usual positivity is coming back.

"There are a couple patterns the Great System always follows. For example, as you were saying, if a resource has a value of 'worthless,' you won't get any essences or tablets."

"Hm, then what's the point of worthless resources even existing?" I asked angrily.

"The Great System knows best how to order our world," Frodi shrugged his shoulders.

I think I know someone who might dispute that assertion. Dalia once mentioned in conversation with my father that there were ancient books that said the Great System isn't so great after all, just a system. And it was created by those we call the Ancients or the Departed. Nonsense and heresy, of course. Father by the way said as much the day he learned it. But right now, there was so much anger pent up in my heart that I wanted to believe Dalia was right.

"Alright, Eric," Frodi said thoughtfully. "Then you stay here and keep working. I'll run off to the village and send someone to hang with you. Just in case..."

"Alright," I agreed without much

consideration. "And does anyone want this moss for anything?"

The fact I cannot use the bonus loot for its express purpose is of course a problem but not a reason to wallow in self-pity. At the end of the day, I would now have a stable source of income. After all, tablets and essences could be sold.

"As far as I know, this moss is useless trash, even though the Great System thinks otherwise. Feel free to just throw it away."

"Gotcha," I mumbled, disappointed.

When my pal was already at the exit, I shouted after him:

"Frodi! Uh... Thank you! I'll never forget what you've done for me!"

The boy turned. For a moment, I thought I saw a strangely acrid grimace cross his face. I blinked. No, it was just me... His face was just as happy and careless as ever. What's with all these glitches today? I'm seeing all kinds of things. Here a club in his hand, there a predatory grin. And all of it from the strange lighting in this cave. Yeah, and let's face it, I'm very anxious.

Frodi gave a friendly wink and waved it off:

"Don't worry about it, friend! Buy me a round when you get rich! Haha!"

A moment later, he disappeared into the tunnel and I was left alone. First of all, I come close to the lake, get down on a knee at the water and wash my very warm face.

Nice! The chill made my scorching forehead

and cheeks tingle. And the water was ice cold. After dousing my neck a couple of times, I finally cheered up. Nothing to worry about! We'll get through it!

After washing up, I crouched on a stone. I needed to look over my trophies more carefully. First, I took out the essences. Little droplets of crystal the size of a thumbnail. In the sun, they shimmered with all the colors of the rainbow. Pretty!

> *- Experience essence.*
> *- Level: 1.*
> *- Effect: +1 to current level progress.*
> *- Weight: None. Takes no space.*

And I had five of them. Now onto the tablets. The thin sheets of clay were the size of my hand. Covered in runic etching. Very lightweight.

> *- Clay Tablet of Agility.*
> *- Level: 1.*
> *- Category: Characteristics.*
> *- Effect: + 0.1 to current Agility progress.*
> *- Weight: None. Takes no space.*

> *- Clay Tablet "Herbalism."*
> *- Level: 1.*
> *- Category: Professions.*
> *- Effects:*
> *- First use activates the Herbalism profession.*

- + 0.1 to current profession progress.
- Weight: None. Takes no space.

- Clay Tablet "Knife Proficiency."
- Level: 1.
- Category: Skills.
- Effect: + 0.1 to current progress in Knife Proficiency skill.
- Weight: None. Takes no space.

I'd have to find out how much tablets and essences sold for in the village.

When I realized I'd have to sell everything, a lump rose up my throat. Fourteen years of anticipation and torment! And now the long awaited level one was slipping through my fingers yet again...

I rubbed my temples and forehead furiously then shot up from the ground. Enough sulking! Time to get to business!

I walked over to the wall and took out Dragonfly. My second piece of moss came a bit easier.

- You have acquired Gray Moss.

- Congratulations! You receive:
- Experience essence (5).
- Clay tablet "Herbalism."
- Clay tablet of Agility.
- Clay tablet "Knife Proficiency."

Woah! Random was feeling generous today! I could feel my hands shaking in overexcitement. Unable to keep resisting the fire in my belly, I got to work double time.

- You have acquired Gray Moss.

- Congratulations! You receive:
- Experience essence (5).
- Clay tablet "Herbalism."
- Clay tablet of Agility.
- Clay tablet "Knife Proficiency."

I looked at the list of trophies. Five essences and three tablets! And again unexpectedly generous!

Alright, let's say I'm still getting bonuses. Everyone knows you always get so-called "bonus" loot for the first things you gather, but the Great System and Random "cut" the trophies after that. Father gave me an in depth explanation once. But I just made three moss cuttings and already had three tablets of Agility. In general though, leveling a main branch is quite a drawn-out process. Sure, I agree. Clay only adds one tenth of a point but, if I dream a bit, another seven like this would add up to one silver.

Maybe Random is just in a good mood today? I really hope so. I'll keep cutting.

- You have acquired Gray Moss.

- Congratulations! You receive:

- Experience essence (5).

- Clay tablet "Herbalism."

- Clay tablet of Agility.

- Clay tablet "Knife Proficiency."

A chill ran down my spine. What is happening? I take another cut, my hand shivering...

And again the same result!

And again... And again...

After my tenth cut, I stopped, breathing heavily in excitement. There are thirty tablets and fifty experience essences in my knapsack. How can that be?! So many cuts and I just keep getting bonus loot like it's my first time!

What if I try like this? I get up a bit higher and reach for the edge of the wall. Now I'm perched like a spider. I can feel my leg muscles cramping. My lower back and shoulders are on fire. I'm pushing my characteristic points for all they're worth.

- You have acquired Gray Moss.

- Congratulations! You receive:

- Experience essence (10).

- Clay tablet "Herbalism."

- Clay tablet of Agility.

- Clay tablet "Knife Proficiency."

- Clay tablet of Strength.

- *Clay tablet of Endurance.*
- *Clay tablet of Acrobatics.*
- *Clay tablet of Flexibility.*

I get down carefully to the ground to refill my flagging energy supply. I grin like an idiot looking over the new tablets. Just like father taught me. Expending more energy, means the loot will be better. But to this degree?! I've never heard of something like this. And I probably never will. Dalia said my case is unique. And I am inclined to believe the healer.

I look at my energy numbers. A bit lower than fifty percent. Within normal limits. I toss a gaze up. Okay... As father used to say, you gotta strike while the iron's hot! Never relax! I have to keep gathering!

CHAPTER 6

I STOPPED cutting when my energy supply stopped filling back up. I pushed my three Strength points for all they were worth, and they were able to cope with the workload for a time. But unfortunately not all that long. I started tiring quickly.

I was only able to gather seven pounds of moss. I could have kept going but there was no more moss left on the lowest level of the wall. I had to cut up high and that took all my strength.

I'd go up, make a cut and come back to the ground with just one and three quarters ounces to restore my energy points. Thankfully, I got more loot for the additional effort.

Frodi never came back, and no one ever came as he promised. I was nursing a vague hope that one of them would bring me some food, but immediately forbid myself from even thinking about it. I was nobody to Frodi and his people. What possible reason did they have to worry about some outsider kid? I have to make it on my own merits.

I pat myself on the back a few times for saving the bread and prunes for later. They were my lunch. Beyond that, I was saved by the fact I had easy access to water. Thirst, as everyone knows, "dries out" your energy and life supplies much faster than hunger.

Although Frodi advised me to throw all the moss away, I just couldn't bring myself to do it. I don't know why. Maybe because it was the first resource I ever gathered on my own that had ever given me anything for the trouble? One way or another, I couldn't come up with a clear explanation.

But my knapsack also wasn't infinite. I decided to set all the moss I gathered on a large flat stone. As it happens, that was where most sun was hitting. Let it sit there, dry out. Maybe it'll be good for something later.

When I finished off the last clump, I fell to the ground tired. I looked at my first haul, an unsightly gray mass covering a flat stone. Hmm... It was only seven pounds, but I was so tired it was like I'd spent all day swinging a pickaxe in a mine.

Now it was time to tally up my results for the workday. Working with abandon, I estimate the totals. And I open my sack with a degree of excitement.

- *Experience essence (400).*
- *Clay tablet "Herbalism" (64).*
- *Clay tablet of Agility (64).*
- *Clay tablet "Knife Proficiency" (64).*
- *Clay tablet of Strength (16).*
- *Clay tablet of Endurance (16).*
- *Clay tablet of Acrobatics (16).*
- *Clay tablet of Flexibility (16).*

I shake my head. I wipe the sweat from my brow and eyes. I reread the whole thing. I feel my heart pounding. It's about to jump out of my chest. My hands are slightly quivering in excitement. My back is soaked in cold sweat.

One of Bug's dirty tricks, no two ways about it. They say he's also quite the jokester. I had to agree with that. My existence was direct evidence.

In the end, cutting just seven pounds of moss landed me clay tablets worth a whole twenty-two points! And of that there was one strength and six agility! If I were level one right now...! I'd...! I'd have...! My heartbeat started racing. I feel tears of rage coursing down my hot cheeks. There they are, my long-awaited tablets and essences right in my hands! But what good are they to me?!

I wanted to cram myself into a dark crack and just bawl in sorrow. Like when I was a child. I had a secret hiding place in our basement. A little cupboard. Every time someone mocked me in school, I would hide out there and sulk in resentment. So no one could see my tears and weakness...

But alas, my parents, our house and that cupboard were all gone now... Instead, I have a gods-forsaken new home where I have to survive no matter what it takes. And I do not intend to sulk.

My fist clenched tight, I angrily wipe away my treacherous tears. If the gods decided I was supposed to be this way, it was meant to be.

I took another quick glance at my trophy list and smiled through the tears. Whoever said it's all going bad for me?! Look at all that loot! I have to admit, it was so much I was afraid...

I imagine Frodi's surprised face when I show him my take. Hehe...

As soon as I thought about my new friend, I remembered a lesson from father. I thoughtfully stroke my chin. Father was always saying not to stand out. If you suddenly get a stroke of good luck, and the gods bless you with unexpected riches or fortune, just keep living the way you always have. Don't rush to show off your wealth to others. Otherwise you're inviting tragedy. That was what he said every time he came back with a new artifact.

I trust Frodi. He gave me shelter. Fed me both yesterday and today. Brought me to this cave. He is a friend. At the very least he acts like one. But I couldn't just ignore father's lessons either.

My unexpected success might draw unwanted attention. I can't forget where I am and what kind of people are around me. After all, when I get down to it, I am only entitled to twenty percent of what I gather. Well, thirty maximum if I consider that today is my first day.

Noope... Father was right. I couldn't afford to stand out, and certainly not go showing off all this loot. No way. Bluster and bravado might come at quite a high price here.

With caution, I look around. I am still alone in the cave. Looks like Frodi really did forget about me. And that's for the best. It gives me time to make a secret hiding spot. See, I'd decided to leave more than half of the loot behind. I'd bring approximately one fifth to the village. That would be more plausible.

My stomach groaned demandingly. I gave it a pat. Yeah, yeah. I'll give you a nice big feast tonight. Plus I have to figure out a place to live. They'd hardly be waiting for me with open arms in the prison laborer barrack. Why would they want more roommates or mouths to feed? They helped me out, gave me a warm place to sleep and fed me, and I was wholeheartedly thankful for that. But that was all. Now it was time to get set up on my own. Thankfully, now I'd have money. Most important would be selling it all without drawing attention. And then if everything goes well, I'd be out of peonage in the blink of an eye.

Hmm, dreaming about nice things is a great distraction from all kinds of gloomy thoughts. It felt easier to breathe.

I spent quite long time searching for a secret hiding spot and was fairly particular. First I wanted to bury it all in the sand, but then I thought about rain. The holes in the ceiling were too big a liability. What if a week-long downpour comes through? The lake level would rise and it would spill out onto the sand. All the shell fragments mixed in with the sand were plenty evidence of that.

The best option was climbing up the wall and hiding it all in a crack. Water definitely wouldn't get in there. But alas, I wasn't up to the task. I'd have to keep looking for something I could actually do.

Just when I started thinking, "to hell with it," about to go to another cave, I found an appropriate place. A very narrow and more importantly inconspicuous gap between two sharp stones caught my eye by complete coincidence. I had a hard time fitting my hand inside. And good. The large hand of a grown man wouldn't be able to fit. Dry inside. Exactly what I need! I take a few steps back. Great! The narrow crack blends in with the wall. I walk a few circles around the cave, looking from various angles. Nope, can't see it. That settles it! I'll hide it here.

I got out the tablets and essences from my sack. I counted out one fifth and put them back. Then I kept thinking and decided not to show them the Strength, Endurance, Acrobatics or Flexibility tablets at all. And I also stashed the corresponding number of essences.

In the end, my sack had just fifty experience essences and thirty tablets left. I stuffed the rest in the hole.

As soon as I took two steps back, I saw some text:

- You have created a simple hiding spot.
- Congratulations! You receive:
- Experience essence (15).
- Clay tablet of Mind.
- Clay tablet "Hiding Spot Maker."
- Clay tablet of Observation.

Would you look at that! A nice little end-of-day bonus! But weird. Why didn't the Great System ever notice my hiding spots before? I made lots of them when I was a child. Maybe the things I was hiding back then weren't worth enough? Or I was choosing overly simple locations?

In any case, I checked the levels of the new tablets and essences. As expected, ones all around. I caught myself on the thought that I was no longer reacting so emotionally to the restrictions. Clearly that was because I finally recognized one important thing — being level zero was helping me. After all, I just got done hiding a large amount of loot and I only got so much thanks to that despicable goose egg.

For the record, I also popped those new tablets and essences into the hiding spot. Sure, maybe I could explain the Observation tablets. The Mind ones as well. But the Hiding Spot Maker tablet would blow my cover.

I drank my fill of the lake's burning cold water before leaving, then headed to leave the cave. My stomach gave a groan of delight, anticipating how soon I'd be eating dinner.

I left the tunnel with mixed feelings. It felt like there was something I was missing, something I hadn't thought through all the way...

As an aside, I was no longer so afraid of the tunnels. Only the distant "howling" passage back at the crossing made my skin crawl now. As for the rest, I was basically used to it.

There are people waiting for me outside. Frodi and another guy. This must be the guard he promised. Dumpy, short. His narrow gray eyes radiate ambivalence. An old ugly scar on his right cheek. The person who stitched it up for him must not have been a very talented surgeon. The right part of his face came out a bit contorted. It gave him a permanent grin. The combination of his cold gaze and predatory involuntary smile really creeped me out.

"You already done, kid?!" Frodi shouted from the distance, smiling openly. "Me and Happy here were coming to pay you a visit!"

"I figured you forgot about me!" I shouted back.

To be honest, deep inside, I was a bit mad at Frodi even though, logically, I knew he didn't owe me anything.

My older pal instantly sussed out my mood.

"Hey, hey, kid! What's with you? You mad?" he asked in a reassuring tone when I'd caught up to them. "I couldn't come any sooner... See, Happy can corroborate. I'm up to my neck in other work. Isn't that right Happy?"

His companion just nodded ambivalently.

"Tired?" Frodi asked compassionately, placing a hand on my shoulder.

"Uh huh... And hungry as a dog... My supply isn't filling back up anymore..." I grumbled.

Frodi loudly cursed and slapped his own forehead.

"Y'know, sometimes I think I've got holes in my head! I didn't even bring food!"

I wanted to be sarcastic and ask something like "then why'd you even come?" But I held my tongue. The last thing I needed was to fight with my only friend here. After all, in the end, he didn't forget about me.

"Let's go to the barrack now. You can have something to munch on there," Frodi rushed and added:

"And Happy can carry your bag for now. That'll make it easier for you to walk."

I didn't even have time to make a peep before my sack was deftly shifted into the hands of the big guy.

"Lotta moss left?" Frodi asked, deftly shifting my attention.

"Not much," I mumbled. "Two days' work."

"Not bad," he nodded and, with a wink, added:

"When you're done with that cave, I'll show you a new little spot. There's plenty of work for you around here."

"Nice!" I said, sincerely delighted.

To be honest, that had me worried. Funnily enough, zero resources with even meagre value are quite the rare phenomenon. Although I might be wrong about that...

The whole way to the village, Frodi was distracting us with conversation. But his idle chatter was just that. Nothing interesting. Just little stuff... Who gathered what, who gathered more, who said what to who and what he got for it... Empty jibber-jabber.

First I tried to carefully listen to him but gradually my attention thinned. I was mentally far from that gloomy place. I was imagining collecting lots of loot and paying off my debt to Bardan. Getting back to Orchus and buying back my parents' house. Getting the farm back up and running and trying to get my past life back. I shot a fleeting glance at Frodi who was still chattering away with a smile. I'll try to help him too. I wonder what sins landed him in this place?

I didn't much believe he was a dangerous criminal. Probably he got locked away on a false accusation while he was a kid. Then landed in forced labor. The debts piled up. And now he doesn't know how to get out of the hole.

That settles it! I'll definitely try and help Frodi! After all, he is my first and only friend! I'll have to speak with him one on one. I think today after dinner I'll tell him my plans.

The village seemed deserted. Frodi explained that by the fact that everyone was at work and the women and children tried to keep their heads down while their men were in the mines. They are afraid of their prisoner neighbors.

At the entrance to the barrack where I spent last night, there is a man perched on the stoop like a throne. A tar-black shock of hair. A thick beard almost up to his eyes. A crooked predatory nose. A powerful torso, also overgrown with black hair. Fists like paving stones. Even sitting, he looked taller than all the prisoners standing around him. There was something animalistic in the gaze of his dark eyes. It was like the look in our cat's eyes before she pounced onto a flock of sparrows sitting carelessly on the windowsill.

Every step we took toward the barrack under his squinting stare made me feel more and more like one of those sparrows. Even the always carefree Frodi stopped chattering and led me up to the stoop in silence.

"Why is he still zero?" the giant asked threateningly.

It was the same raspy powerful voice I heard before falling asleep! Now I knew who it was!

Frodi gave a silent half-turn toward Happy.

And he extended my bag, which a thin frail criminal promptly snatched. Deftly removing all my trophies, he announced:

"Fifty esses and thirty clays."

"What kind of clays?" the animalistic giant asked shortly.

"Agility, herbalist and knife proficiency. Ten apiece," The thin one reported back straight away.

The bearded man had no reaction, just stared gloomily at Frodi.

And Frodi lost all his friendliness and happiness, and snapped angrily:

"It looks like One-ear pulled one over on us. The kid can't use esses."

"Why the hell not?" the bearded man asked in surprise.

The right corner of Frodi's lip slightly contracted. He always did that when I asked him stupid questions.

"The esses he earns are level one."

I saw Frodi holding back a snotty comment by the skin of his teeth.

The bearded man cursed loudly.

"Looks like Knud might have known the little guy can't ding," my friend added fuel to the fire.

More like former friend now...

I stared at Frodi's harsh and angry face and couldn't tell where the happy jokester I had come to consider my best friend had gone. So in the end his good nature, happiness and openness was all fake?

My memories of the last few days all fell into place like pieces of a puzzle. So the club in Frodi's hands back in the cave wasn't just my imagination. This whole act was just something he put on to dazzle me so he could rob me as soon as I hit level one.

My former friend could sense my gaze, looked me in the eyes and gave a scathing smile.

"Nothing personal, kid. You'll be smarter next time. Think of this as a learning experience. You'll be thanking me one day."

The prisoners other than the gloomy bearded guy all whinnied raucously. The scrawny one, throwing my knapsack at my feet, handed all my loot to the ringleader.

He tossed an animal gaze over me and barked:

"Leave him a couple esses. Let him buy himself some food. He's gotta get back to work tomorrow."

CHAPTER 7

I PICKED up the knapsack and squeezed the two experience essences they were "gracious" enough to let me keep, then left the barrack. Was I really that bothered by the lost loot? I don't think so. I followed my father's advice and he was right. Sure I was robbed flagrantly, but most of what I gathered was safely squirreled away in the cave.

To be frank, deep down I was prepared for this. Again thanks to my father's lesson.

But alas, there was something else I was not prepared for. Being betrayed by a person I thought was my best friend... Yes, I understand I had only known Frodi a few hours, too little to consider him even a friend, much less a best friend. But still...

I was also struck by how insanely fast he was able to make me like and trust him. He was so good at it that I was about to help him out of peonage in good faith. It boggles the mind! What a trusting chump I am!

Seemingly, I said the last phrase out loud because I heard a quiet mocking voice behind me:

"Now that's for sure. A real chump."

I turned around sharply.

It was the beggar kid from before with his shock of black uncombed hair and gray wrinkled clothing. He had a joyful smile playing on his grimy face and there was understanding in his chestnut eyes along with, seemingly, sympathy. But I'll try not to pay any attention to that. I've given him enough!

Today Frodi had really taught me one of life's most important lessons. From here on out, the only person I can trust is me.

"Don't let it get to you. You're not the first, not the last," the boy said, wiping his nose on his dirty sleeve. "Frodi's Charisma is sky high. Trusting dopes like you are easy pickings for him. You can't even imagine all the people he left high and dry in the middle of nowhere. Honestly, that was why he bailed on the mines. But the way they took all your stuff, that's bad. Next time try to tuck some of it away."

It was hard to keep a straight face. I hope Crum didn't notice.

"He didn't get everything," I finally spoke up. "He let me keep two experience essences."

"Woah! Two esses! You're a rich man! I wonder why Livid was feeling so generous?"

"Livid?" I asked.

"Yeah," the kid nodded. "The big hairy guy. He's the head honcho of that little operation. All the convicts work for him. Scary dude."

"That's for sure," I agreed and shivered.

"And it's rumored that he's a werewolf," Crum told me softly, looking around in fear.

"Oh yeah?!"

"I mean, you saw him. In a word, a beast. Did you see his eyes?"

"Uh huh," I agreed and took a heavy sigh.

My stomach gave a loud involuntary groan.

"Hungry?" Crum asked understandingly.

"I could eat a horse!"

"You won't be able to buy a horse for two esses around here..."

"So, you been living here long?" I interrupted him.

"Since the day I was born," the kid nodded.

"You know how much everything costs?"

"You offend me."

"Then I've got an offer. You help me turn my two essences into food and find me a place to spend the night and I'll share my dinner with you. How does that sound?"

"Agreed!" A smile of satisfaction played across Crum's grubby face.

As we shook hands, both of our stomachs gave a simultaneous groan.

DUNGEONS OF THE CROOKED MOUNTAINS

* * *

On our way to the village, several times I praised myself for the good sense of having Crum help me find food.

I don't know what my guide spent his tablets on exactly but he was a master negotiator, which led me to other thoughts.

But everything in its turn...

The first stop on Crum's itinerary was someone named Glumb Duckgrass. A gaunt and unwelcoming old man, he raised chickens.

"Ahh... It's you, little scallywag!" he rasped when he saw us in his gateway. "Who's this you dragged to my home? Another shiftless layabout?"

"No, come on!" Crum exclaimed, throwing his hands up cartoonishly and quickly dashing forward. He was talking and didn't kick us out right away. That means we have to get to business quickly.

"This is Eric," the boy continued, pointing at me. "He works in the mine."

And in a reassuring tone, at half volume, he added:

"He's one of Livid's."

The old man's face stretched out slightly in surprise. And Crum shot me a furtive wink and smile.

"Alright, sure," said Glumb, finally having his surprise under control. "And what brought you two here?"

"Well, here's the thing... Livid gave his man here a bonus for hard work. And we wanted to spend some of it on a couple items."

As soon as Glumb heard the magic words "bonus" and "spend," his face lit up. Well, as much as it could.

"Keep going!"

Crum didn't keep him waiting.

"You see, honorable Glumb Duckgrass, my friend has a difficult job. Fraught with mortal danger. He comes back from the mines all tired and beat down. Plus he needs to rest well so he can eat well."

"I see."

"And how can you get good rest without a soft pillow and warm down comforter?"

"You can't!" the old man exclaimed happily. "Look at my chickens, young men! They're white-crested Orchusians! The down and feathers of this breed are used to fill the beds and pillows of our dear baron!"

I shot a glance at the sad scrawny birds and it was hard not to laugh. I wondered if this Glumb had even once seen real Orchusian chickens. They were three times the size of these emaciated fowl.

"Excellent!" Crum feigned admiration and gave me another wink. "Then we would like to purchase some of your outstanding wares!"

"How will you be paying?" Glumb asked, shifting to a businesslike tone. "Copper or silver?"

"We wanted to make a trade," Crum

answered and, seeing his face cringe, immediately hurried to add:

"For experience essences."

Glumb's thin dry lips spread into a smile again. He looked happy. Oh, his little eyes were shimmering. He even rubbed his hands together despite himself. Seemingly the experience essences or, as they were also called here, "esses" were a perfectly valid instrument of exchange.

"How much of your feathers will you give us, for let's say..." Crum pretended to think. "One... No... Hm... How about two esses?"

He said it all with a tone as if we had pockets full of esses.

Glumb's eyes lit up greedily.

"One bale of high-quality feathers!" he shot out instantly and quickly added:

"That, by the way, is enough material for one comforter and one pillow!"

Even I, hardly a sophisticated negotiator, could understand this man was trying to pull one over on us. How obvious it must have been for Crum the ace.

"Yeah, we heard you, mister," he said with a sour face and turned to me:

"Let's go, Eric. Let's see what we can get from Mr. Coalblack Thickman. I wonder how much he'll offer us. They say when there's a windstorm, he has to tie his chickens down so they don't blow away. Can you picture how nice a pillow made of those feathers must be? Eh buddy?"

It hurt to look at Glumb. It seemed like every muscle was twitching on his gray wrinkled face. He was about to have a stroke!

"Two bales of feathers!" he shot out.

Crum pulled me to the exit for show.

"Three bales!" the old man shouted at our backs, nearly weeping.

My new acquaintance turned around. With a chuckle, he said:

"Three bales and ten fresh eggs."

"Three bales and five eggs."

"Let's shake on it!"

Unbelievably satisfied with himself and even more with the effect it made on me, Crum said:

"Now let's go see Mrs. Agneta."

"And what's she got?" I asked, curious and trying to catch up to the kid's fast pace. And that was with him trying to compensate for my rough characteristics by walking slowly.

"Mrs. Agneta is a seamstress. Yesterday, I overheard that she got a big order from Wishstay, the innkeeper. I'd bet my own hand that she needs feathers and down for her new beds."

"I see," I said and asked a question I'd been wondering about for a while:

"Wouldn't it be easier to go straight to the tavern or the inn and just have a nice calm dinner there? Then in the worst case, we can buy some provisions in a store."

"No," Crum shook his head. "It wouldn't be. The tavern and the inn are owned by the same guy. As I already said, his name is Wishstay. That means the prices, as you understand, are the same. For a bowl of vegetable stew, which at most is worth three copper, he'd charge us seven or eight, maybe even a whole ten coins. Two stews would be twenty 'bats' at least."

As I listened to Crum's explanation, I distantly mulled over the fact that copper coins were also called "bats" in this part of Orchus. We also called them "flyers" for the same reason. It was all because the back side of a copper coin depicted the profile of Queen Aslog the Great, who was Duchess of Farmount before her marriage. The coat of arms of her father, Duke of Farmount, was emblazoned with a bat, its membranous wings spread to the sides. Queen Aslog died about twenty years ago, but in memory of her unpopular reign, people continued to call her a bat. And that nickname stuck to the copper coin bearing her image as well.

Meanwhile, Crum continued:

"One stew won't be enough for both of us, so we'll have to order a mushroom porridge, too. And that'll be another twenty coins or so. Then add some bread and milk or berry drink... It all comes to around fifty or sixty bats. And that just so happens to be how much two of your esses are worth."

My stomach reacted with dismayed grumbling to the mention of food.

"Well, what's the big deal then? Let's go eat!"

"Eric, Eric," Crum shook his head. "Don't take cues from your gut. Trust in me! I promise we'll have some food in an hour or two at most!"

To be fair, I should mention that he kept his word. Over a bit more than an hour later, we managed to visit several houses. In every single one, he negotiated furiously and capably, making exchanges and demanding a bit thrown in on top. In the end we had a whole knapsack full of food. And at the bakery, the last point of our journey, Crum was somehow able to sell all the honey we exchanged for sheep's wool from the beekeeper's wife for seventy-five copper. And he got two warm flatbreads thrown in.

"So then," he said victoriously. "Two flatbreads, a quarter wheel of goats' cheese, five apples, five carrots, two onions, a little pot of honey, five eggs, cured trout... Mm, what else we got?"

"A flagon of goat milk and a link of mutton sausage," I said.

"Well and, of course, seventy-five copper coins!" Crum announced with a victorious bow.

"Bravo!" I clapped him on the palm, smiling.

"Of course, we won't be able to get this much every day," Crum started explaining on the way to the barracks. "We got lucky this time is all."

"You're doing yourself a disservice," I

objected. "You were able to turn two esses into copper coins and fill a whole knapsack with food on top of that."

"Nonsense," he dismissed my praise. But I could tell he was flattered by his red face.

* * *

"I don't know how it is for everyone, but to me a full stomach is halfway to happiness!" Crum doled out some wisdom, breathing heavily.

Lying on a small pile of gray rags he used as a bed, he was patting his stomach in satisfaction, now double its normal size. For the record, I was lying on the very same "bed" and my stomach looked about the same as his.

Crum kept up his part of the deal. He found us food and a place to sleep. He had invited me to his little room, which was in the attic of a rickety abandoned barrack on the edge of the settlement.

And though the cold and damp barrack was a pitiful sight, the little attic was warm and even cozy. Crum had put a good amount of effort into improving his living space.

There's a little window with a decaying frame carefully boarded up. Cracks in the walls are stuffed up with rags and moss. To my surprise, there's even furniture. A little table with spindly legs, a crudely jury-rigged chair, a three-legged stool.

But Crum's pride and joy, beyond all doubt,

is a thick trunk with bronze bands and a big old hanging padlock. It was in the corner of his little room in the most prominent place, its rounded sides shimmering. It was immediately obvious that it was Crum's favorite object. The bronze was polished and the lock had traces of grease.

After we went up and Crum pulled up the cleverly rigged ladder, I froze staring at the bronze giant despite myself. I could see in his eyes that he was flattered by my reaction.

When we took the food out of the knapsack and put it on the table, Crum told me about when he found the attic a bit more than a month earlier. The trunk was already here, filled with all kinds of junk nobody would want. It looked horrible, but he put a good amount of effort into getting it up to snuff, sanding it, then polishing all the bronze. He also pulled out all the moldering cloth inside. Lacquered the wood.

He had to bring the lock to a blacksmith. He disassembled it and cleaned the mechanism. And had a new key made. To pay for that, Crum had to run errands for the blacksmith for two months.

When I asked whether it was worth putting so much effort in, Crum answered without hesitation that, if he got the chance again, he wouldn't change a thing. I didn't question him any further. If he was feeling like it, he could tell me later. What difference did it make to me? Some people like horses, some like carving figurines out of wood or stone. Crum here likes taking care of an old trunk. Anyhow, when dinner was ready, I no longer cared.

I lay down sleepy, stroking my distended belly. My thoughts, as usual in such times, were coming one after the next, like a rope of different colored kerchiefs. The kind a magician pulls from his pocket one after the next with a big grin.

The most memorable moments of the day were flying past my eyes. Without a doubt, the most vivid was Frodi's betrayal. Weirdly I didn't feel particular hate or bitterness when I thought about him. It was more the opposite. I was happy that Frodi had shown his true colors. It would have been worse if I only learned it after spending some time with him. My friendly feelings for the rapscallion weren't able to dig too deep.

Mom used to say everything that happens is for the best. I can't say for sure if I agree with her overall but, in this particular case, her expression was on the money.

"Rick, you asleep?" Crum asked, muffled.

"Not yet," I answered, weary.

"Let me ask you a question."

"Go ahead."

"How much do you owe master?"

"Aw, Crum, I can't answer that question..."

"I got it. Don't say. You gave an oath," he easily guessed.

"How much do you owe?" I asked. "Or did you swear an oath too?"

"No," the kid shook his head. "No oaths here.

Or debt."

"What do you mean?" I asked, not getting it.

"Just what I said. I'm a free man."

I didn't fully understand what I'd heard. But when it finally reached me, my sleepiness was snatched away in an instant. Getting up on an elbow, I stared at him in surprise.

"You're just full of surprises tonight!"

Crum chuckled and gave a satisfied burp.

"Yeah, that's the kinda guy I am. I like to surprise people."

Seeing my state, he started to explain.

"Ten years ago, before I was ever born, my father and mother came here with a big caravan. My dad, like yours, was a miner. Like many others, he fell for one of Bardan's tall tales. He was saying there's a rich copper vein here. To be fair, there was a copper vein, but it wasn't as rich as they said. Father made decent money the first year, even got a little house in the village. Mother did some farming. I was already on the way. In a nutshell, a happy family."

Crum spent a bit of time in silence, staring at his trunk. I didn't bother him, knowing firsthand what it was like to divulge such deep emotions.

"When I was two, my father ended up in a cave-in," he continued quietly. "Passed just like yours. Mom was constantly sick after I was born, and she only outlived him by two years. After mother died, I was taken in by one of my dad's friends named Grip. Some might say I got lucky to have any adult watching over me given I was only four. But I wouldn't say so... In the end, Grip and his girlfriend only kept me for one month. That was enough time for them to sell my parents' home and farm along with all their property. Then one fine morning they packed up and got the heck out of Dodge. And as I'm sure you already guessed, no one invited me along on that fine little trip..."

"Jeeze, how'd you survive?"

"Oh, Eric! That is a different and much longer story!" Crum said, smiling. "I'll tell you later some time."

Silence hung over the attic for a while. Crum was first to break it.

"What are you gonna do?" he asked.

"Sleep," I answered shortly.

"Yeah, I figured that... But what about tomorrow?"

"I'll figure something out..."

"I mean, you do realize now that those lowlifes aren't gonna leave you alone now, right? Tomorrow morning, Livid is gonna stick a guy to you and he'll shepherd you around all the way until dark. After that, everything you make is gonna go into the boss's pocket."

I pursed my lips in anger. Bastards! After all, I also have to make my quota. And pay back the debt. Plus I'll need money for food, clothes and a place to live. I can't count on Crum letting me stay here in the attic forever. Today sure. It was part of our deal, but tomorrow I'll have to find a new corner.

"So why does Knud let him get away with it?" I asked.

"Why would he wanna fight convicts?" Crum answered. "Plus there are rumors that he and Livid have a secret arrangement for 'sheep' like you."

"What do you mean 'sheep?'"

"Don't you get it?"

"Are you saying I'm a sheep to them?"

"No more and no less," he nodded without a hint of a smile. "When your wool grows out, they'll give you a shear. Knud gets his, Livid gets his."

"What about Skorx?"

"Oh!" Crum exclaimed and raised a pointer finger. "He's head honcho of this whole criminal enterprise. He gets a cut from everybody. Knud, Livid, the innkeeper, the baker... Everybody..."

Seeing a new question about to tear itself from my lips, he got out ahead:

"And don't even ask about Bardan. It's been working this way for decades. Believe you me, he's no fool. He can't be played so easily. He knows perfectly well what is happening in his domain."

"Is he wetting his beak too?"

"Yep," the kid nodded. "Just like our baron. And if you start unraveling the ball, it'll lead all the way to the king himself... Basically, he's top of the whole criminal heap. And that includes the priests, marshals, generals, ministers. There's lots of them..."

I looked at Crum in surprise. Where would an eight year old boy get such ideas? As if guessing what I was thinking, he smiled and said:

"I heard all that from an old convict laborer. He died last year of consumption. But he used to work a high post in the capital. Then he was cast out to the mines for his sins, whatever they were."

"Not surprised. Anyone who talks like that is liable to get exiled. And by the way, you should be more careful. The wrong person might hear what you're saying."

"Don't worry," Crum waved it off. "Everyone talks like that here. There's nowhere to exile any of us to. This is the edge of the world. Hehe."

"What about death?"

"Oh! Believe you me, Eric! The king does not benefit from his sheep dying. You only get executed when you stop growing wool. Hehe!"

I just shook my head. One of these days, he'd stick his neck out too far. All that said, talk like this cropped up fairly often in our kitchen back home. Especially when Dalia came to visit. The healer shared the latest news in the kingdom, then she and father and mother would discuss it for a long time. Knowing that I had a habit of listening in, father strictly forbid me from repeating even one word. And responsible son that I was, I kept my mouth shut tight.

"For example, let's take me," Crum continued. "I'll be level five soon. I was unlucky when I was born. Random was not feeling generous and only gave me nine tablets. But it was like my mom could sense she was close to the end. So not wanting to leave me with no characteristics, she spent her last years trying to earn as many tablets and essences as possible to give to me."

When he remembered his mother, the boy took a heavy sigh. I kept silent a bit and continued:

"In the last four years, I managed to level up twice. Honestly, I did have to sell most of the tablets and esses. There was nothing else to live on."

"And why do you live here?"

"Where else can I go?"

"Orchus, for example."

"Yeah sure. If a little urchin like me goes to Orchus, they'd put me into peonage faster than you can blink. Then I can kiss my freedom goodbye. But here I can say what I like. If I don't go looking for a fight, nobody will touch me. And I'm making some cash on the sly, getting stronger. When I'm older, then we can see."

"So where do you work? In the mine?"

"No," Crum shook his head. "It's too early for me to go there. The mine is level six."

"Got it."

"Yeah and I don't want to be slaving away for Bardan."

"What do you mean? You're free. It's against the law to take esses and tablets from free people. If you do that, you get sent straight into peonage."

"That's true in theory, but there are a couple

pratfalls. The second I sign a contract, Skorx will get me in debt."

"What do you mean?"

"Well you see, the mine here is a field day for levels six and seven. They get showered in essences and tablets. But starting at level eight, the only people who get bonuses are the ones who leveled their skills. Well, you already know..."

I just nodded in silence. My father was fifteen, but his mining skill was a few points above his overall level. Thanks to those high numbers, he was able to mine faster. And they gave him a chance of bonus drops.

"As for low level workers like me and you," Crum continued. "Skorx has a little job I wouldn't wish on my worst enemy. No-ope, you can count me out of that one."

"What are you talking about?" I asked, my heart pounding.

Crum stared at me and a moment later a fire of understanding lit in his eyes.

"Bug tear them to shreds!" he exclaimed. "Bardan's steward sent you here on Skorx's request?!"

"Yes," I answered in a near whisper.

I felt my throat parch.

"Crum, don't make me wait... Explain what's so bad..."

"Everything!" he spat out in a fury. "The Marked One is a beast from hell! He puts out an innocent request like, 'we need quick workers with a small frame to scout out new ore veins.' But in reality he's looking for something else... You're actually lucky he isn't in the village yet. But he will be before long. Skorx is coming back in a week."

"What is he looking for?"

"No one knows. And anyone who finds anything disappears without a trace. but I..."

Crum started talking, but then sharply fell silent. He looked at me. I saw mistrust in his eyes, which were so friendly before.

"Forget it, Rick," he waved it off and turned his back to me. "It's just stupid rumors spread by people with nothing better to do."

My new friend is afraid. Doesn't trust me. And rightly so. Who am I to him? He's saying things you shouldn't tell anyone. What if I accidentally let something slip tomorrow? That would be it...

"Listen, Crum," after a bit of silence I started. "I understand why you're afraid. We've known each other a bit more than one day and there's no reason for you to risk your own hide for some poor fool. But understand me, too. For the last few days, the only thing anyone has done is scare me with talk about Skorx and his mine. And no one has given me any specific explanations. Just old man Burdoc, the kind soul, warned me to stay away from the northern tunnels. And I can see, Crum, that you know something but are afraid to say..."

"I've already said too much," he cut me off.

"So let's try something else..."

"Are you talking about an oath?" Crum asked, turning in my direction.

"Yes. I'll swear to you that I won't talk, and you tell me what you know. Shake on it?"

"No," the kid shook his head.

"Why not?" I asked in surprise.

"What's in it for me?" he asked matter-of-factly. "An oath is all well and good, but what do I get in return? The information I possess is actually very valuable. In fact, let me take it one further. I don't think even Skorx suspects what he's really looking for..."

What a big-mouth! I mean one day this will bite him in the ass. In the best case, he'll get his tongue cut out. In the worst, it could be his head.

"Let me guess. You heard this from the same old man prisoner from before?"

His frightened face told me that my words had hit their mark. He started to realize what a trap he'd been caught in...

"Listen, Crum," I decided to strike while the iron was hot. "I can see that you already know you've said too much. If I was a scumbag like Livid or Frodi, I already would have started blackmailing you without a hint of conscience."

It felt bad to look at the kid. He was instantly looking peaky. His face pale. His lips quavering. Tears were welling up in the corners of his eyes. Like a little animal backed into a corner, he was all tensed up, clutching his knees with his hands.

"But I am not a scumbag, and not a traitor! I swear that I will never use what you said against you! And let the Great System bear witness!"

Crum must have received a system message and gave a slight shudder of surprise. Smiling, I watched his wide-open eyes run over some invisible text. After he finished reading, his eyes shot up at me in disbelief.

"But..." he started in a quavering voice. "Why? After all, you could have..."

"I could have," I answered seriously. "But only if I was a real bastard."

"So you aren't asking for anything in return? My secret, for example?"

"No," I answered. "I won't ask. But I will make a different offer."

"What?"

"A trade."

"What do you mean?"

"Just what I said. We trade secrets. You tell me yours, I tell you mine. And naturally we seal our trade with an oath of secrecy."

"And you're sure that your secret is as important as mine?"

By the looks of things, Crum had snapped out of it. He has trading in his blood, no bones about it. Just the way his eyes lit up when it came time to negotiate.

"Absolutely," I smiled. "Might even be more important."

Crum looked at my knapsack despite himself. I had some of the leftover food in it. By my calculations, it would only be enough for the next day. I had another seventy-five copper in my pocket, which I wanted to spend on other things. I need stronger clothes and footwear. To match my situation.

A metal flask, fire-starter, pot, spoon... And another couple little things I never considered when leaving my family home. But in this state, I couldn't think too clearly... Too much had fallen on my shoulders in the last few days...

Crum, looking at my bag, understood without a doubt that our previous agreement did not apply to this food or my money. In the morning, he would have no way to get breakfast.

And as for me, I understood that despite his age and poverty, Crum felt at home here. And I need his help.

"Listen, Crum. I have an idea."

He tore his eyes from my bag and turned to me, intrigued:

"Oh yeah?"

"I say we go into business together."

Crum chuckled.

"And what do you suggest we do? Catch fleas? Haha! Or work for Livid and his flunkies?"

He is clearly taunting me. Trying to throw me off balance. Might as well spill the beans. But he's clearly intrigued. Hehe, nice move. Most importantly, he was smart beyond his years. Just the kind of partner I need.

"Nice try," I smiled. "But I'll only go into the details after we swear before the gods and trade our secrets. Then I will explain how we could maybe work together."

The boy, shrugging his shoulders, laughed.

"Well you're not quite as simple as I first thought."

"Make up your mind, Crum," I egged him on. "I promise you won't regret it."

The kid got to his feet. He paced a few circles around the little room and finally sat down on his trunk.

"I agree. But on one condition."

"Tell me."

"I won't play any games that could get me killed."

"Do I look like I wanna die?"

"No, I just wanted to warn you."

"I hear you. Believe me, you won't lose anything. If you don't like my offer, you can say no and we can forget it. So, swear on it?"

"Yes."

After almost an hour hammering out the details, we struck hands and the Great System confirmed the purity of our intentions.

"Well, what now?" I asked when I finished reading the system message. "Who's first?"

"I'll go," Crum answered. "So, as I said, Skorx is not looking for new ore veins."

"Then what is he looking for?"

"That's the beauty of the situation. Hehe. He doesn't even know."

"I am completely lost."

"Let me explain. It all started when the Marked One somehow ended up with a map. Or rather, a small fragment of one. It's a very valuable item. It once belonged to the Ancients."

I unwittingly touched the button on my chest.

"Somehow Skorx got it in his head that the bit of map shows some of the underground tunnels of our mine, which was not actually a mine in the time of the Ancients."

"And knowing that the Departed wouldn't have drawn a map for no good reason, he is blindly trying to find something connected with it?" I voiced my guess.

"Exactly."

I felt a tingle run down my spine:

"And you mean to say that you know..."

"Yes," Crum nodded. "He doesn't even suspect it, but the thing Skorx is searching for is the Temple of the Ancients."

CHAPTER 8

"T HE TEMPLE of the Ancients?" I asked in a whisper.

For a reason I couldn't understand, when I mentioned the temple, all the hairs on my body stood on end. A chill ran down my spine and my heart, beating like mad, was about to burst out of my chest.

I didn't understand what was happening to me but some internal sense helped me to recognize that I needed to reach that place. Maybe there I would finally find answers to all my questions about myself.

Meanwhile, Crum continued:

"The old prisoner, whose name was Targus, is who saved me. A bit more than a year ago, Skorx was putting together his first scout team and I was the first person he asked."

He gave a pensive smile at the memory.

"Oh, Rick, you can't even imagine how proud I was! And that isn't all! Skorx personally offered to make me a scout! Even now I remember how jealous the older boys looked when they made fun of me."

Crum giggled and stroked the back of his head.

"I remember puffing my chest out feeling important and telling Targus the news. But instead of being happy for my success, he started desperately trying to convince me not to agree to the Marked One's offer no matter what."

"By the way, why do they call him the Marked One?" I asked.

"It's an old story. Back when Skorx was in the army, the mages miscalculated a fire spell and accidentally torched his entire unit. He was the only survivor. As a reminder of that battle, half of his face is covered with an ugly burn scar, his mark. He was never a handsome man to begin with, and now all the less so... Let me give you some free advice — when you go to speak to him, never stare at the burn. He hates that with a passion."

"Gotcha. And so how did the old man find out about the danger?"

"As I already said, Targus used to occupy a high post in the Imperial capital. Something connected with roads. Basically, he had a very good understanding of maps and all kinds of diagrams. By complete coincidence, while he was in Skorx's office he saw a fragment of the map. The Marked One didn't much try to hide his treasure. He must have thought that all the prisoners were uneducated."

"And so your Targus was able to determine from the map fragment that it's a Temple of the Ancients?" I asked with mistrust in my voice.

"Ha! That wasn't all he was able to do! He was a very bright old man! He was always trying to convince me to invest more in Mind. Targus sincerely believed that Brother Mage was the most powerful of the brothers. Warrior and Hunter he called half-wits, always landing themselves into scrapes."

I just chuckled in response. I agree, Mage is the smartest of the Three. But the way my father taught me, the strength of the brothers was in their unity. And I was in complete agreement with him. Funny that a simple miner was wiser than some book-smart jerk from the capital...

"Anyway, he explained to me that when he was young and studying in the academy, he was shown some ancient maps. Basically, he knew what he was talking about. Just so you know, Burdoc knew what he was talking about when he warned you not to stick your nose into the northern shafts. According to Targus, the temple of the Departed can be found down there. That, by the way, is where many of the people from the first scout team died. And where I refused to enter, which made all the local boys ridicule me even more. Honestly, when they heard every single scout died, they changed their tune."

"Hmm..." I said. "The old man really did save you."

"And I will be eternally grateful to him for that," Crum nodded seriously.

We spent a bit of time in silence. Crum was clearly luxuriating in his memories while I digested his story and tried to find an explanation for the strange feeling his tale gave me. I felt drawn in by the mysterious temple of the Departed and its riddles... They both quickened the blood and scared me so bad my knees shivered...

"Well Rick?" Crum chuckled. "What do you say? How'd you like my secret?"

"I've got just one thing to say. You shouldn't have been afraid to tell me your story. And to cop a phrase, let me give you some free advice. You're on the right path. Keep on it."

Agreeing, he nodded and said:

"Now your turn. I hope your secret is at least as good as mine."

I smiled.

"We'll see. You recently mentioned that Random didn't give you many tablets? Haha! You're looking at someone who got nothing at birth. Not even level one... I spent a few years confined to a bed. The only indication I was even alive was the meager numbers in my supply bars... Hmm... A living corpse, without any way to use esses or tablets. A pitiful Bug-damned cripple...

Just imagine, I can't even eat complex food! I don't know the taste of candy or cake... And my mother was an amazing cook! Holidays were a torture for me. So many delicious-smelling treats at the markets!"

"If it's any reassurance, I've only ever tried cake once in my life. On my birthday. Back when mother was still alive... But that wasn't what I wanted to say... But I mean, now you can move though, right?"

"Yes," I answered. "Thanks to these items here."

I pointed to my button and ring.

"But how...?"

"They have no restrictions."

"Hold up," Crum got up from his chair in excitement. "Are you trying to say..."

"Yes. These are artifacts of the Ancients."

The boy gulped loudly.

"But those things are worth a fortune!"

"Indeed," I agreed glumly. "Father took some very sizable loans from the bank to give me even this semblance of a normal life. And that is why I'm here. After my parents died, the debt was never fully paid, even after they confiscated all of our property."

Crum whistled.

"And you cannot sell them..." he started thinking aloud. "Otherwise you'll turn back into a vegetable..."

"Exactly," I agreed. "Honestly, I do have one

little item I can sell if I really need to. Here..."

And I handed him Dragonfly.

Crum took the knife with cautious enthusiasm.

"This is the first time I've ever held an item of the Departed! And what does it do?"

"Nothing. For now it's just a very simple item. It can only do two units of damage. Your everyday kitchen knife would hurt somebody more than my Dragonfly right now."

"So then what's the trick?" the kid frowned.

"That's easy. Your knife will always be a kitchen knife, but mine can be improved. Both in damage and characteristics. Though honestly, I don't really know how I'm gonna do that."

"Look at you!" Crum admired. "What else?"

"Items of the Ancients are scalable."

"What do you mean?"

"Let me explain. See this ring?"

The kid gave a captivated nod.

"How many Strength points you see?"

"Two."

"Now you put it on."

Crum's flexible fingers gave a slight shiver. They were thin and covered in small burns and scratches. When he was trying to get that lock fixed, the blacksmith must not have been too worried about his temporary assistant's safety. His right pinky was slightly bent, and his left ring finger had no nail.

"What finger?" Crum asked.

"Any finger," I answered. "The ring will change size to fit you."

"Would you look at that!" the kid admired when he saw the steel band smoothly grasp his middle finger.

"Now look at the ring's characteristics," I said. "How much strength you see now?"

"Six points!" Crum admired. "How'd that happen?"

I chuckled. When father showed me the very same trick, my face looked approximately like Crum's did now.

"Your level is added to the characteristics of the ring."

"Woah!" he scratched the back of his head, stunned. "So that means if I were, let's say, level twenty right now, the ring would change to twenty Strength?!"

"Exactly," I nodded and added:

"And if you improve it, it'll get more characteristics."

"Oh, Great System!" Crum stared at the ring on his finger, struck.

"Now you understand why these items are so expensive?"

Crum nodded fitfully and delicately returned my ring.

"Rick, just imagine what Skorx or Livid would do for these artifacts. Don't even think of trying to sell them here! Even if push really comes to shove! As soon as you show anyone this ring or knife, you'll be a goner! First they'll rob you, then they'll kill you to keep you quiet. I'm surprised your father stayed alive when he bought them..."

Crum's last words put me into a daze... After all, I'd never considered that! For real, how did he ever pull that off?! A chill ran down my spine... After all, my father couldn't have... No! I don't believe it!

Seeing my state, Crum put an arm on my shoulder reassuringly:

"Listen, Rick... Don't pay any mind to what I'm saying... I'm sure your father was an honest man..."

I slowly sat down on the stool. Crum is right. A thousand times right!

"You shouldn't doubt your father," the boy continued. "And especially his actions. In one way or another, everything he did was to help you. I'm afraid to even imagine the kind of risks he had to take."

"You're right!" I answered firmly. "He and mother dedicated their lives to me!"

When I spoke, I felt confidence, but questions remained... Still, at least now I knew who to ask when the time came.

Crum understood that we shouldn't keep discussing my parents and turned the conversation down a different path:

"Hmm, Rick. I have to agree. Your secret is at least as good as mine! Hehe! So then, what was your business idea?"

"Hold up, Crum, I haven't finished yet."

"Woah! You're just like my trunk — filled with all kinds of mysteries! I'm listening."

Rubbing his hands together, the kid crouched down next to me on the chair.

"The thing is, those crooks didn't get all my trophies..."

"So you did manage to squirrel a bit away!" Crum giggled.

"I wouldn't put it that way..."

"What do you mean?"

"Livid only got a fifth of what I made today..."

When I said that, I watched my future business partner's jaw drop.

"But how is that possible?!"

"To be frank, I don't know myself. I spent all day cutting level-zero moss. I suspect the Great System was giving me the maximum possible drop for every resource gathered. I think it perceived every cut I made as the first of my life. I'm sure it's because of my level."

"Agreed!" Crum declared.

He jumped up off the chair and started walking from wall to wall in silence. He must have thought better that way.

"And how much did you get all told?" he finally asked, looking at me and not stopping.

"About seven pounds of moss. All told that's four hundred fifteen esses and two hundred fifty-nine tablets. Well, and as I already said, Livid took one fifth of that..."

Crum stopped dead. By his excitedly bulging eyes, I could see that he was on board.

"That was from one day of work?!"

I once heard my parents use the phrase "screaming in a whisper." Until today, how to do that was a mystery to me... But now I know. Crum had just given a perfect demonstration.

"Oh, Great System! How is it possible?! Rick, you're like that goose from the old folk tale that lays golden eggs! If any of those creeps find out what you're capable of... I mean you... Geeze..."

"I know, Crum, I know..." I answered reassuringly. The kid was about to have a stroke. That was how hard he was breathing. Sweat came up on his brow. His arms were shivering.

"You'd better sit down and calm yourself. If you haven't figured it out yet, I never would have come to you..."

"And where's the rest?" he asked, now in a calmer tone.

"In the cave where I cut the moss. In a hiding spot."

"You made a hiding spot there?"

I can Crum's merchant blood heating up.

"Yes, on my own."

"So it's simple then," he said with vexation in his voice. "For some people in Livid's gang, finding a hiding spot like that would be child's play, Bug damn them!"

"That means we need to hide it in a new spot as fast as possible!" I said, hopping up off the chair.

"We can't," Crum said, sitting me back in place. "If you start messing around, you'll ruin everything."

"Look, it's night out there. Who will ever find out? I'll go over to the cave in secret and take everything out of the hiding spot."

Despite our age difference, Crum looked at me like I was a silly child.

"You'll get nowhere. You won't even be able to get past the guards. Even if they do let you through, tomorrow, Livid and Knud will know that you ran off somewhere in the night. Do you want that kind of attention?"

"No," I was forced to admit he was right.

"Better would be to make yourself appear like the person they think you are. Who are you to them?"

"A sheep?"

"Baaa!" Crum bleated, smiling cleverly. "Exactly! Stupid, frightened and obedient. The last thing you want is to attract the wrong kind of attention. You need to lull them into a false sense of security."

"Do you think they're on the lookout now?"

"Of course! The fact you weren't able to level up means they stand to lose around ten silver tablets. But you left the mine with your hands full. Today you brought the esses and tablets willingly because you didn't suspect you would get robbed. Tomorrow, they'll stick one of the gang to you so you don't get any ideas about squirreling some away. Hmm, Rick... Now I see why you need my help. But I still can't figure what's in it for me."

"I will give you a cut of everything I gather."

"I want half," Crum said with a clever smile.

"Don't you think that's a bit much?" I answered with an equally clever smile. "Did you forget that I'll get a haircut every day from Livid's sheep shearer? And I need to pay Bardan back. Plus pay for a place to sleep."

"Well, don't you worry about where to sleep," he waved it off. "Me and you are in business together now, you can stay at my place."

I shook my head.

"I'd be delighted, Crum, but no. If you do agree to help me, we can't be seen together. Let everyone think I'm working alone. Otherwise, if I'm found out, you'll be next... And I don't want that."

"Hmm, I've gotta agree with you there."

"I'll give you a quarter," I said, extending a hand. "Including what I got today."

Crum gave a cartoonish sigh but then smiled happily and extended a hand.

In the middle of the night, after hammering out all the details, we swore an oath. And after the Great System confirmed for both of us, Crum said:

"You go to bed. I've gotta pay somebody a visit. I think I've figured out a way to trick whoever's gonna be guarding you. But first I'll need all your money."

After Crum left, I splayed out on the pile of old rags and closed my eyes. Only now, alone with my thoughts, did I realize how tired I was. My shoulders, back, neck and legs... My whole body was in pain. It felt like I'd been run over by a carriage going at full speed. And I'd never been so tired before...

But before I got comfortable and fell asleep, I felt an insistent patting on my shoulder. Not opening an eye, I tried to sluggishly move away. But the patting didn't stop. Crum's happy voice joined in.

"Rick, look at you dozing off all sweet! Get up! Time for work!"

What did he mean work? Already?!

Despite myself, I opened my right eye and looked toward the window. He was right. There were tentative rays of morning sun already peeking through the boards.

"Why did the night go so quick?" I asked Crum resentfully as he sat at the table.

"Get up lazy bones," the kid mocked me. "All the amenities are outside. I put down the ladder. You can wash up in the old barrel against the far wall. The water is clean. I fetched it yesterday."

Outside it was quite fresh and damp. I quickly handled my needs, washed up in the ice-cold water and ran upward. It was time to refuel. When I left, Crum was already crunching and smacking away at something.

We ate in silence, just trading the occasional meaningless phrase.

"Eat more," Crum muttered, his mouth full. "My mom always said breakfast should be a big meal. If you don't eat much in the morning, might as well kiss the whole day goodbye. And you know, she was completely right. After she died, my breakfasts were far from ideal. Ah, what can I say? I practically didn't have breakfast at all..."

After we'd eaten our fill, Crum extended me my bag.

"I put some food in there for lunch. More than half of what was left. Cheese, fish, sausage and bread."

"All salty," I scratched the back of my head. "I'm gonna be drinking a lot."

"That's the idea," Crum said with a clever smile.

"I don't get it..."

"I'm almost positive that whoever Livid sends out to shepherd you will take all your food. So take these little sandwiches and this apple separately. Hide them somewhere, and you can eat them once your shepherd dozes off."

"You think he's gonna be napping?"

"Of course!" Crum said in delight. "I'd bet my bottom dollar! But to be sure, have him drink the ale in this flask."

I twirled the container, which we got yesterday, around in my hands.

"I bought some ale this morning in a tavern," the boy explained. "And mixed it with a bit of sleeping potion."

"Where'd you get that?"

"Last week, our healer pulled one of my teeth and gave me a bottle of sleeping medicine... You know, in case it started to hurt so I could get some rest. My tooth stopped bothering me that same day, so I never even opened the bottle until today."

"Hmm..."

"So then... Your shepherd will eat way too much of the salty food, then he'll want to sate his thirst. And believe you me, none of those dummies drink water if there's a flask of nice cold ale to be had."

"Well thought-out. And you're sure you didn't add too much sleeping medicine?"

"Yes," Crum answered confidently. "The medicine man explained it all in great detail. And the cheese and sausage will mask the flavor of the sleeping potion."

"That's very good! You're a smart kid, Crum!"

"You bet I am!" the kid proudly patted himself on the head. "Investing in Mind like old Targus told me was the right move after all... Basically, as soon as your guard starts snoring, get to work. The potion will last plenty of time."

CHAPTER 9

*L*IVID WAS WAITING at the barrack to meet me. As was Frodi, happy as ever and smiling openly. And Happy, yawning wearily. I looked my former friend in the eyes and didn't understand how a person with such a pleasant and kind face could do such nasty things.

Yesterday, Crum told me everything he knew about Frodi. He was born somewhere in the west. In a wagon belonging to some wandering performers. I guess his mother was assistant to a magician and, after performances, he would see if any well-heeled townsfolk wanted to spend the night with his pretty stage-hand for a bit of extra coin. That means Frodi's father could have been anyone.

And starting in early childhood, he also took part in the performances. I bet the young Frodi learned the power of Charisma on that very stage.

You could level it like nobody's business up there.

When he grew and got stronger, he ran away from his mother. In the big city, he linked up with a street gang whose leader had an appreciation for the newcomer's particular talent. Basically, with the kind of life he's had, it's no surprise he turned out the way he did.

"How'd you sleep?" asked the traitor. "Ready to get to work?"

He wanted to give me a friendly pat on the shoulder but I dodged.

"Haha! So you are mad after all!" Frodi said with a laugh. "Ungrateful! I spent all night thinking of ways to help you... I can protect you from all kinds of danger, you know? Happy came to meet you and agreed to keep watch over you. He'll even show you a place where lots more moss grows..."

In my head, I understood that Frodi was mocking me, but his open face and expression seemed to show the opposite. I have to resist! Think about yesterday's betrayal! That way his charisma won't work! As soon as I thought about it, I saw a strange message before my eyes:

- Attention! The Higher Powers have taken note of your accomplishment! You resisted the mind control of a being with Charisma more than 5 points higher than yours!
- Congratulations! You receive:
- Experience essence (50).
- Clay tablet of Mind.

DUNGEONS OF THE CROOKED MOUNTAINS

- Clay tablet "Resistance to Mental Attacks."
- Clay tablet "Lie Detection."

That was followed by another few similar messages which I quickly swiped into the archive, quavering with overflowing emotion. It took some effort not to show it in my face. But seemingly I pulled it off. Beyond that, thankfully, the door to the barrack opened, distracting Frodi and Happy, and I quickly looked down.

"Why aren't you in the mine yet?!" I hear the squeaking commanding voice of the thin criminal who searched my knapsack yesterday with such a deft hand.

"Shut your face, Probe," Frodi answered calmly. "Or is your tongue getting in the way?"

After that, Frodi nodded at Happy.

"If that's the case, my friend here can help you get rid of it. Right Happy?"

The thin convict blew away like the wind.

I took a fleeting glance at Frodi's friend. Crum didn't know a lot about him. There were rumors that, before he became a criminal, Happy served in the retinue of one of the northern Barons.

I was dying of curiosity. What was the message the Great System sent me?!

"Ah, well Probe is right," Frodi said. "You should have been in the mine a long time ago."

Somehow overcoming a burst of emotion, I said:

"I don't think I need to be guarded. I wouldn't want to keep Happy from more important matters."

"Haha! What are you talking about, Eric!? I remember the way your knees shook when we first entered the cave. You aren't being fair to yourself! You're very important to us! We're friends, you and I! Haha! And as you know, friends help one another!"

Frodi was really having fun with me now.

"Then at least let me cut the rest of the moss in the old cave. There's two more days' work there at least."

Frodi glanced at me suspiciously. I have to fix this now...

"You do know after all how hard it is to find resources for my level..."

When I said that, I put on the most pitiful face I could muster. And my final argument:

"All the remaining moss is up high. That means I'll probably get more than just Agility and Herbalism..."

I could sense Frodi's scrutinizing gaze on my skin. He probably used it as a method of detecting lies... But the beauty of what I said was that not one word wasn't true. Sure, I had left out the main reason I wanted to go, but Frodi wasn't all powerful. He could detect a certain lack of truth in my voice, but that didn't eclipse the pure truth he could also sense me speaking.

"Alright," he finally agreed after a few

moments playing the staring game. "You have two days to clear the cave. Now go."

It took a lot of effort to hold back a sigh of relief.

When I took my first step, I just about had a nasty spill. I saw yet another message jump in before my eyes. Without reading it I sent it into the archive.

Now getting further away, I heard Frodi's muted voice:

"I hope that sucker doesn't die before he gets there."

Marching off after Happy toward the mine, I opened the messages from earlier, my heart aflutter. I decided to read them in chronological order.

- Attention! The Higher Powers have taken note of your accomplishment! You resisted the mental control of a being with Charisma more than 10 points higher than yours!

- Congratulations! You receive:

- Experience essence (100).

- Stone tablet of Mind.

- Stone tablet "Resistance to Mental Attacks."

- Stone tablet "Lie Detection."

- Attention! The Higher Powers have taken note of your accomplishment! You resisted the mental control of a being with Charisma more than 15 points higher than yours!

- *Congratulations! You receive:*
- *Experience essence (150).*
- *Iron tablet of Mind.*
- *Iron tablet "Resistance to Mental Attacks."*
- *Iron tablet "Lie Detection."*

- *Attention! The Higher Powers have taken note of your accomplishment! You resisted the mental control of a being with Charisma more than 20 points higher than yours!*
- *Congratulations! You receive:*
- *Experience essence (200).*
- *Bronze tablet of Mind.*
- *Bronze tablet "Resistance to Mental Attacks."*
- *Bronze tablet "Lie Detection."*

- *Attention! The Higher Powers have taken note of your accomplishment! You resisted the mental control of a being with Charisma more than 25 points higher than yours!*
- *Congratulations! You receive:*
- *Experience essence (250).*
- *Silver tablet (3).*

Then, in a lather, I started reading the messages that came after I convinced Frodi to let me stay in the same cave as before.

- *Attention! The Higher Powers have taken note of your accomplishment! Masterfully concealing*

DUNGEONS OF THE CROOKED MOUNTAINS

the truth, you managed to hide your true intentions from a being with Lie Detection 5 levels higher than yours!

    - Congratulations! You receive:
    - Experience essence (50).
    - Clay tablet of Mind.
    - Clay tablet "Charisma."
    - Clay tablet "Power of Suggestion."

    - Attention! The Higher Powers have taken note of your accomplishment! Masterfully concealing the truth, you managed to hide your true intentions from a being with Lie Detection 10 levels higher than yours!

    - Congratulations! You receive:
    - Experience essence (100).
    - Stone tablet of Mind.
    - Stone tablet "Charisma."
    - Stone tablet "Power of Suggestion."

    - Attention! The Higher Powers have taken note of your accomplishment! Masterfully concealing the truth, you managed to hide your true intentions from a being with Lie Detection 15 levels higher than yours!

    - Congratulations! You receive:
    - Experience essence (150).
    - Iron tablet of Mind.
    - Iron tablet "Charisma."
    - Iron tablet "Power of Suggestion."

- Attention! The Higher Powers have taken note of your accomplishment! Masterfully concealing the truth, you managed to hide your true intentions from a being with Lie Detection 20 levels higher than yours!

- Congratulations! You receive:

- Experience essence (200).

- Bronze tablet of Mind.

- Bronze tablet "Charisma."

- Bronze tablet "Power of Suggestion."

- Attention! The Higher Powers have taken note of your accomplishment! Masterfully concealing the truth, you managed to hide your true intentions from a being with Lie Detection 25 levels higher than yours!

- Congratulations! You receive:

- Experience essence (250).

- Silver tablet (3).

Achievements?! Higher Powers?! First I'm hearing of this! I'd never heard the like from anyone — not my parents, not Dalia - I'd never heard anyone talk about them ever before! What is happening to me?!!

Flipping through the strange notifications, I was so stunned that I completely forgot to look where I was walking. And I soon paid for that — my unfortunate carcass splatted awkwardly in a puddle right in the middle of the road.

I hit my right knee on a rock sticking up out

of the ground and it hurt. I swallowed some mud, then slowly raised my head.

I heard raucous laughter from a cart passing by. My view was blocked by the sides of the cart so I couldn't see who was sitting there but, based on the cracking voices, they were probably kids of my age.

"Way to go, kid," Happy grumbled, grabbing me by the scruff of my neck like a kitten.

To my surprise there was no anger in his voice, just slight bafflement and annoyance.

A moment later I was back on my own two. Wet and all covered in mud. I looked myself over and winced bitterly. Hmm... Not a good way to start the day.

After that I remembered why I'd fallen in the mud and my soul was immediately warmed. The loot!

"You're a real freak," Happy threw out after we'd gone a bit further.

"Why?" I made up my mind to ask.

"You just ate a mouthful of shit, and now you're grinning like an idiot," he explained.

"It's just my way of reacting to screw-ups..."

"Got it. You like eating shit. Like I said, you're a freak."

"So you think a person should eat shit with a serious face?" I asked, surprised at my own cheek.

Happy stopped short all of a sudden and gave me an insistent glare. Everything inside me dropped. If he smacked me upside the head even one time with his massive mitts, I'd be a goner.

He spent a long time looking me from head to toe as if deciding whether to smack upside the head me now or save that bit of fun for later.

"Let me share some wisdom with you, kid," he said slowly. "You really shouldn't be eating shit in the first place. Doesn't matter what your face looks like. Does that clear things up?"

"Yes," I answered quietly.

"As for my happiness... You see this scar?"

He pointed to his mouth.

I nodded.

"I used to have a real jolly old soul in my unit. He was always telling idiotic jokes. He was not a fan of me. You know, I never laughed at his moronic stories and all that... The whole unit would laugh their butts off, but I just didn't find it funny, not on my life..."

I lost my breath. Crum told me Happy was the darkest and quietest person in Livid's gang. And here he was walking next to me and enthusiastically sharing a story from his past.

"It happened in the fall," he continued in the meantime. "There was something our Baron didn't share with a neighboring nobleman. And us northerners have a custom. All disputes, no matter how minor, come to war. And so it started. We give them a bump on the head, they do it back to us. In one of those battles, they came for me. My whole cheek got messed up. While I was lying there unconscious, that jolly jerk I was telling you about patched my cheek back up. A few weeks later, when they took off the bandage, the whole unit had a big laugh at my expense. And that joker laughed most of all behind my back, saying now I'd never frown through one of his stories again... Pretty good joke, huh?"

He spent some time walking in silence. But in the pit of my stomach I could feel that there was more to his story.

"And what came after that?" I finally got up the gumption to ask.

"After that?" I saw Happy laugh for the first time in my memory. For the record, it actually made his face look more frightening. "I played a little joke of my own and got him back."

"How?"

"I cut an ear-to-ear smile into his rude face. Hehe. That made him so happy he didn't survive."

We walked the rest of the way to the cave in silence, each thinking about our own thing. I don't know what Happy was thinking about, but there was just one thing bothering me... How to hide all the loot the mysterious Higher Powers had deigned to give me without him noticing? I don't even want to think what would happen if Happy looked in my bag right now.

Walking and pretending to shake the dirt from my knapsack, I took a look inside. Oh, Great System! How can it be?! Only counting experience essences, I have fifteen hundred! And a pile of tablets of various kinds... And six are silver! When Crum finds out, he'll lose the gift of speech! Hmm... If I don't get burned before that...

"When we get there, you're going straight into the lake," came Happy, startling me.

At first I didn't understand what he was talking about but then it hit me. The mud.

Wait... The mud... The lake... That was a way out!

"Yes, of course!" I answered, smiling happily. "Right into the lake, no question!"

Happy shook his head and grumbled under his breath.

"What a dumbass."

Kneeling in the water, I'm pretending to wipe down my bag.

Before that I laid out all the food on the ground for appearances. Out of the corner of my eye, I'm watching Happy. He has forgotten to even think about me. With a hungry gaze, he's boring into the little pile of delicacies Crum gave me. I thought he'd just eat them without asking, but the crook caught me off guard. He hasn't even touched the food. I had to move things along:

"Did you eat breakfast?" I ask.

"Nope," Happy shakes his head, hope in his eyes. I understand. The smoked sausage has a stupendous smell so strong it even reaches me over in the water.

"Then be my guest," I nod carelessly at my stock. "I had a big meal when I got up. Plus this would be too much for just me. I bought it all on those two esses yesterday because I was so hungry..."

It wasn't hard to talk Happy into it. And he fell on the food with abandon. Just wolfing it down.

I was about to mention the flask, but it wasn't necessary. Happy was already sucking down ale with glee.

And shortly after that, he was snoring away heroically, the sound filling the cave and telling me that Crum's potion did the trick.

With a pitiful sigh of relief, I hop out of the icy water. Shivering and clacking my teeth, I walk over cautiously to the sleeping man. After a bit of hesitation, I decide to touch his hand. He just keeps snoring. I touch again. No reaction. Emboldened, I jostle his shoulder. He's asleep.

Great!

With no delay I run over to my hiding spot. While I hid the trophies, I managed to read the properties of a few of the tablets.

- Clay Tablet "Resistance to Mental Attacks."
- Level: 1.
- Category: Skill.
- Effect: + 0.1 to current progress in "Resistance to Mental Attacks" skill.
- Weight: None. Takes no space.

- Stone Tablet "Lie Detection."
- Level: 1.
- Category: Skill.
- Effect: + 0.2 to current progress in "Lie Detection" skill.
- Weight: None. Takes no space.

- Iron Tablet "Charisma."
- Level: 1.
- Category: Characteristic.
- Effect: + 0.3 to current progress in "Charisma" characteristic.
- Weight: None. Takes no space.

- Bronze Tablet "Power of Suggestion."
- Level: 1.
- Category: Characteristic.
- Effect: + 0.5 to current progress in "Power of Suggestion" characteristic.
- Weight: None. Takes no space.

I held the silver tablet in my hand longer than the others. Just think! Six whole tablets in one go! After all, that was more than half of what Crum got when he was born.

- Silver Tablet.
- Level: 1.
- Effect: + 1 to any characteristic / skill / profession.
- Weight: None. Takes no space.

Now I was feeling worse about my inability to use any of this stuff than ever before. But I quickly cast off all my doubts. For now, being level zero is an advantage.

With difficulty, I tear myself from admiring the treasures that unexpectedly fell in my lap, and hide the last tablet in my hiding spot. Still shivering cold, I walk toward the moss-covered wall. As soon as I start working, I'll warm right up.

CHAPTER 10

ESPITE THE MIDDAY snack, my work pace had practically fallen to zero. My supplies just didn't want to go back up. In the end I was able to cut about five and a half pounds of moss. Just over a pound and a half less than yesterday. But it was easy to explain. I was cutting on the upper level.

After fifty cuts, here's what I ended up with:

- *Experience essence (500).*
- *Clay tablet "Herbalism" (50).*
- *Clay tablet of Agility (50).*
- *Clay tablet "Knife Proficiency" (50).*
- *Clay tablet of Strength (50).*
- *Clay tablet of Endurance (50).*
- *Clay tablet of Acrobatics (50).*
- *Clay tablet of Flexibility (50).*

I had an order of magnitude more esses and tablets than the day before. That meant it wasn't the quantity of resources that mattered. More important was the effort it took to harvest. And that effort couldn't just be contrived.

I even tested that. I filled my knapsack with level-zero pebbles and held it in my right hand, then made a cut with my left. But alas, there is no tricking the Great System. My pitiful attempt had no effect. Who knows, maybe I'm doing everything wrong?

Happy is still snoring away, just dead to the world. I decided not to wake him for now. First I have to clean my clothes.

The water in the lake had become a bit warmer. Either that or I was just overheated from all the exertion.

I "admire" my reflection in the water. Hmm, a pitiful sight. My hair is sticking out every which way. My face is glinting with dirt, as if I spent all day working in a barn. As for my "powerful" torso, capable of putting any girl into a lustful daze, I won't even comment. Thin arms, an inverse chest, bony shoulders. Just skin and bones. It creates the impression that Crum and I are the same age.

Seeing the lake, so out of place in this subterranean world, reminded me of Mia the blonde beauty from back home.

UNDERDOG BOOK ONE

Almost one year prior

TODAY I GOT UP a bit early and first thing I did was run over to the window. Glory to the Great System! What a wonderful sunny day! Exactly what I want. Yesterday I finally worked up the courage... well actually it took all year to work up... Anyway, I overcame all my doubting and walked over to the blond-haired Amelia and asked her on a date...

As I spoke, I was alternating between pale and crimson, burbling and hiccupping the whole way. I'm not sure Mia understood all my mumbling but, to my untold delight, she said yes.

I flew home as if I'd sprouted wings! At that moment, I sincerely believed it was the happiest day of my life!

I was picky in my choice of location... Eventually I decided on the shore of a forest lake. It was even called Crystal Lake. The water there was clean and very warm. I loved that place. I had spent a long time there, sitting in the shadow of an old weeping willow and watching the little critters racing around underwater.

I really wanted to show it to my beloved. And for some reason I thought she was sure to appreciate the beauty and purity of this fairy-tale location. In my dreams, I was already imaging her laughing in delight with her magical voice like the peal of silver bells. I was picturing little crystalline tears of adoration welling up in her big sky-blue eyes, her tenderly crimson lips spreading into a sweet and kind smile, revealing a set of pearly white teeth.

Oh, Great System! What a pure and wonderful creature! My love for her was tearing my heart to bits. It was keeping me up at night. And when I did fall asleep, I always saw Amelia in my dreams. Her and I walking hand in hand and talking about anything and everything. I told her I loved her once there in a flash of emotion and she just listened and smiled.

Then I'd wake up and go to school where I would admire her in stolen glances. But consciously I realized we were not fated to be together. Who was she, and who was I?

Beyond that, I saw the way she looks at Haakon, son of Ulvar the hunter. The black-haired handsome lad shot his first wolf at the age of twelve. Now it's long gray tail adorned the young hunter's leather belt. Oh, I would catch her staring at him and wished her nothing but happiness! If she was happy, I'd be happy.

But still I asked her out on a date. I had to tell her how I felt, knowing and accepting the fact that I would never be her choice. Just to let her know that there is a person who would always be there to give her pure and sincere love.

Mia came a bit late for the date. We agreed to meet after breakfast, but it was nearer midday when she showed up. Honestly, I didn't give a crap. It wasn't a big deal! Most importantly, she was here! And I was in no position to talk about lateness. I'd been here since sunup anyway. I was guarding our spot. I picked up all the rocks and dry leaves off the grass. Everything had to be perfect!

Mia walked slowly and proudly. In a cream-white silk dress, she looked like a bird of legend. Her golden locks were up in a high ponytail and there were luxurious white ribbons woven into it. Her eyes and brows were expertly underlined with black makeup, making her facial features even more distinctive. I might even say crisp...

Her deep eyes, the hue of an ocean wave, had an intrigued look. Her little nose was slightly upturned. The corners of her crimson lips were curled upward barely noticeably. A bit more and cute little dimples would appear in her soft cheeks. She is so pretty! Her and this place... Seemingly my heart is about to tear itself from my chest!

"You came," I whispered timidly.

"I thought I was gonna break a heel the whole way," she grumbled unhappily as she gave the meadow and lakeshore a look of scornful disapproval.

"Why'd you have me come way out to the sticks anyway? Was the city not good enough? There are musicians performing on the square today. Everyone from our class is there. It's so nice!"

"I thought it would be nice here too," I burbled, thrown off by her reproaches.

"Well, you were wrong," Mia looked over the

lakeshore again. The scornful grimace just wouldn't leave her face. To be frank, I didn't expect her to react this way to my favorite place in the world.

"Well, what are you so quiet for?" she asked demandingly. "What did you have to tell me that was so important?"

The words I'd spent a whole year carefully selecting got stuck in my throat. I was disheartened. I felt like an animal backed into a corner.

"Actually," she raised a dainty little hand. "You don't have to say... I already know. You asked me out here to tell me you love me. Right?"

"Uh, yeah," I whispered in surprise. "But how..."

"You think I'm blind? And I don't notice you staring at me with those puppy-dog eyes?"

I felt my face burning... I had never felt this much shame in my life... But still I made up my mind...

"Yes Mia. You're right... I love you! With all my heart! When I see you, my heart breaks into pieces! I know it isn't in the stars for us to be together, but I just wanted you to know that there is a person in this world who will always love you!"

I shot those words out and froze, my shaking hands squeezed to my chest. I could read an air of superiority and satisfaction in her sky-blue eyes. And it also seemed I saw a hint of scorn...

"Mia, bravo!"

A loud exclamation behind me forced me to sharply turn around. Haakon came out of the bushes laughing happily. Loudly clapping, he said:

"You were right as always! This freak has a huge crush on you and invited you here to say he loves you! Haha! You win the bet! Now I have to be your slave for seven days!"

Then jester-like, Haakon gave an exaggerated bow.

The bushes shook and the guys from my class all crawled out, laughing merrily.

"He didn't get any drool on you, huh?!" Skeggi shouted.

Everyone found that funny. The raucous laughter of several dozen kids carried over my little meadow. Not breathing, I turned to Amelia and watched with horror as she laughed along with the rest...

I don't remember walking home after that... I didn't go outside for two weeks, burning in shame and crying in anger... Then after some convincing, mom finally got me out into our yard. And another week later I went to school. On the first day, they all laughed at me again, but with less enthusiasm. It probably had to do with the fact that I no longer had any reaction to their antics. Since then, I did my best not to stare at Mia or any other girls. I withdrew into my own mind.

And I stopped going to the lake... It was like they had defiled it with their mocking laughter...

DUNGEONS OF THE CROOKED MOUNTAINS

Present day

"HEY, RICK, what's up?"

A frightened whisper from Crum right above my ear made me shudder.

I turned sharply.

"Why'd you sneak up on me like that?" I asked fearfully. "Yikes! You just about made my heart stop..."

"I snuck up on you?" Crum asked in agitation. "I've been here for an eternity trying to shout to you... Hm... Honestly I was whispering... But still! You could be paying more attention!"

"What do you mean?"

"Just what I said! I came to the cave just as we agreed. First I saw the snoring oaf... Then I noticed you on the shore. Sitting stock still, not moving a muscle. Staring at the water. I shout once... Twice... Zero attention... What's up with you, buddy? And why'd you take all your clothes off?"

I looked around. With a heavy sigh and rubbing my face, I answered:

"Sorry, Crum... Some old memories came over me. I just can't seem to shake them..."

"Don't worry, Rick," Crum waved it off. Then, as he handed me my clothes, he also added:

"And as for memories, here's what I have to say... They'll let you go as soon as you want them to. Got it? Now get dressed quick. Or you'll catch cold... You understand. You can't afford to get sick here."

"Now that's for sure," I agreed, pulling on my pants and shirt.

"How'd it all go?" the kid asked, nodding at Happy, asleep.

"Perfectly."

"He been sleeping long?"

"Since morning..."

"Woah! Then we need to hurry. How much dropped today?"

"See for yourself," I extended him the bag.

Crum gave a whistle of admiration. He quickly counted out a couple esses and tablets then put them back in the bag

"That's Livid's fifth," he explained. "I mixed it up a bit. So he won't suspect anything..."

"That isn't all," I said, picking up the bag.

"I'm all ears," he said, rubbing his little hands together. "Don't draw it out, tell me!"

"You have to see for yourself. Let's go!"

Stopping at the wall with the hiding spot, I stuck a hand into the crack.

"Pretty nice little nook you crafted," Crum praised.

"Thanks," I said and extended him all my stuff. "Here, look."

It hurt to look at the little guy. He quickly covered his mouth with both hands and started bleating. His eyes bulged. Veins popped out on his forehead.

I understand where he's coming from. The

mountain of loot really was impressive.

Finally, the kid got himself together.

"Rick! Where'd you get all this?! Charisma, Power of Suggestion, Lie Detection? Stone, bronze, iron... Six whole silver tablets?! And look how many esses! Just look!"

"Quiet down, don't shout! I'll explain it all later... You've gotta go... Happy is gonna wake up any minute... Take it all and hide it as we agreed..."

"My heart is telling me we're gonna spend another half a night sitting and talking," Crum smiled mischievously, running for the cave exit with our quickly growing stock of capital.

The scene at the barrack was identical to last time. Livid was sitting on the stoop surrounded by underlings.

Happy took my bag unceremoniously and handed it to Probe.

"A bit more variety today!" the thin criminal said, digging inside my bag. "And more importantly, the bag's fatter!"

While Probe sifted through my loot, I tried to keep my cards close to my chest. No one was even talking to me. All questions were directed at Happy, who was answering monosyllabically.

In the end, I had to wake up my guard when our shift was over. That was how deeply he was asleep. When he woke up, he was not the least bit surprised that it was almost evening. Then while stomping toward the village, he said:

"After more than a day on my feet, the silence just made me pass out."

"I'm glad you got some rest," I answered with an innocent look on my face.

"Not a word to anyone about this. Feel me?"

"I'd swear it," I shot right out.

"No need," he waved it off. "You think I'm afraid of any of them?"

"No. I don't."

"Okay then. I'll take you at your word. I bet you've got your own problems to deal with," Happy laughed. "You probably stashed a couple esses away, too. Huh?"

"Just a couple," I mumbled, my head low. But my skin was crawling. Don't blow it! Just don't blow it!

"That's fine," he nodded. "You earned it with your sweat and blood. Frittering some away is your sacred duty. If it keeps up like yesterday, you might keel over. Boss has been shearing everyone clean recently. Not just you. I can see that you're up to something... But just keep quiet about it... Got it?"

"Got it."

"And another thing... Don't forget to beg Livid for some food money. Otherwise it'll look suspicious. If you don't beg, he'll think you're skimming off the top. Feel me?"

"Yeah," I nodded.

And that is just what I did.

After I asked them to leave me something for food, Livid tossed a gloomy predatory gaze over me and said:

"You and that street rat did pretty well on those two esses yesterday. So today you'll only get one. That's all. Get out of here. Tomorrow you go into the mine again."

"Cheapskate," I thought as I placed the essence in my pocket. He already knew. I'd have to tell Crum I accept his invitation. No reason to find another place to live now. Livid has eyes everywhere. If we stopped talking now, it would look suspicious.

The next two days were as alike as two peas in a pod. Happy snored. I cut moss. And Crum hauled away most of what I gathered.

The cave with the lake had more than a day's worth of moss left, in fact there were two. And in that time, I managed to cut down over twelve pounds of moss from the upper levels.

In the evening, Crum and I were going to tally up the results of four days' work. Tomorrow, I'd be going to a different cave. And we decided to keep our first hiding spot as an untouchable fallback for a rainy day.

"So then," raising a finger proudly, my

business partner started. "Let's start with the esses... Considering the junk and grub we bought, and Livid's share... hmm... Three thousand one hundred forty..."

"How are there so many?!" I asked in astonishment.

"It's from the mine," Crum started facetiously. "There's this kid cutting zero moss. He's an idiot, but he got lucky... I'll introduce you to him some time. Hehe..."

"Very funny... I'm just kinda shocked. I didn't think it would be so much yet!"

"And take note," Crum winked. "That's from just four days. And it's only the esses. Now let's get to the tablets... We've got... bum-ba-da-bum... One thousand one hundred twenty-two clay... And six each of stone, iron, bronze and silver..."

While I just stared on, quietly losing my mind, my business partner kept talking calmly. And it should be said that I was somewhat shocked by how little this affected him. Honestly, it was easy to explain... He had seen all the loot in one place already and was used to it, unlike me. And probably, knowing Crum, I could confidently say that he had already calculated our perspectives for the future.

"I already quickly figured out prices... At this pace, in another two weeks, we can probably buy you off."

"And how much could you get for everything I have now?"

"Let me quick do the math..."

Crum thought for a few minutes. Eyes closed. Lips moving. This guy definitely came from a family of traders!

"Okay then," he said, his eyes open. "I made an estimate without my share."

Seeing that I was trying to object, he interrupted:

"Don't argue! You think if you had enough loot to buy your way out of peonage, I'd be demanding my share? You must really think highly of your business partner..."

"Well, it's just..." I started.

"Just shut up," he waved it off and continued as if nothing had happened:

"So then... If we decide to rush and sell it all in this poor market, it'll get us around fifty gold coins."

"Woah!"

"No, not 'woah!'" Crum grimaced, not sharing my enthusiasm. "Just so you have an idea, in Orchus, one silver tablet is worth five to seven gold. And in the imperial capital it's a whole ten!"

"Yeah, but you need to get there first..." I noted.

"Can't argue with that. But still. I think selling silver tablets in this little backwater at just one gold a piece would be criminal. So to my eye, we should sell it all off in Orchus. The esses and the tablets."

"And how are we gonna do that?"

Crum gave a heavy sigh.

"Well, the thing is I can't get there on my own. Only via caravan... But there won't be a caravan for a while. It'll be two weeks. But merchants also drop by sometimes. For the area they pay a decent price but it's still a pittance."

"Hmm..."

"But even if I can get to Orchus somehow and don't get robbed along the way, where's the guarantee that nothing bad will happen in the city? Just imagine... An eight-year-old orphan with pockets full of esses and tablets... I'll either be spotted by a guard or a group of criminals. And either of them will strip me to the threads. "

"Then sell everything you don't really care about here."

"And leave money on the table? Na... I've got a better idea."

"I'm listening."

"Before the caravan comes, I'll look for someone reliable who is also planning to go to Orchus. I'll spin them a yarn about needing to visit a healer or something... And then I'll convince them to also pass by a vendor dealing in tablets and esses. And I'll pay him for his trouble, naturally."

"Is there anyone like that here?"

"There is," Crum nodded. "We can't fully trust anyone, but most people around here are decent. Like Kril..."

"I know him," I nodded. "We traveled here

together. He was also riding with his son."

"Exactly. He's a decent old guy. He's also waiting on the caravan. I'll probably go with him."

"Sounds good," I said. "Let's call that our plan. But for now, let's count out your share and go hide the rest. I've gotta get up early tomorrow. I've got a new cave waiting for me."

CHAPTER 11

MORNING OF THE next day greeted us with a cloudy sky and cold wind. In the mountains something bellowed and boomed. Must have been another cave-in. As a native of the plains, at first such loud sounds scared me half to death but, much to my surprise, I got used to them within a week. I barely even flinched now. Honestly, if there was a loud enough crash, I did still wake up at night. Crum though, as with all the locals, had no reaction to the noise. Seemingly, he didn't even hear it.

We're sitting sleepy around the table. We eat breakfast. Our delicacies of the day are some slightly stale yeast buns, sour farmer's cheese, sweet honey and milk. Despite the constant exhaustion and chronic lack of sleep, we are very happy with ourselves. Finding lots of loot, eating more or less okay and having a soft bed to sleep on does a great job bringing your mood up and keeping it there.

By the way, Crum couldn't resist the temptation and bought us each a pillow and sleeping bag. That comfort ran us a whole three silver coins, but it was worth it. Furthermore, my partner got me all kinds of little stuff like a steel fire-starter, spoon, flask, tin plate and cup and another couple knickknacks. We decided not to buy any clothes yet so we wouldn't stand out. And mine would still be fine for a while.

Last night, we made four hiding spots. Three for me and one for Crum. We decided to follow an old piece of wisdom and not put all our eggs in one basket. For the record, every spot I made gave me the same rewards. And not clay but bronze. That confirmed a guess I had. The more valuable the contents of a hiding spot, the bigger the reward.

"I wanted to ask you a personal question," I turned thoughtfully to Crum as he chewed.

"Go ahead."

"You're four now."

"Sure."

"Yesterday you told me price for silvers..."

"You wanna ask if I sold the tablets I got for levelling?"

"Yes," I nodded. "I mean, you get three every ding. Right?"

"Exactly. If you add it all up, I have earned eighteen silver tablets. That's including the ones I got for being born. Would that be a decent amount of money? Yeah? Hehe."

"Well, I know what happened to your level one silvers. Your parents spent them on you. But the others?"

"I was six years old when I hit level two. I was living at the house of Madam Drina, the bordello owner."

"There's a bordello here?" I could feel my face turn crimson.

"Not anymore," Crum answered, somehow even too casually. "Madam Drina and her henhouse packed up and moved to Orchus."

"And what was it like living there?" I asked, burning in embarrassment.

"You know, Rick, not that bad," he answered. "At the very least, I never went hungry."

"But why a bordello?"

"My mom got me setup there."

I coughed.

"Don't get any ideas," Crum chuckled. "She was earning some side money cleaning up there and I helped. And when she died, Drina took pity on me and let me stay. I was an errand boy. Make appointments, run to the market... Basically, it was a tolerable life. But then Madam Drina moved. Right when the decline started here, she caught wind and got out of town. May Random give everyone her good sense..."

"And why didn't you go with her?"

"She had a condition that I didn't like... And that opened my eyes to a lot of things... When I hit level two and got my tablets, Madam Drina offered to exchange them for clay. She was already level seventeen by then. As you know, clay can only be used up through level fifteen."

"Uh huh," I nodded. "By sixteen, you can only level with stone or above."

"She really sold me on it, saying how we were friends and all that..." Crum continued. "And friends, as everyone knows, are supposed to help one another. She said if I gave her my silver tablets, she would give me an equivalent number of clays. Back then, I was under the spell of Brother Warrior and his heroic deeds. I wanted to become a great hero myself! Hehe! And that snake Drina played on my weakness."

"And what happened?"

"I made the trade. She gave me thirty clay tablets of Strength and I gave her my three silvers. Back then I didn't understand what a simple trick that was. I was such a dumbass. At first I was happy to be able to help her out, repay her kindness. But then when I found out how much silver tablets were really worth, I was horrified."

"Did you talk to her about it?"

"No," the kid shook his head. "What's the point? What could I even say to her? Technically our transaction was honest. If someone is too trusting and doesn't check all the info, that's their problem. Hehe... But that taught me a lesson I'll never forget. Ever since, I can say I haven't wasted another set of tablets so stupidly."

"I can imagine," I chuckled. "So what was her condition?"

"That I keep making the same trade. She would take me with her, give me a roof over my head and food to eat, and help me level up. In return for that, I exchange all my silver for her clay."

"Was it hard to say no?"

"Back then, no," the boy said. "I don't know why... Maybe because I held a grudge for when she tricked me before... When she left, I was all alone with this place. And I regretted my decision on a number of occasions. But eventually I settled in, and now I can see I did everything right."

"If you want to know my opinion..." I said. "I agree completely. Freedom, even if it isn't always with a full belly or warm room is always gonna be freedom. That isn't even all... I'm practically sure that this Madam Drina was only giving you a roof over your head because of those silver tablets."

"You know, Rick," Crum sighed heavily. "Old man Targus thought the same thing..."

And there the conversation ended all on its own, both of us now thinking about their own thing. I don't know what Crum was thinking, but I was mentally transported back to a lesson from my father...

Less than a year prior

"WHY THE GRUMPY face?" asked father, watching

me pick at my plate. "Did you get made fun of in school again?"

"Not too much today," I waved it off. "I don't even notice anymore."

"Good," father nodded. "But remember everyone who insults you. Orchus isn't a very big city. When you grow up, you'll have to do business with some of them. This way, you'll know who to keep your guard up around."

"Yes, father," I nod in response.

"Then tell me."

"You see..." I started with a sour face and fell silent.

"Tell me, son," father encouraged me. "I'm not just your parent. Sorry if this is going too far, but really I hope you can also call me a friend. Right?"

"Of course!"

"Well, if that's so, we should tell each other our problems. What happened? I've never seen mom's quiche sit on your plate for so long."

"Aw, y'know..." I scratched the back of my head. "It's just Haakon..."

"Haakon, Ulvar's son? The hunter?" father clarified.

"Yep," I nodded.

"What's wrong with him?"

"Everything is just fine with him actually," I sighed heavily. "He's already level five."

"Woah!" Father admired cartoonishly. "And all the girls ogle his backside when he's not looking?"

"How'd you know?" I asked in surprise.

"A wise man once told me there is nothing new under the sun. Everything that happens has happened before in some way or another. When I was in school we also had a Haakon, but his name was Drox. He also stole all the women's hearts. He leveled quick, just like your classmate."

"And what happened to him?"

"He left here early," father shrugged his shoulders.

"And why?"

"Because he quickly got up to sixteen, then he couldn't level anymore."

"What do you mean?"

"See, I was thinking you could tell me," father squinted mischievously. "Just think a little and tell me your ideas..."

"Alright," I nodded, straining all my brain cells. This is a game father and I like to play. He gives me a riddle, and I try to untangle its threads. Often, he gives me a bit of direction.

"What happens at sixteen?" he asked a leading question.

"Hm... One second... Let me think... Don't give me any more hints..."

"Okay, you can do it by yourself."

I spent a bit of time thinking then, when it finally reached me, I looked at father:

"He couldn't use clay tablets anymore!"

"Exactly. Keep going..."

"He must have gotten all his level-up bonuses too quickly. If I'm not mistaken, you get forty-eight silver tablets for sixteen levels."

"Correct."

"But I'm also getting the feeling that he wasn't considering the place he lives. I'm surprised he managed to get up to sixteen around here in the first place. If I'm not mistaken, the highest level resource in our lands is lilac sturgeon."

"Right," father nodded and added. "Level eleven. But our Baron decreed them illegal to catch."

"And the highest level land animal is the cave bear I think..."

"Yes," father confirmed. "It's actually level fifteen. Great System give me memory, I believe the last time there was a hunt for one of them was five years ago. And they're also protected by the Baron. After all, the offspring of our ruler need to level too."

"Then how?" I asked. "Was he buying experience essences? How much dough would that have been? Each ding is a thousand points per level. Right? That means going from one to sixteen would have run him... Hm... One hundred thirty-five thousand essences! Was he the son of a rich man?"

"No, a woodcutter," father laughed.

"Is there something you're not telling me?" I asked with suspicion.

"Haha! You're onto something! I had to

slightly tweak Drox's story. He never went anywhere. At the very least on his own two feet. As a matter of fact, he really liked it here."

"So?"

"He was executed," father answered shortly.

Seeing the surprise on my face, he explained:

"Now do you see how he was levelling? It was very simple. He was killing people. He linked up with a group of riffraff like himself and started robbing upstanding citizens. But this isn't what we're talking about."

"Yes, we started with Haakon."

"Exactly," father agreed. "I don't consider Ulvar your classmate's father an idiot, but I do have to admit I don't understand why he allowed his son to level up to five so quickly. After all, you understand that you need to squeeze those levels for all they're worth. And I do not believe that Haakon hit the ceiling on his characteristics and skills. In fact, I'll go one further. It's not possible for someone like him. That means there can only be one explanation..."

"Oh yeah?"

"He disobeyed his father and must have secretly used all the essences he was earning. Sure, he made an impression on his peers. No doubt there. But in the eyes of his father and the other adults, it's just a stupid stunt pulled by a youthful moron."

Father was no longer smiling. There was

sadness in his eyes. His face was sunken. Much to my surprise, I could see how much he'd aged in the last few years. What was the matter with him?

"Did I say there's nothing new under the sun already?" he asked gloomily.

"Yes, father..."

"Well before you were born, your older brother Ivar made the exact same mistake..."

I felt a chill run down my spine. We had a family taboo against talking about my brother. We did talk about him, but very little. Mom usually cries when she remembers Ivar, and father gets mad.

"Was he strong?" I worked up the courage to ask.

"And agile," father confirmed. "But not as smart as you..."

"They say he was the pride of our school... he won tournaments and competitions..."

"All true," father nodded. "He was also a good son. But the constant adoration spoiled him. He used to obey everything I said, but then he got noticed by our baron's scouts at the winter tournament. And those creeps don't give a damn about family ties. Their goal is finding brave warriors for the army of their lord... To achieve that goal, they'll drip as much poison into someone's ear as it takes."

I was listening with bated breath...

"He left home to go serve in the baron's retinue. He abandoned us, you understand? He gave up on everything I taught him..."

"Did you try and stop him?"

"Did I ever... And he had some very choice words for your mother and I in response. That took us by surprise. As it turned out, he hated our life. He was ashamed to come from a family of miners. He envied the sons of the retinue soldiers..."

"And you let him go?"

"We had to make peace with his decision..." father answered sadly. "We thought that if we tried to pressure him we'd lose him... But nevertheless they took him away... He died in the Wastes for a distant patch of steppe no one has ever even heard of... All because the Baron had a little flight of fancy... And now his bones are bleaching under the sun of those accursed lands..."

"I'm very sorry, father..."

"I know, son... You two would have made great friends. He had a kind and valiant heart. I'm very sorry that pride and anger kept me from telling him how much I loved him..."

That was the first time I saw my father cry...

CHAPTER 12

- You have dried Gray Moss.

- Congratulations! You receive:

- Experience essence (3).

- Clay tablet "Herbalism."

- Clay tablet of Mind.

I SAW A SERIES of identical messages raining down on me one after the next as I walked toward the mine. When all was said and done, I counted out sixty-four messages! So that meant my first batch had dried out.

My mouth spread into a self-satisfied smile all on its own. In the end, setting the moss out to dry was the right move!

Yikes! Good thing Happy was walking in front of me and didn't notice anything. He'd have just called me stupid again.

Pretending I was readjusting my knapsack, I

took a look inside.

- Experience essence (192).
- Clay tablet "Herbalism" (64).
- Clay tablet of Mind (64).

I did some quick mental math to see how much money this would be worth locally. Around three gold! And Frodi said to just throw it all away... No way! From this very day, I'd be paying extra attention to every piece of grass I ripped up or stone I harvested! This was a bonanza!

"Listen, Happy!" I turned to my beefy escort.

"Whadda you want?" he grumbled. As always, he was in a bad mood in the morning.

"Wanna take a peek in our cave? It's on the way anyhow..."

"Why?"

"I wanna get some cool water from the lake. Ever since I drank it, the water in the village well tastes like piss..."

"That's true," Happy agreed. "I'm also gonna fill my flask. Lake water is exactly what we need."

When we got into the cave, the first thing I did, as if it was nothing, was to walk over to the stone with the first batch of moss.

"What is it?" my guard laughed, seeing the way I was looking at the dried out gray bunches. "Still waiting for that shit to turn to gold? Haha!"

I tried to squeeze out the stupidest smile my acting ability could muster. It was funny to imagine how he'd look if he found out how close he was to the truth...

I pick up one dried-out clump. All the moisture had gone out of it and it was five or six times smaller than before. It felt soft and dry. It was a bit dark. I took a sniff. There was something very familiar in it... I pulled the air into my nose again... Sniffed... No... I can't remember. And what about the characteristics?

- *Gray Moss.*
- *Weight: 0.175 ounces.*
- *Value: Extremely low.*
- *Quality: Dried.*

I should mention that I was monitoring its transformation every day. In the "quality" line, it was showing a timer for when the resource would change again. To be precise, the quality changed every twelve hours. First it was "not fresh" then "slightly dry." Today the countdown was gone. So the resource had fully transformed. All that remained was to figure out what it could be used for.

I looked at the rest of the moss. The stuff I cut on day two was now at "medium dry." The stuff from yesterday and the day before had just started to lose moisture. Great!

I gathered all the dry moss in my knapsack. It's just over eleven ounces. I'll ask Crum what I can do with it later. I set out the damp moss on the now freed up area. So every little clump got some sunlight.

"Hey, young crap drier!" Happy called. "You gonna get some water?! We've got a long hike ahead of us."

"Yeah, yeah!" I remembered. "I'm coming!"

When I got to the new place, it became clear where all the howling sounds that scared me so much on my first day were coming from. In the middle of the gigantic cave, there was a frighteningly huge fissure in the ground. Like a black tear wound in the body of a gray stone corpse.

Being near it made me feel like a tiny insignificant bug that could be sucked into the crack by a gust of wind at any moment.

"What?!" seeing my state, Happy shouted with a chuckle. "You gonna cry?! Need to change your shorts?! I hope you didn't wet your pants, hehe..."

I fell silent. It wasn't worth replying to this dangerous brute. Though compared to the backdrop, he didn't look quite so fearsome.

I carefully ambled over to the edge of the fault. Roaring like an enraged monster, the darkness seemed to draw me in.

"Hey, kid!" I heard Happy's voice over my head. "Get back from there. It might start to suck you in. Remember the name. There's a reason this place is called Maw of the Demon. Too many people have gone missing here to even count!"

"And what's down below?" I asked when we'd walked over to the far wall of the cave.

"Who can say?" the big guy shrugged. "No one has ever come back. Alright, enough questions. There's your moss..."

I looked where he pointed and gasped in surprise.

"See how much?" Happy asked in self-satisfaction. "I'm the one who found it! You're sure to have a month's work here..."

"Maybe even more..." I answered sadly.

"What's the matter, kid?" I heard notes of concern in Happy's harsh voice. "Something got you down?"

"Why shouldn't I be down?!" I snapped, afraid at my own cheek. Anyway, let it be! To hell with it! I was in pain! Was he gonna kill me?! No way. He was tasked with protecting me!

"What do I have to be happy about?!" I asked, now bolder, meanwhile feeling a chill on my skin. "I'm just a sheep to you! Isn't that right?! I grow some wool, you shear it. I grow some more, you shear me again! Doesn't it disgust you to keep watch over a kid picking up crumbs? And then you shepherd him back to your boss to get robbed blind without so much as a twinge of conscience! How can you live with yourself?!"

Happy listened to me stone-faced. Then after I finished, something happened that I was not expecting. He laughed. Loudly and plainly, clutching his stomach with both hands. His eyes even teared up.

I open my mouth, baffled. What is happening?

When he finally finished laughing, he sat on a stone and pointed me to the one next to him. Not taking an eye off the man, I sat down on the rock where he pointed.

"Okay then boy, listen up," he said calmly, wiping his tears on his sleeve. "About your idea that we're stealing the fruits of your labor... Remember this once and for all... This stuff only belongs to you right up until you give it to us. As soon as you give something to someone else, that's it... It belongs to them..."

"I'm not giving anything to anyone!" I objected. "You're robbing me!"

"Follow the logic, kid," Happy said patiently. "While it is on your person, what you harvest is yours by right. But the second you give it away..."

"Let me repeat!" I started boiling over. "I never gave anything to anyone!"

"Then why is something you harvested in other peoples' pockets?" the man chuckled. "Let me tell you. You gave it away. Right? Obediently, without a word. Like what? Exactly. Like a sheep."

I looked like a fish thrown on shore, my mouth opening and closing in search of new arguments.

"But you can't do that!" I finally shot out. "What gives you the right to rob me?!"

"That's easy," Happy answered. "Might

makes right."

"Wait, wait, wait... So you think that's the way it should be?!"

"Whether it should be that way or not, it's the way of the world."

"But what could I do alone against all of you?" I objected.

"What do you mean?" Happy asked in surprise. "Fight for what's yours."

"But then I'll die!"

"Of course. And as everyone knows, the dead don't need any stuff. That means you made your choice. You opted to give up your goods meekly, but keep your life. Not a bad trade, don't you think? And who ever said might makes right only applies to others? Once you get big and strong, you can take it all back or get payback on whoever took your stuff from you!"

I sat there feeling like I'd lost the gift of speech. No one had ever talked to me this way before. Most surprising of all was the fact that I realized Happy was right.

"Now as for whether I like that or not, well..."

He didn't have time to finish. A new cast of characters walked into the cave. Livid and his gang. Frodi was dragging someone by the scruff of the neck with a grin. When I saw who it was, my heart sank into my toes.

"Crum..." I exhaled.

"Livid, they're in here!" Probe shouted obsequiously.

The whole procession came over to us. It hurt to look at Crum. His right eye was swollen. His nose looked broken. His mouth was all bloody... Our eyes met. He just gave a barely perceptible head shake and lost consciousness... I understood what he was trying to say. The kid was hanging on with the last of his strength just to send me a message. The criminals didn't know a thing!

I clenched my teeth hard... Tears welled up in my eyes...

"What happened to the boy?" despite the calm tone, I could sense some coldness in Happy's voice.

"Nothing he didn't deserve," Livid barked shortly.

"These two shit-eaters are trying to play us for fools, brother," Frodi said, his eyes squinting predatorily.

"This one," he pointed to Crum, lying limp on the rocks. "Was going around town looking for transport. He wanted to run away to Orchus."

"And?" Happy asked. "What is the problem? He's free."

"That's true," Frodi nodded. "Just guess what he was offering in return. Clays of Herbalism and Knife Proficiency. Does that conjure up any memories? He was offering a hell of a lot, by the way. So, it looks like our little sheep has a couple secrets."

The bandits' gazes all turned to me. I

clenched my fists tight, my nails digging painfully into my palms. Bastards!

I looked Happy in the eyes. Surprising! The fearsome and dangerous man was the only one looking at me without any anger... In his gray eyes, I could see sadness and seemingly determination...

"And what?" he asked Frodi. "That doesn't explain anything."

"Why are you defending them all of a sudden?!" Probe squealed and suddenly gave a loud shout:

"Ahh! I see what's going on here! He's working with them! Livid, he's working with them!"

Probe started jumping around like a nut-job, pointing his finger at Happy.

What happened next shocked me. I could only see Happy out of the corner of my eye. Smooth as a droplet of water, he flowed in the direction of the squealing Probe. I saw the steel of a blade flicker, and the skinny gang member fell twitching on the ground, choking on his own blood and spraying a fountain from his throat.

"Hey old buddy, what are you doing?!" Frodi shouted in a daze, looking at the twitching body.

A wide hand lay on his shoulder from behind, Livid's. My eyes climbed into my forehead. The boss's hand was slowly transforming into a deformed animal-like paw.

"I think our old boy just gave us a clear sign that we're no longer on the same path," Livid barked out in an altered voice.

My body was shivering wildly in horror... The crime lord, slowly turning into an animal, took two smooth steps forward. The criminals took a step back almost in time with him.

Happy alone stayed standing in place. Calm, perhaps even no-nonsense, he wrapped a belt around his left forearm. All I could do was envy his guts... Much to my surprise, I realized I admired the man!

"You're right, Livid," he said calmly, not looking at the wolf-man and checking if the leather belt was holding on his arm. "This is where our paths diverge. I don't wish to serve under a mad creature who has stooped so low as to take from the mouth of a half-starving child."

"Mongrel, I'll tear you to pieces!" Livid barked. "I'll eat your heart and liver..."

"Enough prattle, dog!" Happy cut him off. "I'm waiting!"

The werewolf howled in rage and ran forward, claws grating on the stones.

Man and beast jumped at the same time. The lightning-fast swipe of a clawed paw and the flicker of the knife fused into a single motion. A moment later, the two opponents were sent flying in different directions.

The beast almost immediately stood up to his full gigantic height. I saw a knife handle sticking out of his left side and was elated. I looked to Happy with hope. But alas, he was not getting up... He was just lying there breathless, his face down and his arms spread wide. And under him was a slowly spreading puddle, dark and viscous. A few seconds later it hit me. It was his blood...

Livid ran a victorious gaze over his whole pack.

"Anyone else have any doubts?!" he barked.

All the men looked down.

"Good. Then throw this swine into the abyss."

Livid nodded his animalistic head toward Happy's body.

Then the gaze of his yellow eyes turned to me.

"And that little piece of shit too..."

I shuddered in fear... Was this the end?! My life's path would end here in this ghastly place?!

But it immediately reached me that Livid was not talking about me...

"Noooo!!! Cru-um!!! Nooo!!!" I shouted in a voice not my own as I saw one of the criminals, I think he was called Brown, grabbing Crum's bony little body. Then he just unceremoniously chucked him into the abyss a second after Happy's corpse.

Brown wanted to throw Probe's body in too, but Livid stopped him.

"Leave that one. I need to keep my strength up."

He slowly pulled the knife from his side. The wound healed right before my eyes. How is that possible?! Okay, I guess it isn't all that easy to kill a werewolf. Happy probably knew that, but he still answered the call...

"Frodi!" Livid barked. "Have him show you where their hiding spot is. And from there you know what to do..."

* * *

"Their death is on your conscience," Frodi muttered spitefully through his teeth, dragging me down the path toward the barracks.

"Oh no, scumbag!" I spat out. "Don't even try to make me feel guilty! Happy and Crum were killed by the creature you call a master! And you stood by and watched with your arms folded!"

Frodi was not expecting such a bold rebuff and stopped stock-still. Surprise flickered in his eyes.

"You've changed, Rick," he said mockingly. "You wanna live?"

"You think I'm stupid enough to trust you? Even an idiot could see that I'll be a dead man as soon as you find out where the hiding spot is."

Frodi smiled. But it was not the open and kind smile from before. No. Now it was more like an animal baring its teeth.

"That's a mistake," he hissed. "Now you'll die slowly and painfully. And believe you me, you'll tell me everything I want to know. And you could have died quickly, almost without pain."

He wanted to say something else, but three horsemen appeared from around a bend in the road.

"Eric Bergman?" one of them asked. A gaunt warrior with harsh facial features and an aquiline nose. I mechanically note his level — fifteen.

Two others stop next to him. I knew them. Hart and Flea.

"Yeah, Steinn. This is the kid!" Flea squeaked in his terrible voice.

"Is that true?" Steinn asked me shortly.

"Yes, sir. I am Eric Bergman."

"Then you're coming with us," said the warrior and, bending down, grabbed me by the scruff of the neck.

I didn't have time to realize what was happening before I found myself draped over a saddle.

"Steinn, he and Livid have unfinished business. He will be very displeased," Frodi tried to object.

The warrior gave a half turn and said with threatening strain:

"One more word and I'll order you whipped, trash. And send a message to your boss. If he has any problems he knows where to find me."

When we got a bit away, I looked vengefully back. Frodi and I met gazes.

"Rick, if you think you've escaped death, you're deeply mistaken!" he shouted malevolently after me. "People don't live long in the place they're taking you!"

I DON'T KNOW where they took me or how long we were underway. To be frank, I wasn't especially watching the road.

After my rage and fury abated, they were replaced with a wave of apathy and grief. I kept seeing friends die before my eyes time and again. The brave Happy and the no less valiant Crum... They both gave their lives for me...

Much to my surprise, fury and rage again captured my heart. An oath formed itself in my head...

I solemnly swear! As long as Livid and all his gang are still alive, I will not know peace! And let the Great System be my assurance!

To my surprise, after the system message, a certain kind of peace washed over my soul. There was also a feeling of anticipation. Anticipation of revenge...

My eyes closed all on their own and darkness took me into its saving embrace...

I woke up to a pair of dry and heavy hands lightly slapping my cheeks. My eyes open, I see an old man leaning over me. Yellow parchment skin. A thin gray beard. Narrow squinting eyes. His bald head is covered with a wide-brimmed straw hat. Everything about him gives him away as a native of the eastern provinces. His eyes especially stand out. They are a saturated shade of dark blue. Just like Dalia the healer's. That is a feature shared by everyone who has unlocked the third supply — Magic.

"What's the matter with him, Lee?" a harsh voice asked.

"His supplies are puny and exhausted," the old man answered in clean-accented Orchusian. "He needs food and rest."

"Can I count on him tomorrow morning?"

"Yes, sir. He'll be in perfect shape by tomorrow."

I looked around. There were gray cliffs everywhere. Where did they take me? And what would happen tomorrow?

When I heard heavy footsteps, I turned my head. Another person entered my field of vision. When I saw the unsightly burn scar covering almost the whole left half of his face, I finally realized where I was and what I would be doing tomorrow...

I woke up before sunrise. I looked around. I was seemingly in a big tent of some kind. That must have been it. Lying on a reed mat covered with old rags. And my whole body looked like a piece of tenderized meat. My bladder was insistently announcing its existence. That was easy to explain. I had basically slept through a whole day and night. It was all Lee. First he fed me, then gave me something to drink. And then I switched off.

I quietly threw the stinking rags off me and jumped outside. After I drained my bladder, I felt instant relief. But then came another of nature's calls — my stomach groaning.

Commanding myself not to think about food, I took a look around. Alright... What did we have here...? A small travelling camp consisting of a few tents and lean-tos. The biggest one must belong to Skorx. The guardsmen brought me to his camp yesterday.

There were gray cliffs on all sides. I took a closer look. To the left, there was a black hole in the very farthest cliffside. By all appearances it was the entrance to a mine.

"Is he up?" a demanding voice behind me made me shudder. "That's good. Let's go."

It was Skorx. He walked next to me in a quick gait heading toward the large tent. On the way, he tossed out:

"You don't have much time to prepare."

I do my best to keep up. I look over the local boss on the way. Also level fifteen. So he hadn't hit the ceiling in all his characteristics and skills yet. He still levels with clay like the rest of them.

His figure made him somehow reminiscent of Hart and Steinn. The military bearing was immediately obvious. Stands up straight, takes big steps. Torso, legs and arms protected with leather armor. Gives the impression of a man who's always ready for combat.

Yesterday, I caught a fleeting glimpse of his face. I think before he got that ugly scar, Skorx must have gotten quite a lot of attention from the ladies. A powerful chin, high distinct cheekbones, a narrow nose and a stubborn gaze from dark gray eyes. I had seen the way women looked at men like him...

When we entered the tent, someone was waiting for us. A big broad-shouldered bearded fellow, a scrawny, homely, I'd even say ugly woman and a short thin man with a head shining like a cue-ball.

"Skorx! What the hell?!" The big guy roared, his black beard shaking. "Who'd you drag down here?! Miri! Chad! You see this?!"

"Skorx," the bald guy supported the bearded one. "This is just too much."

"He won't even make it to the destination," came the woman.

"What choice do we have, Dag?" Skorx asked softly, walking up to a wide table covered in papers. "Well, you need someone like this to crawl into the burrows, right? What's wrong with this one? The local mothers are in no hurry to surrender their kiddos to be my scouts, so I say he'll do just fine. The only person in the whole work camp who fits the bill, prisoner or peon, is this one. If Knud hadn't told me about him, you'd be going in without a scout."

"That is all well and good, of course, but he won't make it," Miri kept standing firm. "He's nulled! This is the first time I've ever seen such a thing."

The bearded and bald guys nodded in perfect timing.

"Kid," the woman turned to me. "How much have you got in each supply?"

"Ten," I answered. I felt no fear of speaking openly. After what I'd lived through yesterday, these people didn't scare me.

Everyone laughed except Skorx.

"Whether he'll make it or not is your problem," he answered. "I need results. If he dies, we'll find another. But for now, use what we've got."

The bearded guy wanted to say a bit more, but Skorx sharply raised a hand to stop him.

"That is all!" he put a stamp on it. "Not another word! Pick him out some equipment and get on the way!"

Dag went to the door, angrily grumbling under his breath. His friends went after him.

"Let's go," Miri threw out coldly.

"Sir!" I turned to Skorx, who was leaning over the papers. "I have something to say. If I die underground, no one will ever know."

The scouts pumped the brakes at the door and stared at me, intrigued and waiting to see where I was going with this.

"Speak," Skorx nodded, his gaze fixed on the table. "But make it quick."

"My friends died yesterday in the caves. One of them free."

"Names of the deceased?" Skorx asked shortly.

"Crum, and a man everyone called Happy."

"From Livid's gang?" Chad asked.

"Yes."

"How did they die?" Skorx asked.

"Livid turned into an animal and killed Happy, then ordered Crum killed as well. He was just eight years old. They threw him into the Maw of the Demon."

When they heard about Livid, the scouts cursed loudly.

"Where did you learn of this?" Skorx was now standing opposite me, his arms crossed over his chest.

"I saw it all with my own eyes. Livid was forcing me to work in a mine, then taking all my tablets and esses. I had to hide some of them. Crum was helping me. When we were discovered, Crum got beaten half to death. Happy spoke up on our behalf and fought with Livid over it. He did manage to wound the beast, but lost his life. Then Livid ordered Crum thrown into the abyss. And I was saved by your people before it was too late."

"I see," Skorx said. "Anything else? If no, you gotta go."

"No, sir," I answered and headed for the exit.

Crum was right. Skorx doesn't give a crap about what goes on in the village and nearby caves. He is single-mindedly obsessed with his goal and cannot see anything else around him. As he spoke, I could see impatience and annoyance on his face. Like his duties as a steward had been weighing on him heavily for a long time.

Miri brought me to a small wooden barn with all kinds of junk laying around on the floor.

"Pick something out for yourself," she nodded in disgust at the pile of old clothes. "Make sure there's no blood on the clothes. Almost all the subterranean creatures are blind. But they have incredible sense of smell. If they smell blood, we're all toast. Got it?"

"Yeah..."

"Then go find old man Lee. He handles provisions. Buy enough grub for a whole week. Remember, no one will be feeding you even if you start dying of hunger. We meet in one hour at the entrance to camp."

Without waiting for an answer, Miri left.

With a heavy sigh, I looked into the barn. What smells... Some of the items really did have dark brown spots of dried blood. Cold sweat covered my back. I felt a lump rise up my throat. Hopping out of the barn, I spent a long time spewing the contents of my stomach.

While I cleaned myself up, I asked a logical question. If I couldn't take anything with bloodstains into the caverns then why were they keeping all this bloodstained equipment? Wouldn't it be simpler to just burn it all?

"I don't think you'll find anything useful there," old man Lee's voice made me turn. "You'll only attract death."

"But Miri said..."

"That was for effect," the healer interrupted

me. "Even if you did choose something from this rubbish heap, they'd force you to take it off before you went."

"But why?"

"It's like an initiation ritual for the scouts. You have a lot of thoughts while digging through old rags that belong to dead men. You mentally adapt to the job. Get used to the idea that you're worthless. After that, you're easier to manipulate, more pliable."

"I think I'm starting to understand..."

"All beginners do," the old man assured me. "This tradition has lasted many years. I hope your things don't end up in this barn one day... Follow me."

"I'd like to believe your hopes are realistic..." I muttered, following after the healer.

One hour later, I'm at the entrance. An old sail-cloth cloak on my back. My head is covered with a worn out panama hat made of crude leather. That was all I could find there for level zero. But I was thankful even for that. I also have my knapsack in hand, full of food. The old man took me for twenty esses for the items and food. Highway robbery, but better that than nothing. When I heard his inflated prices, I realized why Lee was being so friendly.

When I paid up with the old skinflint, I considered my good fortune. Back in the cave, neither Livid nor Frodi ever thought to search me. After all, there were tablets and essences in my knapsack that I got for drying moss...

Here no one checked or even asked. Although yesterday... Who knows what Skorx's scouts did on the way here...

There was no one waiting for me, so I decided to sit down and have a bite to eat. Among the things old man Lee sold me, I could feel a small cloth bundle. Ah, the sandwiches Crum packed for me yesterday...

My heart ached. A lump rose up my throat. I hid behind a big rock, slowly fell to the ground and covered my face with my hands... I wept silently, furiously wiping away hot tears with my hand...

"I'll get my revenge... One day, I know I will..."

CHAPTER 13

I T'S BEEN THREE DAYS since I was brought below the ground. When I think back the beginning of our strange journey, I shudder. The scouts scared me so bad I felt like death was lurking under every pebble and around every corner. And for the most part, that is accurate... The native creatures of the caverns, starting from plants and ending with animals, are all marked by extreme aggression.

I first noticed it when I just about fell into the toadstool of a lilac fungus. These insidious half-plant-half-animals hunt by luring prey with a light purplish coloration. When their victim leans over to get a closer look at the unprecedented beauty, the fungus releases a cloud of toxic spores. Its powerful poison takes effect almost instantly. And that is where a no less horrid process begins — dissolving and absorbing the prey. Honestly, the ghastly spectacle contained by that particular mushroom saved my life. It was already digesting a cave worm.

After that is when I realized Miri was on alert and keeping me safe. She just wanted to let me see how dangerous this place is for myself without any hints.

The dying cave worm made a lasting impression on me. Its body was short and barrel-like. Its skin was thick and rough. The mouth oozed poison and was dotted with sharp little hook-shaped teeth. I was in shock... Especially in light of the fact that I would soon be crawling down little burrows where monsters just like this one chewed into stone.

The caverns were teeming with creatures one more dangerous than the next... The black megabats hung upside down on cave ceilings and were always on guard with their sharp hearing, ready to fly off after prey at any moment. The giant rats were the size of a wolfhound and always attacked in packs. All it took was one deep scratch and a group of them would crawl out of the rocks and darkness, attracted by the smell of your blood and ready to eat you whole. Beyond that, there were white vipers, fangblooms, coldunes, hexapods and a plethora of other kinds of creatures, which would take more than a day to list...

Gradually my brain started adapting to the stress. A barrier appeared in my mind, very fragile for now, that helped me perceive the potential danger a bit less sharply... Like detach from it...

At first my companions made fun of me. But eventually the mockery fell to zero. Despite their prediction of three hours, I had held out three days.

To be frank, keeping pace with the scouts wasn't such a daunting task. They walked slowly. Softly. Trying to disturb the peace of the cavern as little as possible.

"The caverns don't abide outside sounds and smells," Miri explained to me in a whisper. In the end, she was the one who took charge of me. Dag and Chad didn't take part in my "education." Well, not counting the terrible faces they pulled when I did something wrong.

"Make too much noise, you die," she said. "Start a fire, you die. Deep wound, dead."

For the record, there was no need for fire here. The walls were overgrown with moss that gave off a dull light-green glow, probably the only plant down here that couldn't kill you.

It was fairly chilly, but better to bear the cold than end up in the belly of the cave beasts that would come running as soon as they smelled fire.

Yesterday I got some messages saying the second batch of moss had dried out. Thankfully, they hit while I was lying with my eyes closed. We had just eaten, and Dag announced a one hour break.

All told, my knapsack now had three

hundred twenty-two esses and two hundred twenty-eight clays. Thank the Great System, I still had my bread and butter. As a matter of fact, another two batches of moss would be finishing up soon. I tried not to think about my and Crum's hiding spots. Livid had probably given a command to plow up all the soil near the village. Sooner or later, one of his gang would find the spots.

I had to give the scouts their due. None of them even once tried to steal from me. And actually, I still hadn't figured out why. Either my companions didn't suspect that a street rat like me would have anything of value or they weren't like Livid and his henchmen. Although, based on their faces, it was hard to believe...

By the way, about my companions... And more specifically their equipment... To look at them they were typical hunters, but there were a few peculiarities. For example, they were all wearing arm and leg protectors.

And their torsos were defended by vests of thick leather. The men wielded short spears with leaf-shaped tips and had small arbalests on their backs. Rounding out the picture were the long hunting knives they carried on their belts.

The only difference with Miri's equipment was that she had a short compound bow instead of an arbalest. Father had once shown me something like it at the market. In his words, this was the weapon used by steppe riders. A person has to have a good amount of strength and ability just to pull back the string of such a bow. That made it all the more surprising at first to see such a thing on a small and fragile looking woman. To be frank, I thought Dag was in charge at the very beginning of our journey, but I very quickly realized Miri was holding the reins.

I noticed the way she moved, how she read tracks, oriented herself underground despite the fact her level was no higher than the men's. For the record, they were all fifteen but Miri was without a doubt closest to the ceiling in her characteristics.

They didn't talk with me much. First of all, it was dangerous underground. They would converse amongst themselves in a kind of sign language though, and quite actively at that. Well and secondly, I was of little interest to them.

Just one time, back at the beginning of the journey when we first got to a more or less safe level was I given the honor of conversation. We had a talk about Livid. It turned out my companions hated him no less than me. Honestly though, they never said how he wronged them. For the most part, our conversation about the werewolf was empty chatter but still I learned some interesting things.

"You think you surprised us or Skorx with the news of his abilities?" Dag asked mockingly. "Oh, naive soul..."

"He knows?" I asked.

"Of course," Miri nodded. "And he has

known a very long time."

"Knud too," said Chad.

"Even Bardan," Dag surprised me.

"But then..." I started, shocked.

"You want to ask why a werewolf has been allowed to live as an open secret for so long?" Dag asked, snarling. "Because Bardan sent that creature out here intentionally."

My eyes climbed into my forehead. But that couldn't be. Bardan himself...

"It's like I'm saying — naive soul," Dag chuckled, poking a fat dirty finger into me. "Look at that face!"

"It's all simple, Rick," Miri said. "Bardan is a lanista. He is training himself a new warrior for the yearly championship in the Imperial capital. I don't know how, maybe by oath or some spell, but somehow Bardan convinced the werewolf to join him."

"Clever," Chad nodded. "Livid 'shears' clays off losers in order to raise his characteristics to the ceiling and Bardan meanwhile doesn't have to invest a single penny in his fighter. Beyond that, no one knows about him. He probably has a couple potential fighters training publicly to take part in the championship, but it's all a sham."

"Why make it so hard?" I asked.

"What do you mean?" Dag asked in surprise. "He's hiding his real strong warrior from his competitors. There's still lots of time before the championship, and anything can happen to a warrior. From bloody diarrhea to some supposedly accidental death in a bordello in the big city. Bardan is taking insurance because he is just as much a snake as his competitors."

I was reminded of Happy saying Livid has a plan... So this is why the crime lord acts so greedy. Every clay tablet is valuable to him now. Imagine how enraged he must have been when they took me away. So the criminals weren't going to kill me? Frodi was just trying to scare me... Learning he was a gladiator in training cleared all that up.

"With a fighter like that, Bardan has every chance of vying for the championship," said Chad.

"If he doesn't decide to sell the werewolf to some minor lord who wants to become a mage," Dag inserted and his comrades all nodded in concert.

"Why?" I asked, baffled.

"Well, kid," Dag shook his head. "What do they teach you over in your schools? Werewolves are what kind of creature? That's right, magical. What does that mean?"

"Whoever kills a werewolf might have an Intellect tablet drop..." it dawned on me.

"They say the chances aren't high," said Miri.

"The chances are decent," Dag waved a hand. "What is Livid's level now?"

"Fifteen," I answered.

"Well then if you took him down as a zero, you'd definitely get one," the bearded guy chuckled. "But in your case, it isn't realistic. But for some rich count or duke, it'd be easy-peasy. The beast gets chained down so he won't even dare kick, then some low-level son of a rich man can come and take him down. In fact, it'll still take a lot of effort. Werewolves have extreme regeneration. But sooner or later he will die, even if that requires prolonged torture. And voila, there's your Intellect tablet. Doesn't matter if its clay or gold. The main thing is activating the supply. Then you can have your rich daddy buy you as many tablets as you want..."

Dag sighed dreamily...

"Ugh, it would be nice to be rich... And if I was a duke or something too, or at the very least a baron... Mm-hm... A completely different life..."

At that time, my mind was in a completely different place. Despite how much hate I felt in my heart for Livid, I didn't wish him such a terrible fate...

At first the caves and tunnels were impossible to tell apart from the ones I'd worked in before. In a few of them, mainly on the upper levels, I even saw my beloved gray moss. But they didn't let me cut any. One of the main rules of this group was to always tread in the footsteps of Miri, who went in the front. Any step to one side or the other could be your last. And that meant for me or the whole unit.

Sometime in the middle of the second day, Miri brought us to a tunnel leading down a level.

Although the scouts were more or less relaxed before, after we went down, their behavior changed completely. Their movement speed was almost cut in half and they walked around with arrows nocked. Their heads were constantly turning in search of the slightest hint of danger.

This lower level was noticeably different from the one above it. There was more of the fluorescent moss, making it brighter. Honestly despite all that, the dim green lighting made this place even spookier.

The tunnels connecting the caves also changed. They became wider and larger. All that made the impression that they'd been made out with different technology than the upper level. Later, Chad gave me a short explanation - this level was gnomish handiwork.

"Ha," he whispered proudly. "You should see the beauty of level four... Too bad we aren't going there this time..."

I didn't share his feeling of pity. I had experienced plenty on our "hike" through the second level.

The woman was stopping all the more often, studying some tracks only she could see. Sometimes she gave a command to wait and went forward all on her own. That always put me beside myself. I had a panicked fear of losing Miri. Dag and Chad didn't inspire much trust as trackers. When she came back, I would always steal a sigh of relief. Once I noticed Dag doing the same. After a few hours observing him, I came to the conclusion he had the hots for our archer. She by the way, seemingly knew about the big bearded guy's feelings but tried to pretend she didn't notice.

And then finally, at the end of the third day we reached a big cave with walls like Swiss cheese. There I learned the nature of my new work.

The fairly narrow cave entrance was blocked from the outside by a large stone. Dag and Chad worked up quite the sweat clearing it. A strange fact jumped out at me... From the tracks, I could tell this boulder had been placed here on purpose. And it was moved back and forth often. Based on their dexterous movements, it looked like these two were moving it every time.

There must have been a reason for all this... There had to be a reason... There was nothing like this before...

Before rolling back the boulder, Miri spent a long time straining her ears to hear if there was anything behind the stone. While Dag and Chad dragged it aside, she stood with her bow at the ready.

But despite their fears, nothing came barreling out of the passage. Then in the very middle of the cave, she explained my job:

"See those holes in the walls?" she whispered.

I nodded. Over my three days down here, I'd grown used to not talking much.

"Those are cave worm burrows."

Seeing fear on my face, the woman put her little hand on my shoulder. She had fingers of steel! She could clamp them down pretty hard!

"Don't panic, they haven't been here for a long time. There aren't any other monsters there either. Or any other nasty stuff like fungus or toxic moss. Got it?"

I nodded again. But just for appearances... Say what you like. I'll never believe you. What makes you block the entrance of the cave? What are you afraid of?

"Smart kid," she praised, not noticing my true state. "See how narrow they are? Even I can't get in there. So, see why we need people of your build?"

"Yes," I whispered.

"Your job is to crawl in as far as you can and check where they end. You'll find your way back by a rope, which we'll tie to your belt. If you find a new cave, look for a drawing like this on the wall."

On the ground, she drew a circle with two parallel lines going through it.

"This is our symbol."

"Got it. It means you've already been there," I figured.

"Clever boy, Rick," Miri praised in a whisper. "We have exactly one day to check as many of these burrows as possible."

"Why do we have to work so fast?"

"The caverns don't abide strangers for long," she answered elusively.

Her words made a brigade of ants crawl up my spine.

"You can leave that knapsack here, too. It'll just make you bigger," said Miri, her hand extended. "I promise no one will go through your things."

I bit my lip. No matter how much I wanted to keep my stuff on me, I was forced to admit Miri was right. The burrows were too narrow. The bag would be a hindrance. Well, unless I tied it to my foot. But then it would be a problem to go back. After all, if I didn't find a place to turn around, I'd have to crawl legs first.

"Come on, you got this," the scout said reassuringly. "Don't worry. Everything will be right where you left it. I promise."

Despite myself, I handed her my knapsack. Setting it on the ground, she started deftly tying a rope around my belt.

"The rope is around forty paces long," she explained. "As soon as you feel it pull, come back."

"Good."

"Now signals. Two sharp tugs is an all clear. Three times means danger. Does that clear things up?"

"Yes."

"Then crawl on in."

I adjusted my clothes, nodded and crawled into the burrow. When I was inside the hole, I heard Miri's voice.

"Good luck, Rick. And remember, don't try

to trick us. Do your work the way you're supposed to."

I didn't answer. I just took a heavy sigh and crawled forward. Miri's warning was just an empty vibration of air. I'd already been told what happened to those who played dirty.

They had a boy once who would crawl thirty feet in and stop in the burrow. Then he would slowly pull the rest of the rope to imitate movement while coiling it around his belt. When the line got taut, he would spend some time lying there resting, then crawl back. Once he emerged from the burrow, he'd say he didn't find anything or that the hole was too long.

At first he got away with it. But only until the scouts got a notion they were being tricked. When they decided to test the kid, they pointed him to one of the burrows he didn't know had already been explored.

Not suspecting a thing, he pulled the same trick. When he came back, he said the same old story about the burrow being very deep. But in reality it was only twenty paces long.

The scouts pretended they believed him and sent the little fraudster down a different hole. And when the rope tightened like a guitar string, Dag and Chad pulled back hard, almost instantly yanking the stunned kid outside. By that point, he was already so flagrant that he was stopping around the first bend, just seven paces from the entrance.

When the kid realized what happened, he fell to his knees and begged for forgiveness. And the scouts pretended to forgive him, making him crawl back down all the burrows he'd supposedly checked before. That time he did his job properly, with particular gusto even. And that earned him praise from the scouts.

But this story is the kind that ends with a moral. Once above ground, Dag asked the boy who, for the record, was fully convinced he'd been forgiven, to check one last cave worm burrow. And he eagerly ran off to do that, but it was to be his last... That burrow was still inhabited by the creature that dug it, and the scouts knew that. In other words, they just executed the unfortunate bastard in cold blood. As a warning... Chad told me that story during a break with a bloodthirsty smile...

I checked the first few burrows carefully. I crawled very slowly, listening for a long time and trying to catch even the slightest suspicious sound. The fact that all the passages were old was evidenced by an abundance of glowing moss covering every surface. There was no way not to be happy about that.

The rope would jerk from time to time, telling me everything was fine out there. I would respond in kind. For the record, when it jerked the first time, I almost crapped my pants in surprise. But I got used to it.

After every burrow, Miri would listen

carefully to my report then scrupulously mark my findings on a map. And her map, by the way, was quite detailed. Seeing my interest, she didn't hide the map from me. In fact, she eagerly explained everything depicted on it. That level of trust surprised and scared me at the same time. I really wanted to know what secrets these dangerous people held.

For the most part, the caves I found were already marked on Miri's map. All that remained was to check another six passages and I could head back. I had no desire to hang around any longer than I had to, so I ate a quick snack and headed into another burrow.

There was a constant inexplicable feeling of panic clinging to me the whole time. But there was no justification for it. And I thought it was just me, but my companions also felt something. They were constantly turning their heads and listening for something.

While I crawled, I tried not to think about how much stone, sand, dirt and water was above me. In large caves, such distressing thoughts did not occur to me. No, I only thought about that while enclosed on all sides like a little bug crawling inside a piece of straw. One squeeze from outside and that little bug would be no more...

The burrow came to an end unexpectedly. I was ready for a longer crawl.

It was a small cave with a fairly high ceiling. I looked around. So... No black megabats, though they generally preferred to stay up higher. No toadstools either. Up on one of the ledges, I saw the white tail of a viper flicker past. I froze, holding my breath... A few heartbeats later, the beast was hidden among the stones. Whew... It moved on... Either it didn't notice me, or I scared it... Miri said these snakes never attacked people first. Most important is to keep your distance. If a viper gets too nervous, it might attack.

I turned my head all around. Almost every one of these white snakes is trailed by a coldune, a kind of scavenger that lives down in the caverns. They devour everything that dies by the snake's poison bite. They're fairly cowardly but, if they sense an advantage, they're sure to attack. Strangely, vipers and coldunes have something of a truce... I don't see one anywhere. That must mean the snake is still young and hasn't picked up a scavenger yet...

All clear, I guess... I wanted to dive back into the burrow but out of the corner of my eye I noticed one of the round symbols Miri showed me earlier. Well, more accurately, a small part of one. Black mold had almost entirely covered it. Most likely, the next person to come here won't even be able to see it.

I should clean it off. Thankfully I can. Mold is level zero. Unfortunately, I won't earn anything from it. The Great System doesn't consider this fungus useful in any way.

Doing my best to step quietly, I walked

toward the opposite wall. As I went, I took out Dragonfly. The closer I came to the design, the more saucer-like my eyes became. Impossible!

With a shivering hand, I started scraping the mold off the wall. When I was done, I took two steps back. What I'd first taken for a scout symbol turned out to be nothing of the sort. This was an artistic mosaic made of pieces of pure white marble. It was a strange design. I suspect my companions have nothing to do with whoever created this symbol... And not just that. I believe I may have found a trace of the thing Skorx and his scouts have been searching so long to find...

As I stared, I caught myself on the thought that the pattern reminded me of something. I look closer... Exactly! There it is! It's two fishing hooks connected together! There was the eye of the top one... Next to it the eye of the second. The tips of the hooks had the classic barbs. How did I not notice right away?

And if I connected both barbs with a line, it would form an infinity symbol. And hey, there's a little groove running between them... My hand reached for the image of its own accord... My finger just about touched the shallow channel when suddenly the rope tied to my belt started going crazy, giving three sharp tugs...

CHAPTER 14

DIVING INTO the burrow, I crawled quickly, fitfully scrambling my arms and legs. My little energy supply immediately told me I was pushing too hard. To hell with it! Most important now was getting back before it was too late!

The rope gave another three tugs for danger. I was already pushing my Strength for all it was worth!

My exit from the burrow was comparable to a cork flying out of a bottle of Champagne. The only thing missing was the celebratory pop.

I was so manic and afraid that I completely forgot to take any precautions. Only when I was lying there breathing heavily next to the burrow entrance did I realize how many mistakes I'd made. I was crawling too loudly. Then without looking around, I jumped out of the hole headlong... And that isn't all! I even started sobbing once while I crawled, imagining being left one on one with the nightmares that called this location home! Logically, I understood it was just panic. And sooner or later, I was sure to make a misstep... But I wasn't expecting it to happen at the worst possible time. Precisely when I needed to keep a cool head.

The first thing that jumped out at me was our little camp site. It just wasn't there... Where is Miri?! Where are Dag and Chad?! Where did they go?! If there was a scuffle with some monsters, where are the tracks? Where is the blood? And why is there no stuff?

I looked around in a daze. There was my knapsack... Lying all on its lonesome a few steps from where I left it... By the looks of things, they did rifle through it despite Miri's assurances. I followed the rope. The other end was tied to a big rock. But why?!

Then my gaze paused on the cave entrance... It was closed... The last piece of the puzzle fell into place... I had simply been abandoned. And intentionally. Cynically sending me out to scout, they packed up shop, for some reason tied my rope to a rock and left, blocking the passage. But why?! What did I ever do to them?! After all, I was doing exactly what they wanted! I didn't try and trick them like the boy... Why did they do this to me?!

Behind me came a blood-curdling snarl. I could feel the hair on the back of my head stand on end. My knees buckled all on their own.

Primordial fear paralyzed my whole body.

I turned slowly. A few steps away from me, at the opposite wall of the cave, there was something big and formless standing stock still. Its skin is hairless, wrinkly and a dirty yellow shade. Its wide mouth is full of sharp teeth. Most of all, the beast looks like a flesh-fly maggot, but it's the size of an adult bull.

I forgot how to breathe. The monster stamped its short legs quickly, crawling into the middle of the cave right over to our former campsite and stopped. Its thick head fell to the ground. Only then did I notice that the monster had no eyes. I think that's the very factor that kept me from dying then and there.

A few powerful breaths in and out, and the gigantic maggot charged forward. Toward the door the scouts had blocked. With horror, I watched the monster racing along and following their tracks. Then it hit its foot on the carefully tied rope and started pulling it in.

Much to my own surprise, I started to act at once. Dragonfly slipped into my hand. The narrow strip of steel digs right into the densely woven fibers. But alas, the knife is not doing enough damage for a level-two rope with seventy units of durability. Another couple tugs and the creature would be pulling me.

Miri's complicated knot was not easy to undo. Only one surefire option remained. Quivering fitfully, my fingers somehow undo my belt latch. And I finish just as the last loop of slack rope is pulled in and my belt flies off toward the monster like a spooked gray bird.

Not wasting any more time, I turned around and ran for the burrow I was just in. On the way, I grabbed my knapsack, which had grown a good bit leaner.

My bodily movements didn't go unnoticed. The monster reacted instantly. Turning quite nimbly, it ran backward, determining my location without fail. How can it do that?! Either it wasn't totally blind, or this creature had impressively sharp hearing.

Pushing my meager abilities to the limit, I thankfully won our race to the death. A short awkward jump and I dove back into the narrow burrow. Without stopping, I started crawling forward.

My lungs on fire, joints and muscles just about to snap from strain, my vision starts to fade... No! Just don't lose consciousness! Just not now!

I managed to crawl another three or four paces before the walls were shaken by a blow of monstrous force. After that, a horrifyingly angry roar blasted into the burrow.

Done! I made it! The monster can't get me now!

I heard it slam the wall a few times in quick succession. Then some of the stone above me started crumbling, telling me the bad news.

Apparently I started celebrating too early... This creature was magical... I squinted my eyes and saw it easily tearing through stone and widening the cave worm's burrow to fit its considerable dimensions. Before each gnash of the monster's teeth, I saw lilac bursts of electricity.

Gathering my willpower into a fist, I raced forward.

The burrow quickly filled with dust. Now I was moving by feel. But that was only half my trouble. With every hit, a disgusting and stinking smell wafted out of the monster's mouth. Now I couldn't say what would kill me faster — its tooth-filled jaws or the unbearable stench.

A few minutes later, I realized I had no hope of winning this race. Every yard I crawled, the creature burrowed two. Beyond that, I was growing weaker all the time. And the monster could seemingly sense that, so it was gnawing into the stone with ever more gusto...

Through dust and tears of despair, I saw cracks cover the burrow walls then start getting wider and wider with every terrible blow... For some reason, my flagging consciousness decided that dying in a cave-in would be less painful than getting crunched up in the jaws of a giant flesh-fly maggot. So I started praying to all the gods to cave this whole mountain in on my head. Just so I would die before this bastard got to me.

But my prayers went unanswered. What was more, I could feel something wet and hot touching me... It was greedily entangling my body.

First I thought a viper was constricting my legs and chest with its disgusting white body. I even smiled victoriously... Not a cave in, but a quick death nevertheless — poison... But then the snake started behaving very strangely — dragging me toward the creature which had for some reason gone quiet. And then it finally reached me! That is no snake! It's the maggot's tongue!

I shuddered and started awkwardly grasping at the cracks and stones. The monster did not like that. It started pulling faster. Dragonfly appeared in my right hand all on its own. No, I'm not gonna die like some flea-ridden sheep! I'm gonna fight to my last breath! The way Happy died, knowing he couldn't win!

Take that! And that! The skin of the monster's tongue was unexpectedly thin. The sharp blade of the artifact of the Ancients sank into its stinking flesh time and again like a hot knife going through butter...

- You have engaged Gulper Female (30) in combat!
- You have dealt 2 damage!
- You have dealt 1 damage!
- You have dealt 0 damage!
- You have dealt 2 damage!

I couldn't hit any more after that... The creature's tongue suddenly disappeared and my ears were struck with a piercing shriek of pain. Then I felt a powerful jolt from underground, accompanied by a monstrous cracking and rumbling boom.

While losing consciousness, I start to smile. I'm sure Crum and Happy will appreciate my valor.

My consciousness returned in fits and starts. Dream and reality got mixed together, yielding strange, surreal scenes. Father and mother were in my visions. They were sitting at the fireplace in our house, conversing enthusiastically. I tried to shout out to them but, alas, they couldn't hear me.

Happy was there too. He looked at me for a long time with a harsh but calm gaze. He nodded in approval, then disappeared.

I was expecting to see Crum, but he never showed up. And I wanted to see him so badly. To beg forgiveness for getting him involved in all this shit...

Sometimes my visions were interrupted and before my eyes I saw a thick green fog. It had an unbearable stench and was deafeningly quiet. At such times, somewhere on the edge of my consciousness, the thought would form that I am in the real world. That my tormented body is lying somewhere in the depths of the Crooked Mountains in a gods-forsaken gnomish mine. And that somewhere next to me is a gigantic creature desperately trying to pull me into its mouth with a disgusting tongue.

A message started flickering insistently before my eyes, tearing me from oblivion. And there was also something in the archive. By the looks of things, in the brief instants when I was slightly awake, I had mechanically swiped the new notifications aside.

It took some effort to concentrate on the flickering red letters.

- Attention! Your hiding spot has been uncovered!
- Attention! Your hiding spot has been uncovered!
- Attention! Your hiding spot has been uncovered!

"Hiding spot?" I rasped, baffled then gave a loud cough.

My throat was parched. My tongue was stuck to the roof of my mouth. Sand grating in my teeth. My head splitting.

I look around in incomprehension. Why am I still alive? Where's the monster? And where the Bug am I?

Partially blind, I start feeling around with my hands. Walls, soft moss, dust, rocks... This doesn't seem like that creature's stomach... It's more like I'm still in the burrow...

My hand suddenly hit on something

familiar... Seemingly, my knapsack...

My right hand plunged into the bag. Please tell me they didn't take it... Please...

Awesome! There it is!

I took out the simple little tin flask as if it were an invaluable relic. Still pretty heavy! In fact, I hadn't drunk almost any since I last refilled it. The cool life-giving moisture flooded my dry mouth. I drank a long time, taking big greedy gulps. Oh, Great System! This was the tastiest thing I ever drank in my whole life!

My thirst sated, I spent a bit of time sitting with my eyes closed, sorting through my thoughts and feelings.

I wanted to crawl away from this frightening place but my empty energy supply wouldn't let me. And for the record, I had exactly one point of Life. If not for the recent system message, I'd have died before ever regaining consciousness. So in the end, whoever looted my hiding spots saved my life.

Actually, why "whoever?" By the looks of things, Livid had found my goods. I imagined their ugly mugs when they saw how many esses and tablets I'd stashed! Anyone from his gang would be so happy they'd have a stroke... Hopefully Frodi or even Livid himself...

The dust had settled and I could see that the passage the monster chased me down no longer existed. My dry lips stretched into an acrid smile... Hehe, I guess my prayer for a cave-in did work in the end. Just not on me, it came down on that freak's head!

Although, if I looked at things logically, it was that thing's fault. Miri said cave worms would secrete a special liquid when digging that reinforced the stone. But that monster just went crazy, losing all its fear and chomping through rock with complete abandon. And by the looks of things, it paid dearly for that. Hmm... Miri was right, the caverns do not forgive mistakes...

My thoughts started revolving around what those scouts had done... Bastards! They set all this up! They knew this creature would come... That was why they were in such a hurry...

Hold up... What if I had it all backwards? Exactly! Like in the games I used to play with father, I started "pulling at threads." What if the monster lives in that cave? But sometimes leaves his home for a few days. And maybe it happens with enviable regularity, on a predictable schedule even. Hm... Seems like the truth... And Skorx was even hurrying the scouts along... We must have arrived too late. The creature was already on its way home. Either that or it just got home early...

Now as for me... Well, that was all easy... If those freaks hadn't left poor Eric Bergman as bait, they would hardly have been able to escape the monster... The boulder blocking the passage would have been basically just a pebble to it. I mean, the way it crunched through that wall...

Er... I guess it was a she... I think when I stabbed it with the knife, the messages showed the monster's name and level...

Suddenly it started to reach me... A cold sweat instantly covered my back... The messages!

My heart seizing, I opened my tabs and was shocked...

- You have killed Gulper Female (30).

- Congratulations! You receive:
- Experience essence (6000).
- Gold tablet of Intellect.
- Silver tablet (10).

Oh gods! My body is shaking from the overflowing emotions! After all, this was exactly what the hunting trainers said back home! As long as you do even a little bit of damage, you get loot.

Without particular hope, I open the description of the gold tablet.

- Gold Tablet of Intellect.
- Level: 1.
- Category: Characteristic.
- Effect: +3 to current progress in Intellect characteristic.
- Weight: None. Takes no space.

Alright then... No surprises there... Level one...

I catch myself by surprise... Where is all this icy calm coming from? Maybe I'd already made peace with my situation? Or maybe it was because I was a hair from death and thinking in different terms?

One way or another, the hysteria is over. There's no cause for it here. I should be delighted! I am still alive, and I made a tidy profit! I'm afraid to even imagine how much this slab of gold would be worth... Plus another ten silvers as a bonus!

And look how many esses dropped! What did they teach in school? First take the level difference. Then multiply that by a thousand. And then one fifth of that is what you get...

I was astounded when I took out my flask and the tips of my fingers felt the distinct shapes of esses and tablets. I was perplexed at the idea that those scout bastards hadn't touched my loot... Or at least checked...

Now when I loosened the drawstring, I noticed a strange glow on the bottom of the knapsack... I didn't understand... There shouldn't have been anything luminescent in there... From behind the bundle of crackers, the edge of an item was sticking out, glimmering with all the colors of the rainbow... While I tried to get it out, I noticed the loot from drying the moss was all gone. So they did rob me, the assholes! Then what were these other tablets from? I had noticeably more esses than I got for just the Gulper Female.

Ah, I'm such an idiot! I hadn't read all the messages! I saw the tablet of Intellect and just forgot everything else...

Sitting a bit more comfortably, I opened my knapsack again...

- *Attention! The Higher Powers have taken note of your accomplishment! You defeated a being more than 10 levels higher than you!*
    - *Congratulations! You receive:*
    - *Experience essence (300).*
    - *Silver tablet (3).*

- *Attention! The Higher Powers have taken note of your accomplishment! You defeated a being more than 20 levels higher than you!*
    - *Congratulations! You receive:*
    - *Experience essence (500).*
    - *Silver tablet (5).*

- *Attention! The Higher Powers have taken note of your accomplishment! You defeated a being more than 30 levels higher than you!*
    - *Congratulations! You receive:*
    - *Experience essence (700).*
    - *Silver tablet (7).*

The more messages I scanned through, the more a stupid satisfied smile blossomed on my face... And by the time I reached the last one, I spent a long time unable to believe my eyes... I read it a few times and closed my eyes wearily...

As it turned out, the shimmering glassy item in my knapsack was nothing more and nothing less than a legendary iridescent tablet...

* * *

- Attention! The Higher Powers smile upon you! You have replicated the legendary feat of Agvid the Tracker! You defeated a creature more than 30 levels higher than you without using magic!
- Congratulations! You receive:
- Experience essence (3000).
- Iridescent tablet "Gulper" (1).

My right hand cautiously plunges into my bag. My slightly shivering fingers make contact with the precious slab. My heart is beating out a fervent rhythm like an orcish tam-tam.

After emerging from my bag, the pearlescent glassy sheet shimmered with all the colors of the rainbow, lighting up everything around me. On its iridescent reverse I could make out the outline of a Gulper.

I stared at the lovely item until I had my fill, admiring it. I'd heard so many fairy tales and urban legends about these. Holding my breath, I went to the description.

- Iridescent Tablet "Gulper."
- Effect:
- Unlocks 1 characteristic of your choice from Gulper.
- Unlocks 1 ability of your choice from Gulper.

- Unlocks 1 spell of your choice from Gulper.

- +10 to any characteristic / skill / profession / spell.

- Weight: None. Takes no space.

My memory of the next few minutes is very foggy... Seemingly, giving in to my emotions and throwing caution to the wind, I nearly filled the whole surrounding area with a scream. But I got myself in hand before it was too late and covered my mouth and face with my knapsack. All that came out was a sad muted mooing sound.

Wiping the hot tears of joy from my cheeks, I was panicking in fear I'd made a mistake and read the description of the cherished tablet again and again. My inflamed eyes looked everywhere for a mention of level. But to my immense joy, I couldn't find any.

I wanted to skip! Cry and laugh and the same time! Just pump my arms and legs like an idiot! Was I really going to finally going to break out of the vicious circle?!

I eventually calmed down and took a deep breath. Not delaying for even one more second, as if afraid the touch of luck would abandon me, I mentally wished to use the tablet.

The Great System responded with a blandly phrased question:

- Would you like to use Iridescent tablet "Gulper?"

Oh, how long I'd waited to see these lines!

"Yes..." I whispered in a quavering voice, even though I only had to agree mentally.

- Choose 1 characteristic of Gulper that you would like to unlock.

An impressively long list came before my eyes. This was a pretty advanced creature... Just the sheer number of options... But I only want one! I have been dreaming of it for so long! There it is! Found it!

"Intellect..." I again whispered.

- Attention! You have unlocked the Intellect characteristic!

- Attention! Magic supply activated!

With a stupid smile on my lips, I watched as the third supply bar appeared. There were just ten points in it for now, but this was only the beginning! Suddenly I had a very simple realization... I had just become a mage!

So... What next?

- Choose 1 skill or ability of Gulper that you would like to unlock.

This list was shorter. I was offered a choice of just four options.

- Gulper's Sharp Sense of Smell (anatomically incompatible).

-   Gulper's   Echolocation   (anatomically incompatible).

- Egg Laying (anatomically incompatible).

- Gulper's Lair.

I studied the first two closely. So that was how blind creatures could "see." I already understood that subterranean monsters had a sharp sense of smell. Miri told me about that. But no one said anything about the fact that the echo of their rumbling could tell them where other creatures were located. And not only the location, also the size of their prey. Or based on the description of the skill, at the very least Gulper could do that for certain.

An excellent skill! That would come in very handy... But alas, it was not to be. My body lacked a few of the sense organs Gulper needed to pull that little trick off. Unfortunately, it was the same story with Sharp Sense of Smell. And as for Egg Laying, I didn't even want to consider it...

So the only real option was the Lair.

- Gulper's Lair.

- Level: 0 (0/20).

- Type: Active ability.

- Rarity: Common.

- Description:

- A Gulper can create a temporary shelter in

an appropriate location such as a secluded cave or hidden amongst large stones. Using magic, it weaves a web around itself which provides both defense and a kind of alarm system.

- *Effect:*
- *Absorbs 300 units of damage.*
- *Creator is alerted to unauthorized entry.*
- *+2 life every 30 minutes (while inside).*
- *+2 mana every 30 minutes (while inside).*
- *+2 energy every 30 minutes (while inside).*

- *Requirements:*
- *Intellect — 6.*
- *Expends 70 mana points.*
- *Note:*
- *Duration: 5 hours.*
- *Radius: 6 feet.*

I rubbed my hands together in satisfaction. So this meant I now had protection, though it was a bit fragile. Three hundred points was no obstacle to, say, a Gulper or a cave worm. But a megabat or giant rat would be held at bay. At least long enough for me to try and get out of there... By the way, now I knew how the Gulper Female found out about uninvited guests in her cave.

And I had to give an extra thanks to the mysterious Higher Powers for the fact it could refill my supplies!

Okay, no further questions. I'll take it!

Time to increase my mana supply.

- Would you like to invest 10 points into the Intellect characteristic?

Yes!

- Attention! Your magic supply has increased to 110 points.

Great! Now to handle the spells.

- Choose 1 spell of Gulper that you would like to unlock.

There were only two spells. As it turned out, I was already familiar with both. One I'd even felt being tested on my unfortunate hide. The name of it was "Gulper's Rancid Breath." It means you release a putrid air that, when it hits the lungs, breaks concentration and lowers movement speed several times. So that was why I turned into a fly in ointment. Honestly, to be fair, I should say that with an energy supply like mine, I was never much for moving fast in the first place.

Alas, rancid breath was not a match for a similar reason to egg laying. As far as I understood, magic was merely an enhancement to this spell. The basis of it was a natural ability of the Gulper's body. And to be frank, I didn't much want it... People don't much care for me much as is. If my breath turns "rancid" like that Gulper thing... Hmm... A happy little picture that'd be... Although

I must admit the ability to slow an enemy down would greatly increase my survival chances down here...

And I'd seen Gulper's second spell in action as well... Actually it was tangentially the reason I was now happy owner of an iridescent tablet.

- *Gulper's Shattering Ram.*
- *Level: 0 (0/20).*
- *Type: Spell.*
- *Rarity: Common.*
- *Description:*
- *Using magic, Gulpers can ram their targets with great force.*
- *Effect:*
- *Deals 45 damage.*
- *Sends enemy flying back a few yards, stunning them for 10 seconds.*

- *Requirements:*
- *Intellect — 4.*
- *Expends 50 mana points.*
- *Note:*
- *Cooldown time: 20 sec.*
- *Range: 23 ft.*
- *Radius of effect: 2.5 ft.*

I'll take that one too! Definitely! So this means with a full mana supply, I can land two blows! Honestly, with that kind of damage, I can't do much against the creatures down here. But the ability to send a monster flying back stunned is very useful indeed. Ten seconds to try and run is a mere sliver of time, but still it would give me a chance.

Eventually, I'd increase the spell level, too... There was just one little thing left... Hehe... Finding enough iridescent tablets to fill a small bag...

CHAPTER 15

- Attention! Lair destroyed in 10 minutes.

YAWNING, I stretched and opened my eyes. The five hours flew by like one minute. But I managed to get some rest. Well, that's selling it short — I feel like a newborn baby. The ability I got from Gulper works miracles. My supplies are full and I'm ready to start looking for a way out of these caverns.

But first I need to look through my knapsack. Yesterday I wasn't feeling up to it. Before passing out, all I managed to do was activate Lair.

So then, the gallant and honorable scouts mercifully left me with all the little items like my firestarter, flask and spoon. They also decided against taking my small onion, crackers and carrot.

The rest of the food and loot from the moss drying they took. The moss itself was still there, though. I can even guess who it was that gutted my bag. Probably Dag. The big guy hates vegetables, especially onions. As for the cheese, sausage, dried meat and nuts, that was more to his taste. I imagined him eating my food right now! I hope you choke!

Now for the loot from the Gulper Female...

- *Experience essence (10500).*
- *Gold tablet of Intellect.*
- *Silver tablet (25).*

Everything I'd earned before today, alas, had been lost. Well, not quite... Lost temporarily! If I could get out of here I'd be sure to present a bill to all the scumbags who stole from me! I don't know how yet, but I will make it happen!

Despite the losses, my financial affairs are still completely in order. Just the one gold tablet is worth enough to make this all worth it! And that's not counting the silvers and esses. As soon as I get to the surface, I'll sell all the essences and some of my silver tablets. I'll pay off my debt to Bardan and go back to Orchus. I hope no one bought our house yet. If not, I'm sure I can make an agreement with the bank to buy it back, or at least to rent it...

Slowly eating two crackers and half a carrot, I gently placed the flask to my lips. I have to ration my food and water. I don't know when I'll get another chance to restock.

No, seriously! If Miri, Dag and Chad are eating all my food right now, I hope those creeps choke! Ideally to death!

- Attention! Lair destroyed in 3 seconds.

Okay... Time to get moving...

The cave with the strange symbol greeted me with silence. To be honest, I was expecting all the subterranean flora and fauna to come running when they heard the cave-in. But when I thought some more, I came to the conclusion that it was the exact opposite of what should happen. If you hear a Gulper Female snarling, better stay far away. Out of caution, the only things I imagine would be around here in the near future were the various kinds of poisonous plant. I'm afraid to even imagine the kind of creature that might come running to the sound of a Gulper's cry...

Before crawling out, I cautiously poke my head out... Seems all quiet... I can go. But where to next?

Hm... First I'll take another look at the strange symbol.

Woah! This mold was really quick. The mosaic was covered with black slime yet again. The curve of the upper hook seemed even less visible than before.

I had absolutely no desire to mess with the

mold, but curiosity took the lead. Especially given I didn't know any way back. I had no clue where to go. This cave wasn't on Miri's map so any hint or clue about where to go next would come in very handy.

Dragonfly took care of the fungus fairly quickly. Both fishhooks again shone with the opaque whiteness of marble. Nice material, by the way. Not even a spot of the mold remained. I remember once our neighbor the tax collector complained to his father that builders had been making a racket with sledgehammers in city hall for two weeks. They were pulling old marble out of the walls. It was all to do with that tenacious mold. But here now, there wasn't even a spot left... The stone was as pure white as a maiden. But by all appearances, this symbol was well over a hundred years old...

Again I looked at the little groove connecting the points. Were there once pieces of marble here too? And with time they chipped off? Though, based on the proper shapes and finished look of the design, the unknown craftsman must have intended his creation this way...

I touched my right pointer finger to the channel. It was quite a smooth surface. It wasn't like what would be left behind after a piece fell out...

What the! Something pricked my finger... A tiny little droplet of blood appeared on the tip of my finger. Maybe I cut myself on a sharp edge of the marble? I stuck my finger into my mouth and started carefully looking for the offending rock segment... No... I can't see one...

I was about to dismiss the pointless symbol when a message flew in before my eyes... The surprise made me take an awkward step back... After that, I fell back full-force on my butt...

- Attention! Blood analysis: Positive.

- Mark activated. Would you like to continue route to next mark?

- Cost of service: 50 mana points.

Forgetting the pain, I batted my eyes in confusion then read the strange message again and again... If I had any doubts that there was a mythical temple of the Ancients down here, they all just went up in smoke.

Seemingly I had finally found some kind of route... I weighed all the plusses and minuses and came to the conclusion that it was better to go this way than to slam my head against a wall and try to navigate blind.

As soon as I gave permission, the unknown system quickly emptied my mana supply by almost half. As soon as that happened, a small glowing arrow appeared before my eyes. It was pointing into one of the burrows in the far wall of the cave. Honestly, when I looked closer, it became clear that it was not a burrow. It was a tunnel carved by the gnomes.

The arrow was insisting that I follow that path. Well, alright... Then let's go...

Inside the tunnel, it was quite bright. The omnipresent green moss was perfectly able to cope with the darkness. Miri told me the gnomes had introduced it to the cave system with this very purpose in mind. She also mentioned that the gnomes had gardens on the lower levels where trees were carved of stone but, due to the glowing moss that covered them, they seemed to be alive.

As I walked, I tried to behave the way the scouts taught me. For the record, I was of two opposing minds about Miri: first I felt spite due to the betrayal, but I also felt gratitude for teaching me how to survive down here. Logically, when she was hammering the laws of the caverns into my head, she was essentially helping herself. After all, the sooner a newbie adapts to the rules of the game, the safer everyone will be. But regardless, her advice was a real boon...

I don't know how long I've been walking already. Maybe a day, maybe three. It's just cave after cave, tunnel after tunnel. I lost count a while back...

I was tired both physically and mentally. Constant fear is exhausting. It's one thing to walk in the footsteps of an experienced scout and another thing entirely to wander a dangerous cave system all on your own.

A few times, my journey just about came to an end... First there was a lone megabat. The beast was cunningly hidden between stalactites. But it was too eager. Must have been starving. As soon as I came out of the tunnel, it flew right at me.

That was the first time I used my new Ram skill. It felt strange... I had never experienced anything like it before... Even when I created the Lair...

I saw a sparking cloud of lilac send the bloodthirsty monster flying a few yards back like a ragdoll as it tried to attack. Then stunned, it smacked into the wall and fell silent for a few seconds... It was amazing! It was a pity, but I didn't have enough damage to finish the creature off. I had to retreat...

After that, I just about landed in the web of a hexapod. But I dodged just in the nick of time. From a distance, I saw some giant rats but they were already eating something else. I got lucky...

As I followed the arrow, I was also looking for cozy caves to rest in. I was looking for somewhere with multiple entrances where I could activate Lair. It was easier to keep away from danger that way. Thanks to that useful ability, I was still able to stay on my feet. I ate the last of the crackers and the onion the day before yesterday. There was only enough water left to just barely coat the bottom of the container. Just a swallow...

* * *

By the end of day five the arrow, which I'd grown to sincerely despise, led me to an underground lake. By then, I was looking more like a ghost than any sort of sentient creature. My magic supply is working full bore. I often stop for breaks. As soon as I have enough mana, I activate Lair and just shut down. In those five hours, my supplies somehow fill back up then I continue stubbornly crawling forward...

"Water..." I rasped through quavering lips. I ruthlessly suppressed the urge to run toward the life-giving liquid with the last of my strength. It wasn't easy, but I did it...

First a look around... Miri taught me how to act around an underground water source. First look around the shore from a safe vantage point with plenty of cover. The first sign of danger is lots of bones around the water. That means a predator lives nearby. But even if there are no skeletons, that doesn't mean it's safe. A creature could just be dragging its victim down underwater to eat them there.

The color of the water is also important. Cloudy, green, or oozy? Don't drink it. What was more, there was sure to be something nasty living in dirty water. A muckwalker, for example.

See a little lake with light azure water? Be prepared to counter an aggressive bleaking. And that water is also not recommended for drinking, by the way...

The only water sources worth consideration run clear. And that was exactly the kind I was seeing now. For the record, there were no bones on the shore either.

Although... Over to the left, there was something strange among the stones. First I thought it was just another rock... Hm... Familiar shape... A giant rat? No... Giant rats had different fur and a longer tail. This was like a fish covered in large scales. But it wasn't shiny. It was matte gray. Not surprising I first confused it with a rock.

Lying on its right side. Back facing me. Not moving. And not breathing. Head extended. Powerful neck and broad ribcage. Narrow hips and quite a long tail.

And then it finally hit me! Scales, cat-like body... This was a harn! But it looked dead... A big dangerous creature. We saw one on the second day of our journey. The scouts also called it a cave cat. But that one was much larger. This must be a very young individual. Well, young or not, the size is about like an adult giant rat. Definitely tall enough to come up to my belt at least.

I spent a bit longer lying there observing the scaly monster, then came to the conclusion that it was dead. By that point, I had to go get some water, otherwise I'd lose my mind.

Slowly, trying to make as little noise as possible, I walked to the shore with a shambling gait. Miri told me sounds carry a long way over water. Especially in silence like this. She also taught me that if you're desperate to walk closer to a body of water, make sure to watch the surface of the water closely. Any strange wave or pattern and it's time to run...

To my delight, I saw nothing of the sort. As I carefully filled my flask, I was looking around and often ran back to the safety of the rocks. And let me note that it took some effort not to stick my whole head into the transparent alluring cool water. The urge was so strong I'm honestly surprised I didn't... The harn by the way had yet to move... That means he's definitely dead... At least I could be happy about that.

As soon as I got amongst the rocks, I greedily sucked at the flask. Oh gods! How wonderful!

I sated my thirst then closed my eyes for a moment. This is happiness! I wish I had something to eat as well... When I was filling the flask I saw silvery flickers deeper down. I'd take some little fishies right now... Heh... But it was not to be...

When I thought about food, my thoughts started pivoting around the dead body of the harn. Why not? Was there any reason that couldn't be food? What if it died just a few hours ago? Maybe it got wounded, lost a lot of blood and crawled over to the water for a drink?

But that theory didn't add up. There was no trail of blood. By the way, the fact that a pile of meat like that is lying at the water's edge and nothing came to try and eat it says a lot. Basically, I could call the lake relatively safe for now.

I got tired of thinking and finally got up the gumption to inspect the body.

I cautiously marched over to the monster. I was ready to fire off a Ram at any moment.

Yes, I was right... It was a harn. Still young. Level five. I wonder where he was crawling to? Based on the tracks, he'd come from the same place as me.

If I followed his trajectory... I took a careful look around... I see... This creature was on its last legs and trying to hide among the stones. It just didn't have enough energy to get there...

Huh... What a big powerful beast! Large paws, a broad ribcage. A blue scratchy tongue was protruding from its slightly open mouth, which was full of teeth... Hold up... Looks like he's been fighting a hexapod. After all, they have blue blood. And are very poisonous. Yeah, that's right! I could see blue spots on his claws and sides.

Heh... Mealtime is canceled. This harn's meat is toxic. Although, to be fair, I should note that there was no way I could cut through its scaly hide with my little knife, or even make a deep scratch. It felt like it was made of stone...

Oh, I wanted so badly to eat! The water only gave me temporary relief... Suddenly my head started spinning... My whole body felt weak... My back was covered in cold sweat... My ears started ringing... Familiar symptoms. I was about to pass out from hunger.

Before losing consciousness, I managed to activate Lair. The last thought I had was that the harn's body was apparently also inside the ability's range.

* * *

When I came back to my senses, I didn't realize where I was at first. Getting up on an elbow, I looked around half blind...

Stones... The large scaly body of a harn... Green moss.. A lake... Ah, I remember! I walked over to the water...

I checked how much longer I had before the lair would be destroyed. Another whole hour. Great! Silence all around — I could keep lying here.

As soon as I laid down and closed my eyes, I heard splashes in the water. I crack open my left eye. A fish! Three pinkish transparent fins on the surface. Smoothly they all entered one little inlet. Right near the shore. In fact, I am just about fifteen feet to their right.

What if? Mmm... Hey, that just might work! As if hearing my thoughts, my stomach called back with a demanding groan. If I don't try, I'll never know...

My hand slowly extends in the direction of the shimmering transparent pink spines. After my mental order, a Ram flies toward the bay looking like a cloud of lilac.

A moment later, the place where the three

fish had just been swimming peaceably exploded into a million little splashes mixed with pebbles and sand. When the water settled back down, I saw two oblong bodies sitting still on the shore. I saw the scaly side of the third fish in the water six feet from the land.

- You have attacked Cave Lungfish (3)!
- You have dealt 39 damage!

- You have attacked Cave Lungfish (3)!
- You have dealt 42 damage!

- You have attacked Cave Lungfish (3)!
- You have dealt 22 damage!

Bug take me! Why did I sit down! I only have a few seconds!

With effort, I got up, stumbled and staggered off toward my prey. As I walk, I take out Dragonfly. Just get there... Out of the corner of my eye, I see that the big fish in the water has started moving. A moment later, it was deep underwater seeming to mock me with a flick of its tail.

The ones on dry land had also come to their senses. They were really writhing and twitching...

Hey now! Where do you think you're going?! Pale and pink, the one-and-a-half-foot-long perch-like fish were making a desperate bid to reach the water...

Not today! I'm not gonna go hungry! Twenty

seconds later, the cooldown was over. Another Ram at just about point-blank plastered their squirming bodies to the stone bank.

- You have attacked Cave Lungfish (3)!
- Critical hit. You have dealt 106 damage!

- You have attacked Cave Lungfish (3)!
- Critical hit. You have dealt 103 damage!

- You have killed Cave Lungfish (3).

- Congratulations! You receive:
- Experience essence (600).
- Stone tablet of Agility.
- Stone tablet of Strength.
- Stone tablet of Endurance.
- Stone tablet of Wisdom.
- Stone tablet of Mind.
- Stone tablet of Accuracy.
- Stone tablet of Speed.
- Stone tablet of Intuition.
- Stone tablet "Fisher."
- Stone tablet "Hunter."

- You have killed Cave Lungfish (3).

- Congratulations! You receive:
- Experience essence (600).
- Stone tablet of Agility.
- Stone tablet of Strength.

- *Stone tablet of Endurance.*
- *Stone tablet of Wisdom.*
- *Stone tablet of Mind.*
- *Stone tablet of Accuracy.*
- *Stone tablet of Speed.*
- *Stone tablet of Intuition.*
- *Stone tablet "Fisher."*
- *Stone tablet "Hunter."*

Woah! Would you look at that drop!

So the closer I was to the target, the higher my chance of landing a critical hit... And this lungfish wasn't all that hard to kill. So then, one hundred forty-five health points. Look at how the spell shredded them...

- *Mangled Fish Corpse.*
- *Level: 0.*
- *Weight: 3 lbs., 5 oz.*
- *Value: Low.*
- *Quality: Fresh (will change in 4 hours).*

Four hours? Haha! In five minutes, there won't even be a trace of them! I pop back the head and slip my fingers inside to remove the guts. With a happy smile, I pull the first fish into my Lair. Then I go back for the second.

All that time I was looking around. I wouldn't say I made all that much noise. But at the end of the day a splash, even a loud one, was a fairly normal occurrence near water. But Bug could play all kinds of tricks...

As I butchered the fish, I was reminded of my mom. I tried to remember how she did it and copy that. But alas, it didn't work at all. The Great System or Higher Powers were probably horrified at what I turned their poor lungfish into...

But I didn't give a crap... After haphazardly fileting both of them, I set all the meat on a flat stone. Then I salted it a bit and rubbed it in. Thankfully, Dag hadn't taken the little leather salt pouch Crum bought for me. So today I would feast!

Oh gods! How tasty! The tender meat was only a bit slimy. Almost boneless. I gulped it all down in a matter of minutes and barely even noticed. I have to admit, this was my first time eating raw meat, but I was not in any position to be squeamish. What's more, I liked the flavor.

I watch with satisfaction as my supplies react positively to the food and water. I walk the shore again... But the other fish were long gone... But oh, this won't be our last face-off!

The successful hunting or rather fishing lit a fire in me. First because of the loot, and second because my stomach wouldn't mind a little top-up.

As I buried the fish guts and bones, I was watching the surface of the lake out of the corner of my eye. Pale pink spines sometimes would stick up from the water, but they weren't coming near shore anymore.

I'd have to wait. Let them calm down. And let me save up some mana.

Half an hour later, I renewed the contours of my Lair. I decided not to move to a different place. Here was plenty comfortable. The harn's body didn't smell yet. Beyond that, I always had it for a distraction. Any uninvited guests would first check to see if it's dead or not from a distance. And in the meantime, I could quietly sneak away.

Somewhere around two hours later, there was some action at the water's edge. I rubbed my hands in satisfaction. I had enough mana saved up for two punches. I just had to walk a bit closer.

This time, there were six big fish all together in the little inlet. Slowly, practically without breathing, I crawled almost to the very edge. I extended my hand. I wait for the whole school to crowd up together in one place. I'm practically two paces from them. Now...

Take that!

Great! Two crits at once! Three big fish on shore. The rest in the water. I wipe the sand and small stones from my face. That splash really did the trick.

The next twenty seconds felt like twenty hours. The big fish in the water had already come to and made a deep dive. Seemingly one of the fish split its side on a rock. The water turned a shocking shade of red.

But lungfish I flung on shore were not able to escape. I slammed all of them with a Ram almost point blank.

Food! Loot!

As I pulled my take into the Lair, my gaze caught on something dimly familiar. Sometimes that happens. You look around and everything seems like before, but some insignificant detail shakes your reality to its foundation. And here I noticed something like that, but quickly lost sight of it...

I slowly turn my head, trying to look over my surroundings as closely as possible.

I see stone walls... the cave entrance... the lake... the shore...

Hold up!

Ah, of course! The shore! The water! Waves! Something big is swimming over from the other end of the lake! So, my fishing did attract some unwanted attention in the end.

It happened so fast I didn't notice, but I was suddenly hiding among the stones in the middle of my Lair. There were ten paces separating me and whatever was making those waves, though I also had the fragile three hundred points of defense and the dead body of the harn.

I didn't have to wait long for my guest. Its elongated head appeared right on the surface exactly where I had just stunned those fish.

Hm... I don't get it... What is a bleaking doing here? This lake doesn't seem like the kind of place they would live. There must be an azure pond somewhere nearby. This one must hunt in two places. Also, now I see why it's so deserted here. Bleakings are no joke. He scared away everything in the area.

Meanwhile, its long, fanged head unfailingly determined where I had gone and slowly started lumbering in my direction. And no surprise. Even I can smell the fish blood and guts. What could I say about the bleaking?

Bug take you! Time to move my butt... But I wanted to hang around my fishing spot a while longer.

When I was just about to make a run for it, the predator was distracted by a big splash right next to it. What was attacking now? I stuck out my neck and tried to see where the noise was coming from...

Oh gods! What is happening there! In the place the wounded fish dove down earlier, the unthinkable happened. The water started frothing and bubbling like it was boiling on a stove. A small whirlpool a muddy shade of crimson formed with silvery lightning flickering inside.

What happened next was something I was definitely not expecting. The giant bleaking, terror of all subterranean lakes and rivers fled underwater in shame.

I squinted. What had scared it so badly? Wait... But that's... Yep! Ray-finned wolffish! Little fish the size of my hand. Very quick moving and aggressive. They hunt in packs. Very voracious creatures. Now I could see why the bleaking retreated. A pack of wolffish would eat it up bones and all in the blink of an eye...

Smiling happily at the unexpected help, I lowered myself to the ground. Time for me to replenish my strength, too.

As I sat down on the flat stone, I pulled out Dragonfly. I hope this time I'm not so awkward at butchering. When I reached for the fish, I raised my head and was struck dumb... Right above me were a pair of sloping green eyes... By the looks of things, the harn wasn't all the way dead...

CHAPTER 16

F OR THE FIRST few moments, I stared captivated at the now suddenly living cat. The round black pupils of its emerald green eyes were staring right at me, unblinking. Its wet black nose was slightly vibrating, pulling in as many of the nearby smells as it could. Its small triangular ears looked to be acting independently of one another, moving in all different directions.

When my initial fear passed, I realized the harn couldn't move. It was still affected by the hexapod's paralysis toxin. Honestly, based on the ears, eyes and nose, the creature was gradually starting to come to its senses.

Somehow, the harn's body had resisted the poisoning and was now actively expelling all the nasty chemicals. There was so much blue foam in its fanged mouth.

Realizing it was not going to eat me any time

soon, I quickly started packing up. The harn's black pupils were constantly watching my fitful movements. Every time I took a small step in its direction, I heard a faint gurgling rasp from its fanged mouth.

As I stuffed the fish in my bag, I was periodically checking on my mana supply. Hm... I'd soon have enough for a spell... Other than that, in a minute I'd also have two points more than I'd need for a Lair.

I wonder how many Rams it would take to finish off this burly bastard. If I got up close and slammed one in its head? That would probably be a crit, right? Although, with my damage level, there would be no getting through its hide...

What if I sent him flying into the water? Maybe I wouldn't do any damage, but I could drown him. And let Bug keep the trophies... If I don't deal with this monster now, he'll wake up and be hot on my heels... He's already caught my scent... His nose is really moving around.

And how did he manage to survive? His regeneration must have been sky high...

Oh! There came the long-awaited points from the Lair. Now I'd have the mana for a Ram. Just as I was trying to figure out how far my spell could fling the harn, a message came before my eyes:

- *Attention! The Higher Powers have taken note of your accomplishment! Out of pity for a wounded creature, you kept it alive for several hours.*

- Congratulations! You receive:
- Experience essence (500).
- Silver tablet (2).
- Decrepit amulet of domestication.

When I comprehended the meaning of what I'd read, I gave a loud cough.

What?! So I was fighting for the life of a wounded creature?! How was I supposed to take that? And let me ask — how did I do it?! Sure as fate, one of Bug's tricks.

But then it finally hit me... the Lair! The harn's body was being affected by my ability for so long! The little crumbs of life and energy he was getting from it every half hour were taken by the mysterious Higher Powers as an expression of "pity." Huh... It would be funny to watch the reaction of these mysterious powers if they knew my true intentions... After all, I was about to drown this monster. What could I say? I was still about to.

I calmed down a bit and pulled the amulet out of my knapsack.

- Decrepit Amulet of Domestication of Ferocious Harn.
- Type: Amulet.
- Rarity: Rare.
- Description:

- A magical amulet, which helps a tamer domesticate a Ferocious Harn.

- Requirements:

- Intellect — 2.

- Each attempt expends 15 mana points.

- Note:

- Time before destruction: 23:58:13.

- Number of attempts: 3.

I read the amulet description a few times and looked at the beast. Our gazes met. I could feel its fury and urge to attack in my skin. Was it really possible to domesticate this beast? Although let me say, having an ally like this would sharply increase my survival chances.

Alright, fifteen mana points wasn't such a big deal. Let's activate...

- Attention! You have attempted to domesticate a Ferocious Harn. Unfortunately, you were not successful.

- Remaining attempts: 2.

To be frank, I was expecting something like this. I wasn't even especially surprised. That was why it showed an attempt counter and other requirements. I wonder what I did wrong. Why offer something that had no chance of working? So did I just waste mana for nothing?

Maybe I was standing too far away? I had to try... When I stopped a step away from the animal, he tried to rasp again and exhale more blue foam. That was him trying to roar.

"What?" I whispered. "Don't like being helpless, eh? Ah, if only you knew how much I understand..."

- *Attention! You have attempted to domesticate a Ferocious Harn. Unfortunately, you were not successful.*
- *Remaining attempts: 1.*

What was the hitch? What was I missing?

I took a step back and looked closely at the creature. Our gazes met again... Either because of the magic of the strange amulet or my own anxiety, I suddenly perceived the fear and desperation of a helpless creature in its green eyes. I remembered myself in the years before I had any artifacts of the Ancients. Those old feelings of impotence followed me right up until today. If not for my parents...

Hey, wait... What if there was a clue in the message itself? What did it say there? Hm... Took pity... Kept alive... In essence, that was what the reward was for. So did that mean I had to keep building on that?

In other words, not let this creature die even though it could come to its senses and eat me at any time?! No way... If this were a rabbit or a puppy then it would be another story... But the perspective of owning such a fanged horror really was attractive. Look at those giant teeth... The size of my pointer finger. The claws were impressive too. Even at level five, this monster was capable of doing serious damage. And it was doing pretty well for defense, too. Its whole body was covered evenly in dark-gray scale armor. It was only a bit lighter color on the stomach. Clearly that was the harn's weak spot.

I didn't realize it at first, but I had walked up close to the heavily breathing body. I felt an irresistible urge to touch its uncanny scales. Ignoring the creature's annoyed gurgling, my hand reached out and touched its armored side all on its own.

- Ferocious Harn.
- Level: 5.
-        *Status: Aggression/Fear/Urge   to kill/Thirst/Hunger/Pain.*

I read the lowest line a few times quizzically. So this is how the amulet helps a tamer. It reveals the animal's feelings. I could understand the aggression and urge to kill just fine. You're not alone there, buddy. And I understand your fear as well. I know that fear all too well...

At the very least now I know why the amulet didn't work the last two times. It even made me mad at myself. Dolt! Why the Bug were you in such a hurry?! Now I had just one more attempt. And time was ticking on the amulet itself.

Alright, I can shower myself with abuse

later... Now I need to act. Where to start? Which threads to pull on?

With a heavy sigh, I crouched next to the creature's head. Rasping all the time, it sized me up with an angry gaze.

"Let's start with the easiest part," I whispered and took out the flask.

The harn's black pupils immediately latched into the unfamiliar object. Its nose drew in the scent, trying to figure out what this shiny thing was. A gurgling rasp of its sharp-toothed mouth pushed out even more blue foam.

Opening the flask, I carefully placed it a hand's length from the corner of his mouth. A thin stream of clear water gradually washed all the blue foam off his teeth and entered his mouth.

"Hmm... What a big mouth you have, boy..." I mumbled, feeling a chill on my skin.

The creature first rasped harshly and seethed but when the life-giving water hit his blue tongue and flowed down his throat, he settled down. The flask was drained in a matter of moments.

I placed my hand on his scaled neck and looked at his status. Aggression had been replaced by caution and confusion had squeezed out fear... Heh... Urge to kill was still right there. Just the same as thirst, hunger and pain. However, there was another difference. Before all words of the status were blood red, but the new ones were all orange. That could only mean one thing. I was on the right track.

I spent the next hour carrying water. Carefully walking to the shore, I would fill the flask, come back and pour all the water into the harn's bottomless gullet, then go back to the lake for more. But the animal's status was constantly showing red thirst. Confusion turned to impatience of a corresponding color. Yet he still wanted to kill me. What an ungrateful bastard!

Two times the Lair boosted his energy and life. And mine as well. When that happened, the creature pissed blue liquid. And the last time the piss was a lighter shade. By the looks of things, the poison was gradually leaving his body. But to my good fortune, he was still paralyzed.

Every step of the way, the panic and fear increased inside me. I asked myself: "Eric, what are you doing?! You're sawing the branch you're sitting on! This bastard will soon be able to move, then you're done for! Your supply is already full. You could send him flying into the water with two Rams then let the nearby school of wolffish eat him up." But my intuition, which I was really growing to hate, was insistent that this was worth the risk and the mysterious Higher Powers wouldn't have just done this for nothing. In fact, every time they intervened was to my benefit...

Emptying yet another flask, I glanced at the harn's status again as usual and couldn't believe my eyes. "Urge to kill" was gone! As were thirst, pain, caution and confusion! In their place were now green colored "curiosity" and a deep orange, nearly red "suspicion." Other than that, the creature was still hungry.

That would hardly be enough for the Higher Powers. What now? The harn was curious. That word was green, so it was probably good thing. At the very least I hope so.

But that suspicion is sticking in my craw. It's almost red... And if you add hunger to that, it makes for an unpleasant picture overall.

I scratched the back of my head in thought and reached for my knapsack. The harn's nose greeted the first fish with a gasp of delight. Out of the corner of my eye, I notice the tip of his scaly tail starting to twitch. His spiky ears stand straight up. His pale blue tongue sticks out.

Cutting off a few pieces, I stuck them between its triangular teeth cautiously.

"Go ahead," I encouraged the creature. "Try and swallow. I'm not sticking my hand in any further."

Despite my expectations, the cat's tongue managed just fine. His green eyes were begging for more. I glanced at his status. "Suspicion" had grown lighter, turning yellow. Encouraging.

Another few pieces of fish shared the fate of the previous ones. And it kept going that way right up until all the fish was gone.

"That's all big eater. You really gorged yourself," I said with a shrug. "No more meat."

"Hrn," the cat answered suddenly and slowly

turned over onto his stomach.

His broad clawed paws shiver in weakness and strain. His long tail coils around like a sleepy snake. The cat squeezes its eyes closed and awkwardly braces itself.

I plop down on the ground in surprise. I don't know what his status is now, but I can't keep going so slow... My quavering hand plunged into my knapsack. The harn immediately reacted to the movement. But to my eye, it was not an aggressive move, more like curious. Its elongated head tilted to the side. Its triangular ears stood straight up. A look of anticipation was plastered on its green eyes. Hm... He's probably thinking I'm about to get him out another fish...

I squeeze the amulet of domestication tight in my left hand. My right is ready to fire off a Ram. My heart is about to leap out of my chest. For some reason, I feel the urge to close my eyes tight...

- *Attention! The Higher Powers have taken note of your accomplishment! By showing concern for a wild beast, you have made a new friend. You'll never find a more loyal companion!*

- *Congratulations! You receive:*
- *Experience essence (1000).*
- *Silver tablet (3).*
- *Ferocious Harn summoning amulet.*
- *Removed: Decrepit amulet of domestication.*

DUNGEONS OF THE CROOKED MOUNTAINS

* * *

- Attention! To create a special mental connection with a pet, you must activate a summoning amulet!

I glanced at the harn. He was still lying there looking docile. Just the tip of his armored tail was constantly twitching. Seemingly he was still waiting for a fish. What a big eater!

Making sure there's nothing around to attack me, I get out the amulet. It looks pretty. Still, to look at it, you'd never say it's some badass magical item. It looks like just a little toy in the shape of a harn and made of bronze.

- Ferocious Harn Summoning Amulet.
- Type: Pet amulet.
- Rarity: Rare.
- Category: Perpetual/ Nontransferable.
- Description:
- A magical amulet, which gives you power over a Ferocious Harn. Once summoned, the creature will protect you selflessly and fight on your side.

Remember! Your harn is a living creature, which requires love and care. With training and progress, you can obtain a truly powerful ally!
- Requirements:
- Intellect — 2.
- Each use of the amulet expends 20 mana

points.

- Weight: None. Takes no space.

I feel a brigade of ants marching down my spine. Carefully reading the amulet description again, I leaned my back against the stone wall. The harn meanwhile is placidly crunching through fish heads and guts. And giving a satisfied groan at the same time. So does that mean this big creature is fully under my control? And he will do everything I say like an obedient dog?

By the way, what does the mana cost on the summoning amulet actually mean? Do I have to pay for every command? Or something else?

If I don't try, I'll never know...

- Would you like to recall your pet?
- Expends 20 mana points.

What does it mean recall? I don't get it. But I have to press on. As mom used to love to say: "nothing ventured, nothing gained."

As soon as I answered yes, the unthinkable happened. The harn just disappeared. One minute he's crunching down fish heads with abandon and a moment later I can't see either hide or hair of him! To say I was astounded and spooked is to say nothing!

Getting up off the stone, I cautiously walked over to the place my extremely short-term pet was just lying. Just to make sure, I poked the air with my hand and foot. What if he just turned invisible? But no, nothing.

Shocked, I turned my head and lowered my gaze to the metal animal in my hand.

- Would you like to summon your pet?
- Expends 20 mana points.

Yes! It took effort to hold back and not tear my throat shouting for joy!

The second my supply dropped twenty mana points, the harn appeared at my feet out of nowhere. In fear, I jumped a step to the side. The creature was seemingly no less stunned than me. His scales stood erect; his tail nervously fell to the ground. He tried to hop to his feet but couldn't and plopped down heavily on his stomach.

Our gazes met. Seemingly, we both had the very same question: "What just happened?!"

"Sorry," I said, extending my right hand apologetically and taking a step forward. To be honest, despite the amulet's assurance, I was still a bit afraid of him.

The harn extended his neck, and touched his wet nose to my hand. I wanted to jerk my hand back out of inertia but I stopped myself. The beast's hot breath coated my skin and a moment later I felt the soft touch of his warm tongue. I'd bet my neck that, if my parents were here to see this show, they would never have believed their eyes...

The harn licked me again and his nose

reached for my knapsack in a logical progression.

"Sorry buddy," shrugged my shoulders. "But I don't have any more fish."

I felt an irresistible desire to pet the big old cat. When I placed a hand on his flat head, I was expecting to feel a familiar stony hardness but was pleasantly surprised. The harn's scales were now soft and warm to the touch. And the tongue by the way was not rough. So does that mean my pet can adapt to its master?

He liked being petted, even took it with satisfaction. A deep chest purr bore witness to that. His eyes rolled back, he turned on his back like a cat, revealing a powerful chest and light gray stomach.

"Good boy," I said, smiling. With every second, my fear abated. It was squeezed out by a realization that this dangerous behemoth was now mine.

I wanted to check his status. I was curious what it would look like... When I glanced at the description, I was slightly perplexed...

- *Ferocious Harn.*
- *Level: 5 (130/20,000).*
- *Status: Loyalty to master (permanent) / Hunger / Weak pain.*
- *Strength: 37/75*
- *Agility: 45/75*
- *Animal instinct: 8/10*
- *Speed: 39/75*

- *Flexibility: 41/75*
- *Health: 35/50*
- *Endurance: 35/50*
- *Life supply: 28/400*
- *Energy supply: 32/400*
- *Scale armor: 12/25*
- *Defense: 120*
- *Damage: +97.3...+239.7*

That was followed by a list of twenty abilities and skills like "bite," "paw swipe," or "animal regeneration."

I felt outside of reality for a time. And let me note that this is the first time something like this is happening to me. Seeing a detailed description of another creature including all characteristics and other information is generally an ability reserved for mages. And I am not one of them. So it must be the amulet.

Briefly studying my minion's stats, I managed to cobble together an overall picture. Based on its supply figures, which weren't really that high, the harn was born with fifty life and energy. That, by the way, is twice what a normal person gets. And five times more than I got. I wonder how much the Great System gives a newborn gulper. I don't even want to imagine. I'd die in envy.

The ceiling for most of the harn's characteristics is fifteen points per level. The very lowest is Animal Instinct. His Endurance isn't all that high either, but his low Health is compensated and then some by his Scale Armor. To even get to the cat's life supply, you have to first deal over one hundred twenty points of damage. Anything below that would simply be absorbed by his resilient scales.

Based on the names of most abilities and skills, the harn: is good at camouflage, sees excellently in the dark, and can jump a long way. And for level five, he can do quite high damage. Every "bite" and "paw swipe" leaves nasty bleeding wounds. A flexible, agile, strong and fast creature. Can sit patiently in ambush for a long time. Has high Animal Instinct.

And for minuses, he spends energy quickly and has a small life supply. And also... A terrible hunger! He constantly wants to eat! While I read, he crawled over to where I buried the first two sets of fish guts, dug them up and gorged himself a bit more. Now he's lying on his stomach six feet from the water and closely watching the gray spines of the lungfish.

When four of the big fish swam into the inlet, I felt an uncanny urge to slam them all with a Ram. Something gave me the impression this desire did not belong to me, that it was somehow from without. And furtively so... On the sly...

I glanced at the harn. He was still absorbed in watching the fish. His paws tucked under him, his tail stock still, his triangular ears standing on end. And then it finally hit me! The feelings were coming from my pet! What did it say? A special mental connection?

I decided to see what would come next and estimated the distance to the bay. Not bad. Fifteen feet. Should be plenty close.

I got off a Ram and sent all four fish flying on shore, splashing everything around with water and wet sand. The harn jumped with what looked to be the last crumbs of his energy and caught all the lungfish while they were paralyzed.

Oh yeah! This kind of fishing is fun!

Another thing also made an impression on me. Despite my expectations, the harn didn't start eating the fish right away. He lay next to their shredded bodies sniffing them greedily with his black nose, but he was just staring at me... Is this his way of asking permission?!

"That's all you," I nodded.

After getting the go-ahead, he greedily sank his teeth into the side of one of the lungfish without waiting another second. Now that's discipline!

Due to the level difference, he got no experience, but I was inundated as usual. Scrolling through all the messages, I swiped them aside out of habit. But then my attention was drawn by the now flickering "Pet" tab. Hm... That's new... Let's take a look...

- *Attention! You have successfully fought your first battle with your pet! You now have access to the Pet Training and Progress function!*

I opened the window and was slightly taken aback.

- Available materials for pet training and progress:
- Experience essence (17400).
- Gold tablet of Intellect.
- Silver tablet (30).
- Stone tablet of Agility (9).
- Stone tablet of Strength (9).
- Stone tablet of Endurance (9).
- Stone tablet of Wisdom (9).
- Stone tablet of Mind (9).
- Stone tablet of Accuracy (9).
- Stone tablet of Speed (9).
- Stone tablet of Intuition (9).
- Stone tablet "Fisher" (9).
- Stone tablet "Hunter" (9).

Wait, where were all those esses and tablets from? I read the list again. I hit upon the line with the gold tablet of Intellect and it finally hit me... That's all my loot from the last few days down here in the caverns!

I glanced at the harn as it eagerly ripped into the fish. I didn't think for long... I stroked the back of my head... I looked over all the loot again... Then, with a shrug I whispered:

"Ah, why not?"

CHAPTER 17

- Initiate pet training and progress?

"ALRIGHT," I said, rubbing my hands.

As far as I could tell, the harn had been spending all his experience and characteristic points the way his instincts told him to. He was trying to better adapt to his hunting area and environment.

Although, to be frank, something tells me it wasn't him doing it at all. The Great System was probably doing it for him.

By the way, speaking of Intellect, that reminds me. I now have nine stone tablets of Mind. That's almost enough for two points.

- Attention! You have unlocked your pet's Mind characteristic.
- Present value: 0.2/ 1

Got it. So at the moment, the harn's Mind ceiling is one. Not much, but something... I glanced at the cat out of the corner of my eye. He'd already taken down the three big fish and was tucking into the last. As was his style, he was gorging himself again. Hey, you know what would make a good name for him? Gorgie!

- Would you like to name your pet "Gorgie?"

The unexpected message made me shudder.

"Gorgie?" I turned the word over on my tongue and thought about how it made me feel: "Georgie... Gorgie... Hm... Sure, I'll let him be Gorgie for now. It fits his character well..."

As if he could smell that I was thinking about him, the harn raised his scaly face. By the way, his supplies had already filled out pretty well. Unfortunately, the figures were still far from ideal. He was still hungry. I wonder how many fish this bottomless pit needs every day.

Alright, let's keep going... As soon as I raised the harn's Mind to one, a new message jumped before my eyes which, in essence, was a response to my question.

- Meat required before complete recovery: 33 lbs.

Woah! He'd already downed a bit more than twenty-six pounds. Thirty-three more would make just shy of sixty pounds! Although this was probably only because he was seriously wounded. It was only natural he might need more food than usual.

So that means I would still have to get him another ten fish at least. No problem. As long as the lungfish don't stop swimming into the inlet. But for now, it would be nice if the harn moved inside the Lair. There would be a supply boost soon.

As soon as I thought about that, the creature got up off the ground and slowly walked over to me, staggering and holding the unfinished body of a lungfish in his teeth. Huh... What obedience!

I was astonished. I didn't have to start talking, or even think a complete thought! Looks like Mind noticeably increases the strength of our mental connection.

Within a few minutes, I had thrown almost all the stones into his characteristics and skills. I unlocked another two new characteristics for him and brought them almost up to two.

- *Attention! You have unlocked your pet's Accuracy characteristic.*
- *Present value: 1.8/ 75*

- *Attention! You have unlocked your pet's Intuition characteristic.*
- *Present value: 1.8/ 5*

They told us in school that Intuition isn't strictly required to do critical damage. The chance is always higher than zero. But having Intuition bolsters your chances significantly. It was just unfortunate that the harn's "ceiling" was quite low. A pet that constantly crits would be very cool.

For now, I don't quite know why the harn needs Accuracy. Time will tell. As father always said: "You never know when something's going to come in handy."

After spending the "stones," the picture looked like this:

- *Ferocious Harn.*
- *Name: Gorgie.*
- *Level: 5 (130/20000).*
- *Status: Loyalty to master (permanent)/ Hunger.*
- *Strength: 38.8/75*
- *Mind: 1/1*
- *Agility: 46.8/75*
- *Accuracy: 1.8/75*
- *Intuition: 1.8/5*
- *Animal instinct: 8/10*
- *Speed: 40.8/75*
- *Flexibility: 41/75*
- *Health: 35/50*
- *Endurance: 36.8/50*
- *Life supply: 213/400*
- *Energy supply: 263/418*
- *Scale armor: 12/25*

- Defense: 120/250
- Damage: +98.5...+242.9

I studied his damage figures and considered the best way to invest the silver tablets for a bit. In the end, I came to the conclusion that it was best to improve abilities and skills related to damage. Sure, Strength gave a certain percentage increase, but it was less effective per point than skills. I can't dispute that the ideal option would be to improve both. And probably some rich little baron or count would do just that. But I'm no nobleman... My resources are limited...

So then, what did I know...? The harn has the natural weapons he was born with — claws and teeth. The former did three damage points and the latter ten. Well, discounting the extra points for every level.

Other than that, the Great System had given him a few useful abilities: "bite," "paw swipe" and "pounce."

- Bite: 17/25
- Effect:
- Teeth multiply damage.
- Maximum energy expenditure: 50 points.

- Paw swipe: 22/25
- Effect:
- Claws multiply damage.
- Maximum energy expenditure: 25 points.

- *Pounce: 4/5.*
- *Effect:*
- *Distance: 12 feet.*
- *Height: 6 feet.*
- *+40 to maximum damage.*
- *Maximum energy expenditure: 75 points.*

So that means my new friend can do serious damage, but gets tired very fast. Let's put it this way — the harn was not made to fight for hours. But if a quick deadly attack is what you need, he is the perfect candidate... A lightning-fast jump... Clawed paws that swipe with a vengeance... Powerful jaws that bite down hard... Overall, he expends energy quickly, but gets results almost immediately. All that remained was to learn to use all his plusses while considering the minuses.

The Scale Armor merited special attention. Every point invested in that characteristic gave an additional ten points of defense. If I brought that up to its ceiling, it would give two hundred fifty points!

Hmm... Looking at all these characteristics and skills, I feel like a kid in a candy store... I want to bring them all up right now! But alas... My abilities are limited...

I looked to see what I had left in my knapsack.

- *Experience essence (17400).*

- Gold tablet of Intellect.
- Silver tablet (30).
- Stone tablet of Wisdom (9).
- Stone tablet of Mind (4).

I wasn't able to use the Wisdom tablets; they required Intellect to use. At first I wanted to correct that weakness, but I thought better of it and decided to hold onto the gold tablet for better times. The harn having a magic supply was quite an attractive perspective. But for now with no spells or magical abilities it was a pointless luxury. Furthermore, that tablet was my ticket to freedom.

So I had to figure out what to do with the esses and silvers.

As for the former, I was clear. Let him gain experience slowly the natural way. I wouldn't be able to get him up to level six now anyway. I'm almost twenty-five hundred essences short. Furthermore, based on the experience he had saved up, he'd just hit five. Most likely in battle with the hexapod. The evidence for my theory was him having the skill "Resistance to Hexapod Poison." He has a seven there. He'd brought it up pretty well, actually. I think some of that was my doing.

Alright, we figured that out... Now I have thirty silver tablets left. I think I already know where to invest them. What's most important? Correct. My new friend's life. That means I need to safeguard him as much as possible. Furthermore, I can bring a few things up to maximum.

First things first, Animal Regeneration. It proved itself very effective. Minus two tablets. Next... Scale Armor. Minus another thirteen silvers. And I set the remaining tablets into health, increasing his life supply to five hundred fifty points. I looked on my creation and felt a certain degree of satisfaction.

> - *Ferocious Harn.*
> - *Name: Gorgie.*
> - *Level: 5 (130/20000).*
> - *Status: Loyalty to master (permanent)/ Hunger.*
> - *Strength: 38.8/75*
> - *Mind: 1/1*
> - *Agility: 46.8/75*
> - *Accuracy: 1.8/75*
> - *Intuition: 1.8/5*
> - *Animal instinct: 8/10*
> - *Speed: 40.8/75*
> - *Flexibility: 41/75*
> - *Health: 50/50*
> - *Endurance: 36.8/50*
> - *Life supply: 313/550*
> - *Energy supply: 295/418*
> - *Scale armor: 25/25*
> - *Defense: 250/250*
> - *Damage: +98.5...+242.9*

And some of the abilities and skills caught

my eye once again.

- *Bite: 17/25*
- *Paw swipe: 22/25*
- *Pounce: 4/5*
- *Animal regeneration: 10/10*
- *Hunter: 17.8/25*
- *Fisher: 8.8/25*
- *Resistance to Hexapod poison: 7/25*

His wet nose gently poking my hand distracted me from reading. I glanced at the harn. He was sitting opposite me and closely watching my every movement. And his armor scales had changed slightly. They were bigger and thicker. On his chest and stomach, they'd grown noticeably darker.

"What?" I asked.

A message appeared before my eyes that made me gape in astonishment...

"Fish! Hunger."

"I don't get it..." I whispered, batting my eyes foolishly at the harn.

"Fish. Hunger," came the same message again.

What does this mean?! We can talk like this?! For crying out loud!

I sank down wearily to the ground and closed my eyes. A nice little start...

A moment later, I felt impatient hot breath on my face. There were no more messages, but it was already clear what this buzzard wanted.

I raised my head and tossed a gaze toward the bay. Lungfish. Six or seven of them.

I looked at the harn.

"Ready?"

He just licked my face and stole up quietly to his previous position. Out of the corner of my eye, I noticed that he was no longer shivering at all. Regeneration is already paying dividends.

It's day two of our stay on the banks of the underground river. Ah yeah. I now know it is not a lake, but a river. The harn told me. Our uncanny mental connection occasionally transmitted his knowledge to me. That beyond all doubt useful ability informed me that the river runs many miles west to south-east into the body of the mountain like a giant vein. I was surprised at how huge my new friend's hunting range was.

Beyond that, I discovered why the harn had come here after the battle with the hexapod. Not far from the water, there was a small cave fifteen feet up the stone wall, which served as my pet's den. That was where he was crawling to when he almost died, hoping he could wait it out there. It was hard but, in the end, I also made it up there. And now is the second day in a row we've spent the night up here.

The day I found out about the cave, I

realized one very simple truth — if Gorgie hadn't encountered the hexapod, I'd be dead meat. The arrow was leading me right to his den. Even if he wasn't there at the time, he would have been able to smell me and track me down later...

After the improvement, the harn needed not ten fish as I calculated before but a whole fifteen. I think it was because of his increased armor figures. The thicker scales required more resources from his body.

With time, the lungfish started coming less and less often, and by evening of day two, they'd completely stopped. Either their school had swum further up or down the river or they had figured out that none of their pals ever returned from "our" inlet.

In the end, we caught twenty more fish, fifteen of which went straight down Gorgie's throat. And that was not counting the guts and bones he wolfed down after my barbaric cleaning.

The loot from that allowed me to raise the harn's corresponding characteristics by four points. Except for Wisdom and Mind. And in some way Intuition. It now glowed with its maximum value of five.

I already had enough esses to bring him up to level six. But I didn't give in to the temptation. There's no rush.

The lack of fish was something of a signal. Clearly we'd had all the fishing success this place could offer. Time to pick up and get moving.

I decided not to wait until morning. The meager amount of meat I was able to set aside wouldn't last us long.

"Well, buddy," I said to the harn, hanging the knapsack on my shoulder. "Say goodbye to your home. It's time for us to be moving on…"

Gorgie didn't even bat an eye. Either he didn't really understand that we'd most likely never be coming back here or his loyalty to his master had squeezed out all other feelings.

When the harn got out of the den, I turned around one last time. I bet I'll think back on this place often. If I don't die, of course. Heh… Miri mentioned at some point that the caverns never let you go without a fight. Maybe this was exactly what she had in mind?

And I was back to the travelling routine. Caves gave way to tunnels, then tunnels turned to caves. Only now, with the harn at my side, it didn't feel like such a hopeless journey. In fact, I'll take it further. I had hope.

The whole way, there were two desires struggling in my soul. I wanted unbearably to get to the surface. Thankfully with a guide like Gorgie, finding my way back wasn't such a hopeless endeavor. In fact, he knew approximately the way to go…

But I did have another wish… To reach the mysterious temple of the Ancients. There must have been a reason a person like Skorx had devoted so many years to searching for it. And only the gods know how many people had died in pursuit of his goal. I'm not gonna lie - I was very afraid. But at the same time something was telling me I would find answers to questions about myself. Beyond that, not even two weeks had passed and I had already made it further than anyone Skorx sent. Yes, what can I say...? I was practically being led by the hand... I imagine the Marked One would give anything for a chance like this.

Thus haunted by contradictory feelings, I continued to follow the arrow, which was leading the harn and I farther and farther from the surface. And so I guess I did make my choice, in the end...

Walking with Gorgie was very reminiscent of the way I used to follow Miri. But there was one little difference - the harn was at home here. He could read the caverns like an open book. To him, every smell, every track was familiar and easy to understand. A few times he even deviated from the arrow's instructions, skirting dangerous areas but always unfailingly getting us back on track. The arrow only showed direction. It didn't give a crap about fields full of poisonous thorny plants or paralyzing hexapod spiders. If I hadn't been lucky enough to meet Gorgie, I'd have become some creature's lunch a long time ago. And my search would have ended before it really got started.

But not everything went so smoothly. Sooner or later it had to happen — we were attacked.

It was a viper. I don't know why, but the

harn couldn't sense it. The creep probably had some special ability.

To me, the whole thing felt like a strange fast-paced dream. From somewhere to the side, a toned white body ran over toward the harn. A wide elongated snout with four curved fangs sank its teeth into his scaled side. Or to be more accurate, tried to. The armor hardened at just the right time and deflected the first attack with ease.

- Attention! White viper (7) has attacked your pet.

- Poison Bite!

- It has dealt 170 damage! (absorbed by defense).

At any rate, that was the last thing the viper managed to do. The harn tore its unarmored snake body into a few pieces in a matter of seconds. I didn't even have time to hook in a Ram to earn my portion of the loot, it all happened so incredibly fast.

But that wasn't all. In theory, there should have been a coldune lurking somewhere nearby. And Gorgie had no problem finding the scavenger. With two lightning-fast jumps, he disappeared among the stones.

I was expecting to hear the sound of a fight, but nothing happened. After that, I saw the harn's snout from behind a boulder looking satisfied and caked in blood.

Once I got the all-clear, I decided to see what exactly it was. I glance behind the stones, realize what I'm seeing and am instantly turned inside out.

Amongst the stones, the viper had built itself a nest. But not a regular one, it was right in the stomach of a dead coldune. The creature looked most of all like a gigantic toad and was lying on its back with bony arms flung lifelessly to the sides. Its light gray belly was torn asunder and, inside, the whitish bodies of the viper's young were writhing around like worms.

Based on the blood marks, the harn had already eaten a few of them and was now looking inquisitively on, wondering if I was going to join in the feast.

"No, no," I whispered, clutching my stomach and taking a step back. "That's all you, buddy..."

While my pet champed away loudly, I felt another attack of nausea. I took out the flask and, rinsing out my mouth thoroughly, took a few swallows. Ooh... Much better...

Just for fun, I opened the harn's characteristics. Killing the viper earned him four hundred experience points. Beyond that, he somewhat brought up his speed and agility. In our reckoning, it was on the order of one clay tablet. Basically just crumbs...

But my suspicions were accurate. His tablets are assigned by the Great System. The creature had no say in what to focus on. I praised myself again for not raising his level. Otherwise we wouldn't have even gotten those crumbs.

When Gorgie appeared, impossibly satisfied, I realized too late that I made a mistake with the snake den. I should have given it one good Ram. I don't know what level the baby snakes were, but it was certainly higher than me. I missed out on loot again... Evidence that the harn and I weren't very well coordinated. Not enough experience fighting side-by-side. But no matter. We'll try to make up for the shortcoming. We did a good job with the fish after all, right? That meant we'd figure it out for other creatures eventually.

Gorgie could sense my vexation and rubbed his scaled face on my leg.

"Yes, yes. I understand, buddy... What matters most is that we're still alive... I'll do better next time..."

When I said that, I didn't suspect that my skills would be put to the test so soon... In the next cave, we were attacked by megabats.

The small group of three, peacefully hanging on the ceiling among the stalactites didn't react to Gorgie at all. But as soon as I emerged from the tunnel, they came to life.

When I entered the cave, I had already been warned by the harn, so I greeted my flying visitors with a Ram. They were flying in a tight group so they all got hit.

I see them falling like maple leaves, stunned by the spell. Then Gorgie jumps off after them, and

I realize that we'd both never find better levelling partners.

The big fliers smacked down on the sharp stones almost at once, breaking wings and bones. The harn only needed to finish them off, which he did easily.

- You have killed Black Megabat (8).

- Congratulations! You receive:
- Experience essence (1600).
- Silver tablet (2).

- You have killed Black Megabat (8).

- Congratulations! You receive:
- Experience essence (1600).
- Silver tablet (2).

- You have killed Black Megabat (8).

- Congratulations! You receive:
- Experience essence (1600).
- Silver tablet (2).

The harn was inundated with experience, almost two thousand points. Also, beyond Speed and Agility, his Strength also came up a good bit. What was more, Gorgie's Hunter skill kicked in on one of the megabats, giving a higher chance of dropping bonus resources.

- Attention! Your pet has discovered:
- Red eye of Black Megabat (1).

When I got nearer the scene of the slaughter, I had to pinch my nose with my hand. The bodies of the megabats smelled unbearably of rotten fish mixed with something gnarly and stinky. Even a ravenous eater like the harn would turn his nose up at this nasty stuff.

I hunched over the creature from the message and looked closer. One eye really was red. The other was black as coal. Just like the other ones' eyes.

I read the short description.

- Red Eye of Black Megabat.
- Type: Alchemy ingredient.
- Rarity: Common.
- Requirements:
- Butchery — 8.

I see. I wasn't gonna get anything here. Eight wasn't all that high for a normal hunter. But with my zero, I might as well not even try. I'll just get my hands dirty for no good reason.

When I got up, out of the corner of my eye, I saw Gorgie hopping. The scales on the back of his neck were standing on end, his triangular ears pressed down and his mouth bristling with yellow fangs.

The message that followed made my heart

beat at a frenetic pace.

"Danger! Evil! Fast! Hungry!"

Not asking pointless questions, I hurried to follow my panicking harn out of the cave.

Gorgie was clearly nervous. The scales on his whole body were vibrating periodically. I hadn't seen him this way before. Something had him seriously afraid. And by the looks of things, something was probably tracking us. At the very least that was how I interpreted my pet's emotions.

The fairly long tunnel suddenly ended in a broad ledge reminiscent of a giant tongue. And beneath it was a dark chasm. The arrow was pointing right, toward a wall with more ledges leading down. That means we should go down...

When we reached the precipice, I heard a blood-chilling hiss behind me...

Our pursuer was still in the tunnel, but I could tell we'd been caught up to...

Okay, we'll have to hunker down here. I take a look around. That spot there will do. From the wall to the end of the ledge is a few yards. If I can get a good Ram off, there's a chance of sending the unknown enemy flying into the abyss.

I stood next to the wall and quickly activated Lair. Three hundred points of protection is nothing, but it is my last line of defense.

I glanced at the harn.

"Alright, it's time..."

We can't afford to wait to level you any longer. Every characteristic point could be the deciding factor in this battle.

- Attention! Your pet has reached level 6!
- Free characteristics: 3.

Look at that! I was also allowed to spend his bonus points. So then, together with the silvers, that gives me nine points. I throw all five right into armor. Defense is again at maximum — three hundred points. I still had to decide between forty points of damage or the same into life supply... Every point could be key in both places. Strangely, the harn gave me a hint. He was insistent I increase his damage...

"Okay," I whispered.

I put the two tablets into Jump, raising the ability to the ceiling. I'll pop the rest into Bite. After that, I tossed the remaining stones into Intuition, which was just one away from its ceiling.

Okay... I can't do anything else...

A moment later, when the unknown creature jumped out of the gaping tunnel, a treacherous thought came to mind...

By the looks of things, all our preparations were in vain...

CHAPTER 18

A LL THAT TIME, we had one of the most dangerous monsters of the caverns trailing us — a thorntail. A kind of lizard, they aren't very big but they move fast. It looked somehow like the southern monitor, a creature I'd once seen at a market in Orchus. Though truth be told, the thorntail was three times bigger.

Quickly scampering on its clawed feet, it ran out of the tunnel and stopped with its head outstretched and pointed up. It had a long split-tipped tongue constantly slithering in and out between its sharp teeth.

In fact, the monitor at the market did the same thing. Its master explained that the big lizard was doing that to taste the air.

The delay gave me time to get a better look at our enemy. It had a flexible scaled body, powerful clawed feet, and a long tail with a short spike on the end. It had the same coloration as my harn. It was at level eleven, which could be a death sentence for us. But honestly, Gorgie didn't share my pessimism. In fact, he was raring to rip off as big a chunk of this creature's body as possible.

The beasts exchanged ominous "greetings." The harn gave a warning roar. The lizard responded with a loud hiss.

As soon as I wondered what to expect from the thorntail, I got an immediate but vague answer from the harn. As it turns out, my pet already had some tangential experience with this lizard's kind. Its preferred tactic is lightning-fast bites and swiping its spiked tail.

Basically, Gorgie was in a hopeful mood right up until the thorntail disappeared in thin air... My pet did not see that coming. And a second later it appeared right behind him. Oh gods! It also has magic!

Despite the nasty trick, my harn reacted in good time. A scathing strike of its spiked tail sliced through the air with a whistle but hit nothing. My cat gracefully dodged to the right, and I suddenly felt an urge to blast the lizard with a Ram. To be more accurate, Gorgie was mentally telling me to do it.

But alas, I was so disadvantaged that I reacted too late. My spell also hit nothing but air. And by then, the thorntail was already attacking my pet from the other side. What a nimble beast!

The two armored predators got tangled in a

ball, hissing and roaring in rage. I was standing a few steps from the scuffle, breathless and cursing myself for missing...

The spell's twenty-second cooldown time felt like an eternity. I could sense the harn getting weaker. The enemy's powerful claws and jaws had already pierced his hide a few times. Gorgie was saved by the fact that all its blows were glancing and not doing maximum damage. But he was getting weaker. I think I could feel it in my skin. Another few moments and the thorntail would be through with my protector. Then it would come running after me...

When Ram reloaded, the scuffling creatures were just a few steps from the edge... The chasm will save us!

As soon as I was ready to use my magic, I got a signal from the harn...

"This time I won't let you down!" I exclaimed.

The spell knocked the thorntail off its feet and sent it skidding a few steps across the stones. It did no damage, but did stun it. I bit my lip hard, vexed, and looked on impotently as the lizard's body sat motionless just one step from the edge of the chasm...

The harn, not wasting time, leapt over to the creature and sunk his fangs into its scaled scruff. But alas, the lizard's armor absorbed almost all the damage. The cat was totally unfazed, though. With his last drops of strength, he charged at the enemy on the precipice... A moment later, the still motionless body of the thorntail was careening down into the abyss...

Suddenly all the sounds faded and we were again surrounded by normal silence...

At first I couldn't believe it was all over. The scuffle was just so fast... The harn stood a bit longer at the edge of the abyss, turned and trotted back in my direction with a bold gait...

"You really are something, brother!" I couldn't hold back some praise and embraced my savior by the neck.

He licked my face and gave a satisfied purr.

Then a second later, victory messages started coming in. The thorntail must not have survived the fall.

I quickly opened Gorgie's information. And I exhaled with relief... His life supply, which had drooped a fair amount during battle, was coming back pretty quick. The regeneration was running like clockwork. Checking his energy figures, I didn't realize right away that I was seeing not two but now three supply bars. I closed my eyes and rubbed them with my hands. Clearly evidence of the stress. I'm seeing triple.

I checked again and saw that my eyes were working just fine. It was just that my pet had gained a magic supply! I slid my gaze over the names and, bracing myself, discovered that Intellect now had a two next to it...

The harn's total mana supply was almost two times lower than mine. Just seventy units, fifty of which were from natural traits. But that doesn't matter... My Gorgie is now a magical creature! Too bad he doesn't have any spells or abilities... But that would all come with time...

Beyond that, the harn got eight hundred experience from this battle. Strength, Health, Agility, Endurance and Speed had all gone up by two. And Bite and Paw Swipe each got one.

Looking through the messages from the battle, I was pleasantly surprised. Despite the monitor being level eleven, my cat fought admirably. Another piece of evidence that a high level without great characteristics is just a number over your head.

Despite his little Intuition, the harn managed to get a couple of crits in. I was feeling truly proud of my protector and only friend. A friend that would never betray me.

Deeply touched, I again embraced Gorgie's armored neck... He understood what was happening inside me like no other and gave a reassuring growl... Just then I started to believe everything would be okay and I would certainly be getting home...

Once I calmed down, I finally let go of the beast and sat down wearily on the ground. Now time to sort through my messages. To be frank, I wasn't much expecting much glamorous loot. As a matter of fact, I was expecting no rewards at all. What could I possibly get at level zero? Gorgie had done all the work, the laurels were his to reap.

There weren't many notifications. Well, to be more accurate, there was just one...

- Attention! The Higher Powers smile upon you! You have replicated the feat of the Cunning Lila! You defeated magical creature over 10 levels higher than you without dealing a single point of damage!
*   - Congratulations! You receive:*
*   - Experience essence (1000).*
*   - Gold tablet of Intellect (1).*
*   - Gold tablet "Thorntail's Jump" (1).*

Thorntail's Jump... Thorntail's Jump... I fitfully open the tablet's description.

*   - Gold tablet "Thorntail's Jump."*
*   - Level: 1.*
*   - Category: Active ability.*
*   - Effect: + 3 to current progress in "Thorntail's Jump" ability.*
*   - Weight: None. Takes no space.*

*   - Thorntail's Jump.*
*   - Level: 0 (0/20).*
*   - Type: Magical ability.*
*   - Rarity: Rare.*
*   - Description:*
*   - Using magic, thorntails can jump behind opponents instantly.*
*   - Effect:*

- *Be instantly transported behind an opponent.*
  - *Requirements:*
  - *Intellect — 5.*
  - *Expends 60 mana points.*
  - *Note:*
  - *Cooldown time: 10 sec.*
  - *Range: 15 ft.*

This feat clearly didn't quite reach iridescent level given I got just a gold. But that was a minor quibble... People would rip out my arms and legs to get this tablet. I mean, it conferred a magical ability! Plus I now had two gold for Intellect. That is surely enough to repay my debts and buy off my parents' house.

With a heavy sigh, I glanced over at Gorgie. But I still have to get to the surface... And that ability, beyond all doubt useful, is great at increasing our survival chances. So what's there to think about?

Driving off all doubts, I took the gold tablets from my knapsack.

"Did you see the way that lizard could jump?" I asked Gorgie, who was watching me attentively.

"Hrn," came his affirmative answer.

"Well, now you can too," I said, activating the tablet.

* * *

It's day four since our victory over the thorntail. The day before last, the arrow finally brought us to the long-awaited marker. It was the same kind of white-marble mosaic as the first one... The same fishhooks... I wanted to celebrate but, to my deepest disappointment, after I gave another blood sample, the marker just gave us a new guide arrow and our journey continued...

- *You have dried Gray Moss.*
- *Congratulations! You receive:*
- *Experience essence (3).*
- *Clay tablet "Herbalism."*
- *Clay tablet of Mind.*

The moss drying messages have been following me for a few days now. This, seemingly, would be the last. Number one hundred and ten. I didn't know why they took so long, or why they came so scattershot. Although I did have a theory. It must have been raining on the surface. And because there were cracks in the ceiling of that cave, moisture was seeping inside, putting the moss-drying process on hold. To be frank, I had already forgotten all that. But the Great System sees all...

The first few messages reminded me of Crum and Happy... I wasn't myself that day... But eventually it let go of me...

The cursed arrow was dragging us lower and lower. I was reminded of the gardens of stone the scouts told me were on level four. We left them behind just yesterday. That led me to think the harn and I were somewhere on level five or six of the caverns...

The lower we went, the more dangerous the monsters became. We had to hide a bit and sometimes run... But other times we were able to do some hunting. We'd racked up a good number of kills: two vipers, three megabats, one coldune and one fangbloom, the stems of which have formed the backbone of my diet for two days now. They're absolutely flavorless but have a meaty texture and fill you up pretty well.

Esses aside, I'd gathered fourteen silvers, too. Gorgie and I had to fight pretty gruesome battles to get them. I've been leaning on building up his supplies whereas he's been more emphasizing damage. In the end, we agreed to bring health up to the ceiling, and invest the rest into damage.

Gorgie is ambivalent toward the fangbloom stems. He'd rather have meat. Especially snake meat. It seems to be his favorite. But alas, we weren't coming across vipers all that often, and the stinky meat of the coldunes and megabats was inedible.

So by the end of day four, when the arrow brought us to a small lake we both started licking our lips at basically the same time. Lungfish or in fact any other fish were just what the doctor ordered.

That day just about ended in catastrophe... Gorgie very nearly died.

And there was nothing to predict his brush with tragedy. As we entered the cavern, the harn rendered a verdict as usual. He told me there was nothing around and calmly trotted to the waterline. I kept five steps behind. I already had my flask at the ready. And just then something large and snake-like bolted out of the water in the harn's direction. I was able to see only the shimmering brown side and head, which looked like a catfish.

- Attention! Glitterspark Eel (17) has attacked your pet.

Gorgie calmly, playfully even got out of the line of attack when suddenly the creature shot something pale and blue at him. A moment later I realized it was electricity.

The harn fell like a swatted fly. His body started twitching. His tongue lolled out of his toothy mouth. Not paying attention to the flood of messages raining down on me, I blasted a Ram at the beast as it crawled slowly toward my friend. And without a sound, it flew back into the water looking like a wet brown lump. And it didn't come back out.

In the blink of an eye, I was at my pet's side. And I immediately exhaled with relief. The electricity did no damage to the cat, but it did leave him with a nasty twenty-second paralysis...

When Gorgie came around and could think sensibly again, we came to a mutual decision — we had to lay the smack-down on that creep.

There were a couple reasons. For starters, it was food. We were both so hungry we could eat a horse. Whether the creature had edible meat, we couldn't say. The harn has never seen anything like it before... But to be frank it doesn't matter... The monster would only get in the way of our fishing.

The next reason is trophies. This eel is clearly a magical creature. With a very intriguing ability or spell. Something like that would come in very handy for us. Though honestly, there was one significant "but." The brute was level seventeen.

There was one thing giving us hope — all my Ram's damage got through unimpeded. That means this river predator has no defense. And if Gorgie could get to it, with his very powerful damage, we'd have every chance to win.

Before taking any action, we decided to just watch the shoreline a bit. Sure it looked like a defenseless wretch despite the very effective ability, but it had somehow gotten up to level seventeen. That put us on guard. It must have had other surprises as well.

At the opposite wall, the harn discovered an inconspicuous ledge ten feet off the ground. And it served as our observation post.

I settled in for a long and tense watch but, to my surprise, in less than an hour we had the privilege of watching our first eel hunt.

It was about like we thought. No real surprises.

The aquatic predator's first victim was a coldune. The toad-like creature had come for a drink of water and for a very long time couldn't make up its mind whether to come up close or not. Always on guard and taking shelter the scavenger, which always attacked in secret, got set up behind a large boulder thirty feet from the shore for an ambush.

Too bad we couldn't see what was happening underwater from the ledge. Cross my heart and hope to die, the eel already knew its next victim had come.

The coldune meanwhile made sure it was safe and finally decided to act. Taking cautious clumsy jumps, he came near the water's edge. Just like with the harn, the eel beached itself and immediately used its ability.

The poor coldune didn't even have time to get scared. Twenty seconds of paralysis was more than enough for the lake monster to reach its prey. And then we saw what might have happened to the harn if I hadn't intervened.

The big fish-snake hybrid clamped its wide jaws down on the coldune's body without the slightest effort. And it just popped like a ripe tomato...

My eyes wide in horror, I watched the scavenger's lifeless body disappear beneath the depths. I realized the harn's armor would have made zero difference against a bite like that. Now I see how this creature managed to survive despite its defenselessness. And it didn't merely survive... It was thriving. And it ate very well. Electricity coupled with a bite that did beyond extreme damage, eviscerating its victim's brain - there was the answer to our riddle.

I could sense Gorgie's emotions. He was no less impressed.

"You know, big buddy," I whispered. "That creep is perfectly happy to eat a coldune. I wouldn't like to know what its meat tastes like. Plus, I think with a big fish like him in a little pond like this, there can't be any more fish... The only thing of value is its magical ability. But let me tell you... No ability is worth getting your head bitten off..."

Gorgie was in complete agreement.

"I say we get some sleep here until the Lair wears off then move on. Let's just leave this big fish alone. Play it safe."

I got some good rest in those five hours. I even managed to sleep a bit. Now, the lair was a matter of minutes from expiration. We were just about to leave when suddenly all the scales on the harn's back stood on end. That kind of thing only happened when something very dangerous came near.

"Big! Evil! Strong!" came a brief description of our surprise guest.

Not breathing, we froze on the ledge. And the harn slightly blocked me with his body. Thankfully, his special coloration made us blend into the wall.

A second later, throwing caution to the wind and thumping its big thick paws, a level twenty-five stonehide tusker came out on shore...What a massive creature! Thrice the size of Gorgie, its body is reminiscent of a bear's. Its face is wrinkled and has two sickle-like tusks on either side of a pig-like snout. It also has a large crest of exposed bone running down its spine. Based on the name, its gray hairless skin must be unusually thick.

The tusker stopped next to a bloodspot on the ground, the only reminder of the dead coldune. It gave a loud sniff, then it shook its head carelessly and continued toward the water. I saw a barely visible movement on the smooth surface of the water. The eel was lying in wait. Did it really think it could win? This thing's armored body would stomp the defenseless fish without even wincing.

Holding our breath, the harn and I were waiting to see what would unfold.

The tusker also must have noticed some movement in the water. Its ears perked up, but it didn't slow down one bit. It's waddling forward, seemingly accustomed to relying on his strength and tough hide.

Another two steps and the tusker will be in

the eel's attack zone...

And the huge snake-like fish did attack in the end! To the very last, I still thought it wouldn't do it... But it did... So its instincts must have been strongly geared toward attack. And it doesn't take size into account...

The giant hog took a pale blue bolt of electricity to the forehead and collapsed to the ground, its thick legs splayed awkwardly to the side. The eel, its jaws dislodged, sunk its teeth into the armored forehead of the massive pig. My first thought was, "this thing's met its match now." But I was dead wrong. The bone-chilling crunch of its skull was clearly audible even from way over where we were. I just started gaping, stunned... That thing must have some crazy damage!

Alas, twenty seconds was still not enough for the eel to complete its victory. The giant hog came back to its senses and immediately reflexively shook its powerful head, impaling the slimy brown fish on one of its tusks. But that only made things worse. The mortal wound just made the eel crunch its powerful jaws down even harder...

Unexpectedly, I was overcome with a desire to quickly get down there and slam the half-dead tangle of creatures with a Ram. I glanced into the harn's eyes. These thoughts were clearly not mine... I wanted to tell him to buzz off... But suddenly stopped myself... It finally hit me...

"Hey, that's right!" I exclaimed with a quavering voice, covering my mouth immediately.

The harn, paying no attention to my outburst, was hurrying over to the now motionless creatures. As he went, he was advising me on where best to cast spells and from what distance.

When I reached the scene of the fight, the monsters were still alive. The fish's whiskers and the hog's stomach were still moving, but very faintly. And there was so much blood! Not a sight for the faint of heart... There was something red and gray seeping out of the hog's head. Its right eye had popped out, and a piece of bone was sticking out through its left eye socket. The eel's slippery wet body, impaled on a tusk, had gone limp, lifeless. Guts were spilling out of its slit-open stomach. Somewhere in the intestines, I could vaguely make out the body of the coldune it killed a few hours earlier. I still could not understand — what made the eel attack? After all, it had just eaten... It had to be the predatory instinct the Great System granted it. That had a set of conditions, and they'd been met.

After a bit of thought, I activated Ram, sending the monsters flying a few steps back. I hit just the way the harn told me, almost point blank and right into the creatures' heads. That got me a crit. The damage hit the eel the way it was supposed to. But the tusker's defenses, though seriously harried, only let through four points of damage. That was enough though... Gorgie took care of the rest.

And just in time. I could hear shuffling from

the darkness of the tunnel where the tusker came from, followed by scratching and impatient squealing. A pack of giant rats was coming, attracted by the smell of fresh blood.

Time to go...

I was already underway when I saw the trophy messages and swiped them into my archive without reading. A pack of scavengers that had caught the scent of a dead body was nothing to mess around with. Plus, I figured they wouldn't be following us with such a mountain of meat right under their noses. They'd be more likely to take us for competitors.

The farther we got from the lake, the quieter everything became. As expected, the pack didn't follow us. They must have stayed by the shore to feast.

Five hours later, the arrow led us into a gigantic cave with a huge number of cave worm burrows in the walls. This place reminded me of the gulper lair where Skorx's valiant scouts left me to the hands of fate.

The harn picked out a burrow on the second level, and we climbed in and got set up for a night's sleep.

After a quick bite to eat, a meaty fangbloom stem, burning in impatience, I finally opened my now stale messages.

- You have killed Glitterspark Eel (17).
- Congratulations! You receive:

- Experience essence (3400).
- Gold tablet of Intellect.
- Silver tablet (5).

- You have killed Stonehide Tusker (25).
- Congratulations! You receive:
- Experience essence (5000).
- Silver tablet (10).

- Attention! The Higher Powers noticed you! You have replicated the legendary feat of Espen the Magister! You defeated a creature more than 15 levels higher than you with only minimal spell damage!
- Congratulations! You receive:
- Experience essence (3000).
- Iridescent tablet "Glitterspark Eel" (1).

After reading the last message, I closed my eyes and slowly fell back onto the sleeping Gorgie's warm side.

Yes! There we go! Another one!

Feeling jubilant, my hands shaking, I take the pearlescent slab from my knapsack. The back has a holographic image of a glitterspark eel on the attack.

- Iridescent Tablet "Glitterspark Eel."
- Effect:
- Unlocks 1 characteristic of your choice from Glitterspark Eel.

- Unlocks 1 skill or ability of your choice from Glitterspark Eel.

- Unlocks 1 spell of your choice from Glitterspark Eel.

- +10 to any characteristic / skill / profession / spell.

- Weight: None. Takes no space.

Swiping past the characteristics and skills, my heart aflutter, I open the spell section.

- Glitterspark Eel's chain lightning.

- Level: 0 (0/20).

- Type: Spell.

- Rarity: Epic.

- Description:

- Using magic, glitterspark eels can shoot a bolt of electricity, which immobilizes their target, ignoring all physical and magical defense, then jumps to another target. This spell does no damage.

- Effect:

- Immobilizes an enemy and nearby ally for 15 seconds.

- Requirements:

- Intellect — 7.

- Expends 80 mana.

- Note:

- Cooldown time: 2 minutes.

- Range: 15 ft.

- Nearby ally range: 3 ft.

CHAPTER 19

A FTER LOOKING through the eel's skills and abilities, I closed the last description in disappointment. They were all anatomically incompatible. Too bad...

Of the magical characteristics, apart from Intellect, I could also unlock Wisdom, which governed mana regeneration speed. But I wasn't feeling decisive enough to invest ten whole points in it. In the end, I settled on Health. It was time to bring up my life supply.

- Attention! You have unlocked the Health characteristic!

- Attention! Your life supply has increased to 110 points.

And that was pretty much it. Now to deal with Gorgie. For killing the eel and tusker, he earned six thousand experience and just one point of Strength and Endurance.

Once again, I'm convinced of my own uniqueness. My level zero definitely gives a colossal advantage over other creatures in terms of loot. Beyond that, with all this digging through the harn's characteristics, I somehow started to forget about my own. In the end, what was there to even look at? I didn't have enough data — before you can even count to two, you've read through everything... I increased my life supply and took another look — it was just the same little numbers from my artifacts... Plus ten in Intellect and Health... But then, out of the corner of my eye, I caught a discrepancy. And when I realized what I was seeing, I couldn't believe my eyes. How had I not seen this before?! My Intellect and Health both had no ceiling! More tricks of the Malevolent Bug? Or had the Great System taken pity on its unfortunate freak and decided to grant me some mercy? But regardless of whether a curse or blessing — in my position — it gave me an ideal way to survive... Honestly, there was one big fat minus — you can't just find iridescents lying around on the ground...

Shockingly the harn, who had been sleeping fast until then, sensed that I was about to start giving him silver tablets. He woke up and started singing the same old song about increasing his damage.

This time we found something of a middle

ground. The fifteen tablets were enough to hit the ceiling in both Bite and Paw Swipe. The remaining four I set into Endurance.

Gorgie licked my cheek in gratitude and closed his eyes again. Time for me to get to bed, too. Before I lay my head down to sleep, I looked carefully at my pet, trying to find scratches or other wounds. Not finding anything, I breathed a sigh of relief. And by the way, he'd grown a bit... He was broader at the shoulder. His claws and fangs were slightly larger and had changed color as well. So, tablets change my harn, make him stronger and more dangerous. Curling up next to his warm armored side, I closed my eyes, smiling. The fun is just getting started!

Over the next day, we found a further three of the mysterious markers. That proved only one thing — we were getting close.

In that time, we managed to catch just one fangbloom. So the harn had to shift to a plant-based diet. It seemed I could sense his anger with all of my being.

By the middle of day two, we forgot about hunger. The arrow led us into a small cave and disappeared without a trace. A dead end!

It was such a surprise I didn't even have time to get scared... And when I realized what was going on, I took a sigh of disappointment and sat down on the ground.

"Is this it?!" I shouted in a burst of anger, addressing the unseen forces. "All these days underway right out the window?!"

"Hrn," Gorgie called right back.

"Sorry, buddy..." not opening an eye, I apologized. "It's not you..."

"Hrn," the cat repeated, this time with some distress.

"As I said..."

"Hrn!" Gorgie interrupted with a demanding growl.

I raised my head and froze... My pet was standing at the far wall of the cave and behind his back was the frame of a huge stone door.

All my anger blew away in an instant. I was next to the door faster than I could think. Hm... Up close they were more like gates... How didn't I notice such a huge object right away?! I'd bet my right hand there was no door when we came into the cave! Sure as fate, there was wizardry involved...

Under a small, expertly carved stone ring, instead of any lock, I saw a small impression with familiar lines inside — two fishing hooks.

I extend my hand as usual. The sign didn't mislead. It accepted its "blood tribute" and a moment later gave a positive verdict.

As soon as that happened, the door begrudgingly lit up a dim shade of blue, making me take a step back in surprise.

My initial fear passed and I again came nearer the shimmering archway. The stone gates had seemingly disappeared... They turned transparent... I carefully extended my right arm and tried to touch the clear surface. But my fingers couldn't feel anything and passed through the ephemeral gates as if they were made of smoke...

I glanced at the harn. Much to my surprise, the cat was completely calm, even slightly impatient.

"What do you say?" I asked. "Keep going?"

"Hrn," Gorgie answered affirmatively.

"Then let's go!" I said firmly and took my first step.

As soon as we got past the door, the dim blue glow disappeared and the door turned back to stone. With a shudder of surprise, I took a step back toward the door. But when I saw a carving of the symbol, I exhaled with relief. That means we'll always have a way out.

Leaving the door behind, I turned. Beyond the magical barrier, there was a fairly wide and high corridor. Clearly not of natural origin. Approximately every ten feet, there were stone hooks in the walls for torches or lamps. Though truth be told, there were neither torches nor lamps. Even the hooks themselves were mere contours. Everything was overgrown with the omnipresent glowing moss.

Hmm... Based on the layer of dust on the floor and lack of any tracks, no one had visited this place in a very long time. By the way, the harn immediately confirmed my guess. His animal instinct gave me the all clear... Taking careful steps, we walked forward...

It felt like the meandering corridor was gradually leading us downward. I counted three hundred fifty paces before it came to an end. And the thing I saw at the end of the tunnel made my heart beat even faster.

We were standing on a wide ledge on the top of a gigantic cliff and below us was... Hm... The first association that sprang to mind was of a glass snow globe, a popular children's toy in Orchus. A glass sphere filled with water, they generally had little animals, houses or ship figurines on the bottom and shaking the ball would cause a blizzard of glittery little snowflakes...

I got the impression that we were now inside a toy just like that. But in our case, the sphere was a gargantuan cave with a small village or more like little city on the bottom. Based on the lack of lights in the homes or smoke coming from the chimneys, this little "toy" wasn't exactly as festive as normal...

"Hmm..." I whispered, struck. "Skorx and Crum's friend were both wrong... This is clearly more than a temple of the Ancients."

Tearing myself from the grand spectacle with difficulty, I glanced at Gorgie.

"Well, brother, what now? Wanna go down?"

"Hrn," the cat answered positively and we headed toward the right wall. There on a gentle slope, I could see the next ledge, and beyond it another but lower, then another and another... Something like gigantic natural stairs...

It felt like it took no more than an hour to go down... And thankfully midway, the ledges were replaced with regular stone stairs carved right into the cliffside. I'm afraid to even imagine how much effort the ancient craftsmen needed to make them all...

Then there was a cobblestone path that led right from the stairs to the city. Like a huge stone snake, it wound between the sharp outcroppings of rock that dotted the ground at the bottom. After two hundred paces, I realized they weren't mere outcroppings but gigantic stalactites that had fallen from the cave ceiling. And it just so happened that one was lying right in the middle of the road.

I got the feeling that someone or something was watching us after we walked through the wide-open city gates. For the record, the gates themselves and all the buildings had long since overgrown with the omnipresent green moss. The natives, whoever they were, must have abandoned this place a long time ago. If not for the persistent feeling I was being watched, I would be confident in declaring this city long dead.

Based on the harn's senses, our unseen observer was not aggressive, and was behaving timidly and cautiously. But despite that, Gorgie was prepared to deflect an attack at any moment.

DUNGEONS OF THE CROOKED MOUNTAINS

So accompanied by the mysterious local, probably some little animal, we went further into the little town. Walking the dead, deserted streets between the very old homes and their ghosts made my skin crawl. If not for the harn, I'd have never stuck my nose in here.

The local architecture was noticeably different from that in Orchus. I got the impression that all the buildings were once huge boulders and the doors, windows and livings spaces had been carved into them by the very same craftsmen that made the stairs in the cliffside.

I wasn't feeling brave enough to go into any of the homes. I just glanced into the windows cautiously from time to time. And I didn't much like what I saw inside. Dust and desertion all around. No furniture, no dishes, no things... Empty... Although if I went looking, I'm sure I'd find something... Maybe something useful.

Eventually, the wide street brought us to the central square. Unfortunately, all the buildings nearby had been destroyed by stalactites. Curious that the locals weren't afraid to build their city in such a dangerous location. Did they perhaps have an ace up their sleeve like defensive magic?

After some time strolling the empty streets and not finding a thing other than decay, dust and fragments of stone, we came to the conclusion that it was time to find somewhere to spend the night. Just get some rest and make a more careful survey tomorrow. Maybe we'd be able to find something of value... There must have been a reason we spent so long getting here, risking our lives every step of the way.

We decided to spend the night in the interior courtyard of a small two-story building which was not far from the central square. The building itself and the thick stone walls around the yard were in some way reminiscent of a small fortress. Just about like all the buildings near the center. By the looks of things, this was where the more well-to-do townsfolk lived. The deciding factor in our choice of resting place was a small well in the middle of one of the yards, which by some miracle hadn't run dry like the neighboring ones.

We opted to stay out of the building itself. It looks sturdy still but who knows... Better not take the risk...

Activating lair, we ate some fangbloom stems, drank our fill from the well and went to sleep with our minds at ease...

But alas, we were not able to sleep a full night... A howl rolled through the village. Bone chilling, penetrating all the way to the marrow in fact...

Oddly enough... If I heard that howl in my first few days in the caverns, I'm sure I'd have shit myself. But now, I had a more or less calm appraisal of the new threat... Well not exactly... I was feeling something like anticipation... Or perhaps the thrill of the hunt... But I think the main reason is my armored pet. Our spiritual connection had become too strong. Sometimes I can't even quite tell our thoughts and feelings apart.

"What do you think?" I whispered into the harn's ear when we'd made it to a small hole in the fence. The home we were staying by was on a slight elevation so we had a good view of the central square and all nearby streets.

"*Alone. Strange,*" came the harn's answer.

"Strange?" I asked in surprise.

The loud howling beast being alone gave me lots of hope. But the fact that it was "strange" less so...

When I asked about the creature's Strength, Speed and Magic, Gorgie always gave the same answer.

"Alright, I'm okay with it being strange," I said, making peace with it and starting to observe.

Just then, I felt like someone was watching us again. I even turned sharply. That's how creepy the feeling was. But alas, I still didn't see anyone...

And after that, I was too distracted to care... The harn said the "strange" howling creature had picked up our scent. There was no sense in running, at the very least not with my speed. So we decided to stay and give combat. At least here we have a way to surprise our uninvited guest... And by the way, it didn't make us wait long.

A coal-black blurry spot jumped into the middle of the square we walked across just a few hours earlier. It was the size of a large dog, or perhaps even more accurately a large wolf...

That's it! It's a wolf! And it really was kind of strange. It didn't look like it came from down here. Its powerful muscular body, covered in thick black fur, looked like it was vibrating. When the beast's elongated snout fell to the earth, I realized it was not actually vibrating. The clearly magical creature emanated black steam or perhaps smoke...

A second later, the monster raised its head. Its glowing red eyes stared directly at us. It knew where we're hiding.

With an impatient howl, the wolf tore off looking like a ball of pure blackness. When the creature was just ten paces away, I was able to make out what we were up against. A smoky lycanthrope. Level ten. Eh, we'd seen worse...

The harn shot off from the hole in the fence like an armored bolt of lightning and froze, sheltering me behind his back. The lycanthrope, finally having sighted its prey, was acting utterly careless. With a joyous howl, he started running faster.

When the creature came close enough, I whammed it with a Ram.

- You have attacked Smoky Lycanthrope (10)!
- You have dealt 9 damage!

The wolf was already midjump when my spell hit. It flew a few yards back, and its smoking black body froze in place. Gorgie was immediately on the scene. One long pounce and the cat's scaled body came down on top of its stiff opponent. That is my pet's most terrifying attack. And if it also got a crit... One pounce could possibly be enough to take down this enemy.

Great! It was critical! But the lycanthrope didn't die right away. His flagging life supply quickly started filling back up... I'd seen such a thing before... Livid's wounds healed over just as quickly.

But it didn't look like the harn was too bothered by that. He was tearing and mangling the immobilized monster, dealing insane damage. Even the most advanced regeneration couldn't stand up to something like that.

I jumped out from behind the fence just as the tenth second of Ram ticked over. I got inside the fifteen-foot range and hit the thing with an electric shock. Done. I'm dry. I run back. I gave the harn another fifteen seconds' advantage... But I wasn't fast enough to get back to the fence... A victory message caught me halfway.

- You have killed Smoky Lycanthrope (10).

- Congratulations! You receive:
- Monster Hunter token (10).
- Small ghostly crystal (2).

I don't get it. What about tablets? Where are the esses?! I didn't have time to get really worked up because I suddenly heard a hoarse calm voice behind me:

"Bravo, youngster! Very effective tactic!"

I turned sharply. A few steps away from the lycanthrope's body, which was slowly dissipating, I saw a strange man. Short. Muscular, lithe. Dressed as a scout but more elegant somehow... The stranger's oddest feature was his foxlike ears, tail and yellow animalistic eyes with vertical black slits for pupils.

The harn was behind the stranger in the blink of an eye and landed a lightning-fast paw swipe. But no damage landed. The paw went right through his body like smoke. Just like with the door...

"Looks like your pussy cat's a little hothead," the stranger chuckled, watching Gorgie's surprise.

Then he looked at me and said:

"Young man, would you please be so kind as to recall your pet. First of all, I am not going to harm you, and second your pet will not be able to hurt me..."

"Wh-wh-who are you?" I asked, hiccupping.

"Oh!" the stranger threw up his animal arms. "Where are my manners?! Allow me to introduce myself, Sly Redtail — foxman. I am the keeper of this place."

He gave a slight bow and asked:

"And with whom do I have the honor of speaking?"

"Ahem..." I hesitated. "Eric Bergman,

human."

"Very nice to meet you," the foxman bowed again. "I'd say we should shake hands the way your kind are wont to do but, alas, it won't be possible..."

"Why?"

"Because I am merely a cast of the aura of my physical body which, alas, left this world many centuries ago. The easiest way to explain is that I am a ghost..."

"Ah, there it is..."

"But you needn't fear me. Though I'm sure you've heard many tales about the foxfolk before."

"Yes," I nodded, looking down in embarrassment.

"Is it really that bad?" seeing my facial expression, Sly Redtail was sincerely surprised.

"Not a lot is good," I answered. "You're considered the most dangerous creatures that inhabit the Dark Continent..."

"The Dark Continent?" the foxman asked in surprise. "Never heard of it. I originate from the Emerald Forest, located in the Amberlands."

"Hm... I've never heard of that before."

"What do you mean?" Sly asked, amazed. "Everyone knows the Amberlands, beyond the Lilac Ocean!"

"Did you say the Lilac Ocean?" it suddenly hit me.

"Correct," he nodded.

"We learned in school that the ocean used to

be called Lilac many centuries ago..."

"What is its name now?" the foxman frowned.

"The Dead Ocean..."

Sly fell silent, crestfallen.

"So that means," I continued. "We're talking about the same place..."

"The Amberlands are now..."

"The Dark Continent..." I finished his sentence.

"But why Dark?"

"I don't know much about that... We were told something very bad once happened there... Now they are the dominion of Gloom."

"And the foxfolk have sworn allegiance to Her?" Sly asked, horrified.

"Yes, so it is said..."

The silence held for some time. Sly was digesting the news about his homeland and descendants, but I was burning in impatience. I had so many questions!

"Alright," the foxman finally broke the silence. "I've clearly spent too much time down here..."

"And what is this place?" I asked, quickly taking my chance.

"Once, this place was known as Stonetown. It was the final frontier between our world and the worlds of the monsters."

"And where did all the people go?"

"They died many centuries ago..." Sly

answered sadly.

"What happened?" I asked, my heart skipping a beat.

"A breach... The portal connecting our world with the other worlds started malfunctioning... Then we started getting lots of uninvited guests like that lycanthrope..."

The foxman nodded at the place where the harn had just taken down the fell beast.

"Our mages and craftsmen attempted to fix it, but they couldn't get anywhere. The creatures just kept coming, threatening to drown this world in blood. Magister Ilania suggested we destroy the portal."

"But she wasn't able?"

"No. We were able to alter the way the portal functions, but it came at the cost of all our lives..."

"What about it did you alter?"

"The portal is closed almost all the time now."

"Almost?"

"Yes. It only opens and lets the otherworldly monsters through once per day for a short window of time. Well to be more accurate, it lets through the casts of their auras..."

"Are they also ghosts?"

"No. Something in between... You see, unlike me, they can be killed. They enter our world in order to obtain a body."

"And how are they able to do that?"

"By killing a living creature from our world.

But with one condition — it must be done while the portal is open. As soon as it closes, the monster will disappear..."

Hm... Now I see what the harn meant when he called the lycanthrope "strange." Hmm... What a ghastly little place... Time to haul my butt out of here. Me and Gorgie will go back up to the top levels and hunt some more megabats. Of course, there is always the risk of finding something dangerous like a gulper, but that's still better than here...

"And why did you... hm... stay behind?" I asked a niggling question.

"Before performing the rite, we drew straws. Someone had to stay here to keep watch over the portal. Fate chose me. And as you can see, it had its reasons."

"And why did you have to stay?" I objected. "The portal is broken; you are a ghost. The beasts continue to appear. Sure, I got lucky with that lycanthrope. But if not? A dangerous magical creature would be racing up to the surface right now."

"Well, it's not all so simple," the foxman chuckled. "The door that let you inside is still powered by magic. It is certainly beyond a lycanthrope's capabilities."

"But what if some monster scarier than an overgrown wolf shows up?"

"Now that could be a problem..." Sly sighed heavily. "But in all the years I've been down here, I think I found a way of correcting our error. Though honestly, I lack one very important ingredient."

"What is it?" I asked.

"Ghostly crystals," Sly smiled sweetly. "Lots of ghostly crystals."

"Ahem..." I coughed.

"You got some after killing the lycanthrope, didn't you? Right?" his yellow animalistic eyes stared at me unblinkingly.

"Y-yes..."

"Excellent!" exclaimed the foxman, glinting his fangs. "How many?!"

"Two..."

"Two?! Wonderful! What kind?"

"Small."

"Very good!" the foxman clapped his hands, then his face turned serious:

"Listen, Eric Bergman. I cannot complete my task without the help of a mortal. Alas, I cannot earn ghostly crystals myself. So I have no choice but to ask you for help!"

With an audible gulp, I took a step back.

"Well, Sly Redtail, I'd love to help but I'm in a hurry. That portal of yours is gonna open again soon, and I don't want to become some creature's dinner. And think for yourself... What kind of a monster hunter would I make? After all, I will be eaten for sure... Then a terrifying beast will gain a body and stir up some very serious trouble on the surface..."

The foxman listened calmly, even smiling. It

was written on his sly little face - he'd already made up his mind...

"Yes and beyond that," I made another attempt. "Even if we did stay here, Gorgie and I need to eat something. That's the name I gave the harn here, by the way..."

"Are you done, youngster?" the foxman asked courteously when I fell silent. And after I gave him a cautious nod back, he continued:

"Then I'll start from the top... First... You will not die if you do as I say. Second... Neither you nor your Gorgie will die of starvation... And third... This is the most important. Whether you like it or not, you have to stay."

I felt a lump rising up my throat.

"Why's that?"

The foxman's mouth spread into a predatory smile, revealing a set of sharp fangs.

"Because I have just placed a locking spell on the door you used to get in. So whether you like it or not, you can only leave this place when I allow it."

CHAPTER 20

"**M**ISTER REDTAIL!" I said, glumly addressing empty space. "Are you still here?"

"I'm always here," a creaking voice answered from behind me, and asked with a mocking lilt:

"Well, how'd it go? Get through the door?"

I turned around and all I could do was somberly shake my head. We were not in fact able to do a thing. A few hours ago, after the memorable conversation with the treacherous ghost, Gorgie and I bolted for the exit without another word... But we had no luck... The door wouldn't let us pass... The foxman really had sealed it with magic. And neither my spells nor the harn's claws could help. The door, a monolithic piece of stone, was blocking our only path to freedom... We had to turn back to the city...

"Like I said!" Sly continued, his chin raised

victoriously. "The sooner you realize that helping me is inevitable, the faster we can finish! What do you say?"

"Do I have a choice?"

"No," the ghost answered categorically. "But I will need you to verbally agree to a few things."

"Seeing as I have no other choice, I have to submit."

"So dramatic!" The foxman chuckled. "You can't even imagine how mutually beneficial this will be for us."

"I seriously doubt you can give me what I want..." I burbled, hurt.

"And what is it that you want, if you'll allow me to pry?"

"I want to reach level one," I blurted out my deepest desire.

"Why?" the ghost asked derisively.

"What do you mean why?" I asked in surprise. "To be like everybody else."

"What does that mean?"

"Normal..."

"So you don't want to be special?" Sly's yellow eyes squinted slightly.

"You sound like my parents..."

"Well young man, is that not a reason to listen to what I have to say?"

"So you're trying to say that my freakish nature is somehow special in a good way?"

"I'm surprised you haven't realized it yourself yet... And please, stop calling yourself a freak!"

I had to fall silent. In the last few days, lots of things in my world view had changed. Talking with this strange being had only spawned more confusion.

"Well, alright then," he distracted me from the contradictory thoughts. "We don't have much time... The portal will open soon. We need to be there to greet our guests."

When I heard about the portal and the fact that new creatures would be arriving soon, a cold sweat came over my back.

As if having guessed my thoughts, Sly said:

"Don't you worry, you'll have time to prepare... Let's go..."

"Where?" I asked.

"The statue of Gunnar the Destroyer," the foxman answered, going up the street that led to the center of town.

All I could do was follow him.

I didn't have to walk for long. Once we reached the central square, we ducked down a dark narrow side street that brought us to another square, this one smaller.

"This is the forum of Gunnar the Destroyer!" the foxman said solemnly, extending his right hand forward. "And this is his statue!"

In the center of the small rectangular square, there was a plinth, on top of which towered the stone figure of a man. Quite gaunt, dressed like a normal hunter. A sad, tired face. A short beard covering sunken cheeks and a narrow chin. The eyes had a slight squint. On first glance, I'd have said this stone statue depicted an everyday workman, the kind which came a dime a dozen in Orchus. To be perfectly frank, this old dude looked pretty far from a Destroyer...

"I can see skepticism in your eyes, boy," the foxman said with a mocking lilt. "Were you expecting him to look different?"

I just shrugged, saying nothing. What was there to say...

Strange as it was, the foxman wasn't one bit angry. It seemed he liked my reaction. He looked up at the statue with a sad smile.

"That nickname always brought a smile to old Gunnar's face. For the record, he wasn't only known as the Destroyer. Vanquisher of the Horror of the Depths, Killer of the Black Fear, Vanquisher of Thunder... And lots more of that kind of thing..."

The fox turned sharply toward me.

"For the record, he earned all these nicknames fair and square. He really was the vanquisher of the Horror of the Depths and killer of the Black Fear, along with many other legendary monsters from our world and others. But none of these names even come close to reflecting his true spirit."

"And what was that? His true spirit?" I asked, intrigued.

How could I not be intrigued? This nondescript guy had turned unknown monsters to dust left and right. It sounded like a cute little fairy tale... Honestly, in fairy tales, the main character is about six feet tall and almost always packed into a suit of shimmering legendary armor. This dude didn't quite fit the bill...

"He was a normal man. A loving husband and a doting father. A loyal friend... He led a quiet and inconspicuous life. By the way, he was a fisherman..."

"Wait a second... So that's where all the fishhooks on the symbols are from!"

"Correct," the foxman nodded. "In memory of the true spirit of the founder of our order, our emblem is two fishhooks."

"So why..." I started, but Sly interrupted me:

"You want to ask how it happened that a simple fisherman founded one of the most powerful orders of this world?"

Hm... To be honest, this was the first I was hearing of any order of monster hunters, but still I nodded...

"Alright, I'll tell you," said the ghost. "We've still got a bit of time... Back then, there lived three brothers, identical in face..."

I smiled. Who hadn't heard the tales of the three brothers? So this was the era these tales came down to us from! I wanted to bet five copper it was them, but I bit my tongue. What I heard after that struck me to depths of my soul...

"Let me tell you, it'd be hard to find a collection of more worthless jackasses... The first was a bad-luck hothead who didn't know what side of the sword to grip it by. The second, a simpleton archer... And the third - chief idiot among them - a mage, who dropped out of the academy..."

That knocked the wind out of me.

"So these three dumbasses took a notion in their empty heads to start calling themselves monster hunters. And they started crowing about their imagined feats on every street corner... Any tavern you'd go into, there they were, sitting all puffed up and self-important, listening to wandering minstrels sing songs of their imaginary feats of bravery. By the way, all these singers and performers would earn pretty good money from the brothers for their performances. Those dunderheads were lucky they were born into the family of a well-to-do merchant. But one day their old daddy died, and that was how they squandered their inheritance."

I gulped loudly...

"What?" the foxman asked, raising his right brow. "Did those paltry verses also make their way down to you?"

"Did you know the three brothers personally?!"

"Well sure... And what of it? Wait up..." Sly's face went long. "Are you trying to say that all the little songs and poems about those dunderheads are taken for the genuine article these days?!"

I just nodded in silence. I can feel my cheeks burning...

"What is wrong with you up there?!" the ghost exclaimed in a lather, even stomping his partially transparent feet. "The Amberlands are under sway of Gloom, the foxfolk are used to scare children before bedtime, and the psycho killer brothers are regarded as heroes! I am confounded to the depths of my soul!"

"The brothers are killers?!" I burbled.

"Yes... What else do you think they are? They found some old summoning scrolls and decided to perform a ritual. But their ham-fisted attempt to use the thing got the whole ritual wrong. What's more, the best place they could think to do it was a room in the central hotel... They ended up summoning a pack of otherworldly hellhounds, which escaped to freedom and destroyed the whole city..."

The fox fell silent for a moment, clearly reminiscing. As for me, I was left speechless... To find out that the heroes of your childhood fairy tales were completely different in real life... Try telling anybody — they'll never believe you. They'd even laugh at you. You might even take one to the neck for that.

"But where there's smoke, there's fire," Sly suddenly continued. "Tangentially, those dumbbells are the reason our order was created..."

"How's that?"

"When Gunnar and the other fishermen returned from a swim, they found their city in ruins and the bodies of their families torn to shreds... I was also there... It was a ghastly spectacle... Not waiting for the local baron to help, Gunnar organized the survivors and met the otherworldly creatures in battle! Almost everyone died, but they did fend off the incursion. After burying the remains of their families, the survivors founded our order. And Gunnar became its head."

"And how did you come to be here, beneath the earth?"

The foxman chuckled.

"The powers that be. Nobles. That's the main reason. As the years passed, the order started gaining power. And the bigwigs naturally didn't like that. They started painting us hunters black in the public eye. Inventing wild fables. It reached the point that our brothers stopped coming down to the city and, after a few assassination attempts, Gunnar decided to leave the surface... The order helped the subterranean folk exterminate the Horror of the Depths, in return for which the king under the mountain gifted us this cave and sent us craftsman to build this city. We didn't realize what those little jerks stuck us with until it was too late."

"You mean the portal?"

"Correct," the fox nodded. "That was how we became eternal guardians of the portal..."

Hmm... A sad story... To be honest, I don't think I'd be up to it. Living underground next to a thing that might belch out a pack of blood-thirsty creeps at any moment. Yikes, no thanks. And I love the sun...

"So then, young man, have I sated your curiosity?"

"Completely..."

"Then let's get started."

"On what?"

"What do you mean?" the foxman asked in surprise. "Didn't I tell you?"

"N-no..." I turned my head.

"For your induction into our order, of course!" Sly was shining like a polished copper basin. "Are you ready?"

"No, of course," I turned my head again. "Why do I have to do this?"

The foxman rolled his eyes and rubbed his forehead. Then he asked patiently:

"Young man, do you remember that I told you if you want to survive, you have to do everything I say?"

"Yes, you also promised food..."

"I remember what I promised."

"Then how is that connected with my induction?"

"Oh, believe me, youngster! The connection is very straightforward! You're wasting time. The faster we finish, the sooner you two can go."

I glanced at the harn. Raising his armored head, he licked his lips. My friend hadn't been getting enough to eat for a few days now... I had no choice but to agree.

I raised my head and glanced firmly into

Sly's yellow eyes.

"That's what I like to hear," he nodded. "Then let's get started. Walk up to the statue. Remember, you must answer yes to all my questions."

"Got it."

When we reached the plinth, I looked up. It felt like Gunnar the Destroyer was staring right at me. I could read grief and sympathy in his calm stony gaze...

"Eric Bergman of the human race, are you prepared to walk the Path of the Hunt?!" the foxman recited loudly.

"Yes," I replied.

"Do you choose to walk the Path of the Hunt of your own free will?!"

I fell silent for a moment. I glanced back at the harn... And answered:

"Yes."

"Do you have any proof of your intentions?!"

I stared at the fox in confusion. Opening his eyes wide, he motioned to my knapsack.

All I could think was to remove the crystals and tokens I'd gotten for defeating the lycanthrope and show them to the foxman. With a rapid swipe, he grabbed both of the crystals and said solemnly:

"Okay, I see your intentions are serious! Your contribution to the cause of the Order of Monster Hunters has been deemed worthy! From this day forth, you shall be a brother of our order!"

As soon as the foxman said his last words, a

message appeared before my eyes:

- Attention! You have successfully undergone an induction rite! From this point on, you shall be a Monster Hunter!

- Congratulations! Your reputation with the Order of Monster Hunters has been increased by 20 points! Happy Hunting!

- Removed:

- Small ghostly crystal (2).

"And that is pretty much it, brother," the foxman smiled. "The first step is complete. Now it's time for step two... Let's go."

Not waiting for me to answer, the ghost made a graceful heel turn and in a springy gait walked toward a stone building with massive columns towering at the other end of the forum.

When we reached the central entryway, Sly casually dropped:

"This is our arsenal. After the induction, you are entitled to access it. It is currently limited, but that's a temporary state of affairs..."

As we walked up the stairs, I habitually noted that the building, just like all other structures in this dead city, hadn't been visited by anyone for a long time. Green moss was sticking out of every nook and cranny, making it look more like a huge forest cave than an arsenal.

Once we got inside, I stopped with my mouth open wide. It looked like a gigantic weapons cache. It had every kind of weapon — stabbing, slashing, chopping, bashing, and pointed — and they were hanging on the wall, lying on the ground or standing upright everywhere I looked. My face spread into a dreamy smile... Unable to hold back, I walked up to a sword rack and extended a shaking hand forward. The blade was unspeakably beautiful and drew me in with its predatory shape... As my fingers clenched around its silver gem-encrusted handle, the blade suddenly gave a series of blinks and disappeared. Along with the rest of the weaponry... All that was left was a floor covered in a thick layer of gray dust and the omnipresent green moss on the walls...

"I'm sorry to disappoint you, young man, but that was all an illusion. It was meant as a smoke screen for our uninvited guests."

I looked around, hurt. That was brutal...

"This way," the foxman was already standing next to an inconspicuous door at the far wall and beckoning me with a clawed finger.

I crossed the wide hall and walked through the small doorway.

We went into a small closet with empty stone racks covered in several millennia worth of dust.

"And here is our real arsenal," Sly said with a sad smile. "Or rather, what's left of it. Time, you know... Only a small remnant of our order's former possessions still exists."

After the glimmering majesty of the main

room, this dusty back closet was utterly unimpressive. I looked at the old junk in disappointment and tried to plan out a way out of the crap situation I'd gotten Gorgie and I into...

Meanwhile, diving into some old trash, the ghost suddenly gave a gleeful shout:

"Here we go! Found it! Come over here, youngster!"

Cautiously overstepping the heaps of trash and dust, I came closer to the farthest weapon rack where the foxman was waiting, his face beaming.

"There you go!" he solemnly pointed at a big long doodad which I could vaguely make out as having rectangular outlines.

I walked up closer and stared. The thing the happy ghost was pointing was clearly once a trunk of some kind. Not like Crum's. This one was low and long. Almost completely corroded by mold. Knowing my late friend's passion for all kinds of chests, trunks and boxes, I think he'd have a stroke if he could see this...

"Well young man, what's taking so long?" the foxman flared up. "Open it up, and be quick about it!"

Carefully, or perhaps rather with disgust, I reached for the lid of the box. As soon as my fingers touched the moldering surface, the lid and soon after chest itself fell to dust in the blink of an eye...

"Hmm..." the foxman said, crestfallen. "Time is merciless."

Seeing the cringe on my face, the ghost asked:

"Young man, have you ever heard the old fable of the gift of the jewelry box?"

"The one where the man gets a jewelry box for their birthday? And where he never opens it because he thinks the fancy box is the whole gift?"

"Correct," the ghost nodded. "But the original story was about a foxman... Anyhow, it doesn't matter... So then, have you guessed what I'm talking about?"

I just nodded and crawled over to dig through the dusty remains of the chest. A moment later, my fingers hit upon something hard and rounded. A small vial of dark glass. The size of an apricot.

- Small Potion of Satiety.

- Type: Edible.

- Rarity: Rare.

- Effect:

- Sates thirst and hunger. Restores 50% of life force.

- Quantity:4 doses.

- Note:

- Must be inducted into the Monster Hunters to purchase.

- Not to be taken more than 2 times per day.

- Price: 1 token.

- Weight: None. Takes no space.

I turned to the foxman.

"I see you have many questions," he said, chuckling. "These potions were created by our alchemists precisely for cases such as this. After all, our hunters did not always have access to water and food during their journeys. And in other worlds these were especially necessary. But they also have side effects... hm... if you use this potion more than two times per day, you may develop health problems."

"What kind of health problems?"

"It affects everyone differently. Nausea, vomiting, stomach ulcers, diarrhea. I remember one huntress who overdosed on this potion... She would lose consciousness from time to time. In a word, I don't recommend abusing it."

"Gotcha," I nodded and asked feverishly:

"What about Gorgie?"

The ghost raised its hands reassuringly.

"Your beast can also use the potion."

I exhaled in relief and tried to pull the cork from its narrow opening. But it didn't work.

"Ahem..." the foxman coughed in embarrassment. "Alas, there is one further detail. Items from the arsenal may only be used after being exchanged for hunter tokens."

"Like the ones I got from the lycanthrope?"

"Exactly."

"And how does the exchange work?"

"Oh!" the ghost's arms shot up in relief. "That is very simple! All you must do is select the item and say the word 'purchase' while throwing your tokens into the air. Let's try, shall we?"

"Alright," I replied, taking out one of the tokens and flinging it upward:

"Purchase!"

The small round piece of steel, which had a set of fangs engraved on the back, flew toward the ceiling. And as soon as I said the magic word, they dissolved into thin air...

- Congratulations!
- You have acquired:
- Small potion of satiety (1).
- Removed:
- Monster Hunter token (1).

I immediately popped the cork and brought the vial up to the harn's nose.

"Here, buddy. You need this more than I do."

Gorgie took a meticulous sniff of the new item and, clearly not finding fault, opened his toothy maw. I carefully tilted the vial back and a bright raspberry-colored drop fell onto his wide tongue. The harn's supply figures immediately started going up while he licked his lips happily and stared his emerald green eyes at me.

"Hrn!"

"Well of course, who would have doubted," I muttered, and tilted the vial up again.

When the harn got his second drop, he calmed down and lay down at my feet. A second later, I heard a satisfied belch.

"Alright then," Sly smiled, watching us in silence until then. "And to think you were worried."

I was in no rush to drink the highly valuable resource just yet. I still had some fangbloom stems left. So, corking it back up carefully, I lowered the vial into my bag.

"You're prudent, youngster. I like that!" Sly couldn't hold back a mocking comment. "You'll need more tokens, too."

The edge of my vision slid over the dust heap that was once a chest. There was clearly more than one vial there.

Following my gaze, the foxman said reassuringly:

"Don't you worry, Eric. Everything left in the arsenal can be yours. You simply have to do a few things first. Well, more like just two."

"Earn a high reputation with the order and get enough tokens?" I asked.

"You're catching on fast!" Sly flitted his yellow eyes and quickly added:

"Unfortunately, only a pittance remains of what the order once possessed... But even it can significantly lighten a Hunter's heavy load!"

After finishing his melodramatic speech, as if remembering something important, Sly turned toward the short stone weapon rack.

"There they are!" he shouted and, in a second, was next to a section of stone. "Over here, Eric!"

Emboldened by the first discovery, I was there in the blink of an eye.

"Take a look at that," said the ghost, pointing a clawed finger at a thick bundle of cloth.

This time without fear, I touched the unknown material. As absolutely expected, it instantly fell to dust, revealing a small hollow containing around thirty semitransparent spheres of a murky brown shade. Each was the size of a large apple.

- Blot.
- Type: Trap.
- Rarity: Rare.
- Effect:
- A creature caught in a Blot will lose 20% total energy.
- Note:
- Must be inducted into the Monster Hunters to purchase.
- Price: 4 tokens.
- Disappears after triggered.
- Weight: None. Takes no space.

"Here's everything I can offer right now," Sly said with a shrug of his shoulders. "You've gotta agree, it's pretty good, eh?"

"True," I agreed. "But I'd like something that can do a bit more damage."

"Increase your reputation! Earn tokens! Then I'll try to find you something else..." the foxman answered evasively.

What a jerk! Can't give me everything right away...? But more things could increase my chances of survival. Thankfully, none of this claptrap had any level restrictions... That was nice...

As if reading my thoughts, the ghost said in an apologetic tone:

"Unfortunately, the magic of this location will not allow me to take more than allowed... And alas, I have no authority in the matter..."

Uh huh... Keep talking... You want me to do what you ask for treats like a trained dog...

Trying not to show my true feelings, I pretended to understand everything and that I was ready to work together. I took two of the spheres and threw eight tokens into the air while saying the magic word.

- Congratulations!
- You have acquired:
- Blot (2).
- Removed:
- Monster Hunter token (8).

After that purchase, I had just one token left in my knapsack. I wanted to get another potion, but I reconsidered it and decided it was better not to waste the token. What if the clever foxman has something even nicer in his bins?

I suddenly felt a strange feeling... It was as if

the air suddenly became heavier. I lost my breath for a moment. My eyes went dark. The hair all over my body stood on end...

A moment later the delusion subsided...

"What's wrong with me?" I rasped out with my suddenly parched throat.

"The portal!" the ghost exclaimed. "It's opening soon! Let's go, I'll show you where best to activate the Blots!"

CHAPTER 21

THE PORTAL to the world of the monsters was outside the city and was nothing more than a giant crack in the cliffside. The inside of the fault oozed with greasy-looking liquid, somewhat like an infected wound in the body of a stone giant.

The dark ooze flowed down off the walls to the ground in big sticky drops, congealing into a smoking puddle with an uneven surface. Weird that the liquid didn't flow out any further... Clearly, the magic the foxman mentioned earlier was doing its job.

"Nasty thing, isn't it?" Sly commented, his face scrunched up.

"Not much to like about it..." I agreed, squirming. "When does it all start?"

"Any minute now," the fox answered. "Let's go!"

"But where?" I asked in surprise. "Isn't it

better to meet the creatures here, while they're still disoriented after going between worlds?"

"I like the way you think, but no," the fox man threw out as he walked back toward the city. "The monsters gain their power from the portal. The closer they are to it, the stronger they become."

"Then why did you bring me here?!" I shouted, baffled.

"So they can catch your scent, obviously!" Redtail answered with no compunction.

"Got it!" I shouted after him. "You want to get me killed!"

"Not in the least!" Sly answered, shaking his head. "I'm trying to help you survive!"

We walked through the rest of the city without another word. I was wheezing in anger, while the foxman in front of me was whistling a happy tune. When we were past the wall, my guide stopped, turned and said:

"We're here. See those somewhat rickety floorboards on the ground?"

"Yes," I mumbled.

"Beneath them is a pit trap, with long sharp stone stakes on the bottom. There are stairs next to it. You must go down them to the bottom of the pit. There you will see a narrow opening that leads away from the pit. You can take it outside. But before you do, break two Blot spheres in the center of the pit."

"Ahem..."

"Is something bothering you?" the foxman raised his right eyebrow.

"You want me to be bait?"

"And hunter at the same time! Any creature from the portal is much stupider than its true incarnation. The portal sort of forces them to move fast, and often they are just too rapacious. We took advantage of that and made a few different traps, often fairly primitive ones like this pit for example. Heh, we learned in practice that this kind of trap is the most effective and reliable. But there are exceptions..."

"Like what?"

"Higher creatures. They're stronger and more cautious. When you hunt them, you've gotta really think on your feet. And use magic..."

"Are there many traps down here?" I asked with hope in my voice. I was already so scared I was hiccupping, and then he tells me about these "higher creatures..."

"Oh, this whole city is one big trap!" the foxman smiled ravenously and quickly added regretfully:

"But alas, most of them are too degraded to use. And it would be a problem for you to activate the rest of them with your reputation and small mana supply. The only option for now is the classic... This trap pit here..."

A wave of unpleasant fatigue came over me again. When my vision brightened back up, wincing, I turned to the foxman who was looking at me with compassion:

"Why didn't I feel these creepy sensations before the wolfman appeared?"

"Because you hadn't been inducted into the monster hunters yet. From now on you'll be able to sense manifestations of otherworldly magic. Whether its portals, monsters that acquired a body or their offspring... And otherworldly objects as well... For now the feelings will be fairly chaotic but, the higher your reputation, the stronger that sense will become..."

Despite my nausea and spinning head, I understood that I had received a very useful ability.

Arsenal items, a special sense — those would be two significant pushes toward improving that pesky reputation. Ah! And the traps... Three altogether...

Unbeknownst to me, I realized the foxman was right. This could be mutually beneficial for us. I just had to take care of one little thing — try not to end up in some otherworldly creature's stomach.

I suddenly got a bad taste in my mouth as if I had bit down on something bitter, and at the same time rotten... I winced...

"Can you taste bitterness and rot?" the foxman asked.

"Did the portal open?" I answered with a question of my own.

"Yes," answered Sly, disappearing into thin air. "Alas, during battle I will merely be an observer and cannot speak with you... Good luck, Eric!"

When the foxman disappeared, I glanced over at Gorgie.

"Well, buddy, looks like we're alone again. Let's do it..."

I ran over to the barely visible hole in the ground, saw the stone stairs and, after a moment's thought, started down. When I was in the middle of the stairs, I heard a distant powerful roar from above. A brigade of ants marched down my spine. The harn jumped forward, his scales standing on end...

"Big, evil, strange," came Gorgie's laconic description of the large monster on our trail.

After reaching the bottom of the pit trap, I froze, stunned.

"Woah!" I couldn't hold back an exclamation. "This is easily big enough even for a gulper!"

As Redtail warned, the whole bottom of the pit was filled with sharp stone spikes of various heights and diameters. This trap was clearly made for creatures of all shapes and sizes.

Carefully maneuvering between the spikes and stakes, I broke first one sphere then, two steps later, a second.

- Attention! You have activated a Blot!
- Attention! You have activated a Blot!

Done... In theory, the creature would fall on a stake and end up in at least one of the Blots I had thrown.

I looked around... Ah, there's the little hole the ghost was talking about...

Once I was inside the fairly wide tunnel, I started to feel the earth shaking, first weakly but gradually growing stronger.

"Great, just what I needed... An earthquake," I grumbled but then caught myself.

It actually wasn't an earthquake! There was just something big and heavy bounding this way! A powerful roar up above chilled the blood in my veins, confirming my guess. And a moment later, the pit trap behind me was filled with terrible shaking and a thundering sound, which was quickly eclipsed by a soul-shattering squeal of pain...

As soon as it happened, a waterfall of damage messages cascaded down on me! Alright, the Great System considers the pit trap a way of me dealing damage...

The exit from the hole was twenty steps away from the trap. Incidentally, something truly astonishing happened inside the trap! The millennia of dust stirred up by the still unseen giant, which the Great System identified as an Icy Rover, flew in all directions like a wild hurricane! The aggrieved roar, shriek and rasping were intermixed with the crunching and scraping of stone!

The more the dust settled, the less sound the level-sixteen creature made. First to get up the nerve to go over to the pit was the harn. Very cautiously, crawling, he walked over to the edge and peeked inside. Based on the lack of victory messages, the monster was still alive. So I did my best to tell the cat to be careful.

After I got the go-ahead from Gorgie, I also walked up to the pit. My first impression was of a living block of ice stuck on a fork like a baked apple... Hm... Or rather maybe a few forks.

Its hefty white body was giving off a thick steam. Clearly the world this monstrosity jumped here from could not boast of especially sunny climes.

The rover was living out its last moments. Honestly, it tried to get free to the bitter end, but that only made things worse. Every time it got up on its stumpy legs, it fell back down impotently, again sliding down the stone stakes and doing additional damage to itself. What's more, my Blots did their modest part, snatching forty percent of the monster's energy, which noticeably weakened its position. Hmm... I must admit the foxman knew what he was talking about... I was impressed at how effective the pit trap turned out to be.

After it so joyously raced here for my soul, and so stupidly fell into the primitive trap, we did not spend much time watching the otherworldly monster agonizing. After a bit more moving around, the rover drew its last breath, and its ghostly body crumbled to bits like a smashed ice cube, then immediately dissolved into thin air.

- You have killed Icy Rover (16).

- Congratulations! You receive:
- Monster Hunter token (20).
- Large ghostly crystal (2).

Despite the message that the battle was over, my body was still trembling savagely. Either it was the cold emanated by the otherworldly monster, or the fear which would not let me go. I think it must have been the latter... There couldn't be the slightest doubt — if not for the pit, that chunk of ice would have ended both Gorgie and I.

Our specialty is fast, powerful attacks that deal lots of damage. That tactic would not have worked against the rover. Based on the system messages about the damage from the stone stakes, the creature's supplies were simply too high. We'd have lost our breath before draining them. By the way, I took another glance at the Blots... They took forty percent of the monster's energy instantly... I have to quickly scoop up the rest of the arsenal's stock!

Weird. What's taking so long for Sly to come back? I was expecting him to have come already to blurt out one of his stock phrases... I wanted to summon him, but suddenly my ear caught a sound I was not expecting to hear in this gloomy place... From the direction of the city, I heard the echoing frightened scream of a little girl!

Forgetting everything, I dashed off toward

the sound. As I ran, I cursed myself for being so slow... The thoughts that entered my head were one more unbelievable than the next... How can this be?! Had the portal accidentally brought someone else here with the monster? A person from the other world? And just where was that foxlike bastard?!

Passing through the city gates, I jumped onto the main street and froze like a statue. A girl of unusual beauty was standing in the middle of the causeway. She had a short slim little body. Her hair was pure white and wavy, falling delicately over her fragile shoulders. Her slightly sloping eyes were the color of a cornflower. Her light yellow dress, like a bright sunbeam accidentally shot into the kingdom of darkness, gave me feelings of hope and serenity.

"Where am I?!" she screamed sonorously. I could hear notes of fear and panic in her voice. "What is this place?!"

She was hugging herself at the shoulders with arms thin as twigs and, shivering in fear, looking around hauntingly.

Still not believing my eyes, out of inertia, I took a few steps forward. She immediately noticed me...

"Where am I?!" she shouted, her voice quavering. "What is this place?!"

"Good day," I rasped, my throat parched. And I quickly started telling myself off mentally... What do I mean "good day?!" What am I talking about?!

"Where am I?!" Not paying attention to my words, she repeated her question, stunned. "What is this place?!"

"Calm down," I said, raising both hands and taking another few steps forward. "You're in Stonetown... Don't be afraid... I'm not gonna hurt you... What is your name? My name is Eric..."

She just kept standing there embracing herself and repeating the same fearful phrases as if she was very spooked:

"Where am I?! What is this place?!"

The closer I got to the girl, the more clearly I perceived one strange aspect. Her face... It seemed to be replaying the exact same emotions over and over. And the precision is astounding. The corners of her mouth, the dimples on her cheeks, the frightened gaze of her cornflower-blue eyes, the movements of her brows... It was all the same as a minute earlier... Add to that the repeating vocal intonations...

When I was no more than fifteen feet from the girl, my mouth suddenly filled with bitter and rotten saliva... What happened after that seemed like a strange dream...

The harn appeared behind the stranger like a supple armored shadow and, to my immense horror, his big teeth crunched down on her fragile feminine neck.

Stunned, I opened my mouth in a muted scream! No! Gorgie, what have you done?! The harn's armored head jerked a few times, trying to tear off her lily white head... Well, that's all... This is the end...

Once I thought the harn and I had just murdered a defenseless girl, the "defenseless girl" started undergoing a strange metamorphosis that made my insides go cold.

Her cute little dress, her golden curls, her skinny little body — they all dissipated. The harn's powerful jaws were now crunching down onto the neck of a strange pale-skinned creature. And its final predeath rasps were fighting to escape its fanged mouth. It was lying on the earth, held down by the cat's scaly body and impotently scratching the stone causeway with its long gaunt appendages. My mad gaze fell on the extremely long claws, which were leaving deep scratches in the paving stones.

Just five more steps, and I'd have been turned into a bloody shredded rag...

But as soon as I thought the creature's time was up, it managed to surprise me. It wriggled with utterly unbelievable effort and, despite the scrawny body, was able to give a powerful burst and cast the harn aside... The creature's neck and sunken chest were gushing a thick dark-blue liquid... That must have been its blood...

It had a decent shot, but the creature wasn't even thinking of running. It just took one abrupt motion and jumped off the ground, turning its nasty fanged face in my direction... However, that was all it had time to do before I sent it flying with a Ram.

>*- You have attacked Snow Ghoul (19)!*
>*- You have dealt 33 damage!*

Its long legs splayed awkwardly, the creature flew a few paces back like a ragdoll, which the harn immediately took advantage of, enraged by its recent stroke of bad luck. A long jump and Gorgie's fangs again sink into the elusive monster's neck... A jerk upward and the creature's bald head is rolling over the paving stones... Alright.. You're done, freak...

>*- You have killed Snow Ghoul (19)!*

>*- Congratulations! You receive:*
>*- Monster Hunter token (30).*
>*- Large ghostly crystal (5).*
>*- Small vial of Snow Ghoul Spirit.*

Swiping the victory message aside, I walked over to Gorgie on rigid legs and embraced his broad neck passionately.

"Thanks, bro..." I whispered, my voice quavering. "You saved me again. I'm such a dummy... Sorry I doubted you..."

"Youngster!" I heard Sly shout behind me agitatedly. "Your carelessness just about pulled up our mission by the root! If not for your amazing pet... Everything would have fallen through..."

"I know," I whispered back, stroking Gorgie's armored neck as he groaned in pleasure.

Then I turned my head to the ghost and said:

"Well, you've gotta admit you weren't doing great either..."

"Where is this coming from?" Redtail's face stretched out in surprise.

"Would it have been so hard to warn me?"

"Like I said," Sly began to justify himself. "I am not allowed to interfere in your battles... Not by word and not by deed..."

"Who says?" I squinted.

"I am also not allowed to divulge that information," the foxman shrugged his shoulders. "I can only give you advice before battle... During combat, I'm out of the picture... The battle is yours and yours alone.."

I had lots more questions and complaints for the fink, but decided to keep them to myself. He'd twist out of them no matter what. Instead I said:

"Well, now I have some crystals for you."

"Now that's a different conversation, youngster," said the foxman, rubbing his hands together in delight.

"What's more, I got one of these..."

I take the small elongated vial from my knapsack.

"You managed to capture the spirit of an otherworldly creature," Sly nodded with a mysterious smile. "Let me note — that is a ve-ery rare trophy..."

"Okay, what can I do with it?"

"You, I'm sorry, but nothing..." Sly answered, shrugging his shoulders.

"But why?" I asked in disappointment. "It doesn't have any level restrictions, after all..."

"That's true," Redtail agreed. "But it has a different problem..."

"What?"

"Absorbing a spirit is risky business... Only the most valiant of us ever had the courage to do it... Although when a hunter succeeded, they received a modicum of the otherworldly creature's power. We used to call those warriors ghostkin."

"How do you do it?" I asked firmly. "If there's a way to become stronger, I have to take advantage of it."

"Eric, you don't understand..."

"Not allowed again?" I asked derisively.

His head tilted to the side, the foxman squinted his yellow animal eyes and answered:

"I see you're feeling determined... Alright then, if you please... But first let me tell you what you stand to lose."

"Okay," I nodded. "But you must know - I am not planning to change my decision. I have to risk my life here every minute as it is, something you've played no small part in. And if these spirits you're talking about can increase my survival chances, I simply must try."

"Then you must know that a hunter has to pay dearly for taking the spirit of an otherworldly creature," the foxman said, flashing his sharp fangs.

"What is the price?"

"Their life," the ghost answered threateningly. "In the truest sense of the word. Before you absorb a spirit, the creature it belongs to tries to take as much life from you as it can in one blow. But it's never more than ninety percent of the total."

Trying not to show my anxiety, I clarified:

"So you just have to start with a full life supply?"

"Exactly."

"Then I'm in. What do I need to do?"

The foxman just shook his head, but still answered:

"You must perform a ritual before an altar in our temple. But let's deal with something else first."

I chuckled acridly.

"Are you afraid I'll bite the dust before I give you your crystals?"

"Honestly?" the ghost asked in annoyance. "You're the first mortal the Door has allowed to enter in nearly one thousand years! Of course I'm afraid of missing my chance!"

"By the way, why did it let me through?" I asked a question that had long been bothering me.

"Your blood..." the ghost said and quickly

stopped himself.

"What?" I grabbed at the thread. "What about my blood?"

"Alas," the foxman answered, shrugging his shoulders. "I cannot say..."

"Not enough reputation? Or has someone forbidden you?"

"Neither... I simply do not know... I only have my own conclusions based on what has happened."

"What does that mean?"

"Well, you followed the ancient markers here, didn't you?"

"Yes..." I nodded.

"The only reason they brought you to the city was because they analyzed your blood favorably. And don't ask me how that happened... Magister Ilania herself created the spell... As much as I'd like to, I simply cannot explain what it's based in... For the very simple reason that I myself know nothing about it..."

Alright, he doesn't want to talk now, he'll tell me everything later... Although he's already said plenty. Honestly, it was all stuff I already knew.

"Here, take this," I said in an appeasing tone, extending the seven large crystals to the foxman.

Seeing my loot made him noticeably excited.

"Woah! Seven just like that! And they're large! Are you sure you want to become... ahem... what was it you said... Ah, right! Normal?"

- Congratulations! Your reputation with the Order of Monster Hunters has been increased by 140 points! Happy Hunting!
- Removed:
- Large ghostly crystal (7).

I opened the reputation tab.

- Reputation "Monster Hunters."
- Present value: 160.

"Bravo, youngster! Your reputation with the order has grown significantly!" the ghost praised me. "I believe I'll be able to find something more for you in the arsenal."

"Then what are we waiting for?!" I smiled.

The thing turned out to be magic scrolls. I couldn't imagine how they'd survived so many years without crumbling to dust.

"Take them, take them," seeing my hesitation, the foxman encouraged me. "Don't pay any mind to how they look. They won't disintegrate. Their magic is still strong!"

Cautiously picking up one of the scrolls, I took a look at the description.

- Hunter's Fury.
- Type: Magic scroll.
- Rarity: Rare.
- Effect:

- First strike or spell after use will do critical damage.

- Note:

- Must have reputation 100 with the Monster Hunters to purchase.

- Price: 10 tokens.

- Weight: None. Takes no space.

"Well, what do you say?" Sly asked. "Quite a rare item. There are just twenty of them left in the arsenal."

"Very interesting," I answered. "But I don't really need them yet... My damage is still pretty low... But I will take as many of the Blots as I can. After seeing them in use, they're really nice..."

"If you say so," Sly said, shrugging his shoulders.

Setting twelve brown spheres aside, I took out forty-eight tokens and made the purchase.

- Congratulations!

- You have acquired:

- Blot (12).

- Removed:

- Monster Hunter token (48).

Carefully packing the spheres into my knapsack, I turned to the ghost, who was watching me attentively.

"I wanted to ask," I started. "Is all this token juggling necessary? It seems so silly..."

Sly laughed at my question, clutching his stomach with both hands. His eyes even teared up.

"I thought you'd never ask! Of course it isn't necessary! You don't even need to say anything... Haha! It's enough to simply choose an item and mentally wish to make the purchase! Haha!"

"Then why..." frowning, I wanted to ask a question, but Redtail interrupted me:

"Don't be angry, young one! It is an old tradition of ours! All the newbies go through it... I fell into the same trap once upon a time... Haha!"

Sly laughed it off and said in an apologetic tone:

"Well young man, I've been locked up all alone in this little hole for over a thousand years. You have to agree I deserve some entertainment."

Ah, a joker. At least he didn't push me too hard. Out loud, I said:

"Now show me where a guy can absorb a spirit around here..."

The hunters' temple was on the opposite end of the city, in the outskirts. It was a fairly wide platform with a stone block in the center that looked like an anvil.

"So, here is the altar," the ghost said, pointing at the block. "Are you sure you want to do this?"

"Yes," I replied firmly.

Sly just sighed heavily and said:

"Then walk up to the altar and, when you're ready, pour the spirit out of the vial and into the stone basin."

I nodded and took a few steps forward. After that, I checked my life supply. After taking some absolutely flavorless satiety potion, it was filled to the brim. I gave an order to Gorgie to stay where he was and not intervene no matter what. He agreed uneasily, and I activated Lair. Not looking back so I couldn't see the concerned faces of the harn and foxman, I uncorked the vial.

As soon as it happened, a message appeared:

- Attention! You are attempting to initiate the process of absorbing a Snow Ghoul spirit!
- Attention! To be sure you complete the process successfully, your life supply should be 100% full!
- Continue?

I checked all the bars again and, my heart aflutter, gave my consent. A second later, the transparent pale figure of a ghoul was hovering over the altar. And a moment later, it attacked...

Before the darkness engulfed me, I saw its eyes. They were filled with blue blood...

CHAPTER 22

I CAME BACK to my senses gradually... It felt like my body no longer belonged to me... My limbs heavy and disobedient, there's a cloudy veil before my eyes, as if I'm looking at the world through a pane of mica. My ears feel all plugged up, but I'm starting to hear familiar sounds...

"Eric... Eric..."

"Hrn... Hrn..."

"Shoulder..." I rasp. It's like there's sand in my mouth.

"Thank the gods!" came Sly's voice.

"Hrn..." came Gorgie. I was suddenly flooded with feline emotions. And they ran the gamut from adoration to reproach. Briefly, Gorgie told me I was a real jerk...

"Sh-shoulder..." I repeated, sluggishly fending off the cat's warm tongue with my left hand. "Right..."

"Did you think there would be no consequences?!" the foxman started trying to teach me a lesson right away. "You just about got

371

yourself killed! If not for that Lair of yours..."

"What's wrong with my shoulder?" I rasped, trying to see why my right arm was weirdly numb.

"The ghoul left a mark on you," the foxman explained. "Those marks serve as a reminder that us hunters always walk a razor's edge..."

I slanted my eyes to the right and tugged my shirt back a bit with my left hand. I could see a scar on my right shoulder left by the teeth of the snow ghoul. And the raw tissue was not red but an icy shade of blue.

With a heavy sigh, I closed my eyes. Time to see what I got for risking my life.

- Attention! You have absorbed Snow Ghoul spirit!

- Congratulations! Your reputation with the Order of Monster Hunters has been increased by 200 points! Happy Hunting!

- Present value: 360.

- Snow Ghoul Spirit.

- Type: Magical spirit.

- Rarity: Rare.

- Effect:

- Vampirism.

- Description:

- Summons a spirit that attacks an enemy one time, reducing their life by 35% and using that to replenish your life supply.

- Summoning requires 500 mana points.

Remember! You may only appeal to the power of the Snow Ghoul 1 time every 5 days!

"Huh..." I rasped.

"Well, what is it?" I immediately heard an acrid question. "Like what you see?"

"Are you mocking me?" I burbled.

"Not at all," Sly chuckled.

"Five hundred mana..." I moaned. "That would take fifty Intellect points! Where am I supposed to get that?! I don't know if you know this, but iridescent tablets aren't exactly just lying around on the side of the road..."

"Oh your tender years, youngster," the fox continued mocking me.

"And all for one attack once every five days..." I mumbled.

"But you must agree, it is quite an attack!" Sly exclaimed.

"That's true..." I sighed sadly and asked:

"How long will my arm be like this?"

"I think it'll get better tomorrow," the ghost answered, shrugging his shoulders.

Out of the corner of my eye, I looked at the Lair figures. So I was lying there unconscious for just over four hours. That means I still have some time to relax before the portal opens. As soon as I thought about that, Sly upended my expectations:

"Youngster, you have less than an hour to come to your senses. We have lots to do."

Paying no mind to the foxman's

commanding tone, I uncorked the vial with my teeth and swallowed the last drop of satiety potion. My supply immediately reacted positively to the liquid.

When the empty vial disappeared into thin air, I fell back wearily onto the warm armored back of the harn, who was lying nearby and closed my eyes. Done... I need to get some sleep...

After a bit of rest, the foxman again ratcheted up the pressure. First of all, he dragged me back to the dusty arsenal closet.

"Seeing as you earned another two hundred reputation points for absorbing the spirit, you now have access to another item from our secret treasure," he said as we walked.

When I heard the last two words, I chuckled skeptically.

"I understand your sarcasm, young man," he commented bitterly on my reaction. "If only you could know what our order used to be capable of... The look on your face... But alas, time is merciless..."

Back in the closet, the ghost walked over to the far wall and pointed at a hidden niche almost at ceiling level.

"That's where the last item I can give you is located..."

"What if I bring up my reputation more?"

"Alas, this is the last secret this place holds," Sly shrugged.

Hm... To be frank, I was hoping for more.

"Well, alright," I said, sighing heavily. "Let's see your secret..."

The secret was a narrow scroll that gave off a pale blue magical glow.

"Is that some kind of spell?" I asked, coming to life.

"Better," the foxman smiled. "It's a map."

"A map?" I asked, not understanding.

"Yes, a map," the ghost nodded. "A map of Stonetown and all its traps. As you remember, I myself was preparing to show you but alas, I was mistaken in my calculations."

"What calculations exactly?" I asked, my ears perked up.

"Hm..." Sly stumbled. "You see, Eric... Here's the thing... I'm going to have to leave you..."

"What does that mean? For long?"

Closing his eyes guiltily, the foxman said quietly:

"For good..."

"What do you mean for good?!" I shouted, baffled.

"If only you knew how bad I feel about this whole thing, youngster... I have expended too much power keeping you in this city... And I overshot... The spells that hold me here are breaking. I cannot continue to power them. Heh... Old Sly the trickster played one last trick — on himself..."

"And what about your mission?! The portal is still open! And what, if I may be so bold, are Gorgie and I supposed to do?!"

"Alas, I cannot unlock the Door. It will only open after the portal has been sealed. You'll have to continue our mission without me... I sincerely believe in you, my brother!"

Oh, go screw yourself! You're no brother to me! Brothers don't lock each other in a gods-forsaken tomb to be devoured by otherworldly creatures!

Eric, Eric... Looks like this is becoming tradition...

But out loud I asked:

"How can I seal the portal?"

"Did you see the puddle beneath the crack?"

"Yeah, looks sticky and nasty," I nodded. "I saw it. I was surprised that it didn't all drip out."

"Sealing magic," the foxman confirmed. "But the spell needs more power. You need to feed it ghostly crystals."

"But how...?" I started, but Sly interrupted me.

"Simply throw them into the puddle."

"And that's all?" I asked in surprise. "That's the secret method it took you over a thousand years to come up with?"

"Yes," the ghost answered. "I think it should work."

"And you're not even sure?!" I exclaimed,

thunderstruck.

"Well I really hope it will work... It has shown promising results."

"What results?"

"That puddle used to be the size of a small pond. That must give you some hope, doesn't it?"

"How many crystals have you fed to that thing so far?!" I asked, astounded.

"Many. Very many," Sly answered sadly. "Your predecessor almost completed the mission, but alas he died. And the monster that killed him acquired a body and escaped to freedom. By the way, I see you are using one of its abilities. It must have adapted to the caverns pretty well and multiplied."

"I don't understand," I shook my head. "Are you talking about the gulper?"

"Exactly."

The ghost nodded and suddenly his body started fading.

"Well, seems like that's about it..." Sly Redtail announced sadly, glancing at his quickly disappearing hands. "My thousand years of imprisonment has come to an end... I hope you can cope with your mission, brother... Farewell..."

I stood there not saying a word, watching my sly and cunning jailer disappear into thin air. It would be even more accurate to call him the one who doomed me to die and yet insisted on calling me a brother.

I had no desire to say farewell to him. So I

turned and walked toward the rack of potions of satiety. The map ran me two tokens, so I had enough for one more of the vials as well.

AFTER THE GHOST disappeared, Gorgie and I first ran for the Door one more time. I wouldn't exactly be surprised if the fox played one last trick on us before leaving. But alas, that cunning jerk's magic was still active... I had to go back down with a heavy heart and get ready for more uninvited guests. I decided to start with the map...

To be frank, when I unfurled the ancient scroll, I was afraid it would turn to dust like everything else around here. But the magic artifact didn't let me down.

- Attention! Would you like to use item: Map of Stonetown?

As soon as I gave my consent, the scroll disappeared and I got a new message.

- Tab created: Map of Stonetown.

My heart aflutter, I opened the new tab. Before my eyes appeared a diagram of the whole city. The foxman wasn't lying. This place really was one big trap. For example, I was standing not far from the statue of Gunnar the Destroyer, and it was actually a device for killing otherworldly creatures. According to the description, the stone image of the order's founder would turn into a battle golem upon activation. To be fair though, that place on the map was marked gray and labeled "out of order." To my deep disappointment, almost the whole map was covered with gray spots.

But there was also good news. The pit trap which had so effectively handled the ice rover was still marked with green and labeled "in operation." There were maddeningly few such places on the map. But still there were a few more, which was hard to be upset by...

Other than green and gray spots, there were also a few blue ones. In their description, it said they were magical traps, requiring mana to activate. And I must say, a huge amount of mana! I had never heard of anyone with such an insanely large mana supply. So I didn't really understand how the former masters of the city ever managed to use them.

So in the end, as the fox said, I could only use the very simplest devices.

Within an hour I had visited all the green spots. There was some good news and some bad news. To my eye, it was good that the ancient devices were in decent shape, murderous and quite simple. But most of them could only be used one time - that was the bad news.

But in one way or another, the devices significantly improved our chances. All that remained was to decide which of the traps we would lure the next monster into. And based on the sudden onset of queasiness, we weren't going to be kept waiting long.

* * *

- Attention! You have absorbed Longtailed Ysh spirit!

- Congratulations! Your reputation with the Order of Monster Hunters has been increased by 200 points! Happy Hunting!

- Present value: 860.

- Spirit of Longtailed Ysh.

- Type: Magical spirit.

- Rarity: Rare.

- Effect:

- Snakeskin.

- Description:

- Summons a spirit that surrounds you with a magical shield capable of absorbing 20000 units of damage.

- Summoning requires 600 mana points.

Remember! You may only appeal to the power of the Longtailed Ysh 1 time every 5 days!

It's been seven days since the fox disappeared, may the abyss tear him to shreds... In that time, I earned fifteen large and ten small crystals. And I managed to buy up all the Blots and potions from the arsenal. The only things left were the scrolls of Fury, which I had no need for yet. Starting today,

I'll start spending tokens on them as well.

Right now, I have twenty vials of satiety potion in hand and fifteen energy traps. Well, and seventy tokens. For the record, that's enough for seven scrolls...

A few hours ago, using a trap with a falling spiked ceiling, Gorgie and I took down a giant snake, and it's what dropped the second spirit vial. I won't hide it, I was nursing a hope in my soul that I'd get something with more basic requirements this time. But alas, summoning the snake's spirit cost even more than the ghoul's.

And a new mark appeared on my body. On my stomach, legs, sides and, by all appearances, back there was now a green imprint from the Ysh's scaly body. When I drank the vial on the altar, its spirit tried to constrict around my body. And this time I had worse luck. I never lost consciousness, so I experienced the whole thing... I felt like a wet rag being wringed out...

One drop of potion and my supplies were full again. Phew... I felt better right away...

"Hrn," Gorgie quickly piped up as if to say, "don't forget about me.".

"Well of course," I muttered sweetly, pouring the rest of the potion into the cat's mouth. "How could I forget about you?"

Getting up heavily, I slowly walk over to the crack. There are five large crystals in my knapsack, which I got for defeating the Ysh. I'd have to throw them into the puddle which, by the way, had grown noticeably smaller in my seven days here.

I opened the map as usual. There were just three green spots left. The first pit trap, where the ice rover died ignominiously. And another two deadfalls. The rest of the traps have either been activated or were destroyed by the monsters caught in them.

In my time here, I'd seen my fill of otherworldly creatures. If not for these devices, Gorgie and I would no longer be among the living.

"Hm, bro..." I said sadly to Gorgie, walking next to me. "What are we gonna do when we run out of traps?"

"Hrn," the cat answered calmly.

"Hunt like we used to?" I chuckled. "Without traps, how would we have ever killed the Ysh for example? You saw that giant snake! Or that slimy thing we stuck on the spikes? Its blood was clearly toxic. Remember how it ate through the rock?"

I pointed at the fearsome tracks left on the street by the Acid Worm.

"One bite and you'd be beyond saving."

"Hrn..."

"And don't argue. You know I'm right."

Chatting calmly like that, we first reached the arsenal, where I bought seven scrolls of Fury, then walked toward the portal.

We had a few hours before it would open again, but my mouth suddenly filled with bitter saliva with a slightly rotten taste... How?! But that was all I was able to think before my mind was plunged into darkness...

I woke up to someone slapping me on the cheeks. And they weren't trying to be nice about it. The slaps were straight from the shoulder, impertinent. I opened my eyes...

There was a dead pale face hunched over me. Ears sticking up, a bare scalp, eyes narrow and black, a straight nose. Thin bloodless lips clamped shut in impatience.

Seeing that I'd come to my senses, the being addressed me in an unfamiliar language. I couldn't shake my head because I was completely immobilized. The unknown figure repeated its question, but the intonations and words changed. I still don't understand... I noticed out of the corner of my eye that the harn was lying next to me. His chest is rising measuredly. Thank the gods, he's alive! Clearly he's also immobilized like me. I can't sense his emotions. That must mean he's unconscious.

I slanted my eyes right. The paleface isn't alone. There's two more with him — a man and a woman. Like the first, there's not a single hair on their heads. Their figures are lithe. Gaunt, but strong. Based on the gear, these are not hunters or scouts. These are warriors. For weaponry: short curved swords, taut bows and daggers. All the items the uncanny strangers carry are coal black.

The paleface that tried talking to me turned to his companions and made something like a croak and a hiss. Based on the intonations, he's very mad. While he was busy chatting, I lowered my eyes. Hm... Doesn't seem like I'm tied up... Then... It finally reached me — magic...

I open my messages. Strange... The Great System says the harn and I were immobilized and made unable to use spells by some unknown sorcery. So that means one of these three is a mage.

They work quick... They got the drop on Gorgie... He didn't even manage to get one kick off...

"You understand me, worm?" the stranger asked, changing to Orchusian. "I see that you do."

He ran his hand smoothly before my face and I gave a loud cough.

"Who are you? And what do you want?" I rasped.

"Shut your mouth, worm," he rudely interrupted. "I'll be asking the questions here."

The paleface squinted in anger and I saw four sharp fangs.

"Are you alone here?" he asked.

I fell silent, but the stranger seemingly took that as enough. He turned to his companions and said something in his vile tongue. They just gave a short nod, and something happened I was not expecting. Faster than a bolt of lightning, they all reached for their blades and started attacking one another.

My mouth gaping, baffled, I watched them fight.

It was everyone for themselves, sometimes turning into two on one. And the former allies, their eyes peeled for good opportunities, would turn back into opponents in an instant.

The palefaces fought in silence using weaponry and magic. The spell flickers, clang of steel, and heavy breathing all blended together into a whirlwind of death. They're so blindingly fast, it's hard to follow their movements.

Based on the bitter taste in my mouth, these things must have come from the fissure. Hm... But why didn't they kill us? Why are they fighting each other?

A sonorous feminine scream of pain announced that the woman had taken a wound. Her left arm was hanging down limp as a lash. But that didn't stop her from making a long lunge and sticking her curved blade deep into the one who wounded her... The thin coal-black strip of metal went straight into his heart.

Fortunately for me, that was the mage who rendered Gorgie and me motionless. As soon as his body disappeared, I was able to move again. And I was overcome with a desire to slam both of them with a Ram.

"Gorgie," I whispered, activating the Fury scroll and a spell. "Glad you're awake."

- *You have attacked Twilight Vampire (16)!*
- *Critical hit. You have dealt 83 damage!*

- *You have attacked Twilight Vampire (17)!*

- Critical hit. You have dealt 79 damage!

The two remaining vampires, no longer fighting, were caught completely off guard by my attack. Tossed a few paces back like broken dolls, they were frozen in awkward poses.

The harn was on the scene in a second. A long pounce and the cave cat's scaled body landed on the nearest vampire's chest. A moment later, the Great System informs me the first kill has been made.

Meanwhile, the vampire lady came to her senses and easily dodged the harn's claws, running in my direction with unexpected speed. Her pale face turned into a grimace of death.

She shouted something in her croaking language. I meanwhile took out another vial of potion and took a sip. My life and energy supplies jumped upward, restoring my mana instantly.

The body of the running fury was enshrouded in black smoke. Probably some ghastly spell.

The harn, angry that he missed, was already a step away from the attacker.

A ravenous smile appeared on the woman's pale grinning face.

"Is that all you have in your bag of tricks, worm?!" She suddenly screamed.

When I was just fifteen feet from her I answered, my voice quavering:

"Not quite."

DUNGEONS OF THE CROOKED MOUNTAINS

The eel shock, a bolt of pale yellow lightning, streamed off toward the vampire, making her stumble and somersault a few yards ahead out of inertia. Then Gorgie, feisty and hot on her heels, capped off our standoff with a big fat period.

With a heavy sigh, my legs shaking, I fell to the ground... My heart was about to burst out of my chest.

- You have killed Twilight Vampire (16).
- Congratulations! You receive:
- Monster Hunter token (30).
- Large ghostly crystal (5).

- You have killed Twilight Vampire (17).
- Congratulations! You receive:
- Monster Hunter token (40).
- Large ghostly crystal (6).
- Ephemeral Backpack of the Twilight Warrior.

More loot? I wonder what the vampire lady shared with me.

- Ephemeral Backpack of the Twilight Warrior.
- Type: Magical object.
- Rarity: Epic.
- Effect:
- + 10 ephemeral inventory slots.
- Items may be stored 2 times as long.

- Carried items weight 2 times less.

- Note:

- After equipped, becomes part of wearer until death.

I took the strange glowing item out of my knapsack and twirled it around in my hands.

- Attention! Would you like to use item: Ephemeral Backpack of the Twilight Warrior?

After I gave my agreement, the uncanny bag dissolved into thin air, and a new message appeared before my eyes.

- Tab created: Ephemeral Backpack of the Twilight Warrior.

Spellbound, I open the new tab and see ten empty slots. And below them is a list of items I can place into these slots. And wouldn't you know it, all my stuff is there. For curiosity's sake, I choose one ess and move it into an empty slot. I look into my knapsack and one ess is gone. It's like it just turned to smoke!

Hm... One more... Two down in my knapsack, but plus two in one of the backpack slots... It suddenly started to reach me just what kind of item had fallen into my hands...

Overjoyed, I moved my most valuable stuff into the ephemeral backpack and breathed a sigh of relief. Just try and rob me now!

After I finished sorting through the drop, I walked up to the portal. Redtail was right. The fissure seemed to be gradually closing. The black ooze turned to viscous tar right before my eyes, then that tar at some point turned to stone. Seemingly, the ancient evil would cease to exist in just a tiny bit.

I took out all my crystals right away. After killing the vampires, I had twenty-one. The small puddle, now more like a spot of tar, gave a slight vibration when it sensed the magic of the crystals I dropped into it.

At first nothing happened. I had already started thinking it was time to get ready for the next incursion when suddenly the fissure went into motion and started to contract.

I ran a few steps back, my heart aflutter and watched the jagged cliff edges join together as the disgusting ooze turned to black steam. A few heartbeats later, the ancient portal, which had served as a passage for all kinds of horror over the millennia, ceased to exist.

I glanced at Gorgie and, in a quavering voice, said:

"That's all, buddy... We did it... Time to get out of this place..."

CHAPTER 23

- Attention, Hunter! For valor displayed in combat with ancient evil, your reputation with the Order of Monster Hunters will be increased by 2000 points!

- Current reputation: 3280.

- From now on, you will receive a 50% discount on all items available in any of the order's arsenals!

- From now on, the brothers of our Order regard you as a Hero!

- Congratulations! You receive:

- Monster Hunter token (500).

I SCRATCHED the back of my head, baffled. To be frank, I was expecting something more significant. I mean really, no matter how you slice it, we vanquished an "ancient evil..."

I think if some other hunter were in my

place, this process would have taken much more time. I don't believe my predecessor was getting showered in crystals at the same rate as me. Sly himself was constantly hinting at that in our conversations.

And well really, what good was so much reputation with a dead order? It also left me with a large number of these tokens... Heh... Discounts are sweet, no doubt. But what's the point if all the goods have turned to dust? By the way, I shouldn't forget to grab all the Fury scrolls from the arsenal before I leave. With my new reputation, they would run me five tokens a piece now.

There was one part of the messages that had me confused — "in any of the order's arsenals." Does that mean that Stonetown isn't the only place the monster hunters lived and worked? If that's so, where might the others be? And importantly, what condition are they in? Honestly, to be perfectly frank, I did not want to fall into the hands of another Sly Redtail just yet... Although I would be happy to dig around in the other locations' arsenals.

The Maps tab was blinking, which drew my attention. Let's open it up... Woah! Look how much stuff! Up until then, there were only trap markers. Now all the main city buildings were labeled. Almost all of them were on the central square. There's the statue of Gunnar the Destroyer... There's the arsenal... There on the outskirts is the temple... The portal, by the way, is no longer there.

Wait... What's that? My heart started beating faster... Bank? Ba-a-ank!

"Hrn?" Gorgie was surprised to see me start my fast-paced duck-walk toward the central square.

"Old buddy!" I shouted as we went. "If even a tiny bit of what should be in that building is still there, we'll be set for life!"

I'll admit that, for the last few days, never losing hope that I'd find something of value, I had rigorously checked every building in this little town. While Sly was with me, I tried to find out where the former masters might have hidden their things, but the ghost refused to help in any way. His argument was that stealing would be disrespectful to his fallen friends and brothers in arms. And that, by the way, just served to convince me even more that this little town was stuffed to the gills with valuables.

And alas, all my attempts to convince him such as: "I might find things that could help in battle with monsters" had no effect on the tricky foxman. He just laughed his crafty laugh and told me that traps are the best way of vanquishing otherworldly creatures. Well that and "quick thinking and valor..." May the abyss take that little geek!

Still, I can't say my searches turned up nothing... Many times I discovered very simple safes and hidden wall niches but, alas, there was nothing in them except dust.... Beyond that, I saw a few traces of prior looting. Clearly my predecessors, luckier and with higher Observation or Treasure Hunter levels, had already checked these places. Honestly, it makes me wonder... If they died in battle, where did the valuables they found wind up? Heh! More questions... I guess I now have more than I did before I came here.

And now the map gives me a long-awaited hint! Stonetown had its own bank! Wonderful news! I'd even say stupendous!

Just imagine how many hunters once lived here... And where must they have kept all their trophies? Correct! The bank!

In school, we were told that bankers used special gnomish magic to keep their depositors' valuables safe and sound. Maybe this bank was the same? The perspective of it made a chill run over my skin!

When I reached the central square, opened up the map and found the place where the Stonetown bank should have been - I wanted to rip my hair out.

The only thing there was a big hill of giant stones overgrown with a thick layer of green moss. The shapes of the stone fragments hinted at some particularly long stalactites. I looked around, as if seeing the square again for the first time. The town hall, bank, temple, and another dozen or so buildings were destroyed and buried under gigantic rock fragments. Only now I noticed that almost the whole city was in good condition, except for the most important structures. It was as if someone was intentionally using destructive magic to make the hanging rocks fall off the ceiling.

Hmm... I looked in disappointment at the piles of rock and, rubbing my chin, thought. With my current figures, I wouldn't be able to clear these hills even if I had several lifetimes. I was reassured by the fact that the map still showed active blue points under the rocks. That must mean the ancient hunter traps are still active. So the bank safe must be on a lower level. I really want to believe that something is still down there...

Hmm... Despite the oath I swore to myself never to return here, I have to admit — this place doesn't want to let me go. When I get stronger, I'll have to come back.

Taking in the stony hill that kept the hunters' treasure safe from outsiders, I sighed in disappointment and marched toward the arsenal. I'll buy up the last of the scrolls and be on my way.

The foxman did keep his word in the end - the Door let us leave! When I got outside, it felt like a stone had fallen off my shoulders...

We're free!

The overload of feelings made me hug the harn's armored neck. He immediately licked my face all over, also glad at our deliverance...

It's funny to think how hard I'd have laughed if some joker told me just a month ago that I'd be happy to find myself on level seven of the caverns of the Crooked Mountains.

DUNGEONS OF THE CROOKED MOUNTAINS

Filling my lungs with air from the caverns which now felt like home, I turned and looked back at the closing Door. I have mixed feelings about leaving this place. Disappointment — I didn't find what I was secretly hoping for... Joy — we survived and escaped the trap... Comprehension — the only place you can find free cheese is a mousetrap... Next time, I'll think twice before I decide to enter some ancient location...

It's been five days since we left the ancient city. Yesterday we got past the pond where the eel used to live. We still didn't enter the cave. We were avoiding it. The harn told me that, despite how many days had passed, it still holds the smell of rot. There must have been a pitched battle for the bodies of the tusker and eel and, ever since, there had been more squabbles over the bodies of the losers.

On our way, we did get some hunting in. We ended up with a big reserve of fangbloom stems. For the record, after the flavorless satiety potions, I was shoveling them down like the finest delicacy known to man.

And the harn was able to treat himself to some viper meat. Two times even. Beyond that, we took down a small flock of four megabats and one vile coldune.

Gorgie was improving gradually, and I

played no small part. By amicable arrangement, we invested all silver tablets in his magic supply. We were gradually improving the other characteristics the natural way, but Intellect needed a bit of a kickstart.

And the battle with the vampires proved that every point of Intellect could be very important. That day, in just two thorntail jumps, the harn had practically emptied his mana supply, by the same token giving the vampire lady a window to take me down... Now though, he has twenty-six points — enough mana for five jumps.

My thoughts had returned to that memorable tussle on a few occasions. I took some time to think over the vampires' strange behavior and came to the conclusion they were fighting each other for the right to kill Gorgie and I. One of them was going to have to disappear so the other two could acquire bodies.

And that led me to the conclusion that these beings must have their own code of honor. What was stopping the mage from quickly cutting me down when he realized that there were just two of us? Then he could have just watched his two companions hack each other down for Gorgie's body. But he didn't... He first announced the news to his friends, then the whole scuffle started...

The "odd man out" scenario was also supported by the fact that, as soon as the mage died, the other two stopped fighting.

My father once told me that sometimes it's

useful to look weak. He said it could be a way of gaining an advantage. The true meaning of his advice only reached me now. I was lucky that the twilight warriors underestimated the nulled "worm" and his level-six pet.

Overall, I'd basically cracked it. But now the question: "How did those freaks get into the city?" remains open. I definitely remember the portal closing after the Ysh died. That means the vampires didn't come from its world like the snow ghoul had, jumping in after the icy rover. There was definitely something more at play here... Something the damn foxman never warned me about...

I have a few guesses, one more unusual than the next. I'm inclined to think the twilight vampires have a way of controlling portals. When Sly was describing the Potions of Satiety, he mentioned that hunters could travel to other worlds. That led me to a logical conclusion — sentient otherworldly creatures must be able to do the same thing. All that remains is why I never sensed the portal opening. Maybe I didn't have enough of the foxman's precious reputation?

"Hrn," Gorgie distracted me from the heavy thoughts.

"Yes, you're my pretty boy," I whispered into his ear and admired his now higher figures.

- *Ferocious Harn.*
- *Name: Gorgie.*

- *Level: 6 (13600/27000).*
- *Status: Loyalty to master (permanent).*
- *Mind: 1/1*
- *Strength: 48/90*
- *Agility: 55/90*
- *Accuracy: 5.8/90*
- *Intuition: 6/6*
- *Wisdom: 5.8/12*
- *Animal instinct: 8/12*
- *Speed: 49.1/90*
- *Flexibility: 41/90*
- *Intellect: 26/60*
- *Mana supply: 310/310*
- *Health: 60/60*
- *Endurance: 49/60*
- *Life supply: 650/650*
- *Energy supply: 540/540*
- *Scale armor: 30/30*
- *Defense: 300/300*
- *Damage: +140.6...+451.4*

- *Bite: 30/30*
- *Paw swipe: 30/30*
- *Pounce: 6/6*
- *Animal regeneration: 10/12*
- *Hunter: 21.8/30*
- *Fisher: 12.8 / 30*
- *Resistance to Hexapod poison: 7 / 30*
- *Thorntail's jump*

I glanced into my ephemeral backpack.

DUNGEONS OF THE CROOKED MOUNTAINS

- Experience essence (59660).
- Stone tablet of Mind (24).
- Clay tablet "Herbalism" (110).
- Clay tablet of Mind (110).
- Gold tablet of Intellect.
- Monster Hunter Token (505).
- Hunter's Fury (19).
- Blot (15).
- Small potion of satiety (18).
- Ferocious Harn summoning amulet.

After we took down our first viper after leaving the town, I noticed something strange with the backpack. And to me, it was cause for celebration. First came a message asking whether I'd like all new loot to go into my new backpack from then on. I agreed to that with pleasure, forgetting that all the ephemeral slots were already occupied. I recognized my mistake when a new item dropped. I quickly opened the backpack tab, but froze with my mouth wide open. Now there were eleven slots?!

After that, the overexcitement behind me, I was able to think normally again and realized what was going on. Everything I put into the ephemeral backpack was labeled "Weight: None. Takes no space." So in other words, I have ten more ephemeral slots!

I just left a bunch of junk in the old knapsack as a diversion. If someone else got their hands on that, it wouldn't be so bad.

"Hrn..." Gorgie told me quietly.

"Yes... I taste it too..." I whispered.

The thing is, on day five of our journey, my mouth filled with the familiar bitter saliva... First I couldn't believe it, thought it was just in my head, but the harn confirmed — there's something evil and ravenous lurking nearby. However, Gorgie didn't call this unknown creature "scary." He must have tussled with one before.

And now we're sitting fifteen feet off the ground on a wide ledge. We're waiting to ambush the offspring of an otherworldly creature that acquired a body and escaped to freedom.

Below us is a large and damp oval-shaped cave. The walls contain a few cave worm burrows, but they're practically choked with green moss. The cave is surprisingly humid... But how could the air be so moist without a water source? There isn't even a little puddle...

Suddenly the scales on the nape of the harn's neck started vibrating... Aha... So the unknown animal was coming to pay us a visit. At first I tasted bitterness, then a hint of decay.

First I heard a loud gurgling breathing, then some pattering footsteps. The first thing that came to mind was that the unseen creature was not used to walking on land.

A few moments later, the monster appeared from a gap in the opposite wall. Heh... So, looks like it's a muckwalker! I myself had never seen one but, based on the distinctive features Miri told me about, this must have been one. I just don't understand one thing — what is an aquatic creature doing so far from the putrid waters it calls home?

I took a look. The thing was like a big old toad, or maybe a fat lizard. The skin on its body was all cracked, even broken in a few spots. On its right side there was a deep scratch that oozed with thick green slime. Ha! Looks like this thing is injured!

Unexpectedly, I got a vague explanation from the harn.

"Hunting spot. Battle. Rival."

"Are you trying to say he lost his swamp to a stronger rival?" I asked in a whisper.

"Hrn," Gorgie answered affirmatively.

The harn also let me know that the muckwalker was worn out by the fight. It was wounded and had lost lots of blood. Now it was looking for an aquatic home-base where it could recuperate. That was why it came into this damp cave, in hopes of finding some water to wallow in. In other words, Gorgie was suggesting that we attack the wounded critter before something else did.

When the monster came up closer, I saw that he was not wrong. A muckwalker. Level twenty-one. Whooping, burbling, and squelching heavily, it was heading for the middle of the cave.

Gorgie suggested we act immediately.

"Wait," I whispered. "Let's play it safe."

I take out two brown spheres and throw them under the feet of the slowly shuffling creature.

The spheres broke open silently and the muckwalker caught the full brunt of the energy traps. The Blots instantly drained forty percent of its energy supply. The monster, not expecting such a dirty trick, gave a wheeze and its big fat body was instantly enshrouded in a murky green haze.

And that was all the master of the swamp was able to do. A moment later, it's jelly-like body fell down heavily to the ground and a long slimy tongue rolled out of its wide toothy maw.

Gorgie was next to its round head in a few leaps and dealt several lightning-fast blows with his clawed paw. I forbid him from biting the creature — I didn't want him to get poisoned. So the harn was acting cautious.

The pale green smoke that puffed out of the muckwalker after every one of the cat's blows was slightly flickering. And somewhere around the tenth swipe, it completely dissipated.

That was the end. The muckwalker's magic shield was down. Powerful blows rained down on the creature's head, turning it into a pile of green jelly in a matter of seconds. Near the end, I also made my mark. I blasted the monster with a Ram, placing a period on the end of our skirmish.

Breathing heavily, my eyes wide in excitement, I looked at the harn. The cat was also breathing heavily. His feet and body were vibrating intensely. My pet was really going all out.

- *You have killed Muckwalker (21).*
- *Congratulations! You receive:*
- *Experience essence (4200).*
- *Gold tablet of Intellect.*
- *Silver tablet (6).*
- *Monster Hunter token (30).*

- *Attention! The Higher Powers noticed you! You have replicated the legendary feat of Sigrun the Sly! You defeated a creature more than 20 levels higher than you using surprise attacks!*
- *Congratulations! You receive:*
- *Experience essence (3000).*
- *Iridescent tablet "Muckwalker" (1).*

Before I could get appropriately happy at the new iridescent, Gorgie gave a sudden jolt! And a few moments later, the cave was filled with hissing and shrieking!

Giant rats! A pack of three!

Thinking for a moment, I uncork a vial of potion and take a swallow. The harn bristles up and stands at my side. Two drops and our supplies are filled to the brim.

A short glance back - I won't be fast enough to reach the ledge.

We'll have to meet the enemy right here.

- *Attention! You have activated Gulper's Lair!*

While the giant rats stood frozen in place, studying the battlefield, I take out the iridescent tablet, my hands shivering. There's no time to read all the muckwalker's spells, skills and abilities now. But before the giant rats went on the attack, I managed to toss ten points into Intellect.

Two hundred ten points into my magic supply! Now I can fight properly!

The big old rats jumped almost simultaneously. Two of them were immediately flung back by a Ram reinforced with Hunter's Fury.

- You have attacked Giant Rock Rat (9)!
- Critical hit. You have dealt 75 damage!

- You have attacked Giant Rock Rat (9)!
- Critical hit. You have dealt 83 damage!

The third creature jumped right at me, but was knocked out of the air by Gorgie's armored body. The two dark gray bodies intertwined into one squealing and growling ball, then flew a few steps aside. Despite the level difference, the giant rat was clearly losing the squabble. Gorgie's scaled paws flickered like the wings of a dragonfly, turning the side and chest of the subterranean scavenger into a bloody mess.

The harn won but, it was unfortunately too slow. The ten-second stun passed like no time at all. Turning their whiskered heads, the rats went back on the attack. But this time they took a more devious approach. They split up.

One of them dashed off to help their mortally wounded friend, and the other was at my side in two jumps. It was over so quickly that I didn't even have time to kick, though that was partially thanks to my delayed reaction speed.

The giant rat's first blow was absorbed by the Lair, giving me time to come to my senses. Then I was left defenseless!

Ram! Squealing in distress, the rat again flies a few steps back and stays there next to the dead body of the muckwalker.

I look over to the harn. He's lurching between the two creatures, a blistering-fast shadow landing powerful blows left and right.

I cast eel lightning in that direction and the giant rats get stuck in stupid poses. And that is their death sentence. Gorgie, enraged, rips through their throats one after the next and, without even a second of delay, turns toward the last rat just as its starting to come to its senses.

A Thorntail's Jump and the harn is behind the giant rat, which was caught completely off guard. The cave cat's fangs clamped down on the scavenger's neck in the blink of an eye. Even I could hear its spine crunching.

That takes care of the last one... We won...

Not truly realizing what was happening, I got a warning from Gorgie. It's time to run. A whole pack of rats would be coming here soon.

We left quickly. Well... As quickly as possible with my speed... Contrary to my fears, none of them followed us. Clearly the giant rats were just fine eating the bodies of other rats. Beyond that, there was also the muckwalker. They weren't above eating it either. After I saw the sheer satisfaction of a rat pack devouring the remains of a megabat, I'm confident they would eat anything.

I finally got around to looking through the loot back at our camp site. My third iridescent tablet delighted me with a new spell.

- Muckwalker's Defensive Aura.
- Level: 0 (0/20).
- Type: Spell.
- Rarity: Rare.
- Description:
- Using magic, muckwalkers can create a defensive aura.
- Effect:
- Absorbs 2000 damage.

- Requirements:
- Intellect — 9.
- Expends 100 mana.
- Note:
- Cooldown time: 3 hours.

Beyond that, happily, one of the swamp creature's abilities was not labeled "anatomically incompatible."

- *Muckwalker's Aquatic Regeneration.*
- *Level: 0 (0/20).*
- *Type: Active ability.*
- *Rarity: Rare.*
- *Description:*
- *When exhausted or wounded, Muckwalkers will search for an appropriate body of water, submerge themselves and magically speed up the healing process.*
- *Effect:*
- *+20 regeneration.*

- *Requirements:*
- *Intellect — 11.*
- *Expends 120 mana points.*
- *Note:*
- *Duration: 1 hour.*
- *Ability may be used no more than 1 time every 12 hours.*

"We got so lucky to find that wounded muckwalker," I whispered into the dozing Gorgie's ear, rubbing my hands together.

"Hrn?"

"We got a very useful tablet. You might say it saved my life today."

"Hrn?!"

"Of course, of course! How could you think such a thing? If not for you, I'd have died long ago. You're my main defense! What can I say! You're my closest friend in the whole wide world!"

"Hrn," Gorgie answered, licking me on the cheek.

I patted him lightly on his scaled neck and thought...

What is waiting for me up on the surface? How would the valiant scouts take my resurrection? I wonder what they told Skorx? Although, what am I talking about? Those bastards had already buried so many innocent souls — one more wouldn't make a difference...

CHAPTER 24

You have killed Black Megabat (8).

- Congratulations! You receive:
- Experience essence (1600).
- Silver tablet (2).

- Attention! Your pet has reached level 7!
- Free characteristics: 3.

"**C**ONGRATS ON the level-up, brother!" I embrace Gorgie, who'd grown a good deal stronger in the last few days.

"Hrn," the cat nuzzled my cheek with his wet nose.

"Agreed! You're my pretty boy! Come over here so I can pet you…"

- Ferocious Harn.
- Name: Gorgie.

- *Level: 7 (0/ 36000).*
- *Status: Loyalty to master (permanent).*
- *Mind: 1/ 1*
- *Strength: 51.5/ 105*
- *Agility: 58.5/ 105*
- *Accuracy: 5.8/ 105*
- *Intuition: 6/ 7*
- *Wisdom: 6/ 14*
- *Animal instinct: 8/ 14*
- *Speed: 51.5/ 105*
- *Flexibility: 41.3/ 105*
- *Intellect: 28/ 70*
- *Mana supply: 330/ 330*
- *Health: 60/ 70*
- *Endurance: 52.5/ 70*
- *Life supply: 650/ 650*
- *Energy supply: 575/ 575*
- *Scale armor: 30/ 35*
- *Defense: 300/ 350*
- *Damage: +144...+462*

- *Bite: 30/ 35*
- *Paw swipe: 30/ 35*
- *Pounce: 6/ 7*
- *Animal regeneration: 10/ 14*
- *Hunter: 22.8/ 35*
- *Fisher: 12.8/ 35*
- *Resistance to Hexapod poison: 7/ 35*
- *Thorntail's jump*

It's been nine days since the memorable

battle with the muckwalker and giant rats. We're now in the cave where I found the first Monster Hunters marker. There beyond that rock wall is the former lair of the gulper female. The place where the scouts abandoned me.

In the last few days, we hunted fairly successfully. Megabats, vipers, fangblooms, coldunes, giant rats — I don't even remember how many. Unfortunately, as in the battle with those three rats, I was not always able to do damage, but even so I had fifty-four silver tablets in my backpack awaiting their hour.

Gorgie was now able to take down monsters without any help from me so, by mutual agreement, we decided to save the silvers for level seven.

Today, we'll use some to improve Thorntail's Jump. With a heavy sigh... Goodbye, seventeen tablets... Still, I can't afford not to...

- Attention! You have enhanced your pet's spell!

"Alright, let's see what that got us," I whispered.

"Hrn..."

- Thorntail's Jump.
- Level: 1 (0/40).
- Type: Magical ability.
- Rarity: Rare.

- Description:

- Using magic, thorntails can get behind opponents in an instant and become temporarily invisible.

- Effect:

- Be instantly transported behind an opponent.

- Temporary invisibility duration: 5 seconds.

- Requirements:

- Intellect — 5.

- Expends 55 mana.

- Note:

- Cooldown time: 8 sec.

- Range: 20 ft.

Rubbing my hands together in satisfaction, I read the description one more time. Now the harn can jump one yard farther. And it isn't much, but recharge time and mana expenditure came down a bit as well. And last... But not least... Gorgie will now be invisible to the enemy for a few seconds after he jumps!

"Beautiful!" I commented. "Darn, I guess we should have improved that spell earlier..."

"Hrn..."

"I agree... How could we have known?"

"Hrn..."

"Yes, yes, buddy.... I haven't forgotten about your damage. But we have thirty-seven tablets left... We need to make sure we spend them intelligently."

"Hrn!"

"But we agreed! Defense and health come after the spell. You're able to handle the little stuff around here easily as it is. And it's only little to you... What if, all the gods of this world forbid, but what if you die doing something reckless?! How do you suggest I live with that?! Just so you know, I wouldn't make it long here without you... I'd last as long as it took to find one of those coldunes..."

Gorgie just frowned and placed his scaled head on his paw.

"That's better..."

And before he started protesting again, I brought his scale armor up to max. That quickly brought the protection up fifty points. Then ten tablets into health — life supply hit the ceiling for this level — seven hundred fifty points. I glanced into the backpack. I had twenty-two silvers left.

As soon as I started thinking about the best way to invest the rest, a wet nose nuzzled my palm.

"Alright, if you say so," I nodded, raising all the harn's combat abilities to the ceiling. Eleven more down...

What now? After he got what he wanted, the harn closed his eyes and began dozing off peacefully.

I chuckled then got deep into his info again. There are a few characteristics and abilities I could bring up to the ceiling. I noticed that the Great System hadn't once deigned to improve them in all those battles. So I'll do it. One point into Intuition, six into Animal Instinct and four into Animal Regeneration. Alright... No more silvers... All that's left is to use up the three points the System gave Gorgie for hitting level seven.

The battle with the Muckwalker gave Gorgie two points of Intellect so, with the spell improvement, his magic supply was now high enough for six jumps, which was one more than before.

If I increase the supply now, thirty extra mana points wouldn't be enough for a seventh jump anyway. Sure, the surplus isn't exactly bursting my pockets, but we're in no position to just go wasting valuable points willy-nilly.

Strength, Agility, Endurance, Speed. These characteristics are improving at an acceptable pace as is. But Wisdom had practically not moved. I'll bring it up - that'll increase mana restore speed.

That settles it! Three points into Wisdom.

Now let's see what that gets us.

- *Ferocious Harn.*
- *Name: Gorgie.*
- *Level: 7 (0/36000).*
- *Status: Loyalty to master (permanent).*
- *Mind: 1/1*
- *Strength: 51.5/105*
- *Agility: 58.5/105*
- *Accuracy: 5.8/105*
- *Intuition: 7/7*
- *Wisdom: 9/14*

DUNGEONS OF THE CROOKED MOUNTAINS

- *Animal instinct: 14/14*
- *Speed: 51.5/105*
- *Flexibility: 41.3/105*
- *Intellect: 28/70*
- *Mana supply: 330/330*
- *Health: 70/70*
- *Endurance: 52.5/70*
- *Life supply: 750/750*
- *Energy supply: 575/575*
- *Scale armor: 35/35*
- *Defense: 350/350*
- *Damage: +171...+541*

- *Bite: 35/35*
- *Paw swipe: 35/35*
- *Pounce: 7 / 7*
- *Animal regeneration: 14/14*
- *Hunter: 22.8/35*
- *Fisher: 12.8 / 35*
- *Resistance to Hexapod poison: 7 / 35*
- *Thorntail's jump (1).*

I glanced into my backpack with a sigh.

- *Experience essence (103460).*
- *Stone tablet of Mind (24).*
- *Clay tablet "Herbalism" (110).*
- *Clay tablet of Mind (110).*
- *Gold tablet of Intellect (2).*
- *Monster Hunter Token (535).*
- *Hunter's Fury (17).*

- *Blot (13).*
- *Small potion of satiety (17).*
- *Ferocious Harn summoning amulet.*

I wasn't using the traps, scrolls or potions from Stonetown anymore. There was no need. The harn was able to take down enemies without artifacts just fine. I'll save them for later. Who knows where we'll end up next?

The harn gave a signal, tearing me from my thoughts. He heard something. But not here, not in this cave. A bit further away. Back where the tunnel ends.

"Scavenger. Hunter. Female. Same kind as you."

At first I couldn't believe my eyes. "Scavenger" is what Gorgie called coldunes. That means some coldune was hunting a human! A woman!

At the moment, I only know one woman who is likely be anywhere around here. Miri! If it really is her, then why isn't she with Dag and Chad? But Gorgie was pretty clear that the woman is alone...

A few seconds later, I distinctly heard the sounds of weary footsteps and a heavy breathing coming from the tunnel. The woman was running this way, right into the cave where we were planning to spend the night. And she was bringing that creature with her.

There's one thing I can't understand. If it is Miri, then why is she running away from a mere coldune? That doesn't sound like her. A cowardly scavenger like that would be easy pickings for her. And the fact that she's alone doesn't mean anything. Back when I was still with her, at times I caught myself thinking that Dag and Chad were weighing her down.

My guesses turned out right. The small thin woman that jumped out of the dark yawning tunnel mouth didn't even come close to the fearsome scout lady.

A mane of tangled dirty hair, a pale exhausted face, and raspy breath tearing its way out of a wide open mouth. Clothes extremely worn, a lean knapsack hanging off her back. Despite the obvious fear and bewilderment, her hands are grasping a short little spear tightly.

She runs with a slight limp, constantly turning and looking back.

"*Female. Lots of noise,*" the harn tells me, upset.

"Well, what did you expect? She's afraid. There's a monster coming after her," I whispered.

When the harn heard the word "monster," he just gave a scornful cackle.

I shook my head. If I had big fangs and claws like him, I'd probably be laughing too.

Knowing the coldune's cowardly habits, we were in no hurry to intervene. Let the woman who, by the way, hadn't noticed us yet, run a bit past us. That way she could lure the cautious creature out of the tunnel.

Ah, of course... I jinxed it...

The lady ran into the middle of the cave, stopped with her spear held in front of her and started looking all around. Just then, she saw Gorgie up on a narrow ledge six feet off the ground and getting ready to pounce.

So sharp-sighted...

Her thin arms fitfully squeezing the spear and shivering hard, her mouth flew open in a muted scream. When she saw her new enemy, she put her back up against the opposite wall. The hair falling over her face made it impossible to see her eyes, but it was clear nevertheless that she was horrified. But not enough to drop her weapon or scream in fear, thus inviting more hungry guests to the cave...

I have to admit - she's doing very well!

Meanwhile the coldune, not suspecting a thing, finally emerged from the tunnel. When it saw its prey frozen against the wall, it took a few cautious jumps to close the gap.

The woman, not knowing where to point her spear, was turning it from side to side.

Another jump and the scavenger was in Ram range. I used the spell immediately, tossing the frog-like creature over toward some sharp stones. A second later, Gorgie was at its throat.

- *You have killed Cave Coldune (7).*
- *Congratulations! You receive:*
- *Experience essence (1400).*

- Silver tablet (2).

The woman, seeing the predator slaughtered so quickly, pressed her back even harder against the wall, preparing to make her life come at the highest possible price. Her chest heaving faster and faster, her legs slightly bent at the knees, the tip of her spear was pointed at the harn, who was approaching slowly.

"Don't be afraid! He won't touch you!" I said as friendly as possible and not all that loud, coming out from my cover.

The lady shuddered in surprise and the shaking tip of her spear was instantly pointed in my direction.

"Don't be afraid!" I repeated. "Neither me or my friend here are gonna hurt you!"

To confirm, the harn stopped and started licking his scaled side. That put the strange lady into an even bigger tailspin.

"May I walk up closer?" I asked. "So we can talk without making too much noise."

Breathing faster and faster, she just nodded in a daze. But she was still holding her spear in front of her, turning it from me back to the harn, who had lost all interest in her.

Based on the very rough tip, this weapon couldn't even get through the cat's scaly hide, but I won't say that out loud. If it makes her calmer, let her hold it.

Slowly, not making any sudden movements,

I walked forward. When I got up close enough, I was finally able to make out that she was level five. With such a mop of red hair in her face, there was no seeing her eyes. Her sunken cheeks were caked with dirt. Her pale dry lips were quavering. Her thin arms were covered in abrasions.

Her and I are approximately the same height. And she's just as thin and frail. But she looks seventeen years old. On her thin waist, I notice a rope cut at the base of a familiar knot. Now this is interesting...

"I couldn't cut the rope myself," I said, nodding at the girl's waist. "I had to undo my belt."

She looked down, not understanding, then glanced back at me. She peered into the darkness... Then shuddered and opened her mouth in a daze...

"Eric?" Much to my surprise, her voice was dimly familiar. "Eric Bergman? Is that you?!"

"Yes," I nod in surprise. "Do I know you?"

Instead of answering, she threw down her spear and was at my side in a few steps, then gave me a firm hug and burst into a fit of bitter tears.

"Those scoundrels, animals..." she sobbed. "They used me as live bait... Left me there to die... The bastards..."

Still not understanding what was happening, I stood there like a statue, afraid to move.

"Oh gods, Eric," she suddenly exclaimed, backing away. "So they did the same with you!

They spun me a whole yarn about you being careless and said you got eaten by cave beasts!"

I just nodded and shrugged my shoulders.

Clearly finally having noticed my crazy facial expression, she backed away and put her disheveled hair behind her ears. Then baffled, she asked:

"What, don't you recognize me?"

I shook my head in silence even though her voice was dimly familiar. Wait... Not just the voice now... I finally saw her eyes... Swollen with tears, they were still very familiar... Like two dark emeralds!

"J-Jay?" I asked perplexedly. "Jay, is that you?"

"Well finally," she smiled, then something strange happened. Her eyes rolled back and she slowly started sitting on the ground.

The harn was on the scene in an instant. Placing his back below her, he helped me hold up the now unconscious Jay. Otherwise, with my Strength, I'd never have managed.

"Poor little thing, she's been through a lot," I whispered, looking the girl over for wounds. "And those bastards probably cleaned her out just like me. She must be hungry..."

Thinking briefly, I took out a satiety potion and dripped some of the magical elixir into Jay's slightly open mouth. A minute later, the blush returned to her cheeks. The dry cracks disappeared from her lips. Her breathing evened out. I smiled and activated Lair, let the poor thing get some rest.

* * *

Jay woke up seven hours later. Seeing the harn, she gave a muted gasp but, clearly having remembered the night before, she calmed down a moment later.

"How are you feeling?" I distracted her from staring at Gorgie's fearsome fangs.

She turned and, seeing me, breathed a sigh of relief.

"I thought I dreamed you..."

"To be honest," I scratched the back of my head. "I can't believe we ran into each other down here either... After all, didn't you get carted off to serve in the master's residence? How'd you end up in the caverns?"

Jay gave a heavy sigh and clenched her lips angrily.

"It was all Ing!" she spat out.

"Ing?" I asked. "Bardan's chief steward?"

"Yes," she nodded. "That lascivious old brute! He thinks he can do whatever he likes, the creep! I may be a peon, but I'm no slave! He doesn't have the right to treat me that way!"

I couldn't quite tell what she was talking about, but I was listening very carefully. After so many days of loneliness, talking with a living person was a breath of fresh air.

"Then one day he made a pass at me yet

again..." she said, turning all red and faltering for a moment. Then she continued:

"Basically, I slashed his vile face and said I'd tell everything to Mrs. Emily, Mr. Bardan's wife."

"And did he back off?"

"For a while..." Jay answered sadly. "But just when I thought it was all over, he struck back. He set it up so Mrs. Emily's earrings were found in my belongings... I was accused of theft... They found witnesses quick... Hrika, the jerk... And Valgard too..."

When Jay mentioned the larger scoundrel, she just wilted. Even I could clearly tell she had fallen for the handsome redhead. That made his betrayal all the harder on her...

"And you were sent to Skorx..."

"Yes," she nodded. "Only now did I understand how Ing got revenge on me."

We spent a bit of time in silence, each thinking of our own thing. Then I asked:

"How long since the scouts left you?"

"It was yesterday," she answered, clenching her fists. "They sent me into a burrow then cleared out my bag and put a big stone over the cave entrance and left me to perish. They even tied the rope on a rock for some reason..."

"Was it a huge cave? Lots of burrows in the wall?"

"Yes," she nodded. "One wall was caved in. That really surprised the scouts."

I chuckled. Those bastards sure are true to

themselves.

"What are you smiling about?"

"Your good luck," I continued smiling.

She flickered her eyes.

"So you think I'm lucky?"

"If you knew what they left you to get eaten by, I think you'd agree with me."

Jay's face changed. I meanwhile continued:

"The monster is called gulper female. Level thirty, for the record. And the cave you were brought to is no more and no less than her lair."

"And they know when the monster is not in her lair?" she asked, pale.

"Yes," I nodded. "They also knew the monster would be alerted as soon as they entered the cave."

"So that's why they blocked off the cave entrance! To stop the monster!"

"Oh no!" I chuckled. "Did you see that huge cave-in?"

"Yeah..."

"That was all the handiwork of the gulper female... Well... ahem... not exactly handiwork. She didn't have hands... But she did have huge teeth, killer magic and a long slimy tongue. She also had a sharp sense of smell and could use the echo of her roar to discover the location of living creatures. Believe me, despite all her agility, even Miri couldn't run away from that creature. And the little rock at the entrance is nothing to her."

"They cover the door so the bait won't run

away!" Jay said in a shivering voice, comprehension dawning. Wrinkling her forehead, she glanced at me:

"Then where is the creature? Seeing how they ran away, she should be showing up at any minute, right?"

"Well, so they thought," I nodded and smiled. "But she didn't. And well, that isn't the whole story... The gulper female was in the cave the whole time."

Jay's eyes now looked like saucers...

"Or rather, her dead body," I continued. "Right under that giant cave-in. Now do you understand why I said you got lucky?"

She stared at the wall with an unseeing gaze. Her lips were slightly pursed. The pallor returned to her cheeks. Looks like she's starting to see what a scrape she landed in...

"Wait..." she suddenly began. "How do you know all that? About the creature, the cave-in, her abilities and level?"

"It's all simple," I said with a shrug as I got off the ground. "When the scouts fled, I was left one-on-one with the enraged beast. I dove into a burrow. She followed me. She started smashing the rock wall. And then the stones collapsed on top of her."

"Okay," Jay nodded. "But what about her habits and abilities?"

"I heard about them from my father and his friends," I lied without a blink, adding as I took a step toward the cave exit:

"He was a miner."

She wanted to ask something else, but when she saw me quickly leaving she shot to her feet and asked in fear:

"Eric, where are you going?!"

"What do you mean?" I feigned surprise. "The surface. Where else? Well, good luck to you. Bye!"

Then I walked forward at a slow pace.

"What about me?! You're just gonna leave me all alone down here?!"

I turned around and slightly tilted my head toward my right shoulder. Jay was standing and embracing her own shoulders. Tears started welling up in her eyes.

"Do you really want to come with me?" I asked, trying to make my voice seem dispassionate.

"Of course!" she exclaimed. "Please take me with you!"

"Are you sure?" I asked firmly.

"Yes!" she took a step forward, her chin raised.

"Then I have two conditions. First... The surface is still a ways away. In order to survive, you have to do everything I say. Do you agree?"

"Yes!"

"And second... You're going to see a lot of weird stuff on the way..."

"Wait, Eric..." she squinted suspiciously. "So

you were never going to abandon me, were you? Right? That whole spectacle was all so I'd give an oath not to tell anyone your secrets?"

"Basically yes..." I said, embarrassed. "But oaths are serious business. I cannot force you..."

I didn't have time to finish. She interrupted me:

"I'll do whatever it takes! And I'll swear an oath! Just so I can see the sun again..."

An hour later, the specifics of the oath agreed upon, the Great System confirmed Jay's words, and we started toward the cave exit. By the way, she had never noticed the hunters' mark — the symbol was covered reliably by black mold. And all the better... One less dangerous secret.

"I think we're going the wrong way," she started looking around excitedly as we walked through a small cave with three exits. "I definitely remember the scouts taking us that direction."

She pointed toward the far tunnel.

"I know," I answered calmly. "Gorgie is leading us to a different way out."

"Are you trying to say we aren't going to Skorx's camp?" Jay asked in surprise.

"I know I'm not. There's nothing for me to do there."

"And what about your oath to Bardan? Or don't you owe him money?"

"I do owe Bardan," I nodded. "Not Skorx."

"But you were transferred to Skorx by Bardan's people. You are obliged to do as he says."

"True," I agreed. "And technically, all the time I spent under the ground I was carrying out his only order — go with the scouts and do as they say. They said to crawl down burrows and look for something unusual. But my oath says that I must do that only until I am able to repay my debt in full. The main argument in favor of my interpretation is that the Great System has never made a peep. That must mean I'm doing everything right."

"Do you mean to say you're ready to pay back your debt to Bardan?"

"Exactly," I answered. "But there's a problem."

"As soon as you show up in Skorx's camp and announce that you're ready to pay back your debt, they'll come after you even harder," Jay stated the obvious.

"Exactly," I answered. "A zero, who miraculously survived the caverns, is suddenly able to pay off a huge sum... Sorry, I can't say how much..."

"I understand. You're bound by oath," she nodded.

"Heh... Can you imagine what they might think?"

"Beyond that, I have every reason to believe that as soon as Bardan finds out about my miraculous resurrection he'll do everything to try and hold onto me. He's probably already been told about my unique and interesting specialty."

"You can say that again..." Jay chuckled unhappily. "But still, you'll attract attention when you show up to pay back the debt."

"I have a plan," I answered. "There's someone I need to find. An old friend of my parents. A respected healer woman. If someone like that pays off my debt, even if it's with my money, there shouldn't be any questions. Well, they might ask, but at that point I'll be free! Do you understand?"

"It's a risky plan," Jay stroked her chin in thought. "It has lots of holes, but it's still better than going back to Skorx. And you have an advantage. Everyone thinks you're dead. No one is looking for you. It's too bad you can't just run away. The Great System won't allow it. But as long as your attempts to honor the oath remain pure, it will keep quiet. It must know you have enough to pay him back in full, that's why it isn't saying anything. By the way, what clever scheme did you come up with to earn all that money so fast? I wouldn't mind a bit of advice."

"Hey, how much do you owe? If it's not a secret?"

"Oh, it's not," Jay chuckled bitterly. "My stupid boozehound of a daddy took a ten-gold loan from Bardan's shady outfit."

After a bit of thought, I said with a smile:

"We'll be stomping around here a few more days before we reach the surface. So I think me and Gorgie can help with your problem."

CHAPTER 25

- You have acquired Gray Moss.
- Congratulations! You receive:
- Experience essence (5).
- Clay tablet "Herbalism."
- Clay tablet of Agility.
- Clay tablet "Knife Proficiency."

"**D**ONE," I said to Jay, who was sitting nearby. "Twenty-four cuttings."

She was nestled up near a large stone in the middle of the cave and absorbed in trying to mend her clothing. When she heard me, she nodded respectfully and got back to her activity.

Heh... So facile... After all, just a few hours ago she tried to object.

I saw a wall with a small outcropping of gray moss and said we should take a quick break. Jay quickly started whining and hurrying me along, saying we're losing valuable time on worthless gray moss.

I responded that we were actually not in a hurry, but she ignored me. And I wasn't feeling like pressuring her or being rude. I had to make a clear demonstration of why I was not going to move until I cut all the "worthless gray moss."

When Jay saw how much loot I got from each cutting, at first she couldn't believe her eyes. But when it finally hit her, she spent a bit of time in contemplative silence. And for the record, she hadn't said anything about it since...

I often catch her looking at me pensively. As if she's seeing me for the first time. And I understand why... When she first met me I was just some kid, a zero and a cripple. But now she saw me wandering dangerous caverns as if they were my home, and with a terrible monster for company. Seemingly, she didn't believe the significantly redacted story of how I met Gorgie, from which I removed all mention of magic.

To be frank, I didn't believe it either. I mean, I said I saw a half-dead predator and just decided to take care of it, then we became fast friends... Heh... But very soon, in our first battle, she will see my spells in action...

Well, not counting when we killed the coldune. That was very fast-paced. Jay might have thought it was Gorgie who sent the scavenger flying with his magic. And I hadn't activated Lair again... Basically, I know I need to tell her about my magic, but I keep stalling. I'm afraid of her asking questions... The less she knows, the better for her. I had already lost two friends over my secrets...

"Why are you doing that?" Jay asked, tearing me from my thoughts.

"To dry it," I answered, carefully setting the pieces of moss in what was, to my eye, the driest part of the cave.

"So you get tablets for that too?" she asked, baffled.

"Yes," I nod in response. "And esses, too."

Jay just shook her head pensively and continued sewing up her jacket. I took a fleeting glance in her direction. She cleaned herself up. She looked like the girl from old man Burdoc's cart again. Her mess of red hair was hidden beneath a braid. The grime was gone from her face. Her clothing was neat and tidy again...

"By the way, I wanted to ask. When you worked in Bardan's residence, you probably heard all the latest news... What's been happening out in the world?"

"All kinds of stuff," Jay nodded. "They say the frontier with the steppe has been restless."

"Sure, it's always a bit unruly out there..."

"It's different this time," she objected. "An orc chieftain is amassing a horde..."

That's bad. The last orcish incursion happened a few decades ago. After that, the eastern Barony of Arundel ceased to exist. Those were the lands we now called the Wastes.

"This year our Prince Albert is getting betrothed to the daughter of the Iron King, Princess Anna."

"I've heard..." I said. "Bardan is preparing soldiers for the yearly Games, which will be held in honor of their betrothal."

She nodded and continued:

"Bad news came from the west. The expedition to the Dark Continent, which was organized and led by Count Milon, ended in failure. Only one of their several dozen ships returned. The surviving sailors all say that the rest of the expedition was engulfed by Gloom..."

When she mentioned the Dark Continent, a chill ran down my spine. I wonder, does Count Milon know the true name of those lands?

"Eric, what's going on with you?" Jay asked in surprise.

I shuddered.

"What?"

"Well, you look like a sparrow in the cold. Like your feathers got ruffled... You're suddenly all tense..."

Trying to affect a casual voice, I answered:

"Oh, yeah... I just remembered a scary story. Wanna hear it?"

"Oh gods! Of course not!" she waved it off and, pointing her hand around the cave, added:

"I'm trying to get out of a scary story right now..."

"You can say that again," I answered and

asked:

"Has anything changed in our Barony?"

"Baron Corwin refuses to make peace with our barony."

"The old Raven still lays claim to part of our lands?" I asked in surprise.

"He died last month," Jay told me. "There's a new Raven now. Well, more like Raven chick. They say young Corwin has already threatened to cross the border with a mercenary army several times."

I chuckled.

"Sounds like our Bear will have to go pluck their feathers again."

She sighed.

"Oh, I don't know... I overheard Bardan telling his wife that Baron Berence has some kind of ailment. He's not the same old Bear as he used to be... And unlike the young Corwin, our baron's son is a real dunderhead. He has no interest in anything but wine and women..."

I took a heavy sigh. This was reminding me of my parents... Our cozy family evenings next to the fireplace... Mom, tired but happy, wrapped in a blanket with a glass of astringent Orchusian wine in her hand... Father enthusiastically explaining some aspect of the way of the world to me... Sorrow suddenly pierced my heart... Tears welled up in my eyes all on their own... So that Jay wouldn't notice, I pretended to wipe sweat from my forehead with my shirt sleeve as I wiped the treacherous moisture from my cheek...

When I finally finished arranging the moss, I got up and asked:

"You ready to keep going?"

With a silent nod, she quickly shot to her feet and we were back underway.

A FEW HOURS LATER, the harn led us to a wide lake. We stopped right at the entrance to the cave. I looked around. The bright azure water came up to the walls almost everywhere. There was just one narrow strip of dry land, to the right. We'd have to walk it to reach the exit.

"What a spooky place..." I mumbled quietly. "Is there no way around?"

"Hrn," Gorgie answered negatively.

Out of the corner of my eye, I caught an admiring glance from Jay.

"Water!" she gave a muted squeak. "Finally I can wash up!"

"No you can't," I brought her from the heavens back down to earth.

"W-why not?" Jay asked, perplexed. "Are you not planning to stop here? This is water, Eric! If I don't take a swim right now, I'll just die! I smell like..."

I didn't let her finish:

"No. We will not be stopping here. As a matter of fact, the faster we get out of this cave the better."

"But why?" she asked, disappointed.

"I can see you didn't listen to Miri very well..."

"She didn't really say much to me, actually..."

Jay shrugged her fragile shoulders, winced and added:

"Dag was more the one creeping around me... A real lecher, that guy..."

"Ah, I see..." I nodded, understanding. "It all makes sense now..."

"What makes sense?"

"I'll tell you later..." I waved it off and started quickly explaining:

"Now listen and remember. Look at the water. If water is this color, never go near it. Better to run away..."

She gulped in fear.

"W-what's in there?" she asked, her voice quavering.

"A bleaking," I answered shortly and added:

"The problem is that this is the only way to the surface. Gorgie was always keeping us away from dangerous places before... But alas, not this time..."

"We have to walk that strip of dry land?" Jay asked with horror in her voice, nodding at the path. "So close to the water?"

I chuckled mentally. Just a few seconds earlier, she couldn't wait to take a swim. But out loud I said:

"Yes... But..."

I led a thoughtful gaze over the shoreline once again, the narrow path, the lake... Hm... Too risky... We'd have to think something up... And by the way, Gorgie was in complete agreement...

"W-what's th-the m-m-matter?" she asked, now slightly rattled.

"We can only walk after we fight."

"You're going to fight the monster?!"

Jay's eyes looked like two saucers. She was staring at me as if I were mentally unstable.

"Yes," I nodded. "Look around. Here on this strip of dry land, we have an advantage. Bleakings are kings of the water, but weaker on land. Here they go much slower. We have to lure it on shore."

"You've lost your mind!"

"Perhaps," I nodded back. "But we don't have any other way out. If we don't take it down here, the creature is sure to catch us on the narrow path."

"Are you even sure there is one?" she asked, shaking and tilting her head toward the lake cautiously.

"Yes. Gorgie can smell it. He says the bleaking already knows we're here, too. It's swimming over..."

"And we can't go back?" she made her final attempt.

"Better to just prepare for a fight at this point," I said and added:

"If we work together, we'll survive."

That's only if we win. But I didn't say that out loud. Jay was about to fall unconscious in fear as it was.

"By the way," I said, taking some Blots out of my backpack. "Remember when I said you'd see lots of weird stuff? Don't forget the oath you swore."

Jay said nothing back. Her mouth open wide, she was captivated, watching the brown spheres appear in my hand one after the other as if from thin air.

When I activated Gulper's Lair, she reacted with a muted whimper.

"Three hundred points of defense is not much," I commented calmly. "But in a pinch, it could be the difference between life and death. Believe you me, I've had it happen before..."

She now resembled a mechanical porcelain doll, only able to give identical nods until the spring inside stops bobbing.

"Hrn..." Gorgie warned and the scales on the back of his neck immediately stood on end.

I glanced toward the water and, not turning, said over my shoulder:

"Get ready. The bleaking is coming on the attack."

If not for its excessively mobile tail, the body of the reptile swimming in our direction could be confused with a big piece of driftwood.

When Jay saw the monster, she gave a muted scream. Hm... I'm afraid to even imagine her reaction if she saw an Ysh or an Acid Worm...

Meanwhile, the bleaking swam up to the shore and froze for a few seconds. After it realized we were not planning to walk any closer to the water, it crawled onto the land, slithering smoothly. The curved claws on its short feet gave an unpleasant screech when they touched stone.

"Level nineteen..." Jay whispered with horror in her voice.

The lizard's long flat body was covered in pale scales. And for the record, they didn't look all that tough. An oblong, extended snout... Jaws lined with triangular teeth... A ridge of bone running from the back of the head all the way to the tip of the tail... The bleaking was in some way reminiscent of a Red Alligator that jumped out of the portal. I'm reminded that we didn't even need to activate a trap to kill it.

I swallowed some spit. No taste of bitterness or rot. No... Bleakings come from our world. But that won't stop us from using the same tactic that helped us take down a similar creature before.

When the lizard reached an acceptable distance, I threw all three Blots one after the next. Losing sixty percent of its energy had an immediate effect on the monster's movement speed.

Five steps... And the Eel's Chain Lightning immobilized the predator completely. On the edge of my perception, I hear Jay breathing fitfully.

The harn slammed full force into the stock-still reptile's scaled side. The bleaking was turned onto its back, revealing a poorly defended white stomach. Gorgie immediately crashed down on it from above. It was an obvious crit...

The thin scales, torn up by the teeth and claws of the cat were turned to bloodied scraps in a matter of moments. Its guts fell out of its belly and hit stone.

Okay... The fifteen seconds are up. The

bleaking will come to its senses now. The harn made a long jump to the side. And just in the nick of time... The reptile's toothy jaws, despite the ghastly wound and loss of over half its energy, gnashed loudly just a millimeter from the cat's back paw.

The attack made me shudder... Phew... Gorgie could have easily lost a limb...

Not wasting any more time, I activate a Fury scroll for extra power, then land a Ram right on the bleaking's exposed belly as it tries to dodge.

- Critical hit. You have dealt 102 damage!

Taking a few somersaults, the lizard again froze in place. His intestines, outside his body, were wrapped around his scaled body and mixed together with blood, slime, sand and pebbles. A nasty smell of decay reached my nose. I heard a characteristic sound; seemingly Jay is nauseous.

Gorgie continued to attack, not wasting any time. All caked in monster blood, he looked like an ancient demon of the caverns as he mangled his old enemy's unprotected stomach. Based on the harn's emotions, a creature just like this had once almost killed my four-legged friend...

The bleaking, coming back to its senses, started moving dully but it was in death throes at that point... A puddle of its sticky blood was quickly forming beneath it.

The harn didn't jump again. His head

plunged instantly into the now large wound. A strong burst... A nasty crunch... And I see the reptile's heart in Gorgie's satisfied mouth.

I turned.

Jay was leaning on the wall and not breathing, frozen. Her dark emerald eyes contain disbelief and shock.

"Listen," I turned to her with the most calming voice I could muster. "If you want any loot, you'll have to hurry. The bleaking is gonna die soon..."

"Are you a mage?" Jay asked timidly.

After finishing off the monster, we sat at the water's edge and waited for the harn to eat his fill of the fresh meat. All caked in lizard blood, he'd make the perfect bait for all the local predators, so I was going to get him in the water before we left. Thankfully there would be nothing else living in the water where the bleaking was. It's best not to drink, but it's just fine for washing up.

Still, Jay refused to swim outright. To be frank, this place would soon be packed with scavengers, so I had to agree. Time to move our butts...

"Probably," I shrugged. "Although to be honest, I'm still very far from the official rank... But I do have a magic supply. And a few spells too."

"So you are a mage," Jay said affirmatively and asked a question I also wanted answered:

"But if you're a mage, why aren't your eyes blue?"

"That I do not know."

But I do have a guess... I think the reason is that I have only ever used iridescent tablets. But I decided not to tell her that.

"Gorgie is also a magical creature, but his eyes are green," I said.

"Maybe it works differently for animals?" Jay suggested and suddenly said joyously:

"You know, that's actually cool!"

"What exactly?" I didn't get it.

"Well, your eyes..." she said, then facepalmed:

"I'm such a silly girl! After all, that's why you asked me to take an oath of silence!"

"Exactly," I chuckled. "I don't want the attention."

"Honestly, a powerful mage could tell in two shakes..."

"Believe me, I have no intention of encountering powerful mages any time soon," I objected with a smile.

"Good," said Jay. "Alright then, now I understand about you. But what are you planning to do with your Gorgie?"

I glanced at the harn, now bathing in the water.

"Oh! That's actually no problem at all. You'll see when the time comes."

"Hrn..." Gorgie told me, his ears perked up.

"Okay," I said, getting up off the ground. "We've gotta go. The scavengers will be here soon."

DUNGEONS OF THE CROOKED MOUNTAINS

I WAS STANDING on the top of a cliff and taking in the sunset! At that moment, I sincerely believed I was seeing the most beautiful, captivating spectacle of my life!

The sun, gigantic and fire red, was slowly drifting into its heavenly palace, bidding a fond farewell to the world below. It seemed to have been waiting to give me a little bit of its warmth and light before going away for the night.

Jay was perched on a small boulder next to me. There were tears of joy and relief rolling down her pale cheeks...

We made it out! The caverns took pity on us in the end and let us go!

After the battle with the bleaking, the harn led us another two days. Sure there were several megabats, fangblooms and two vipers, but I have to admit they were the calmest days of all the time I spent underground.

Jay was jumping for joy. She had never gotten so many esses and tablets before. We did the math and just the reward for the bleaking covered most of her debt. Too bad the lizard wasn't magical... Then she'd really be in luck... But even still she had to be counting her blessings. The last few days had brought her more money than she could even imagine. If she pays back the debt, she'll still have a decent amount left over. Now it's just the small matter of selling all the loot at a good price.

We admired the sunset then decided to continue and spend the night somewhere down below.

Cave cats are frequent visitors to the surface, so Gorgie didn't feel any discomfort. He quickly found a fairly comfortable path and was confidently leading us along, giving occasional warnings when we reached somewhere dangerous.

"You recognize any of these places?" I asked Jay in the early evening when we were standing on a wide cliff overlooking a valley below.

"Yes," she nodded. "See that river, it's called the Swiftwater. The forest to the right we call White Glade. We used to collect birch sap there."

"And what's over there?" I asked, pointing to a pillar of black smoke in the distance.

"That's Fisham, the village where my aunt Vasilina lives. I was actually going to suggest we go see her. She lives alone. We could get there in a few days. We can take a breather... And you know, she cooks so well! Mmm! You'll be licking your fingers!"

"I'm not opposed. We could use a rest. And I really miss normal food. But I'm worried by that smoke..."

"It's just normal smoke," she waved it off. "Somebody's hut must have burned down. It's been a dry autumn this year. They probably weren't being careful..."

I looked around. So the mining village was behind us and we had emerged on the other side of the Crooked Mountains. All we can hope is that we won't meet any old friends over here.

When we reached the foothills, it was already

night. We mutually agreed to keep walking and not stop. With a guide like Gorgie, going through the woods at night would be a walk in the park.

In fact, that's basically what it was... We walked a fairly wide path while talking in muted tones. Well, Jay did most of the talking. Heh... I wasn't expecting her to be so chatty. She was trying to keep quiet in the caverns...

She told me about her family, sisters, mother, good-for nothing father who was still a kind man deep down... About her former fiancé who stopped talking to her once he found out she was being given up into peonage. About her girlfriends, who also turned against her.

"Oh gods!" she exclaimed. "I was such a fool then! I sobbed indignantly!"

"And you're not a fool now?" I chuckled.

With a laugh, she gave me a light pat on the shoulder.

"No, now I'm not a fool anymore. You know, I've been one step from death for the last few days, and that gave me a chance to rethink a lot of things. I feel like my life is starting over. All my troubles from before the caverns seem so minor and insignificant..."

Suddenly the harn, who was walking in front, stopped sharply... And we quickly saw and did the same...

"What is it?" Jay whispered, on edge.

"Gorgie smells death," I answered gloomily. "There are a few corpses in the next glade."

"What are we gonna do?"

"There are lots of tracks, but he doesn't smell any living people," I answered and suggested:

"We should take a look..."

We smelled the nauseating stench of rotting corpses as we approached the glade. And a few minutes later we found the source...

It was a wide-branching old oak with people hanging on ropes, swaying. Five. Men. Undressed. The oldest, I think fifty or so. The youngest still just a boy.

"Robbers?" I asked, turning to Jay.

But she didn't answer... She was standing with both hands covering her mouth, a river of tears gushing from her eyes...

"Do you know them?"

"That's... Michal..." she pointed at the boy, sobbing. "I've known him since childhood... And that old man is his father... They aren't robbers... They're from Fisham... Simple folk... Who would want to kill them?"

Not knowing what to do, I took a step forward and gave the silently weeping girl a timid hug. There was no reason to say anything. Silent, I started stroking her hair reassuringly.

She sniveled and pressed her whole body up against mine. I feel my shirt get wet on my right shoulder from her tears.

"Listen, Jay," I said quietly. "I'm really sorry about your friends... The gods saw what happened to them. I'm telling you the whole truth... But it's too late to help them now. They're dead. We need to get out of here. It's risky to stay here too long."

She raised her head and backed away.

"We're not gonna take them down and bury them?"

"No," I answered. "We shouldn't draw any attention now. What if the authorities did this? You know it's illegal to cut down hanging men without permission. But I promise you — as soon as we reach the nearest village, we'll tell the local elders."

"You promise?" she asked, wiping her tears away.

"I promise," I nodded. "Now let's go..."

It was around morning when we reached Fisham... Or rather what was left of it... We saw another couple impromptu gallows along the way, too. And every time Jay recognized an acquaintance or childhood friend. There were no women among them, either. Whoever did this was clearly only killing the men.

We walked through the village, burned to the foundations, and tried to figure out what happened. Gradually we made our way to the center where Jay's aunt's home once stood.

"Did your aunt live in the center of the village?" I asked in surprise. I just couldn't forget the ramshackle hut old man Burdoc picked her up from. And her lonely aunt lives in a mansion in the middle of a village...

"Yes," she nodded, looking at the black smoldering pieces of wood with tears in her eyes. All that was left of Vasilina's home. "She was a miller's widow."

Hm... It suddenly occurred to me that a well-heeled aunt could have helped get her niece out of peonage. But I kept tactfully silent...

"And what's that?" I asked, pointing at a long post towering in the middle of the small square.

"That's where the elder used to proclaim orders from the Baron."

"See that? Is there something hanging there?"

Our interest piqued, we walked across the square and stopped five steps from the pillar. The unknown item was a wooden shield cloven in two. The shield boss, which survived intact, was engraved with a grinning bear, the emblem of our Baron. But that wasn't so interesting... In black ink, there was a raven drawn on the shield itself with its wings spread wide.

I took a heavy sigh and lowered my head.

"What does that mean, Eric?" Jay asked, agitated.

"You can't guess?" I answered with a question of my own. "It looks like the young Raven brought that mercenary army he promised. And based on what we've seen today, we must be just behind the cutthroat army's back lines."

END OF BOOK ONE

Want to be the first to know about our latest LitRPG, sci fi and fantasy titles from your favorite authors?

Subscribe to our **New Releases** newsletter:
http://eepurl.com/b7niIL

Thank you for reading *Underdog!*
If you like what you've read, check out other LitRPG novels
published by Magic Dome Books:

Level Up LitRPG series by Dan Sugralinov:
Re-Start
Hero
The Final Trial
Level Up: The Knockout (with Max Lagno)

Adam Online LitRPG Series by Max Lagno:
Absolute Zero
City of Freedom

**The Way of the Shaman LitRPG series
by Vasily Mahanenko:**
Survival Quest
The Kartoss Gambit
The Secret of the Dark Forest
The Phantom Castle
The Karmadont Chess Set
Shaman's Revenge
Clans War

Dark Paladin LitRPG series by Vasily Mahanenko:
The Beginning
The Quest
Restart

Invasion LitRPG Series by Vasily Mahanenko:
A Second Chance

Galactogon LitRPG series by Vasily Mahanenko:
Start the Game!
In Search of the Uldans

**The Bard from Barliona LitRPG series
by Eugenia Dmitrieva and Vasily Mahanenko:**
The Renegades
A Song of Shadow

Interworld Network LitRPG Series by Dmitry Bilik:
The Time Master

In order to have new books of the series translated faster, we need your help and support! Please consider leaving a review or spread the word by recommending *Underdog* to your friends and posting the link on social media. The more people buy the book, the sooner we'll be able to make new translations available.

Thank you!

Till next time!